SEP   2016

P9-DED-759

Assassins:
Discord

ERICA CAMERON

TRITON
BOOKS

YA
FICTION
Cameron, E.

Triton Books
PO Box 1537
Burnsville, NC 28714
www.Tritonya.com
Triton Books is an imprint of Riptide Publishing.
www.RiptidePublishing.com

This is a work of fiction. Names, characters, places, and incidents are either the product of the author's imagination or are used fictitiously. Any resemblance to actual persons living or dead, business establishments, events, or locales is entirely coincidental. All person(s) depicted on the cover are model(s) used for illustrative purposes only.

Assassins: Discord
Copyright © 2016 by Erica Cameron

Cover art: Damonza, damonza.com
Editors: Sarah Lyons, Carole-ann Galloway, Kate DeGroot
Layout: L.C. Chase, lcchase.com/design.htm

All rights reserved. No part of this book may be reproduced or transmitted in any form or by any means, electronic or mechanical, including photocopying, recording, or by any information storage and retrieval system without the written permission of the publisher, and where permitted by law. Reviewers may quote brief passages in a review. To request permission and all other inquiries, contact Triton Books at the mailing address above, at Tritonya.com, or at marketing@riptidepublishing.com.

ISBN: 978-1-62649-422-0

First edition
September, 2016

Also available in ebook:
ISBN: 978-1-62649-421-3

Assassins: Discord

ERICA CAMERON

MORRILL MEMORIAL LIBRARY
NORWOOD, MASS 02062

For Michael and Danielle, who started me on this particular story, and for Sarah, who gave my characters a home when I wasn't sure how to find them one.

It is not true that good can only follow from good and evil only from evil, but that often the opposite is true.
—Max Weber

TABLE OF
Contents

Chapter One

For the first time since she was ten, Kindra almost dropped her knife.

Breath catching in her throat, she stared at her hand and willed herself to calm the hell down. Sure, this had been an effing weird week, but what she had to do here today wasn't anything new. She knew the drill. Get in, get done, get out, get gone.

The slip had happened in less than a blink, her fingers sliding on the ribbed handle of the blade. Anyone skilled with knives would've noticed the near-miss. And there was no reason, not in anything Atropos held holy, for Kindra to have almost dropped the knife.

The guy strapped to the chair in front of her wasn't skilled. Even if he had been, Kindra was pretty sure Mr. Bernard Gasper had other things on his mind right now. Like figuring out how to *not* die in the next sixty seconds.

Tightening her grip, Kindra strode forward. The chill crept through her thin gloves, numbing her fingers, but that was the downside of abandoned warehouses in winter—people noticed if you turned on the heat. She ignored the biting air, the smell of old fish, and the annoyingly loud creaks the roof made as the wind battered it. Instead, she concentrated on her assignment. Her target. The one her father had missed.

Kindra refused to acknowledge that tonight, for the first time in her life, her hands were shaking. She refused to even consider the possibility that her father's affliction had hit her.

There was, however, another possible cause that she couldn't discount: Bernard shouldn't be here. It was possible that Kindra's hands were shaking because she *shouldn't* kill him. Because doing this would permanently damn her already bloodstained soul to Hades.

She cataloged the sprinkling of gray in his otherwise dark-brown hair, and the sheen of sweat on his copper skin—sweat, in a room that couldn't be above thirty degrees, because he was still struggling.

Bernard Gasper fought the thin ties binding him to the chair bolted to the floor. The gag kept him mostly quiet, but he battled his bonds so fiercely that they were cutting into his skin. Blood dripped off his wrist and into small puddles on the stained concrete.

Kindra eyed the growing patches of evidence with distaste. Guns had never been her favorite weapon, but there was definitely something to be said for death by sniper rifle: a lot less cleanup for the assassins.

The gag would have to go, because she needed information, but for a moment she stared into his dark eyes. There was terror there, but he also seemed to be pleading for her to listen. To hear him. But he didn't want to *talk*, he wanted to *beg*. For his life and for the protection of his cause.

And because this job had, for the first time in her life, given her a reason to think maybe disobedience would be worth the risk, she was actually contemplating listening.

Oh, bad idea.

Ripping the gag out but holding the knife to his throat—hoping it'd be just enough of a threat to keep him from screaming—Kindra watched Bernard suck in air and try to speak.

"If I—I tell you what I know, they'll kill you too," he wheezed, his voice so raw Kindra could barely make out the words.

"They could *try*." Kindra pressed her knife harder. *Whoever "they" are.*

Bernard opened his mouth—to argue? To plead? To scream?

The door blew off its hinges. Brutal heat filled the once-freezing warehouse. Debris flew across the room, and Kindra wasn't quick enough to dodge it. Not all of it. Something heavy slammed into her shoulder, and her head cracked against the cement floor. The air carried a blast of burning clay.

Shit. Was that C-4? The ringing in her ears and the darkness encroaching on the edges of her vision swamped her thoughts. She fought against the dizziness, trying to push it back. It took far longer than she liked to open her eyes.

When her eyes focused, a familiar face hovered above hers. One that shouldn't have been anywhere near here.

"Baby, we've really got to stop meeting like this," said a girl with dyed-black hair—her brown roots peeking through—and teasing moss-green eyes. A familiar endearment on the wrong tongue, and familiar eyes in the wrong face.

Finally, the aha moment she'd been waiting for but never thought she'd get.

He was in disguise.

It was her last coherent thought before everything went black.

One Week Earlier

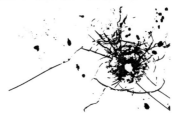

Chapter Two
1812 : TUESDAY, FEBRUARY 9

"**C**an I be the one *not* in the van next time?" Seraphina's voice sounded even drier than usual over the open comm line.

Kindra shifted on the wooden bench, turned a page of the college-level finance textbook on her lap, and tilted her head as though cracking her neck. Scanning the courtyard between two office towers, she wondered how long the team would stay near Manhattan after the job.

Maybe if everything goes well, they'll actually let me play tourist this time.

Maybe, but probably not. Downtime wasn't something the Westons saw much of. There were always places to go and people to kill.

"Concentrate, or you'll be kept on surveillance for a solid year," Odira said.

Not like Sera would ever lose focus on a mission. The girl was more clearheaded in a crisis than any of them. Even at fifteen.

"I can bitch and work at the same time, Mother," Seraphina shot back. "Multitasking is a wonderful thing."

Kindra tried not to react to the conversation playing through the tiny comm in her ear, not even to roll her eyes at her sister's complaints. Instead, she cataloged the eleven people in the courtyard—two tourists poring over a map, one nanny with two toddler charges, five men in suits using a trash can as an ashtray, and one girl shooting pictures of the courtyard's statues with an old-fashioned Nikon, the patch on her camera bag declaring in neon-green letters, *Nerd? I prefer intellectual badass.* None of them registered as a threat.

Odira grunted. "I'm not joking, Sera. If—"

"ETA three minutes," Amett cut in.

I should've stolen an art book instead, Kindra thought when she tried to read a paragraph of the text-filled pages spread across her lap. Finance was boring even when she was only pretending to study it. Letting her eyes wander, she watched the two toddlers chase each other in circles and shriek with laughter. Then Amett mumbled something over the comm, pulling her attention back to the mission.

"Repeat?" Odira requested.

"Nothing." He cleared his throat, and Kindra heard the shifting of cloth, probably as he settled into position. She glanced up at the office building across the street.

No. Stop. Her part of the job was down here. Watching for cops. For danger. For anything that might interfere with the successful completion of the job.

She looked away before her eyes locked on the cracked-open window on the fifth floor or spotted the glint of her father's customized L115A3 AWM sniper rifle. Despite visual obstruction from the trees, the shot was basically seventy feet of open space. Not exactly a challenge for her father.

The client didn't want silent or secret or subtle. They wanted untraceable, but loud and public. That was fine. The Westons could do showmanship just as well as they could do invisible, but . . .

Her eyes found the kids again. Good. The nanny was leading them out of the courtyard. Orders from the client for a clean hit should keep the collateral damage at zero, but accidents happened. It'd be better if they were gone before the strike.

"ETA two minutes," Odira said.

Odira had hooked in to the internal security system of Gasper Exports last week and had been using it to track Bernard Gasper's daily schedule. To the minute. Now it was helping Sera choreograph his death.

"No change inside." Seraphina moved heavily enough that the squeak of her chair came through the comm. "He's taking the information—papers; still no flash drive seen—out of the safe. The packet is in the inside pocket of his overcoat. Multiple pages."

Oh, thank Atropos, he's taking it all with him. Kindra had *not* wanted to sneak into the building to steal his physical backups of the files he'd received several days ago.

"Stall him ten paces west of the trash can on the east side of the square. We'll go for phase two after retrieval," Odira said. "In and out. I don't want you within fifty feet of him when the bullet hits."

Sera cleared her throat. "Keys and wallet are in his right coat pocket. Sixty seconds and counting. He's following his normal route. Looks stressed. Won't be for much longer though."

She laughed. No one joined her, but no one told her to stop, either.

"He's in the elevator. Alone. Aaaand . . ." A few quick snaps and clicks, and then Sera laughed again. "Ha! Nope! No elevator for you, bitches. Express service for Mr. Gasper."

"You messed with the elevator?" Odira's tone barely changed, but Kindra had practically made an art out of deciphering her moods. There was definitely a threat running through her words now. "Unnecessary, Seraphina. If the tamper is found, I'm feeding you to Atropos."

And that would be different from every other day how exactly? Kindra kept her grumbling to herself.

Sera wasn't so circumspect. "Leave the Fates out of this. They've got better things to do. We don't want him exiting the building with a crowd, do we? Besides, no one finds my hacks."

"Don't get cocky." *Like your brother was*, Odira left unspoken.

There was a moment of silence, a breath everyone should've taken but didn't.

"Ten seconds to exit." Sera sounded smooth and clipped now. Professional.

This was always the interesting part for Kindra: getting close enough to the targets to look into their eyes and try to guess what they'd done that was heinous enough to end up on someone's hit list. Closets weren't big enough to hold the skeletons lurking in the eyes of any mark Kindra had ever targeted; each of them had needed catacombs.

Standing, she adjusted her scarf to cover the bottom half of her face. The recent snow had melted, but it was still effing cold. It didn't hurt that the bright-red scarf distracted people from her actual features.

Holding the book open in front of her, Kindra pretended to read as she crossed the courtyard, but her attention was on her surroundings. Bernard exited the building when she was halfway across. He stopped at the top of the stairs to glance at his watch. His yellow tie was crooked, he was frowning, and it might have been her imagination, but his hair seemed grayer than it had a few days ago. He looked harried; when he tried to smile at someone he passed, the lines around his mouth appeared noticeably deeper. For a moment, Kindra wondered why.

She shook the moment off fast. Sera was right. It wouldn't matter for long.

Closing in, Kindra gauged the distance between the marker her mother had given her and Bernard's path. Adjusting her pace, Kindra timed it exactly right and—

Slam.

Her shoulder collided with Bernard's so hard he started to lose balance.

Thud.

Her heavy finance book dropped to the ground.

"Oh, hell! I'm so sorry!" Kindra draped a heavy Brooklyn accent over her words and made her eyes wide as she reached out to steady Bernard. He didn't seem to notice her hand dip inside his coat and lift the packet of papers out. "You okay?"

He smiled and nodded. "No harm done. We're in one piece." Bending down, he picked up the finance book. He never even flinched as Kindra lifted his key ring from his pocket, muffling the clinking metal against his leather wallet, and dropped them into the pocket of her coat. His smile was a little more relaxed when he straightened. "How are you doing in this class? I had to take it twice before I passed."

"Really? Well, that makes me feel better." Kindra smiled back at him, trying to guess what darkness lurked behind his calm facade. Nothing about the way Bernard reacted to the setup fit within the scope of her usual targets. The last guy she'd tried a version of this pull on had almost shot her. This guy *couldn't* be so fundamentally different from the rest. "Sometimes it looks like everyone gets it but me."

"It may feel like it, but I promise you're not alone. Everyone else is just really good at pretending." His smile turned into a smirk. "Or they cheat."

Laughing to hide her confusion, Kindra took the book. "I better get going. Sorry again."

"Good luck," Bernard said. "It gets better after graduation."

"Thanks! I'll keep that in mind." She began to move away.

"Hold on a moment!"

Kindra's heart stalled. *Oh shit. Has he already realized his wallet is missing?* Maybe now the threat would darken his eyes.

She could run. Even if Bernard chased her, Amett could make the shot. The problem was the attention. If he died chasing her, people would remember her.

Please don't let it come to that, she prayed to Atropos as she turned and moved back to where Bernard stood, keeping the smile on her face but ready to fight her way out if she needed to. "Yeah?"

Bernard's smile *had* changed, but not in the way she expected—it was softer, not sharper. Taking her textbook and using a pencil trapped between the pages, he lightly wrote two names, one of them his. Under Bernard's name was a phone number. "I've had more than a few female interns tell me how hard it is for them to find people who take them seriously. If you need a finance-related internship, there's a friend I could call. We did our MBAs together eons ago, and he still owes me a favor. Call me when you're ready to get started, and I'll introduce you. I'm positive he'll at least give you an interview."

"Really?" Kindra couldn't keep her eyes from widening. Realizing neither a fight nor a threat was coming was like missing a step in the dark. It threw her off-balance. It threw her out of *character.*

She scanned his face, looking for the microexpressions that would give the gesture away as a trick or a trap. It seemed honest and without condition, an offer made in the hope that it would help out another human being.

When she accepted the book and pencil back, an unfamiliar and uncomfortable amount of guilt churned in her stomach. She smiled at a man about to die. "Wow, um, thank you."

She took a breath, swallowing the momentary—*and suicidally insane*—urge to suggest Bernard run like the Erinyes were after him, change his name, and never resurface again. It wouldn't work. They were being watched and listened to far too closely. Kindra had no chance of sneaking him a message he'd understand in time. Warning him would mean Amett's rifle scope focusing on a new target, and she wasn't sacrificing herself to commit some random act of kindness.

"Well, ain't he a sweetie," Sera said as Kindra waved and walked toward the crowded sidewalk bordering the uptown edge of the building, moving just a bit faster than might be normal. Even for a native New Yorker.

Yeah. He was. So what did that *guy do to deserve this?*

She would never know. Closing her eyes, she, for the first time in her life, prayed for the soul of a mark.

May Charon's guidance come at a price you can pay, your journey across the Acheron be swift, and Hades's judgment be forgiving.

Odira started the countdown. "Three, two—"

Crack.

A gunshot. A bullet striking stone. A chorus of screams.

Everyone in the courtyard, including Kindra, ran. She ducked her head, covering it with her finance book, and bolted for the street.

"What the— Amett! You fucking *missed?*" Odira screamed loud enough for Kindra to hear over the racket, but it took a second for the words to sink in. Her steps slowed, and she looked back.

Missed? Amett Weston didn't miss. He'd never missed an actual target. Especially not one as beautifully lined up as this. But it had to be true. The screams of the crowd definitely didn't have the tenor they usually did when someone's brains created an impressionist painting on stone.

Another shot cracked through the air. Kindra's flinch wasn't an act this time.

Odira kept cursing. The second shot hadn't found its target either.

Kindra dove into an alcove, pretending to cower as she watched people on the sidewalk flood in both directions. No one seemed sure what had happened or which direction would be safe. Like startled herd animals, they were guided by fear and hope alone.

"Should I try for an up-close?" *Run, Bernard. Run now, because I don't want to have to be the one who kills you.*

"Damn it!" Sera this time. "He's back inside. Cops are already on their way."

"Clear the hell out of there, Kindra. Now!" Odira barked out her orders in the same voice she always used when she was so pissed Kindra could practically see steam rising from her skin. "Before they block you in."

Kindra joined the crowd rushing away from the madness in the square. The subway station was half a block away. She shoved her finance book into her mostly empty backpack, sprinted down the stairs, swiped her MetroCard, and pushed through the turnstile. Pulling her hat lower and her scarf higher, she moved to the far end of the platform and waited. The next train was still two minutes out. She sat on the bench to avoid pacing nervously.

What had she seen in the split second she looked back, the split second after the bullet should have hit Bernard Gasper square between the eyes? Nothing. Definitely no blood. The shot had to have either nicked the side of his head or missed him entirely.

He missed. Amett Weston effing missed.

The words were still running through her mind when she dropped onto the subway car's hard plastic seat. Round and round they went, each repetition chasing the next until it too closely resembled the annoying music she'd heard at carnivals. It became a chorus of "He missed?" played to the tune of those screams. Bernard's random act of kindness acted as the bridge.

Kindra closed her eyes and stuffed her hands into the pockets of her coat, reassured—but not much—by the papers, keys, and wallet she felt there. Despite the absolute effing disaster of the last few minutes, she assumed her task was the same as it normally was—copy the stolen documents while "keeping your eyes firmly fucking off information that you do *not* need to know," and return to base.

Grinding her teeth, Kindra adjusted the papers. She'd slipped them in quickly and one hadn't quite fit, the corner catching on the pocket and refusing to move. The only way to fix it was to pull them out entirely and refold them fresh.

In the middle of trying to do just that, her gloved fingers slipped. One page nearly fluttered to the floor. She grabbed it, scanning the passengers quickly to make sure no one was paying attention. Then she made the mistake of glancing down.

She sucked in a breath so fast she almost choked.

Atropos bless.

The details of the black-and-white picture were too grainy to be sure, but the size of the bodies in relation to the car in the foreground, the building behind them with the word "school" written in Spanish, the woman on her knees bent over one of the small, bloody corpses . . .

What she was looking at wasn't like the Westons' jobs, isolated deaths that had been scattered across continents and years. It definitely wasn't the elimination of someone twisted enough—or stupid enough—to get themselves caught up in something that would land them in the Westons' sight lines.

This was a massacre. Of *children.*

She flipped the page over. On the back were two much clearer, full-color shots. One focused on the woman grieving over a girl whose once-white dress was now mostly red, her dark eyes wide and unseeing. The second showed a woman slumped over the body of a boy whose head hadn't survived a close-range shot from a high-powered weapon.

Those really are kids. Fucking hell. Kids. Is this Bernard's work?

It was difficult to fathom the depth of the split personality that would take. Not many people capable of ordering a schoolhouse massacre also fought for feminism in the business world, but she'd seen scarier levels of depravity in her life.

Below the picture that was now shaking in Kindra's hand were the words *G. H.'s latest scare tactic in E. B caved to R. W. (R's E business partner) 2 days later,* written in a barely legible scrawl. The *B* might mean Bernard, but that didn't necessarily implicate him in this bloodbath. If anything, it hinted that he caved to someone else *because* of it.

Kindra couldn't find it in her to blame him for that. The collateral damage—the ones who were in the wrong place or related to the wrong people, and the kids who hadn't yet had time to pick a side—*those* were the ones that twinged the last bits of a conscience Odira and Amett hadn't yet beaten out of her.

The train began to slow. Kindra folded the paper with the others, keeping her expression blank as she slid them back into her pocket. As though it weren't important. *Nothing to see here*, she tried to project. *Don't notice me, and I won't have to kill you.*

Odira had found a town house in the West Village for their stay—the owners spent winters in Florida or France or some place with an *F* and left the property to the care of a vacation rental service—but Kindra got off the train one stop early. She needed fresh air. And time. And a copier old enough not to keep records of everything it scanned, which was getting harder and harder to find. Luckily, all of those things were available in the blocks between this subway station and her family's temporary mansion.

She made it all the way to the street before she came within five feet of another human, but she still felt crowded. Nearly claustrophobic.

Staying near the edge of the sidewalk, she locked her hands in her jeans's pockets and away from the blade hidden in the right pocket of her coat. Keeping her hands away from her knife wouldn't stop her from reacting, but it would add one more step between instinct and bloodshed.

She kept her chin just low enough to seem as though she were watching the ground pass beneath her feet, not carefully tracking her surroundings. Within ten minutes, she'd passed twenty-five people and cataloged them in her periphery. She'd walked seven blocks, passing four buildings that could've served as short-term hideouts if she'd been on the run from the cops, and a restaurant that she was pretty sure existed solely to launder money. She noticed it all with the small corner of her mind that was always *on*, always active, but now it was almost drowned out by the merry-go-round:

Amett missed.

Is that school of dead kids why we're after Bernard?

Atropos bless it, Amett *missed.*

Taking a shaky breath, she tried to clear her mind as she turned toward the local library, jogging up the steps of the ornate building. It was a bastion of brick and ivory-colored stonework from a much older era, and she focused on the detailed carvings around the front door and forced the muscles in her face to relax until she could pull up something that felt like a convincing smile. Warm air hit her when she stepped through the doors, the sudden change in temperature making her shiver. The woman behind the desk in the lobby smiled in welcome.

Kindra clasped her hands in front of her face. "*Please* tell me you guys have a copier."

"Kind of." The librarian grimaced. "It's ancient, but we can usually get it to work."

"I'll take my chances." Kindra pulled the finance text out of her backpack. "I've been to three places I thought had copiers, and I'm running out of time to get this book back to my friend."

Chattering away, the librarian led Kindra to a slightly battered Xerox machine. Kindra picked a page of the finance book at random, placed it on the glass, crossed her fingers, and pretended to hold her breath. When the librarian pressed Copy, it took a minute for the machine to decide whether it wanted to work. Finally, the whole thing shuddered, and a thin beam of light began scanning the page.

The librarian grinned. "Must be your lucky day."

"Must be." Kindra forced a laugh. A few more pleasantries, and she was alone.

Moving the book to peer through the glass, Kindra spotted the mirrors installed only in pre-hard-drive copiers, but better safe than in serious shit. She popped the side panel open, looking for the serial number and manufacturing date. *Yes.* The model just missed the cutoff for the installation of hard drives.

After she closed the panel and straightened, she hesitated before pressing any of the worn buttons on the keypad. A green *1* was already lit up on the screen. It would only take a moment to switch that number, to add a second set to the copies she was about to make—and keep it for herself. A backup plan in case this job went any further south than it already had.

You might not even look at it. They can be destroyed later if you don't want to know, but you'll never get another chance to make a copy if you don't take it now.

The logic didn't do anything to soothe the nervous tension vibrating under her skin like electricity through a metal fence as she slipped the first page of the documents under the textbook and hit the faded *2*. It shuddered and slowly spit out two copies.

Most of the twenty-three, double-sided pages she refused to glance at—the memory of that picture still too fresh—but one word on one page caught her eye.

Redwell.

Atropos bless it.

She didn't read the rest of the page, but she thought about the scrawled words under the picture. "*G. H.'s latest scare tactic in E.*" G. H. could be the client, and E? Considering the Spanish signs in the picture and non-European architecture and flora, it had most likely been taken in South America. Probably Echemorro, the tiny nation on the northwestern coast of the continent, or its neighbor Ecuador. Kindra couldn't begin to guess the location if it was referring to a city instead of a country. But the last part? "*B caved to R. W. (R's E business partner) 2 days later.*" R for Redwell? B might refer to Bernard, but she couldn't be sure. *R. W.* meant nothing with so little to work with.

The thought almost made her laugh. Little? Normally, Kindra didn't even know who they were working for. Comparatively, she was overloaded with details now.

"The more you know, the more danger you're in," her brother used to tell her. "Amett and Odira keep secrets because it makes us a little bit safer."

It was a nice lie, one she and Ryce had believed because they'd needed to, but it was definitely a lie. If safety had been what Odira was after, she never would've forced her children into this life.

Two weeks ago, though, Kindra had been in the room when Odira got a call. Her mother's side of the conversation had been terse, one-word answers, but when it ended, she'd looked at Kindra with something very close to regret in her eyes.

"Tell Amett that Redwell called," was all she'd said.

Person? Company? City? Code name? Kindra hadn't been sure. Still wasn't. Whoever or whatever they were, apparently there were a lot of dead kids tied to that name.

And that's *who we're working for? Shit.*

Another line added to the chorus of the damned merry-go-round of unwelcome thoughts spinning on high speed inside Kindra's head, but she knew what happened when she prodded Odira for information. There was a scar on her thigh from a night she'd asked too many questions.

If she wanted to know anything, she'd have to figure it out herself.

It took time, more than she had to spare, but Kindra managed to copy all the pages and separate them into two stacks before the librarian came back to check on her. "What do I owe you?" When the librarian gave Kindra a number, she quickly passed her twenty dollars, waved, and ran out. "Keep the change! Thanks!"

On the sidewalk, she slowed her pace to carefully fold the extra copies and slip them into a hidden pocket of her bag. In fifteen minutes, Kindra would be late for the rendezvous. From here, without running, it would take her almost exactly that long to reach the base where Odira would be waiting to claim everything Kindra had stolen. Expecting her to hand it all over and then forget.

She wasn't sure she could this time.

Redwell. Dead kids. Amett missed. Redwell. Dead kids. Effing missed?

The thoughts kept whirling, but the revolutions didn't bring any new revelations.

What's the stronger sign of the apocalypse: working for a client who kills kids, or Amett missing *his target? Maybe this is what they meant when they said ignorance is bliss?*

But she'd always been lacking information, and she'd *never* felt anything close to bliss. Now all she had was guilt, or something like it.

But then she'd never had a mark offer to get her an internship either.

Three doors away from their rented town house, Kindra realized she hadn't paid attention to anyone she'd passed since the library. She could only vaguely picture their faces or what they'd been wearing. The buildings had melded into one long strip of brick and stone and glass. She'd been a walking target with a pocketful of papers that might incriminate a powerful client, and a wallet belonging to a man who shouldn't have survived an assassination attempt.

"Shit." She climbed the stairs, shaking her head and yanking herself by force out of her spinning thoughts.

"Afternoon, Mackenzie!" The neighbor stood at the top of her own steps, holding the leash of her ridiculously coiffed Standard Poodle. "How was your day, dear?"

"Just lovely, thank you," Kindra said with a smile and a perfectly cultured English accent. In the eyes of the neighbors and the rental agency that managed this property, she was the eldest daughter of an English family on extended holiday.

"Stay warm, dear," the old woman said as her dog politely tugged her toward an inviting tree.

Kindra nodded and unlocked the wrought iron gate and the glass-paneled door. Both were fancy as hell, but neither was all that great at keeping people out. Not the ones who knew what they were doing, anyway. If the Westons had decided to break in and claim the place instead of faking paperwork with the agency, it wouldn't have been difficult. The security system was overpriced and useless. The owners had to be gullible as hell.

As she shut the front door, Kindra caught the familiar scent of Seraphina's bidis. She padded through the elegantly dressed rooms toward the back of the house and then leaned against the frame of the open back door. "I still say you shouldn't smoke those."

"And I still say that if I don't have at least one bad habit, I'll go crazy . . . *er* than I already am." A shaft of sunlight caught Seraphina's hair, turning the dyed highlights blonder than usual and bringing out the flecks of amber in her otherwise dark eyes. Sera smirked and blew a perfect smoke ring into the air. "Drugs make people stupid, alcohol is a waste of time, and sex is overrated. Leave me my stupid bidis. You're the only one who nags me to quit."

Anymore.

The word went unsaid, but she knew both of them heard it. Kindra was the only one who mentioned the bidis *anymore*. Their brother, Ryce, had never approved of the habit either, especially since Sera had picked it up at age ten. But he'd been dead for four years.

And his name has been verboten ever since.

"Upstairs," Odira called down. "Sera, put that thing out."

Though she looked longingly at the half-smoked bidi, Sera put it out and placed it in her pocket. No chance of accidentally leaving one behind for DNA evidence that way.

"Is this going to be as bad as I think it's going to be?"

Kindra glanced at her sister, more surprised by the thoughtful tone of her voice than by the words. "Yeah. It's probably that bad. Maybe worse."

"He *missed*," she whispered as they got closer to the third-floor office that had been turned into a surveillance suite.

Nodding but hiding her own confusion, Kindra kept pace with Sera on the last few hardwood stairs and filed into the room after her.

Amett wasn't there.

"Did you kill him?" Sera asked.

Kindra held her breath, waiting for the answer; the same question had popped into her head.

"No." Odira adjusted a setting on the additional security system they'd installed inside the house and shook her head. "I might still, though."

Kindra wanted to read sarcasm into that, but there was too strong a chance that Odira was being completely serious. "Where is he?"

"With Doc J."

In New York City area, if the Westons were bleeding, unconscious, or dying, they went to see Doc J. They didn't know his real name, and he didn't know theirs. Patients met him in an old building, in a scrupulously clean apartment, and he did what he could. For a price.

"Amett was hurt?" How had that happened? *When* had it happened?

"If he wasn't, he will be," Odira muttered. "Sit down."

We're doing the review without him? Kindra barely kept the question in her head. The only times that had ever happened were when someone was literally on the verge of death.

They always did this: reviewed any tapes or audio recordings they had of the hit, even when the job went off almost exactly to plan. For Odira, "*almost* exactly to plan" wasn't good enough.

Today they didn't have "almost" to fall back on.

With a few quick clicks, Odira pulled up their surveillance feeds from the courtyard. The official cameras had all been adjusted slightly, making their angles wrong to catch sight of Kindra or what happened to Bernard, but Odira had installed an extra camera last week, one hooked straight into the Westons' system. A better and safer way for them to watch not only the job, but the investigation that followed.

Seemingly unconcerned with Amett's absence, Sera flopped into the second chair at the desk. Kindra placed her bag on the floor and then leaned against the wall nearby, her hands in the pockets of her coat.

According to the time stamp in the corner of the video, the image was current.

Uniformed patrol officers and besuited detectives crawled all over the square, interviewing the smoking businessmen, but there was no bloodstain. No body bag.

Because he missed.

Odira pressed a button and the video reversed. People walked backward, and then they ran backward. The cops reversed down the street, lights flashing. Crowds fled, reversing in both directions, no one sure which way safety lay. Then the courtyard was quiet and calm and moving on the right temporal track.

Kindra saw herself and the photographer. She watched herself cross the square and run into Bernard, could even pick out the moments she lifted the packet of papers from his coat and the wallet and keys from his pocket. Not because they showed up on camera—which would have been a failure of epic proportions—but because she remembered the whole encounter with brutal clarity.

"You did well enough," Odira said as Kindra saw herself stroll off camera. Practically gushing praise from Odira. "It would have been perfect if someone *else* had held up his end."

Kindra nodded, but her eyes were on the photographer. The girl wasn't taking pictures anymore. In fact, she seemed to be watching Kindra walk away. *Interesting.*

Bernard called her back and wrote the message in her textbook. There it was, the damnably honest surprise on Kindra's face when he explained what the number was for. An act of kindness from a man who didn't know he'd been marked to die.

But apparently Atropos disagreed with that plan.

The bullet hit the stone statue behind Bernard. He fell. The photographer flinched, but she didn't start screaming. And when she ran, it wasn't away from the courtyard.

She ran *toward* Bernard.

The photographer grabbed Bernard's arm and yanked him to his feet with capable efficiency. The second bullet struck the ground six inches off her shoulder. She ran to the building, dragging Bernard along.

"I hate Good Samaritans." Sera had watched the same thing as Kindra, but apparently had seen something completely different. The photographer didn't look like a Good Samaritan. She looked like a bodyguard, shielding Bernard's body with her own as they ran. Or maybe Kindra was the one interpreting it wrong. But then Sera rewound the footage and squinted at the screen. "Or maybe not. Are we sure she isn't someone we need to be worried about?"

"Not sure, no, but we'll keep her as a low priority. If she's a Good Samaritan, she doesn't matter. If she's working security for him, we'll find her again. The important thing right now is fixing the fact that our primary target is still alive." Odira's last two words were pushed through gritted teeth.

Kindra locked down her muscles to hide the shiver of fear that went through her, concentrating on the looped footage. She watched the photographer run toward Bernard again. Maybe the girl really was one of those strange people who, when bullets started flying, saw only the people who needed help to get out of the way.

"Why didn't he take a third shot?" Kindra asked. There had been enough time for him to pull the trigger again before the photographer reached Bernard.

"He said he couldn't without missing again." Odira jammed her finger on the space bar. The picture froze just as the cops began to arrive.

For a moment, the entire room was silent. Even Sera held back her normal commentary.

Odira lifted one hand and traced the short, not-quite-invisible scar behind her right ear, a nervous habit that she rarely let herself give in to. "The client was already impatient before today. After this screwup, we're going to have a hell of a time keeping them from bringing in another team."

Another team? That was so brainless—and dangerous, and expensive—it was practically unheard of.

"Even if they do, it'll take anyone else a while to get as integrated as we already are," Sera said. "It'd be imbecilic to try to pull us back."

"What have I always told you about people who let stress and fear make their choices for them?" Odira crossed her arms.

"They end up dead," Kindra supplied. It was an outcome that was a lot more likely with a second team in the mix.

Unless they were working together from the start, two teams on one job meant exponentially more chances for something to go wrong. Or that the team who *didn't* get the job done would retaliate by reporting everything to the cops, the Feds, and anyone else in a position to fuck up everyone's lives.

"Exactly. Because they're making *stupid* choices." A muscle in Odira's jaw twitched—never a good sign. "That's where our client is because of what happened today. Stressed and afraid."

Our client. G.H. or Redwell? Kindra's hands clenched inside the pockets of her coat, one closing around Bernard's papers and Odira's copies. She didn't look at the backpack by her feet, refused to acknowledge the copies hidden there.

It always played out the same. Odira would demand the stolen documents and the copies, and they would disappear into the system of files her parents had hidden in safe-deposit boxes all over the country—the world, maybe. The originals would go to whomever had ordered their retrieval.

Curiosity about the jobs and the targets and the *why* of it all had been almost entirely beaten out of Kindra, but in that moment, the need to know ate at her like rust in iron, slowly disintegrating her control. What had a man like Bernard, the kind of man who was willing to use a long-owed favor from an old college friend to help out a stranger, done to warrant making a public spectacle of his death?

Odira tapped her right index finger on her left biceps a few times and then nodded. "We have to move forward from here. For now, we're doing it without Amett."

"Are we leaving him behind?" Sera asked.

Kindra tensed. Sera didn't sound like she cared either way; she asked more like she wanted to make sure she was in the loop.

We wouldn't, right? We wouldn't just leave him behind because of one mistake . . . It was unthinkable. Kindra didn't *want* to believe it. They weren't just a team, they were family. Weren't they? Dysfunctional, yes, but still family.

But for a moment, Odira really looked like she was considering it. Like she wished she *could* just leave him behind as easily as an empty magazine. "No, but until we figure out what the hell happened, he won't be in the field."

Kindra relaxed a little. No one was being abandoned. She'd already lost Ryce to a stupid mistake. She couldn't handle it if what was left of her family fractured further. But when she looked at the expressions on Odira's and Sera's faces . . .

They really don't care one way or the other, do they?

She almost snorted at herself for the sentimentality. She knew well that Odira didn't waste her time on things that weren't useful.

They don't care about Amett any more than they do about Bernard.

"Kindra, you're going to have to take point on this one," Odira said. "Sera will stay on tech, and I'll keep running logistics until we know whether or not Amett can take over. We don't have time to wait. The longer we delay, the tighter Bernard's security is going to get and the harder this job is going to be."

"What's the new plan?" Kindra asked.

"Capture, kill, and dispose," Odira said.

Sera pushed her hair back and looked up to the ceiling. "And I'm going to be stuck in the van for the fun part again."

"You'll be exactly where we need you to be, and you'll shut up about it," Odira snapped. "We've got enough to deal with already. Don't make it worse."

Though she opened her mouth, for once whatever Sera had been planning to say didn't leave her lips. Shrugging, she grabbed a knife off the side table and began idly flipping it over the back of her left hand.

"Where are Bernard's personal effects?" Odira demanded once she seemed certain Sera's mouth was going to stay shut. Kindra pulled out the thick stack of paper, the wallet, and the keys. And forcefully ignored the existence of the second set of copies in her backpack as she turned it all over.

After tossing the wallet and keys onto the desk, Odira flipped through her copies and the originals, her eyes skimming the contents but her face revealing none of her thoughts. Kindra relaxed against the wall. There was nothing in those pages to give Odira a single hint about what Kindra had done. Nodding once, Odira folded the documents, slid them into her back pocket, and raised her eyes to meet Kindra's.

Oh hell. What did I do?

"Why are you wearing that?" There was a dangerous undertone to Odira's question.

Kindra glanced down, barely suppressing a cringe. The bright-red scarf she should've hidden in her bag as soon as she was out of camera-sight in the subway station was still around her neck. *Shit.* She had to force herself to face Odira again. "I . . . forgot."

Odira never took her eyes off Kindra's as her hand swung up and connected with the side of Kindra's head. The force sent Kindra staggering sideways a step, but it wasn't as bad as last time. No black spots and no blur. Then again, last time Odira had been holding a small stone statue they'd just discovered was a fake and thus not worth a tenth of what they'd been told it would fetch.

"We do not *forget*." Odira's brown eyes were flinty, and her jaw was clenched. "You won't like it if I ever have to tell you that again, Kindra."

I don't like it now. She was effing tired of being punished for bullshit reasons, and she was *sick* of working without ever seeing the whole picture—who was pulling the strings and why. It had been the status quo for years, but she couldn't not dig for answers. Not this time. Not on this job. Not when she would be taking her father's place and trying one more time to end Bernard Gasper's life.

Most of the time she could make herself not care. It was always her life or the target's, and she saw nothing in any of them worth mourning, let alone worth dying for. But Bernard had been kind and generous in a moment when neither was necessary and in a situation where most people wouldn't have been. He'd offered a potentially life-changing leg up to a stranger, and that earned him at least a breath of a chance in Kindra's eyes.

If Kindra was going to take this one out, add him to the list she'd been growing for years, then she was going to make sure his was a life worth taking. Or a life worth dying for.

Jacksonville, Florida

Sunlight streamed in through floor-to-ceiling windows, illuminating the spacious office on the top floor of Redwell's corporate headquarters. The eighty-eight-inch flat-screen TV mounted to the wall had been on since early that morning, four news channels displaying simultaneously with captions running across all four windows. Each time the man behind the massive mahogany desk looked up, he scanned the stories on the screen before returning to the documents splayed across his desk and the spreadsheet open on his computer.

This time, something on the screen caught his attention and held it. A smile grew on his face, adding creases to slightly age-weathered skin, as he picked up the remote, selected one of the four stations, and unmuted the TV.

". . . but only two shots were heard, and no eyewitnesses or security personnel seem to have spotted the shooter or the weapon." The reporter, a grim-faced woman with bronze skin and dark, narrow eyes, gestured behind her. On the bottom of the screen, the headline read *Anna Maria Cortez reporting live: Shots fired in the middle of Manhattan.* "The scene itself is still in chaos, as you can see, and a sweep of the surrounding buildings is currently underway."

Dropping the remote to his desk, the man watching exhaled slowly, the sound almost like relief, and ran a hand over thinning, light-brown hair liberally streaked with gray.

"What came to light is that this may not have been a random shooting at all. Witness statements lead us to believe there may have been a target of this seemingly random act of violence."

A picture popped up in the corner of the screen. It showed a man with copper skin, gray-sprinkled dark hair, a broad smile, and wide, dark eyes. A man the caption named Bernard Gasper.

The smile on the watcher's face dimmed a little, and his eyes narrowed, his focus on the screen seeming to sharpen.

"This man, Bernard Gasper, the current CEO of Gasper Exports, Inc., is reported to have been standing directly in the projected path of the bullets," Anna said. "Though the shots appear to have missed, Gasper himself has not been seen since the incident, and we have learned that attempts to contact him by members of his staff as well as investigators—"

The man hit the power button on the remote, and the TV went black.

"Fuck." His hands clenched on top of his desk, but for a few moments after, he neither moved nor spoke. Forcibly deep, even breaths were the only sound in the room. Then he held one longer than the others, closed his eyes, and exhaled slowly. When his eyes opened, he sat up and pulled an out-of-date cell phone from his pocket, dialing a number from memory.

"You disappoint me, Odira," he said a few seconds later. "I thought what I had was worth more to you than what you showed me today. Fix it. Quickly."

Hitting End on the call, the man gripped the phone tight in one hand and rubbed the other over his face.

"*Fuck.*" Grunting, he adjusted his hold on the phone so he could dial again. "Matthew had better be right about you."

He lifted the phone to his ear and waited. "A mutual acquaintance gave me your number. I might have a job for you. Call this number back in the next six hours and we'll talk."

He hung up, slid the phone into his pocket, and returned to the work spread across his desk. "Surrounded by fucking incompetence, I swear to God."

Chapter Three

Movement caught Kindra's eye. Just crossing into sight of the cameras Odira had installed on their street was her father, no sling or bandage in sight. Each step looked heavy, but he held his head high, like he refused to break under whatever invisible weight he carried.

What in Tartarus is happening here?

Amett Weston did not *miss* a shot for no reason. His visit to Doc J had made her assume something was physically wrong, but apparently not. He moved without limp or hitch, his stride even and steady, if a little slower than usual. The sight of Amett whole and unharmed should've been a relief, but worry only dug its claws in deeper.

Clearing her throat, Kindra pushed a button on the comm. "He's on approach."

"The prodigal returns!" Sera was a block away, on a street where the higher number of businesses meant their service van blended in a little better. She and Odira had been updating some of the software, but that project was instantly put on hold. Family business took precedence over the Family Business in this instance.

No longer wanting to watch Amett's plodding advance, Kindra shifted her attention to the screen showing the courtyard of Bernard's office building. It swarmed with people, but not cops and investigators. Now, tourists shuffled through the space, eyes wide as they took pictures and stared at the wounded stone statue—the bullet had shattered the thing's foot instead of Bernard's head.

Kindra pushed out of the chair, casting one last glance at the screens. Someone caught her eye.

A guy eased his way through the fringe of the tourist crowd, moving with careful casualness. His attention seemed to be focused on the crime scene to his left, but when someone shifted too close to him on his right, the guy dodged without hesitation. That kind of awareness wasn't instinct—that was training. And his ball cap and hooded jacket kept most of his features concealed from the cameras, even Odira's hidden one.

New security for the building? Or Redwell's second team scoping the place already?

No time to think about it now. Amett had almost arrived. Kindra made a note of the time stamp and the question on their log sheet, then headed downstairs.

Odira and Sera met Amett at the door. Their procession inside was nearly silent. The Westons knew how to move quietly, and they all must have felt the need for stillness just then. When the door shut behind them, most of the sounds of the city were gone. They stood in a loose circle, watching each other. What Amett said next could change everything. Kindra didn't want to hear it, but she knew they couldn't delay it forever, either.

"What did Doc say?" Odira went straight for the bull's-eye, as usual.

Amett glanced up at his wife, his soft brown eyes meeting her dark ones for less than a second before he looked away. "There're two options, and he isn't sure which one it is."

"Two options for what?" Sera asked.

"Why I can't stop this." Amett removed his hand from his pocket and held it out.

His hand was trembling.

Seraphina went still, her eyes just a touch too wide.

This didn't compute. Amett Weston didn't have weaknesses. He was in complete control of his body and, thus, his world. He accepted nothing less from himself or his family. This? It wasn't possible. But that didn't make it go away.

"Bottom line?" He was staring at his hand like it had betrayed him. "It's Parkinson's or essential tremor. Out of the two, we're supposed to start praying for the tremor."

"Atropos bless it." Odira's voice was hoarse, but Kindra couldn't get a read on what emotion danced in the muscles lining her sharp jaw. Anger? Distress? Possibly some combination of the two. "How long?"

Amett hid his hand in his pocket again. "It's been about a month. I thought it was getting better, but yesterday . . . I couldn't get it to stop."

Odira closed her eyes, and froze statue-still. It seemed as though she was on the verge of cracking and losing her infamous control.

"Is there treatment?" Odira's face still betrayed no emotion that Kindra could decipher, but . . . she had to feel something, didn't she?

"I have a contact for a prescription, but it's not one hundred percent. Especially since there's no way to be sure which condition he's trying to treat. I . . ." His broad shoulders rose, his back curved, and, for the first time, his head fell just a little. "I can't guarantee aim or accuracy anymore."

Odira's expression pinched, and Kindra heard muttering that sounded like a string of inventive curses. It only lasted three seconds before Odira's control was back in place, efficiently snapping together like a Paratus-16 rifle.

"Fine. New plan." Odira took a long breath and let it out slowly. "Amett is going to take over logistics on all operations from here on out. Sera still has tech. Kindra and I will switch on the wet work as needed."

Kindra saw a chance, a small one, and took it. "I probably shouldn't be the one if we're going for an up-close. He's seen me."

"He's seen a version of you," Odira said, dismissing the concern and Kindra's possible escape route from this job.

It was true, though. If there was a god, Greek or otherwise, hovering somewhere above earth, he'd built Kindra's entire family with an eye to blending in anywhere. With the right clothes, hair, and makeup, all of them had the features to be from a hundred different places. Whether they needed to be part of the Spanish aristocracy, hide in the slums of Singapore, infiltrate Saudi Arabian royalty, or stroll unnoticed through South Florida, the Westons had it covered. Middle-of-the-road skin tone and facial features, plus a collection of well-crafted wigs, made it easy for them to highlight parts of themselves and hide others. Easy for them to be anyone from anywhere.

It was all true, but this time, with copies of papers she shouldn't have hidden in her borrowed bedroom, and too many dangerous thoughts still running like a broken carnival ride in her head, that truth didn't make Kindra feel any better.

Chapter Four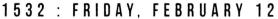

1532 : FRIDAY, FEBRUARY 12

On Tuesday, Kindra had been going for "college student." Today her look was more "teenage jet-setter." She was on recon only while Odira checked their bugs, which was good because fashion-centric disguises rarely lent themselves well to running. Or walking. Luckily, she wouldn't have to go far. The glass-walled tower that housed Bernard's condo was across the street, soaring above her head to make the most of the view over Central Park.

There was no logical or logistical reason for them to be here as far as Kindra could determine. The bugs were more of an excuse than a reason; Odira just didn't want to admit that she had no effing clue where the target had gone.

First Amett and now Odira. They are absolutely losing their minds.

Bernard might be as naive as he seemed to be when it came to the tar-like criminal underbelly clinging to the business world, but Kindra didn't think he was stupid. If someone made an obvious attempt on your life, you didn't go home—they probably knew where you lived. If Bernard Gasper had *any* brains whatsoever, he'd be miles away. Possibly in another country if he could make it across the border without raising alarms—legal or otherwise.

So unless Odira and Amett had a secondary plan they'd declined to share, there was no good reason for Kindra to be suffering the cold in clothes more pretty than practical.

Tapping the toe of one fur-lined, stiletto-heeled boot with not-so-feigned impatience, she began a new text message on her jewel-bedecked smartphone. For once, the character Kindra was playing was oddly aligned with her actual mental state.

I can't believe my father is keeping me waiting this long!

Sera's response came fast. *Seriously. Your dad is a crap weasel.*

Kindra almost snorted trying to hold in her laughter.

Don't let him see you say that. Kindra scanned her side of the street for any changes even as her fingers moved across the touch screen. *Daddy is "connected."*

Please. That hit man thing only happens in movies. ;)

This time Kindra did laugh as she scanned the street again. The weight of the KA-BAR Tanto inside her fuzzy boot and the Glock 17 9mm hidden under her down-filled coat made that statement a huge, flashing lie.

Only training kept her from reacting when her eyes landed on a familiar figure about to cross to Kindra's side of the street.

Without a decent shot of his face, Odira and Seraphina hadn't been able to identify the possible security guy Kindra had spotted. He hadn't appeared here or at Bernard's office building on Wednesday, but that was definitely him strolling down the street with too-careful nonchalance. He looked younger than she'd first thought. His smooth brown skin was almost the same rich fawn color as his leather coat. The coat and the jeans were civilian, but the military-style boots and the wrist cuff that Kindra knew could fit a small blade weren't.

So, training, but not necessarily a lot of time undercover. He obviously couldn't hide from people who knew what they were doing. Probably not part of another hit team, then. Not a good one, anyway. Kindra was leaning toward the security theory. First job maybe. Otherwise he'd probably have gotten himself killed by now.

Is he why they wanted us out here? A heads-up would've been really effing appreciated.

OMG you should see the hottie at nine! Kindra typed. She was mic'ed, but she didn't want to speak aloud unless it was absolutely necessary.

"I'm tracking, but there's no good angle of his face," Sera said. "Not from our cameras or any of the ones we tapped. The guy knows how to keep his face off a screen."

"Get close," Odira ordered. "We need a picture. His wallet would be better."

Smiling, and relieved at actually having something to do, Kindra tossed her blond hair over her shoulder—a ridiculously heavy wig that she hoped she would never have to wear again—and stood. She walked about fifteen paces before *crack*!

Oh, shit!

She started falling sideways. For no apparent reason.

Before she could twist and save herself, arms wrapped around her waist. Her descent halted, then reversed, until she was locked tight against someone's chest.

A tenor voice laughingly said, "If you wanted to catch my attention, all you had to do was smile."

The guy who'd caught her was only an inch taller than Kindra in her three-inch heels. Five eleven, maybe. He had a teasing light in his eyes—gorgeous, dark, moss-green eyes—and strands of black hair poked out from underneath his red beanie. His skin had a golden-brown undertone that could easily have been either a genetic gift or a tan, and his fine-boned features made him seem almost delicate, but he was strong enough to keep her easily trapped against a chest covered in a puffy black North Face jacket. To get away, Kindra would have to pull some moves that a jet-setter wouldn't know or likely feel compelled to use when faced with a cute rescuer.

There was something off, though. Looking at him was like playing a complicated game of "One of these things is not like the other." Kindra couldn't put her finger on what had caught her attention, but she didn't mind staying where she was to figure it out. Those laughing green eyes were fascinating.

She swallowed to clear her throat and smiled. "Thank you. Obviously my father overpaid for these boots." Still leaning on the stranger's arm, she held out one foot and sent an entirely unfeigned glare at the snapped heel that had sent her careening off-plan and out of control.

"Were you headed somewhere important in those stupid shoes?"

They really are stupid shoes.

Forcing herself to stay in character, she turned the glare on her rescuer. "They're *designer*, I'll have you know."

"Like I said. Stupid shoes." Green Eyes laughed when Kindra playfully pushed at his shoulder. "So? Were you? Maybe I can help you get there."

She didn't think it was her imagination that turned that offer into a proposition.

"Walk away, Kindra." Odira's sharp tone made her flinch, but she hid it by wiggling and ineffectively trying to get out of the stranger's hold. The guy loosened his grip, but didn't release her, as though he didn't trust her to keep her balance on her own.

"Target is stationary, but might not be for long," Sera said.

Odira nearly growled. "We *need* that picture."

"Well . . ." Kindra looked toward Possible Security Guy. He was making himself comfortable on a low wall on the edge of the park, his face still too shadowed for her to make out details. "I thought I saw an actor."

Following her gaze, Green Eyes shook his head. "That guy? No way."

Kindra hoped Sera would give her a name, because she couldn't think of a single actor who even somewhat resembled Possible Security Guy.

"Mention *The Following*," Sera said.

"Really. I think he was in *The Following*." Kindra could picture the actor now. Possible Security Guy did have the same build and skin tone—she just didn't know his name.

"Michael Ealy?" Green Eyes shook his head as he finally released Kindra.

Mentally, she checked her weapons to make sure they hadn't been lifted, but she kept her eyes on the Ealy look-alike. "I should introduce myself. He looks *so* much like Michael Ealy."

Green Eyes smirked. "Baby, if he's your type, I am going to be sorely disappointed."

Kindra blinked and smiled. Not the jet-setter's smile, either. "Just because he's *a* type doesn't mean he's the only one."

That wasn't part of her character, but it had slipped past her lips regardless. To Kindra's mind, a pretty face was a pretty face, no matter the gender or what color the skin, hair, or eyes attached to the body. Green Eyes fell squarely inside Kindra's wide parameters. Bisexuality had its perks, making her job a whole lot easier. And far more enjoyable.

"Enough, Kindra," Odira snapped.

"Kinny's got a cruu-ush," Sera sang.

"*Focus*. Now!" Odira's orders sent Kindra's pulse rate jumping and made it a struggle to hide the tension coiling through her body. "The target is moving. *Go*."

Kindra shifted away from Green Eyes, tracking Ealy as he walked away. "I have to—"

She stopped. Have to *what*? What did Odira expect her to do with one working shoe? She couldn't chase after the guy, hobbled as she was.

"Have to what?" Green Eyes asked. When Kindra shook her head, he smiled. "Unless you're dead set on throwing yourself at the doppelgänger of a married actor, feel like joining me for something hot and hopefully caffeinated?"

"Tempting though that might be . . ." Now that Ealy had disappeared around the corner, Kindra really *was* tempted to join Green Eyes. Instead, she waved a careless hand at the glass-walled building. "I'm waiting for Daddy to finish a meeting. He's late. As usual."

"Too bad. Guess I'll have to hope I'm there to catch you next time you decide to fall." He smirked, the smile and the gleam in his eyes both teasing, but the kind of tease that invited you to join in. "My name's Dru, by the way, baby."

Kindra forced her face into a frown even though the easy way that endearment tripped off his tongue was oddly intriguing. "And my name *isn't* baby."

He laughed. "Yeah. I know."

With a mock salute and that same smirking smile, Dru shoved his hands in the pockets of his black jacket and sauntered across the street. A disconcertingly strong surge of disappointment filled her chest as he walked away. *He didn't ask my name.* Which was a stupid thing to be disappointed about. It wasn't like she could have given him her real one.

"Having fun?" Sera asked.

"Say another word and you're going to be in as much trouble as Kindra is, Seraphina." Odira's tone was so even and dry that Kindra knew she was fucked.

She shook off the encounter with Dru. "Not my fault the shoe broke."

Odira said nothing. *Fantastic.* Endless hours of drills would be the best-case scenario. Twice now Kindra had made a mistake during this job, so it was likely Odira would come up with something awful when they were done. Only the scarf had been Kindra's *fault*, but that never seemed to matter to Odira.

Getting locked out in the snow when they left the city for a new base (in the name of endurance training, of course)? Adding a new poison to the list of daily ingestions in hope of eventual immunity (Odira's ode to outdated mithridatic beliefs)?

Whatever Odira's punishment, it was worth it.

Excellent self-control was the only reason Kindra could keep the stupid smile off her face. She was *glad* her shoe had snapped. When was the last time she'd talked to someone just to talk to them? Not as part of a job or to get close to a target or because she needed to grill them for information. Elementary school? Probably. In the middle of third grade, Odira and Amett had pulled her out of school for good.

Yes, there was something strange about Dru, something that seemed familiar or wrong—Kindra wasn't sure which—but right now it didn't matter. He had caught her when she fell and smiled at her for no reason. It had felt nice.

Is that what normal life is like? Is that what I could have if I ever find a way out?

It wasn't worth thinking about because it wasn't ever going to happen.

I really hope Daddy is going to bring me new shoes, Kindra texted as she limped back to the benches. It was hard enough to run in these when the heel was attached.

So far the only good thing about today—this *week*—had been meeting Dru. She'd likely never see him again, which was for the best, considering the roads that relationship could possibly travel. It would either be a one-night stand or involve some level of bloodshed. A "meet the parents" dinner was certainly impossible.

Silently laughing and then cringing at *that* image, Kindra sat down to watch for Bernard, for official investigation teams, and for any possible freelance security. So, everything. She was watching for everything.

A tour bus stopped across the street, releasing a far larger stream of tourists than others that had made the same stop recently. It was that oddity which kept Kindra's eye fixed on the spot, and it was the excess of movement that helped her pinpoint the unexpected stillness. *Oh.*

She typed into her phone, *Did you see anything odd today on channel three?*

"Checking." Sera's keyboard clicked in the background. "Shit, he's moving, he's— Nope! Gotcha, fucker. Running facial rec, but I think I know this guy. Swear I've seen his face before. I'm sending everyone a screenshot."

Kindra's phone buzzed, and she swiped at the notification to bring up the picture. A close-up of an oval-faced Hispanic man with deep-set dark eyes and a cleanly shaved head.

"Well. Guess we know who Ealy is working with." Amett's voice sounded off, somewhere between amused and annoyed.

"He can't be serious." Odira almost sounded offended. Indignant. "Javier can't even stay out of sight in the middle of a crowd! He thinks *Javier* is going to—" She cut herself off with something close to a growl.

"Who is Javier?" *And if "he" isn't Javier, who is she talking about?*

"Working on it." Sera huffed, and then her tone shifted into the professional, obviously reading from something. "Javier Martinez. It looks like everything we have on him is from when Odira and Amett ran into him last year during that Tunisia thing. Twenty-seven, ex-military, and widowed—no kids. Seems to usually run with one guy he served with and— Are you guys serious? This scruffy, white frat boy is *actually* named John Smith? Okay, then. Last year you thought they were working with two others—a Chechnyan couple you ID'd as Bashir and Nuura Umarov. If Kinny's escapee is working with them now, he wasn't in Tunisia."

Why is Javier . . . Oh.

A realization lit up like the flash of gunfire on a dark night. Odira had already said it, hadn't she? *"After this screwup, we're going to have a hell of a time keeping them from bringing in another team."*

Javier's team was on the job, so taking out the Westons was almost certainly on their to-do list. Kindra would bet her life and Odira's wrath that Javier Martinez was spending his afternoon doing what they were doing: gathering intel.

The "he" Odira had been so indignant about? The client. Odira couldn't believe whoever was pulling the blood-covered strings inside Redwell thought Javier would be able to take out the Westons. Kindra would be a little offended by the idea too if she weren't royally pissed the fuck off.

Would Odira and Amett share anything with her and Sera? This had to count as an exception to their usual ask-no-questions policies. This wasn't a client thing; this was Damocles's sword in the form of a hot Spanish ex-military grunt with a gun and backup. Yes, he could possibly be here on a job that had nothing to do with Bernard and Redwell, but Kindra didn't put much stock in coincidences.

So what's up? Do we have a plan tonight? Kindra sent the text and then scanned Columbus Circle, looking for anyone else who felt out of place.

"Stay exactly where you are." Odira's order came through sharp and clear. "Amett, see if you can deliver a love letter."

That confirmed it. If Amett and Odira were paying any attention to Javier at all, it meant they believed he was here for them.

"Warning or wound?" Paper crinkled through Amett's comm.

"Warning. For now." Odira grunted, the noise carrying a level of dissatisfaction that she rarely allowed to escape.

They were letting Martinez walk away? Death sent a much longer-lasting message, especially when the message was for people who'd been sent to kill them.

Amett didn't argue the orders. Then again, no one questioned Odira, not even her husband. Maybe especially not him.

From her perch on the bench, Kindra watched Amett move in. He was dressed in a blue suit with a huge black coat, but curled over a walker, looking so gray and frail that even she had to stuff down the urge to help him cross the street. Amett shuffled slowly down the sidewalk, approaching Javier. The limited space and shifting pathways of the crowded sidewalk made it easy for him to step ever so slightly closer to Javier than was usually polite. Even knowing what Amett was going to do, Kindra couldn't spot it. The drop was that clean.

Kindra shifted her position, holding her phone up as though taking a selfie, so she could watch Javier through the camera's enhanced zoom. It was a couple of minutes before Javier lifted his fingers to his mouth, blew on them, and then stuck them in the pockets of his slate-gray duffle coat. He jerked his hand out again like it'd been scalded, his eyes darting from face to face in the surrounding crowd. When he pulled out the paper—a scrap clearly torn from something—his body stilled.

"He can't decide if he's pissed or impressed." Sera laughed and then started humming "One Way or Another." With the song playing in the background.

"Almost finished." Odira's lack of comment on Sera's musical interlude was conspicuous. "No one has gone into Bernard's condo since he left Tuesday morning. We're not going to get anything else from this location."

"At least we figured out who Ealy is probably working for," Sera said.

Kindra wondered if Sera guessed the truth. Would the danger worry her at all even if she had?

More keystrokes on Sera's line. "Martinez is on the phone. The angle isn't great, so I can't catch everything. He's ordering a regroup, I think. Something about a raven? Maven? Something. Call ended. He's leaving. Headed downtown by foot, but he's scanning the street aaaand, yes. Hailing a cab."

Amett had been silent since before his brief contact with Javier—Kindra still couldn't believe they'd left the guy alive—but only when there was a noticeable click on the comm line did Kindra realize it was because he'd muted his mic.

"New orders." Amett's voice was even, giving little away, but Kindra still got the impression that he was annoyed. "Back to base ASAP."

Kindra looked down at her broken shoe and contemplated the various ways she was *supposed* to make it back to the town house from this position. The one plan that allowed for a cab also involved a police tail and a potential threat to her life. None of her escape plans took wardrobe malfunctions into account.

Standing carefully, Kindra hobbled toward the curb and held her hand up. She was already in trouble today, so screw it. She couldn't miss Amett briefing Odira. Hopefully he'd fill everyone in now, since the whole thing had already gone so far down the paved road to Tartarus, but . . . well, given the way the rest of this job had been going, she wasn't exactly holding her breath for that.

If Kindra wanted information, she was going to have to take it. This time around, holding on to the memory of Bernard Gasper's random act of kindness and Dru's inviting eyes, she was oddly okay with that.

But having information didn't mean anything would change. Even if she did find out that Bernard didn't deserve to die, what the effing hell was she supposed to do to stop it?

Balama, Echemorro

E ven with a suppressor, the distinctive echo of the eight gunshots made the man watching from the shadows across the narrow, cobblestone street flinch.

No sounds or people escaped the building for the next several minutes, but the man waited, still and silent. His patience was rewarded when three men filed out of the building, one leading and the others following close behind. None of them seemed to notice the man across the street raising his camera.

"We could have hired someone else to do this, Alejo," one of the men muttered in Spanish, distaste coloring his words.

"It's the devil's work, and I'll not dirty anyone else's soul with it." Alejo removed the magazine, the only part of the weapon that might hold his fingerprints, and placed it in his pocket. After wiping down the gun, he tossed it in a gutter. From the shadows, the man recorded it all.

Alejo and the others got into the car parked on the road, and left. The driver crossed himself as they passed the building. In the backseat, Alejo stripped off his leather gloves and stared blankly at his own hands.

When the car turned the corner, the man moved silently across the street. He followed the small alley dividing the buildings to a garden in the back. Using the balconies to climb up to the third floor, he entered the apartment Alejo had just left.

In the living room of the small but meticulously kept apartment, a man lay on the wood floor. His hands and feet had been locked behind him, and three others had been bound and gagged on the couch—his mother, his wife, and his son. Tears had flowed down his cheeks, leaving dark circles on the wood floor. The blood had left stains far darker.

Each room had been obviously and thoroughly searched, their contents scattered across the floor like trash. Jaw clenched, he documented the carnage but touched nothing. No mere human could save the poor souls who had once resided there.

Leaving as quietly as he'd arrived, he traveled through side streets and back alleys until he was well away from the bloodshed. Then, hands stuffed deep in the pockets of his jacket, he hummed while he strolled down the narrow, inclined streets of Balama. Neither the music nor his easy, loping strides could disguise the strength of his frame or the wariness in his dark eyes.

Several minutes later, his breath caught when something scuffed against the cobblestone street, the sound like a missed step. Still humming, he walked backward for a few steps, his chin tilted up as though his attention were on the shimmering wash of stars spread out across the sky like glitter spilled on construction paper. His eyes kept their focus on the earth, on the extra shadow spilling onto the street from the alley where his follower hid.

"I hate being right sometimes," he muttered as he resumed walking forward. In the pockets of his coat, his hands closed on what was hidden there—a flash drive in his right pocket and a gun in the left.

Quickening his pace, the man ducked into an alley, one that led away from his rented room. He hid, gun drawn and ready. A minute later someone crept around the corner. The weak slant of light from the street was just enough to reveal the gun.

The man lunged, grabbed his stalker's gun hand, and drove him back—*hard*—into the opposite wall. The stranger grunted, and his gun clattered to the ground. He didn't try to free himself—not after the cold gun barrel pressed against his throat.

"Why are you following me?" The man spoke Spanish fluently, but not with the accent of a local.

The man pinned to the wall sneered. "You're not as good as you think you are, Special Agent Isaac Marks. Especially not when we know who we're looking for."

There was a moment then when neither of them moved or blinked, as though both were waiting for the words to settle, both holding their breaths to see what the reaction would be.

Pressing the gun harder against the man's throat with one hand, Isaac began searching with the other. He found his own picture in an inside pocket of the jacket—an official headshot from his FBI personnel file—rope, zip ties, several knives, and two flash drives. He dropped everything but the drives and the picture to the cobblestone.

"If you're going to shoot me, do it already," the would-be assassin ground out between clenched teeth.

"I haven't decided yet."

"Shoot me now. It'll save you time—I'm not telling you shit."

Isaac tilted his head. "What do they have on you? Who are they threatening?"

When the man against the wall laughed, it sounded painfully close to a sob. "Everyone," he gasped. "Everything."

He took a deep breath and held it. Then, in a flash of desperate motion, he grabbed Isaac's hand on the gun and forced him to pull the trigger.

Warm blood splattered across Isaac's face, coat, and hands. For several seconds he stood motionless, but then he turned, pocketed his gun, his ID picture, and the extra flash drives, and sprinted down the alley. He ran, breathing hard and harsh, taking back routes and shortcuts to lose anyone who might still be following.

As soon as he was 'ocked inside his rented room—a heavy dresser shoved in front of the door—he stripped and stumbled into the shower. The water was only lukewarm and the pressure barely adequate. Isaac cursed at it constantly, fluently, in five languages as he scrubbed his skin nearly raw.

Several minutes later, dressed and restlessly pacing the tiny room, Isaac began to mutter.

"They know. Didn't expect to hear your real name out of his mouth, did ya, Isaac? Didn't expect him to blow his own goddamn head off either." He shuddered, a full-body tremor that left him looking a little nauseated. "So is the leak in your office or Bernard's? And you're talking to yourself again. Jesus. Altair would laugh his ass off if he saw you like this." He chuckled and rubbed his hand over his face, but the sound and the gesture were shaky. "'All your training just goes right out the window when you're working alone, doesn't it?'"

He climbed on top of his bed and pried the casing off the broken window AC unit, retrieving the laptop stashed in a waterproof protective case. Though he took the newly acquired flash drives out of his pocket, he put them down without inserting them into the computer. Instead, he plugged in his own flash drive and his camera's memory card and began uploading everything to a new email message. In the "To" column, he typed an address made of a seemingly random series of numbers and letters. Though the body was blank, his mouse hovered over the Send button.

"They'll track you as soon as you hit Send," he muttered. "Okay, okay. So, what? Dead man's trigger? Might work."

Still mumbling, Isaac composed a short message and clicked Schedule instead of Send, setting it twenty-four hours ahead. His sigh when he closed the program and shut the computer down was almost like relief.

After hiding the laptop again, Isaac settled into bed, but it was a long time before sleep found him. And even longer before he loosened his grip on the gun under his pillow.

Chapter Five

1814 : SATURDAY, FEBRUARY 13

Certain Bernard wouldn't return home, the Westons were devoting only a small portion of their attention to the security feeds from his condo. That changed when every camera and microphone started acting up at 18:14:32. First flickering. Then static. Pure static.

"Get your gear, Seraphina." Odira's voice was as grim as her expression. "We're heading over there."

"Have you completely lost your mind?" Sera's voice rang off the hardwood floors and high ceilings.

Yes, Kindra wanted to say. *They really, truly have.*

After the new orders from Redwell, the situation had become more ludicrously impossible to pull off. Because of Amett's screwup, they now had a specific list of questions for Bernard, aimed at ferreting out what information he'd had time to pass on to whom. The Westons had to capture, interrogate, eliminate, and dispose of a target that they couldn't even *find*, and they had to do it before Javier's team eliminated them.

Kindra knew better than to comment on the stupidity of any of it, but the facts and speculations about this job were like angry wasps trapped in her mind. They buzzed and stung and wouldn't be forgotten.

What makes Bernard Gasper dangerous enough to warrant a public execution? What does he have that someone else wants this bad? And how is torturing him before we kill him going to make the slime he dug up any less dangerous?

The answer to that last one? It wasn't. It would just make Bernard the first in a much longer list of people Redwell needed to eliminate.

Worse than the deaths she could see lining themselves up like dominos was that neither Odira nor Amett seemed concerned that all of the client's moves since Amett's missed hit—demanding interrogation of the target, threatening their lives with another squad, having that squad *in town already*—absolutely *reeked* of desperation. The client wasn't holding anything back now. Anyone who remotely resembled a threat was in their crosshairs.

Like the Westons.

The Westons knew about the hit on Gasper. They knew—or Odira *probably* knew—the identity of their client. They *knew*, and so if they couldn't do the job they'd been hired for, they would have to go.

Though Kindra tried to get a read on Odira, it wasn't possible. There was no expression on her face, no signal to show how far south this job had gone.

"Looks like we have a lead." Odira blinked and looked away from the screens. "We better move fast if we're going to follow it anywhere useful."

"You know what those cameras going dark means, right?" Sera asked. "No way in hell was Bernard the one who found them *and* a blocker that would work. That static means pros, Mother."

"Did I *ask* for your input?" Odira's voice was as dangerous as the slide of a pump-action shotgun. Sera and Kindra froze, staring as though she'd actually pulled a gun. When Odira spoke again, the words were only slightly more level. "If someone is bothering to take out our surveillance in the condo, it means there is something important in there they don't want us to see. And you both better stop questioning orders and making rookie mistakes, because failure is not an option on this job."

"I think our reputations would survive one missed hit," Sera muttered after a few seconds of silence.

Kindra held her breath. Would Odira fill them in on the danger they were facing?

No. Odira remained silent, staring them down with no obvious inclination to share.

Another beat of silence, and Kindra broke. For her sanity and for Sera's life, the truth—this *one* truth, at least—had to be acknowledged. "Javier is waiting for a kill order, isn't he?"

Odira's eyes were stonier than ever. "I'd bet every bullet in this house that they called Javier's team the second Amett missed."

Hearing the threat admitted aloud might've been a relief if Odira hadn't acted like it was something they should've known already. Like informing them was tedious and unnecessary, despite the fact that the playing field had changed. Their world was now full of unknowns and blind spots. The Westons were being forced to make assumptions about the opposition, and it made staying ahead of it all a challenge at best. Impossible at worst.

It pissed her off.

From the information Odira and Amett had gathered on Javier's team, patience was not their defining characteristic. Javier had likely jumped with appalling enthusiasm on the order to take the Westons out, and would be aiming to eliminate Bernard too. It'd be a double payday.

"Comms will be useless until we get that jammer fixed, so we'll call you every ten minutes to check in," Odira said as she turned and walked out of the room.

"This is such a nightmare," Sera muttered, trailing obediently after.

They grabbed gear and pounded down the stairs. The door slammed shut.

Kindra was suddenly alone and, for the first time since the hit, had an indefinite stretch of solitude ahead of her. The prescription Amett had started taking seemed to exhaust him. He'd gone to bed, likely for the night. It might be safe enough to remove the copies of Bernard's papers from their hiding place in the bedroom she shared with Sera.

Moving silently, she retrieved the copies and hurried back. She closed the door to the surveillance suite and slightly adjusted the chair sitting against the wall, just enough to make a noise if someone entered the room.

She sat down in front of the monitors that once peered into Bernard Gasper's daily life; now they showed only glimpses broken by heavy static. Although her thumb ran down the edge of the stack of paper in her lap, she couldn't make herself look at them yet. *Once you read these, you won't be able to forget. It'll only make dealing with Odira more difficult.*

Kindra had watched Odira and Amett to see if and how things would change after Amett's relegation to the background, if they would include her in their planning sessions and tell her more about the job. But they hadn't. Asking wouldn't help—she'd heard the fight the day Ryce had asked too many questions. She'd seen the careful way he held his fork at breakfast the next morning, as though his hand hurt too much to grip the utensil properly. She bore the scars of her own attempts to ask why, too.

But she couldn't *not* know. Especially not after she'd watched how reluctantly Odira shared something as crucial as the truth about Martinez's team.

If keeping secrets was more important to Odira than sharing information that could save Kindra's life . . . fine. Good to know. She obviously thought Kindra was an idiot for asking, which made it easy for Kindra to justify going behind her parents' backs without apology. She was part of this team. Information that belonged to one belonged to all. Right?

It effing will now. What belonged to one now belongs to me.

Determined—and determinedly ignoring the shiver of fear that ran through her—Kindra waited until Odira confirmed their arrival at Columbus Circle and then unfolded the papers.

The first page was numbers. Hundreds of numbers laid out in columns and rows that were labeled with coded combinations of letters and numbers. Some of the boxes on the sheet were circled, and those cells were marked with handwritten number-letter combinations. Invoices? Financial data? Export records? Without context, it was meaningless.

The next page. A death certificate issued in Echemorro for Maria de Abaroa Abreu, a name listed again on a deed selling land owned by Maria and her husband, Vasco Espinosa Abreu, to Rose Water Farms. There were sixteen more pairings—death certificates and land deeds. All of the deeds were dated after the deaths. By days. A week at most.

What the hell? Kindra stared, trying to connect the dots. A schoolyard massacre. Spreadsheets of coded numbers. Death certificates. Land deeds. How did it connect to each other? Or Redwell?

Another page, this one with photos of two very brief handwritten letters. The dates on the letters predated every single death certificate, but not by long.

3 November
To: Redwell, Inc.
Attn: Mr. Garret Hadley

I received your communique and will attempt to address the concerns regarding soil erosion of the coastal farmland you were interested in purchasing. With careful planting, and a little ingenuity in our construction plans, we should be able to combat this issue to everyone's satisfaction.

God bless,
Eduardo Melo Santos
Psalms 2:8

November 8
To: Rose Water Farms
Attn: Mr. Eduardo Melo Santos

Thank you for taking these concerns so seriously. While our agricultural department is genuinely interested in the land and eager to begin work on the plant life your teams have discovered, we simply cannot fund the project until we know that the property will remain workable throughout all phases of the research.

Have a blessed day,
Garret Hadley
Hebrews 9:22

Redwell is a company, then. And Garret Hadley . . . G. H. The client? Eduardo has to be the one in control of the enterprise in South America. Shit. I wish I could search this.

On each letter, the Bible reference had been highlighted, and both the first and third letters of the book name had been underlined, those letters written in cursive instead of printed. Nothing else had been marked. Was that the signal that the message was coded? There were at least five she could think of that might have been used, but it wasn't like she had the Bible memorized. She couldn't test the possible ciphers and codes without the correct passage, but for that she'd have to look it up. The computer wasn't an option because Odira would find it, but maybe there was a Bible on the bookshelf downstairs.

After Sera and Odira checked in, Kindra looked at the door. Even lightly drugged, Amett woke up at the faintest noises. Retrieving the papers had been safe because she'd only had to go to the next room. To get to the bookshelves, she'd have to pass the master bedroom where Amett was sleeping. It was a risk, but she might not get another chance to search, and she knew she had ten minutes before the next call.

Worth it.

Before she could get up, the doorknob shifted.

Heart thumping dangerously fast, Kindra folded the papers and slipped them under her thighs. The door opened, catching the corner of the chair. Amett nudged the chair aside, casting a vaguely confused look at it as he passed, before his gaze drifted to the static-filled screens and then at Kindra. All he asked was, "All quiet?"

"Yes." Kindra swallowed. Her left hand trembled just slightly on the arm of the chair. She reached with her steady right hand for her mug of coffee and cursed herself stupid for taking the documents out when she wasn't completely alone in the house.

Amett picked up a comm unit and placed it in his ear, his eyes scanning the staticky screens like they displayed a code he could decipher. Kindra sipped her coffee and watched him review the log. It was a series of gibberish numbers and letters to most people, but each set of eight characters she wrote when Sera checked in indicated their progress, their location in relation to the target, and their estimated time of arrival. Amett nodded as he glanced over the page.

"Couldn't sleep?" Kindra asked.

"I slept enough." He pulled a chair closer and settled down.

Then she asked a question she never would have *dared* ask Odira had the situations been reversed. "How are your hands?"

Amett's reaction was small—a blink that lasted just a touch too long and the faintest of lines forming around his eyes—but it was as telling as a full-body flinch. Slowly, he extended his left hand. At first he seemed steady, but then the tremor appeared, almost as though it started in his wrist and traveled down to the ends of his fingers.

"You really are off fieldwork?" She was pushing her luck, but Amett didn't often backhand her for daring to ask. He simply puffed up, used his intimidating, broad-shouldered, massive frame to its best advantage, and retreated into stony silence.

He shot a glare at her and pulled his hand back. "What do you think?"

Kindra met him glare for glare. "I think you should have told us before this job went to Tartarus at supersonic speeds. *Sir.*"

Amett looked away first. "Learn from my mistakes." His voice was quiet and a little rough. "This is what happens when you ignore what your body is trying to tell you. And when you keep secrets from family."

In that instant, her training slipped. She recoiled and barely kept herself from shifting her weight on the chair. The packet of papers was thick enough that she could feel its edges pressing into her thigh. Though Amett couldn't possibly see it was there, some irrational portion of her brain was sure he *knew*. Somehow.

"They're due in another ten, right?" Amett glanced at the time displayed in the lower corner of the screen and back at the log sheet. "If they haven't made progress by then, she—"

One of the feeds went black.

Amett's mouth snapped shut, and they both leaned closer, watching three more small squares of static blink to black. The cameras weren't being blocked anymore; they were *gone*.

A quick command called Odira. She answered on the first ring. "What?"

"If you don't get everything unblocked in the next sixty seconds, we're going to lose the chance we have at seeing who's taking out our tech," Amett warned.

This can't be Martinez's team. They wouldn't be disarming the bugs; they'd be trying to hack them.

"Almost there," Odira said.

One of the screens flickered. A tenor voice filled the room. "How long will they try?"

Kindra jumped, almost spilling coffee down the front of her shirt. A picture appeared, but not the one she'd been expecting. This camera should have had a perfect view of Bernard's desk in his home office, looking over his shoulder for the clearest shot of his computer screen and desk. Instead, the picture blurred, smearing across the screen.

Amett yanked the keyboard away from Kindra and adjusted the settings.

"Until he's buried alive, drowned, or burned at the stake. This one may be a long-term thing." This deeper voice laughed, the sound mirthless. "Make yourself comfortable, sweet pea."

"Odira, you hearing this shit?" Amett demanded.

"Yes." Odira's tone turned the word into a curse.

"There are worse places to get stuck," Tenor said. Something scraped, and the camera shifted. There was a wall and, at a very strange angle, a bouncing foot hanging in midair. No, not midair. The camera was on its side, catching part of someone who'd propped their feet up on Bernard's desk.

"At least Bernard's using his time wisely."

Amett swore, his eyes locked on the screen as he ran his hand over his shorn hair.

Almost in sync with Amett's imprecations, Tenor snorted. "Wisely? I know the Bible passages are code, but come on. Studying that book won't actually do much to help."

That's all you're going to give me? Kindra leaned forward an inch, holding her breath. *C'mon. Give me the key.*

"It gives him a way to keep busy. Tiffany never did keep a man entertained."

Amett grunted. The sound seemed to be part surprise and part satisfaction, but Kindra couldn't read his facial expression.

Inside Bernard's condo, there was a moment of silence, and then Tenor asked, "You think we found all of them?"

"Maybe." Deep Voice sighed. "Hopefully."

"Fifteen bugs in a three-bedroom condo is overboard," Tenor said. "How did they even get them set up?"

"They're ghosts, and they don't leave things to chance."

Another grunt from Amett, but no words. His attention was wholly focused on the screen and the strangers who seemed to know Kindra's family.

"You talk about them like they're the bogeyman," Tenor said.

Deep Voice snorted. "They're worse. Bogeymen only come out at night."

"She didn't seem that bad," Tenor said.

"She's a bogeyman in training," Deep Voice warned. "If she figures out who you are, she'll slit your throat first and question why later. Or never, maybe."

Slit their throat? Are they talking about . . . me? But how could they possibly know her penchant for knives? She glanced at Amett again. His jaw clenched.

"But R—"

"Not the same, and you know it. That was voluntary, not forced."

Tenor sighed. "It's not fair. It's like those kids in Somalia. They don't know what they're doing. Or why."

"Yeah, well, don't—"

The door opened, and a woman wearing jeans and a flak jacket walked in, her face out of frame. "Odira is still outside. Won't take her much longer to crack this blocker."

The words spurred a list of physically impossible curses from Seraphina, curses that only got more interesting when the camera moved, the picture going dark. There were shifts and clicks, like something electronic was being taken apart.

"Just heard," the woman said. "Isaac Marks is landing on Wednesday, so we'll arrange the meet as soon as possible after that. Daelan checked in, and everything is quiet with Tiffany. Later we can—"

The sound cut out.

Kindra set her mug down with a too-loud *thunk.*

"Get back here." Amett's hands were shaking so badly they rattled the keys they were resting on. "Now."

"Already on our way," Odira responded.

Amett ended the call and slumped back in his seat. "I think I'm going to have to kill them this time." He lifted one hand to trace the line of his eyebrow. "Or you will."

"This time?" Kindra stilled as one brain cell nudged another and created an actual thought. "You know who they are?"

He nodded once. "Second and third to speak, at least."

Tenor had sounded vaguely familiar to Kindra, but she discounted the possibility. It couldn't be. Tenor was slightly higher pitched than Dru, and the accent was different. Plus, if Dru had been Tenor, there would've been absolutely no reason for Kindra to have survived the encounter.

"Who are they?" Kindra doubted he'd answer.

But he did. "Your mother and I used to work with them. Hugo and Cassidy Calver."

Calver? No . . . it can't be them. Memories of a barrel-chested man with wiry dark curls, bronze skin, and a broad smile standing next to a tiny woman with pin-straight brown hair, pale beige skin, and hazel eyes popped into her head. She hadn't seen them since she was eight or so, but she had once known the Calvers well enough to call them Uncle Hugo and Aunt Cassidy.

And now he's going to kill *them?* Kindra held back a shudder. Barely.

Her family had ended so many lives in the past decade that Kindra couldn't keep count. She'd personally been the tool to help Atropos take at least thirty-six souls. It was so very different to consider killing someone who had held her as a child and made her laugh when training stressed her out.

They both fell silent, but their thoughts probably spun in very different directions. Kindra could barely imagine how different today would be if Amett hadn't missed. She likely wouldn't have fumbled the papers on the subway, and she wouldn't have ever considered keeping a copy of the documents. There wouldn't be another team on their asses, and they wouldn't be facing off against people who had once been part of the team. The family.

If Bernard had died on Tuesday, they'd probably never have known the Calvers were in town. She also wouldn't have known anything more about their client than a name. Right now she'd be trying to extend their stay in New York so she could explore the art museums and the architecture and the inane tourist stuff they never had the chance to do between jobs.

But, no. Amett had to miss that shot.

Seventeen minutes after the sound had cut out, Odira and Sera came in through the back door of the town house.

Amett moved to the top of the stairs and called down, "Were you followed?"

Kindra used the brief moment of inattetion to shove the folded papers into the waistband of her jeans at the small of her back, thankful she was wearing a jacket thick enough to hide the outline.

"The Umarovs were on us as we left Columbus Circle, but we lost them on the Upper East Side," Odira said as she ran up the stairs. "Javier is getting uppity. He might need another reminder of how this business works."

"One mess at a time." Amett ran his hand over his head again and then tilted his chin up, sighing quietly.

As she appeared on the landing, Odira's narrowed gaze flicked between Kindra and Amett. When she glanced down the stairs, toward the master bedroom, Amett shook his head. "They need to know this."

Odira's jaw tightened just a fraction, a signal that Amett would be catching hell later, but she didn't protest as she followed Amett into the surveillance suite. Seraphina was close on her heels.

"The Calvers are Bernard's new security team?" Odira said it less like a question and more like a statement in need of confirmation.

Amett shrugged. "Looks like it."

"How did he even *find* them?"

"My guess?" Amett glanced at the blank screens. "They found him and offered to keep him out of our crosshairs."

Odira cursed, and her right hand lifted to trace that scar behind her ear.

"We always knew it would come to this," Amett said, his voice softer than Kindra had ever heard it.

"*Bastards*," Odira muttered, her hand dropping. "Atropos bless it, I wish I'd been able to take a shot at them the last time they interfered."

They interfered with our jobs before?

The Westons hadn't ever botched a job, but there were oddities in their record—a few jobs where the target had gone missing or died an accidental death before the hit could be set up. There weren't many that fit either scenario, but now Kindra looked back on them with a whole new eye.

"It's been a year since we've even heard a rumor about them." Amett looked regretful. Almost. "I was hoping someone else had taken care of it."

"Who are the Calvers?" Sera's expression turned from confused to determined as she started complaining. "Why do I feel like I'm the only one in this room not hearing half this conversation? You guys suck when you do this."

Amett simply said, "We brought them in from time to time when we needed backup."

It was such an understatement, it was practically a lie. They hadn't just been team members. The Calvers had essentially been family for a long time.

At least, they had been for Kindra.

"All right. Whatever." Sera shrugged, seemingly indifferent. "One more complication on an already botched job. We'll take care of it. I don't see the problem."

Would Kindra have been that blasé if she didn't remember Hugo's easy laughter or Cassidy's oatmeal-chocolate chip cookies? Or if she hadn't found out what kind of client Odira had contracted them to?

How does this job keep going from bad to worse? Kindra closed her eyes for a moment, reining in her frustration and fighting to keep it off her face.

"'Taking care of it' might not be that easy." There was something close to reluctance in Odira's voice. And maybe grudging respect. "The Calvers are *very* good, and they know how Amett and I work. Getting ahead of them won't be easy."

Sera grinned. "You know how I like a challenge."

Kindra pressed her lips shut tight and quickly suppressed the urge to slap some sense into her sister.

"This won't just be a challenge. This will be . . ." Amett grunted. "We've changed a lot of our techniques in the past eight years, but they know *us*. They were always able to predict us."

"So? That means you guys know *them* too, right?" Sera's eyebrows arched. "I can't believe you two spent more than a week with these people and didn't figure out how to get inside their heads."

"To a point," Odira conceded. "But they didn't always do what we expected them to. It's part of the reason we finally split. They were dangerously unpredictable."

It was hard for Kindra to see either of the people in her memory as dangerous, but people didn't usually think any of the Westons were dangerous either—until they were about to die.

Kindra had learned a long time ago that the most dangerous people in the world were often the ones you'd smile at on the street, the ones who could sidle up to you without awakening a single hard-won survival instinct. The most dangerous people in the world were the ones who passed unnoticed through the crowd and were gone before anyone saw the blood spreading across the floor. She'd met those people—been raised *by* those people to *become* those people—and those people scared the shit out of her.

She'd never been scared of the Calvers. Not once.

Odira glanced at Amett. "They don't know about you. They don't know what changed or why you missed. They'll expect us to set it up for you to try again."

A slow smile spread across Amett's face, his teeth glinting against his tanned skin. "So they won't see Kindra coming."

Everyone turned to face Kindra. A shiver started at the base of her spine that raised goose bumps on the back of her neck.

Bernard's life or yours?

Under the weight of her family's eyes and the pressure of their expectations, all Kindra could do was nod. "Just tell me what the plan is. I'll take care of it."

Chapter Six
1442 : SUNDAY, FEBRUARY 14

One thing Kindra could say for sure about this disguise was that it was incredibly comfortable. Slightly baggy jeans, sneakers with two-inch lifts to make her taller, her hair hidden under a scruffy brown-black wig. Teen boy, pixie-cut girl, or none of the above? Kindra played the androgyny of the outfit to her benefit and let people make up their own minds.

The gray skies blocked what little warmth the sun might have bestowed on the city, so Kindra flipped the collar of her black coat up and then tightened the cobalt-blue scarf around her neck, raising it to cover her chin. Like most of the pedestrians on the street, she moved deliberately to avoid the patches of ice last night's brief rain had left on the sidewalk. Unlike them, her eyes took in everyone while she mentally noted three different conversations in two different languages, listening briefly for the hint of anything odd.

A separate part of her mind worked on solving the puzzle of the Calvers.

Their team was at least four: Hugo, Cassidy, Daelan, and "Tenor." It'd be five if the Michael Ealy look-alike worked with them instead of Javier. Six if Amett was wrong about "Tiffany."

The jewelry store Kindra was here to case was at the end of this block, but considering how vague Amett's hunch had been, she was pretty sure this would be a massive waste of her time and energy. The plus side of following a very vague hunch? There was no way for Martinez's team to be here. Even a few hours ago, the Westons hadn't known anyone on their team would be walking down this particular street.

It would be, while not quite impossible, not at all easy for anyone to have figured out where she was headed or to have followed her here. Kindra was keeping an eye out for Javier, John, the Michael Ealy impersonator, and Nuura and Bashir Umarov, but she truly doubted she'd spot a single one of them. She was more worried about the two members of the Calvers team whose faces she didn't know—Daelan and Tenor were unknown entities in this game.

The Calvers' involvement had given Kindra a brief moment of hope that Amett and Odira would finally bring her and Sera into the loop, but everything after that reveal had happened like it always did.

After they'd listened to the Calvers' conversation several times— often enough that the voices rang in Kindra's ears—Odira and Amett had retreated to the master bedroom and shut the door.

"Typical," Sera had muttered. "Why should we be in on the meeting? I mean, it's not like we're risking our lives or anything. Oh, wait!"

Kindra had hesitated, considering telling her sister exactly how much they weren't in on, but as much as Seraphina bitched about getting left out of the loop, she never seemed to actually mind. She tripped along happily behind Odira and Amett whenever they offered her a new puzzle to crack. There was a chance that Sera would be upset about Odira holding back crucial information, but dead kids in some country she'd never visited? Probabilities were higher that Sera would think Kindra had her priorities all sorts of twisted and then tell Odira that "Kinny might be crackin.'"

It hadn't been worth the risk. She wouldn't ever have to regret something she didn't say.

"Can you take tech?" Kindra had asked. "I need to move, or I might lose my mind."

Nodding, Sera had plopped onto the desk chair and adjusted the controls to suit her preferences, even though the only screen showing anything was the hidden camera outside Bernard's office building. In the middle of the night, watching that screen was like watching a movie on pause. Nothing but the leaves on the trees moved.

"We might have to stage a coup d'état if this goes on much longer," Sera had said as Kindra left the room.

You don't know the half of it. I'd tell you if I thought you'd care.

All Kindra had said was, "Let me know when you start the weapons cache."

Out of Sera's visual range, Kindra had moved as quickly and silently as possible on the wood floors until she reached the room next to her parents'. The interior walls of the house were thin. Pressing her ear against the drywall, she'd been able to make out the conversation on the other side.

"You can't really think they still use that code, do you?" Odira had asked Amett.

"'Tiffany' wasn't one of their codes."

"Doesn't matter. It follows the same pattern and is thus crackable. They're not stupid."

"Or they know we'd expect them to change everything from the ground up because that's what we did," Amett had said. "But I'm almost certain Hugo would keep pieces of it. Change some things, keep others, and leave everyone else guessing. And do you not remember how often Cass watched those Audrey Hepburn movies? Especially—"

"*Breakfast at Tiffany's*," Odira had supplied. "That's still a stretch. You know what he threatened if we get this wrong."

"He" who? Hugo? Javier? The client?

"What else do we have?" Amett's voice had dipped to just above a whisper. Kindra missed some of the words, but caught the end of the sentence. ". . . doesn't happen, because you're right. Hugo and Cassidy have Bernard—they've probably had him since Tuesday, if that photographer we spotted was one of theirs. If we don't finish this before they get Bernard to that meeting with Marks and the other Feebs on Wednesday, he'll make good on those threats."

Shit. The FBI? Wait . . . Cassidy mentioned Isaac Marks arriving Wednesday. Is he a Feeb? Maybe that's who Bernard is working with.

Kindra hadn't heard any more. Mind spinning, she'd gotten the hell out of there before Odira and Amett saw her lurking.

Two minutes later, Odira and Amett had returned to the surveillance suite and declared that "Tiffany" was code for a hideout in a jewelry store. They'd sounded a lot more certain than Kindra knew they were, and the FBI hadn't been mentioned. Not once. Neither had the Wednesday deadline they were apparently operating under. Kindra had swallowed the questions she'd wanted so badly to ask. At least until they'd pulled up a list of jewelers and jewelry stores in Manhattan and the boroughs.

"Over five thousand?" Sera had stared at Amett and Odira, her round eyes a little wider than usual. She'd waited as though expecting them to say it had all been some strange joke. They hadn't. "Are you two brain-dead? Even if we take the code literally, there are still, what? *Six* Tiffany & Cos. in the city?"

"They're not at Tiffany's." The conviction in Amett's voice had seemed unfeigned that time. "They're somewhere smaller. An old building with thick walls and, most likely, a basement that has a connection to another building and, thus, another exit."

Kindra had crossed her arms and leaned against the wall, watching her parents carefully. "How can we be sure she's even referencing *Breakfast at Tiffany's*? That can't be the only classic movie that uses the name."

"It's the best lead we have," Odira had said, her finger tracing the scar behind her ear. "We're following it. Get onboard fast, girls."

Odira had looked one loud noise away from using somebody as a living punching bag. Kindra had even kept her breathing quiet for the rest of the night, watching as Sera had hacked the city's records for every jewelry store Amett and Odira thought might be a possibility.

Architectural plans had narrowed the field to fifty. Drive-by sweeps had whittled that list down to twenty. Logic had arranged the final seven, and Odira had picked the two most likely stores for Kindra and Sera to recon.

Which was why Kindra now found herself walking down this icy, crowded street alone.

With their tech, time, and resources stretched thin, Kindra had no cameras watching her, no backup within shouting or shooting distance, and no real hope that she would actually find something useful here today. Her only connection to the others were the tiny comm and mic she wore.

A man lingered a little too long on the curb. Kindra watched him shift uneasily. He could be adjusting the fit of a hidden holster and— No. He was trying to fix a wedgie without using his hands. Huffing an annoyed breath, she moved on, meandering down the street.

Despite the frigid temperatures, several vendors had sidewalk tables set up, including a woman selling used books. Kindra glanced at the titles, her eyes briefly clinging to an oversize coffee-table book on surrealist art, but it was only when she noticed a pocket-size Bible sitting on a corner of the table that her attention shifted completely off her surroundings.

Kindra picked up the Bible and raised an eyebrow in question.

"Two," the old woman said with a smile.

Handing over two dollars, Kindra walked away before the woman could say anything else.

"What was that?" Odira asked.

"Someone tried to sell me a book," she mumbled.

"Don't draw attention," Odira warned.

This is New York City, she wanted to say. *I could have purple hair, a magician's cape, and a huge sign that says, "Follow me to Wonka's chocolate factory," and people* still *wouldn't pay attention.*

She bit her tongue to keep the words in. It was a near thing, though, and that was worrying. Keeping her emotions in check, or stuffing them down so deep she forgot she had them, wasn't usually a problem. Now she had a Bible that probably wouldn't get her any closer to answers, and she was mentally barking at the only people in the whole world who knew the real her—the only ones who knew she was alive.

Harsh as Odira could be most days, this was the only family she had.

How sad is that?

The thought jarred her, but it didn't stop her from opening the Bible and searching for the passages she needed. She found Psalms 2:8 first: "Ask of me, and I shall give thee the heathen for thine inheritance, and the uttermost parts of the earth for thy possession."

It didn't mean anything to Kindra, and seeing the passage didn't give her any clues that broke the code. She read the passage until she had it memorized. Frustrated, she flipped pages until she found Hebrews 9:22: "And almost all things are by the law purged with blood; and without shedding of blood is no remission."

Blood. Twice in one passage. That couldn't be good.

As she slipped the small book into the inside pocket of her coat, Kindra shook her head. She knew nothing useful *and* had one more thing to hide from her parents. At least the Bible would confuse rather than infuriate them.

Letting the Bible quotes fall into her subconscious, Kindra concentrated on her mission: scope out Amour Pour Toujours (specializing in antique jewelry since 1940), find out that nothing was happening worth noting, leave, and maybe steal some time to swing by the Met and decompress before she headed back to the town house. That was her plan, and it was a good plan, until she noticed a familiar camera bag bearing a patch that said in bright-green letters, *Nerd? I prefer the term intellectual badass.* move past her on the sidewalk.

The Westons habitually called on one of the three Greek Fates; Kindra had long since been trained out of believing in coincidence.

It was the photographer. How many camera bags in the city had that particular patch sewn on? The height was right and so was the way she moved: an easy, almost skipping gait. A lime-green hat covered her hair, a thick black coat obscured her figure, and the turned-up collar hid most of her face.

Trailing at a short distance, she watched the girl greet a few people like she knew them, with warm smiles and lingering hellos. Coincidence solidified into purpose when the photographer entered Amour Pour Toujours.

Clearing her throat, she murmured, "The hunch might've been right."

"What?" Something thudded on Odira's side of the comm. "Report."

Kindra turned as though the bakery's display window had caught her eye. The Bluetooth earpiece kept her from looking like she was talking to herself. "I'm just saying that the Good Samaritan moment from last week didn't go over well, and repeating it now won't be any better."

"She's there?" Odira cursed. "Is she near the store?"

"It's not *near*; it's a direct hit."

"Sera! Anything?"

"A whole lotta nuthin," Sera said. "Want me to head uptown?"

"Yes. Get nearby fast for backup."

"And me?" Kindra leaned closer to the window and examined a brightly decorated cake. It had swirls of yellow and green frosting that built up in the center to look like an abstract bouquet of flowers. It was cool. For a cake. It reminded her of a piece she'd seen in a Parisian gallery two years ago. She'd liked that painting so much, she'd been tempted to steal it.

"Move in," Odira said after a moment of silence. "Recon *only*. Confirm."

Kindra rolled her shoulder, settling deeper into her disguise and the substitute personality that came with it. "Whatever you say."

"And Kindra?" Amett this time, his voice slightly softer than usual, almost . . . hesitant?

"Yeah?"

"Be careful." There seemed to be *concern* in Amett's tone. "Get out of there if you even *think* they might make you."

"Gotcha." Today was not the day Kindra wanted to die. Not in a jewelry store with backup miles away. Not here. Not for this job. "I'll talk to you later."

She smiled at the baker when his eyes met hers, but shook her head when he tried to wave her inside, pointing instead at the cake and giving him a thumbs-up. The man grinned.

Keeping her smile on like a mask, Kindra kept walking, moving closer to Amour Pour Toujours two shops down.

When she opened the glass-paneled door, a tone rang through the shop—an electronic notification trying to sound like an old-school bell but never quite achieving its goal. A woman in a red blazer and black silk blouse raised an eyebrow when Kindra stepped in, and her professionally detached smile never reached her eyes.

"Can I help you, sir?" Her voice was just as smoothly silky as her blouse.

Guess I know what part I'm playing now, Kindra thought. "Valentine's Day blindsided me somehow. Again. I need something before dinner tonight."

"You've come to the right place." Her smile became a little more genuine. "What kind of stones does your love prefer?"

Kindra sidled closer to the counter. "Well, he's not a fan of yellow gold."

"You're in luck. Many estates we've purchased from recently have contained a lot of work in silver, white gold, and even titanium in some of the newer pieces."

Kindra perused the displays on the walls first, giving herself a chance to check out the security cameras discreetly hidden in the corners. Two more cameras than a store this size had any use for. The extras had wide-angle lenses—a different make and model than the rest.

"Do you have anything with the tree of life on it?" Kindra turned her attention to the wall behind the counter. "Or something a little . . . whimsical?"

"Hmm." The woman walked along the glass case circling the room.

Kindra peered down the hallway behind the counter. The photographer stood there, talking to a guy with olive-tan skin and dark-brown, curly hair. He leaned against the wall, his arms and his ankles crossed, and he had a crooked half smile that reminded Kindra of Sera's.

"What about this?" The saleswoman took a pendant out of the case. Kindra pulled her attention away from the hallway just as the photographer glanced in her direction, missing making eye contact by milliseconds.

"A distinct possibility." The circular silver pendant had a beautifully engraved Pegasus in the center. With options like that, Kindra was beginning to think she'd actually buy something. "Do you have anything else along those lines? His tastes run simple rather than elaborate, so this end of the spectrum is perfect."

With a satisfied smile, the woman replaced the pendant. "I have another one that is a bit more Celtic, but you did ask about the tree of life."

She moved toward another case, and Kindra glanced at the hallway. The guy was gone. The photographer had taken his place, leaning heavily against the wall to watch the store. Watch *Kindra.*

Their eyes met, though at this distance Kindra couldn't tell what color hers were. Kindra smiled and waved. Because that's what people did. Normal people didn't hide or slink about in the shadows. They went places and made friends. Even when those friends were strange girls who lurked in hallways behind jewelry stores and stood watch over a door with a really subtle trip wire rigged to . . . *shit*. To something that looked like a strip of C-4 molded to the doorframe and then painted to blend in. Anyone who tried to walk through that door without permission wouldn't just be bleeding, they'd be broken and burning.

The girl in the shadows didn't twitch an eyebrow in response. She stared with the kind of focused attention that made Kindra's skin itch, and Kindra knew it was time to get out.

"Might these work?" The saleswoman passed her a silver necklace first. Like the Pegasus pendant, this was a silver circle, but the design was a tree surrounded by intricate Celtic knots. The silver cuff bracelet in the woman's hand was clearly made to match, the design elongated but otherwise identical.

The level of detail in the etchings alone was gorgeous. "That is *perfect*. Can you wrap those up? I'll take both."

The slight widening of her eyes was the only indication that Kindra had surprised the woman. She covered it up quickly. "Of course."

In the hallway, the photographer stepped closer. The move brought her deeper into the patch of shadow under a blown lightbulb, so Kindra still couldn't see her. Not well enough to sketch her later.

After handing over a credit card and a fake ID, Kindra kept the corner of her eye on the girl in the shadows. She hadn't moved, and Kindra didn't like feeling analyzed. As soon as Kindra had the receipt and the bag in her hands, she left the store and walked briskly down the street.

"Hey, guys?" she quietly said. "I think I'm going to head home and watch Jeopardy."

"Get out." Amett was supposed to be nearby, but Kindra knew he couldn't risk showing his face on this street in *any* disguise. "Sera is almost on-site, and she'll take over observation."

A cab rolled to a stop half a block up as Amett spoke. Only the girl's purse—a beat-up black leather bag that they'd repurposed for a hundred different disguises—identified Seraphina. The wig she wore was dirty blonde and slightly stringy, and her clothes were simple— boots, jeans, a gray shirt, and a black coat. The way she moved and stood somehow made her look small, exhausted, and absolutely harmless. It was weird to see.

Sera plodded up the block on the opposite sidewalk, and Kindra ran across the street, flagging down another cab before it could pull away from the curb. Opening the door, she slid into the backseat and rattled off an address eight blocks from the town house. Out the window, she watched Amour Pour Toujours pass by.

The photographer was standing at the window, her eyes following the cab until, at the last second, they switched to Sera, watching her progress and judging her, measuring her the same way they'd weighed and measured Kindra.

"Be careful," Kindra said.

"I got this," Sera mumbled.

But she didn't have anything, and it took less than ten minutes to see that.

"Shit." After Sera's curse, shuffling of fabric and quick footsteps echoed through the comm. "Our Good Samaritan has looked out the window in my direction too many times, and I can't be one hundred percent, but I think I just saw John Smith drive by in that Mini Cooper. There's a tiny chance I'm wrong, but fuck this. That's not a chance I'm taking today."

The only way anyone on Javier's team could've known where they were was if someone told him. The only people who could have done that were the Calvers. At this point, being anywhere the Calvers *or* Martinez's crew could pinpoint was a *bad* idea.

Amett immediately ordered the retreat that Sera was already making.

"Do you think Cassidy would reach out to Javier?" Amett asked. "Why risk giving their position away?"

"All they had to do was get news to Javier that we'd been spotted in the neighborhood. If Cassidy did it right, John and Javier have no idea who tipped them off *and* she got to make it clear that she knew we were there without talking to us directly." Wary admiration seemed to be layered under Odira's words. "Looks like she's still thinking like me."

Amett grunted. "Best way to win a two-front war is to get your enemies to fight each other."

Kindra listened to it all as the cab dropped her off on a nearly deserted residential street. Without having to worry about anyone else's eyes judging her, and less of a need to care about mussing the swaths of makeup on her face, Kindra gave in to the temptation to rub her hands over her face. The groan she bit back, though—her comm was still active.

"Get back to the base," Odira said once they were sure Sera had made it out of the area safely and—as far as they were able to tell—without a tail. "We need to regroup."

Kindra agreed and then went silent. As if regrouping would help. This whole job seemed to be one fiasco after another. If the Calvers were willing to point Javier's team in their direction, their lives had just gotten ten thousand times more difficult.

Across the street from Amour Pour Toujours, a man who bore a striking resemblance to Michael Ealy waited. A black beanie, black Yankees hoodie, and a slate-gray scarf obscured most of his features—everything but his amber eyes. He'd followed a girl here from the town house in the West Village. The girl with a long braid of hair had left the house dressed in black skinny jeans and a black coat buttoned up, but had transformed along the way into a scruffy-haired guy in baggy jeans who'd sauntered into the jewelry store about ten minutes ago.

Now, that guy/girl/person was jumping into a cab. The cab disappeared and the only other empty cab on the street was already too far off for him to jump into.

"Fucking hell." Nose wrinkling in frustration, he pulled a phone out of his pocket and slumped against a blank stretch of brick wall, keeping one eye on the jewelry store. He entered a phone number in a new text and then began typing.

Situation is complicated and search is ongoing. Still alive, though. Please don't hate me.

The first response came back in less than a minute, and then they kept coming.

WHAT DO YOU THINK YOU ARE DOING?

YOU'RE GONNA GET YOUR PUNK ASS KILLED.

TELL ME WHERE YOU ARE RIGHT THE FUCK NOW, ASSHOLE.

DO YOU EVEN CARE HOW FAR UP MY ASS GUNNY MOORE HAS BEEN SINCE YOU WENT AWOL?

The smile on his face somehow looked both fond and pained as he read the messages. It got even more pained when he typed an answer.

I don't want you involved in this, Geo.

Grinding his teeth, he scanned the street and checked Amour. There was a girl standing in the window, her eyes locked on something on his side of the street. He followed her gaze, confusion creating furrows between his brows when he spotted a different blonde girl. His phone's vibration drew his attention down.

Aaron, no. I'm serious. Come home. Or let me help.

He cringed. *I can't.*

If you love me at all, you won't leave me here wondering every second if you've finally gone and gotten yourself killed.

I love you enough to keep you well away from this shit. I'm turning off the phone and changing numbers. Don't send anything here. I won't get it.

He pried off the back of the phone, but it vibrated before he removed the battery. A little warily, he turned it over and opened the new text.

Die on me and I will never forgive you.

Eyes closed, shoulders curled in, and phone pressed to his forehead, he breathed deep. A few seconds later, he dropped his hand to slowly, reluctantly type one last message.

I know.

Before another message could arrive, he popped the battery out, changed SIM cards, shoved the phone into his pocket, and glanced back at the blonde girl.

She was in motion, booking it down the street almost at a jog. In the jewelry store's wide front window, two people watched her leave: the same girl who had been standing there earlier, and a broad-shouldered man whose long-sleeve button-down shirt wasn't baggy enough to hide the gun holstered on his belt.

He shifted away from the wall, moving as though to follow the girl, but then he glanced back at the jewelry store and subsided.

As he settled against the brick again, his thumb absently traced the casing of the cell phone in his pocket. However strong the temptation might've been for him, he didn't take it out.

Chapter Seven

The plan had been simple: wait for the Calvers to move Bernard, and then ambush them. Transit was always dangerous when trying to protect a civilian, a fact that would work to the Westons' advantage. As long as they were in the right place at the right time.

To that end, two of the team had been within a block of Amour Pour Toujours ever since the cameras had been installed. It was where Odira and Sera were now: one of them watching the front exit of Amour's building, and one watching the street a block uptown. Amett had been right—the basement of Amour connected with the basement of the store behind it.

It had only taken an hour to set up cameras. Kindra had thought that everything would move fast after that. Almost a day and a half later, nothing had changed except her caffeine intake.

The jamming signal they'd expected was in place, one they'd partially foiled by running their equipment on as many different frequencies as possible. The signal seemed to emanate from somewhere in the vicinity of Amour.

Now, three of the six cameras were pure static. This jammer, or something like it, must have been running on Sunday when Kindra had cased the store too. She'd been surprised when Odira stayed silent through her recon run, but it wasn't until they regrouped that Kindra had realized her comm had dropped out the instant she stepped inside the store.

Even after the fact, it scared Kindra how entirely alone she'd been in there. If she'd died or disappeared, they probably wouldn't ever have known what happened. She would've vanished, leaving, at most, a little blood in her wake.

Just like Ryce.

Kindra shuddered; the motion shifted the small Bible still hidden in her coat pocket. Luckily, it was freezing inside the house and everyone had more important things on their minds, so no one had questioned why she was wearing it. She glanced over her shoulder as though she could see through the walls to where the copied documents were stashed. She hadn't had a chance to finish going through more than half of them.

So many secrets. They felt like acid bubbling under her skin, some slow-acting chemical that was beginning to eat away at her sanity and her control.

The door behind her slammed open so hard it bounced off the wall. Kindra jumped, a good quarter of the warm coffee in her mug splashing onto her coat, her shirt, and the desk, barely missing the two keyboards sitting there.

"I don't think I've ever said this before, but it's true right now," Sera said. "I hate my life. Everything *sucks*."

Kindra grabbed a tissue from the box on the corner of the desk. Sera stopped next to Kindra's chair, eyeing the coffee stains though they barely showed up on Kindra's black shirt. This was why almost everything they wore when not in disguise was dark—easier to hide the stains.

"You're mainlining caffeine again, aren't you? You always get hella jumpy when you're hopped up on coffee." Sera smirked. "That's another reason why bidis are better."

"A caffeine addiction is more manageable." Kindra tossed the wet tissues into the trash. "And it smells better. Why didn't you guys call in your return?"

"Odira is even jumpier than you right now. She thought she heard a click on the comm."

"A click?" Kindra faced her sister with wide eyes. "I thought no one could find your comm frequency?"

"Yeah, well, either Odira is beyond mental, or she was right when she said that Cassidy Calver is a tech genius."

"So are you." That'd been Sera's thing. Tech and sharpshooting. She was slightly better on the tech, but she had more fun with the guns.

"Odira makes this woman sound like a combination of Bill Gates, Adrian Lamo, Gigabyte, and the goddess Athena herself." Sera sank to the hardwood floor and plopped her legs open to a middle split as wide as her dark-wash skinny jeans would allow. The heels of her combat boots thudding against the floor wasn't enough to mask the loud *pop* of her hip joint or the grateful groan Sera gave as she folded over and pressed her cheek to the cool floor. Then she sighed. "I'm not sure how much of it is paranoid bullshit and how much we should be taking seriously, Kinny."

"Given this"—Kindra waved her hands at the monitors blinking in and out of static—"and how fast she was able to get a message to Javier without giving away their location, it might not be a horrible idea to err on the side of paranoia."

Sera thumped her forehead against the floor once. "I *hate* going up against a pro team! Especially when we're on the wrong end of the informational scale."

Kindra used another tissue to sop up a little of the coffee that had soaked into her coat. "The what?"

"Informational scale." Sera shifted positions, stretching over first her left leg and then her right as she watched Kindra out of the corner of her eye. "Right now it's weighted out of our favor. The Calvers know who we are, how many we've got, and where we have to go to get what we need. We've got pretty close to jack shit. It's like they dropped completely off the grid after Odira cut them out."

"Thought you liked a challenge." Kindra lobbed the tissue into the trash can.

"*Challenging* is not the same thing as *impossible*," Sera griped.

Kindra hummed agreement, but said nothing. Her caffeine tolerance must be getting pretty damn high, because her thoughts felt like they were moving through mud. Her body sagged, exhaustion weighing on her like a metric ton of snow—a feeling she knew from experience. That had sucked, but this was worse. She couldn't dig her way out of this one, and even sleep probably wouldn't alleviate her fatigue much.

For a second, maybe less, Kindra reconsidered telling Sera, sharing the burden.

A figure moved into view on one of the few cameras transmitting. The caffeine Kindra had thought wasn't working surged through her bloodstream at full strength. "Is that *Amett*?"

"Is he wearing body armor?" Sera sprang up from the floor. "I don't think he's wearing body armor. He's fucking exposed, without a disguise, in full view of a known enemy camp, without his body armor." There was no snark this time. Incredulity filled her face and her voice. "Are we sure his disease isn't neurological? Or terminal? Because I think he's trying to commit suicide by security team."

"Where's Odira? Is she downstairs?"

"No, she . . ." Sera's face blanked. "She said they had an errand to run."

Amett strolled across the street, inconspicuous until he tossed something through the front window of the store.

"Was that—" Kindra blinked as the storefront exploded.

The blast was small, more for fire than for destructive force, but Amett and Odira weren't done. He ran, aiming for a van she didn't recognize. Odira was waiting there, half of an arsenal emerging from the open side door Amett dove into seconds before she drove the van out of camera range.

"They've lost their minds. They've *lost their fucking minds*!" Sera screamed.

Kindra's finger was on the comm's Talk button. Amett's voice boomed through the speakers before Kindra could say a word. "If this goes south, grab as much cash, weapons, and clothes as you can carry and *run*." The words were harsh with static but intelligible.

"And if it *doesn't*?" Kindra demanded.

Amett laughed. "Then you'll be joining the fun."

Fire climbed up the front of the building. The van reappeared in a different camera, turning onto the street one block uptown.

The basement door of Amour opened. Odira fired. Each round from the AK-47 reverberated through the speakers, echoed from both Odira's and Amett's comm mics. The bullets lodged in the quickly closed door, buried themselves in the brick face of the building, shattered second-story windows, and probably killed a handful of people in those apartments. People who shouldn't have died tonight.

Kindra's stomach rolled. So much collateral damage. Too much.

Lights flipped on up and down the street, and the police scanner in the corner crackled to life with a dispatcher calling in all cars. Multiple gunshots. Possible explosion. Fire trucks needed to respond to a two-alarm fire, possibly three.

That street would never be the same again.

"You're about to have a lot of very unwelcome company," Kindra warned. A lot of it. If Javier Martinez even wanted to *pretend* to be a legitimate player, he was hooked up to the police scanners too. He'd know exactly where to find Odira and Amett, and if he could mobilize fast enough, he'd be ready to swoop in and finish off the Westons and the job.

"Lima Charlie." Amett huffed the "loud and clear" signal as though he was running. With all the chaos on screen, it was hard to tell if he was still in the van or not.

"It's been too long since we did a full-frontal assault." Odira sounded like she was on the verge of laughter as she pulled her guns into the van and closed the sliding door. "I missed explosions."

Amett *did* laugh. The sound made Kindra and Sera glance at each other, jaws slack.

Sera recovered first, clearing her throat and pressing the comm button to ask, "Who the hell are you lunatics, and what have you done with my parents?"

"Gear up, girls." Still laying down suppressive fire on the rear exit, Odira rattled off a list of ammo, guns, knives, and clothes that had Kindra scrambling for a pen and paper. Kindra's memory was good— they'd trained her too well for it to be anything else—but forgetting something important seemed like a pretty solid possibility right now.

"Most of it is packed and ready in your room," Amett added. "Less than five minutes. Be ready."

The line went quiet.

"Why do I have the feeling at least one of us is going to die tonight?" Sera asked.

"Because you were right." Kindra stood and strode toward their bedroom. "Our parents have lost their effing minds, and they're dragging us along for the ride."

All Kindra could hope was that she could get herself—and, with any luck, Sera—out of this alive. She hoped, but she wasn't planning on holding her breath for it anytime tonight.

Chapter Eight

K indra had very little in the way of personal possessions: a favorite customized Colt 1911 handgun, a *fantastic* collection of knives she'd stolen over the years, a few changes of practical clothing in different shades of dark, and—after this job—a Bible, a jewelry set, and a stack of stolen documents. All of that had to leave the house with her. Even if the Westons all survived to see the sunrise, Kindra had a feeling that packing up camp was going to be a rushed affair. She wanted everything that mattered with her *now*.

Sera had bolted downstairs as soon as she grabbed the duffel waiting on the floor on her side of the bed, but Kindra aimed for the bathroom. The weapons she strapped to herself, the clothes she stuffed in the duffel on top of the gear and cash, but the Bible, the jewelry, and the packet of paper she hid. Gearing up had only left her a couple of minutes to work with. Moving quickly, she cut a 4-inch slit in the lining of an empty side pocket of the bag, slipped her contraband inside, and used wide stitches to sew up the gap with supplies from her med kit.

"Hurry your ass up!" Sera shouted up the stairs seconds before Kindra finished. As soon as the thread was tied off, Kindra threw the bag over her shoulder and sprinted to the front door.

"Okay, fine." Kindra met Sera on the town house's tiny stoop. "Bidis *are* better. Coffee makes me pee."

Snorting, Sera ran down the steps and dove into the van idling in the street, Amett at the wheel. It wasn't the same one he'd jumped into earlier, and Odira wasn't with him.

"Why do I have the feeling at least one of us is going to die tonight?" Had Sera's question been more prescient than they'd realized?

"Where is she?" Kindra demanded.

"Watching the escape routes and getting a tracker on any person or car that tries to leave." He drove far faster than Kindra had ever traveled the streets of Manhattan, even at this hour of the night. "All in all, it's gone to plan."

"Plan? You guys call this mess a *plan*?" Sera had clambered up front to sit in the passenger seat. Her fists were clenched on her thighs. Kindra knelt between the seats. "This was *not* a plan. This was a botched suicide attempt."

"No, this was us flushing out a target before someone flushed *us* out." Amett's fingers tightened around the wheel. "When you're running your own team, you'll get to make the calls. Right now you're still under our command, so shut up or find yourself dumped in military boarding school."

"Like that wouldn't be easier than dealing with this shit." Sera pulled her Kevlar on, strapping it into place with violent jerks.

"Easier"? Most days it would probably feel like a vacation.

"This has something to do with that call Odira got while we were out, doesn't it?" Sera asked. "She got weird as soon as she hung up with whoever that was."

Was it Garret? What the hell could he have possibly said to prompt this descent into insanity?

"Bernard Gasper cannot make it to the meeting with Isaac Marks tomorrow. Everything else is now a secondary concern." Amett reached back to hand Kindra a comm. "Here."

"I have one."

"This is tweaked." Amett let go of the device, and Kindra barely caught it before it hit the metal floor. "Odira set it up to shift frequencies every few seconds. Hopefully that will make it harder for anyone to listen in or block it."

Switching it on, Kindra peered at the tiny earpiece for a moment before fitting it into her left ear. "Cassidy is really that good?"

Amett nodded as he handed a second comm to Sera. "Both the Calvers are really that good. And whoever they're working with probably is too."

"We have movement," Odira said. The shifting frequencies warped her voice slightly, but the words were clear. "Three cars. I count six people. One of them has to be Bernard. Javier is late, but I'm sure we can expect him any second."

Amett pulled over next to a black, midnineties Honda Civic. "Kindra, hot-wire it and follow the tracker Odira gives you."

She grabbed her duffel bag, slid the door open, and hopped down to the street. When she turned to check for any last orders, Amett tossed a handheld GPS unit out the window and then he and Sera were gone, racing toward their targets at a speed just shy of noticeably dangerous.

None of them had time to waste. Bernard and the Calvers were getting away.

Extracting a wedge and a slim jim from her bag, Kindra pried the door open a crack, slid the slim jim inside, and had the car open in about fifteen seconds. She shut off the dome light, using a small flashlight instead, and removed the cover from the steering column. It took her another minute to bring the car to life. There was a rattle to the engine she didn't like—not surprising in a car this old—but the thing ran.

"I'm in motion." She pulled out of the parking spot, but didn't turn the headlights on until she made it halfway down the block.

"Follow the car marked Tango-One-Mike-Three," Odira ordered. "You're looking for a white Mercedes coupe. Confirm target is present before contact, and keep your eyes on the rearview for unwelcome guests."

"Lima Charlie." Kindra set the GPS in the convenient cell-phone holder mounted to the windshield and navigated toward the aforementioned target. A minute later, Odira barked out two more tracking markers—one for Amett and the other for Sera. Her sister must have swiped another ride.

Following the little white dot on the screen wasn't easy, since the coordinates on the map didn't care about insignificant things like one-way streets or solid buildings. It took her ten minutes to catch up. The coupe was on the Upper East Side and heading farther uptown.

"I think my target might be heading for LaGuardia," Kindra reported. "Or at least a hideout in Queens. It looks like they're aiming for the Kennedy Bridge."

"Stop them before they get anywhere near that airport," Odira bellowed. "If Bernard gets on a plane—"

A screech of tires cut off whatever she'd been about to say.

"They're two blocks away from me." Kindra took a sharp right, the car skidding into the turn. "Still about a mile to go before we hit the bridge."

"Mask, Kindra," Amett snapped. "Do *not* let them get a good look at you."

"Lima Charlie." *Because partially obscured vision is always helpful when driving.*

Kindra grabbed a full-head mask from her bag and pulled it on one-handed, making some quick adjustments as she swerved through the predawn traffic. When her visibility was as good as it was going to get, she returned both hands to the steering wheel and picked up speed. There was a white Mercedes coupe ahead.

Her target was finally in sight.

In that moment, everything else disappeared. Her parents' insane behavior and stupid decisions, the Bible quotes and the stolen packet of papers, Amett's disease and the missed shot—it vanished as years of training took over. All that mattered was the mission.

Reach the car, identify the occupants, kill someone.

The Mercedes sped up, but Kindra was already too close. She pulled alongside the car, and Bernard Gasper's wide eyes stared back at her from the passenger seat for a second before a hand on his head shoved him out of the window frame. In the flickering light that entered the car, Kindra couldn't identify the driver. She didn't think it was the photographer.

The coupe's engine roared, and the car shot ahead of Kindra's old Civic.

"Bernard is inside." The faster Kindra drove, the more the ancient machine groaned in protest. "How the hell am I supposed to keep up with a Mercedes in an effing *Civic*?"

"So steal a better car!" Sera shouted.

"And lose time switching all this gear and shit?" In an intersection, she swerved around a limo meandering down East Ninetieth Street and spun onto Park, sliding between two cabs. "How is that better?"

"You let them get on the highway, and choices are only going to get worse," Odira warned.

"No shit." Something caught her eye, movement that didn't fit the normal patterns of traffic as she crossed an intersection. "Oh *shit!*"

She stomped the accelerator to the floor. The Civic shuddered but sped up. The blue SUV that had been aiming for her clipped the back of her car instead of ramming the side.

The impact slammed Kindra to the right, but she kept a firm grip on the wheel with one hand, steering into what the car wanted to do anyway while simultaneously drawing her Colt. She fired three bullets through her passenger window.

Glass exploded. She heard a second crackling crash and hoped at least one of those shots landed in the SUV's driver and not just the windshield.

She pushed the car as fast as she could, following the white dot. The Civic had taken the hit surprisingly well, only a slight grinding noise from the rear end to show for the crash. She got lucky. When she spotted the Mercedes again on East 106th Street, it was stuck behind a slow-moving delivery truck with oncoming traffic blocking the other lane. But they were about to reach the turn onto First Avenue. From there, it wasn't far to the ramp to Kennedy Bridge.

The truck moved. So did the coupe.

Kindra rammed the rear end of the Mercedes at close to fifty miles an hour. The Mercedes didn't stop; it sped up.

The Civic limped along, a tiny bit of smoke trailing up from the engine. Kindra pushed the car harder and caught up again, this time when a wall of cabs gave the coupe nowhere to run. She checked the rearview again, but the blue SUV with the shattered windshield didn't reappear.

Ramming into its quarter panel, Kindra sent the coupe into a spin.

She drew her gun and fired through the windshield. The shots missed the driver's head, but their body jerked like impact had been made somewhere, just before the coupe slammed into the cars parked along the side of the road. The driver slumped over the wheel. In the passenger seat, Bernard looked close to panic.

"Can I end this now?" As uncertain as she was about their client, and despite knowing the change in orders, right now ending this fiasco of a job before one of them died sounded like an effing *brilliant* idea.

"No!" Odira shouted. "If he's still alive, you grab him."

Kindra jumped out of the car, shooting over the heads of several people who rushed out of a diner. They screamed and scattered. Kindra's next two shots went through the passenger window of the coupe, high enough to be well clear of Bernard's head as he ducked low in the seat.

"Get out or I shoot you here." Kindra modulated her voice to a lower timbre. With her long hair hidden and her small breasts unnoticeable under body armor, most people assumed she was a guy. That was okay. She *wanted* him to think that right now.

Trembling, Bernard unfolded and slowly reached for the handle.

"Move faster or I'll shoot you."

With a jolt, Bernard jumped from the car. She dragged him toward the beat-up Civic. Sirens were approaching in the distance.

Kindra opened the trunk and shoved Bernard inside, cracking him on the head with the butt of the gun when he screamed. It didn't knock him out, but it sent him reeling. And it shut him up.

"More headed your way, Kindra, and we've got Javier's team on our asses." Amett sounded close to frantic. "Move!"

After slamming the trunk shut, Kindra got back in the car and stomped the accelerator to the floor. The car shuddered, and the smoke pouring from the accordioned hood thickened.

"I need a new car. Fast," Kindra growled and drove toward the Bronx. "This thing is like a big neon sign saying, 'I'm the one you're looking for.'"

"Take Walnut Ave north until it dead-ends in a parking lot." Now that they had the target in hand—or in trunk, really—Odira sounded more like herself. Calm, detached, and all-knowing. "Switch cars there if you can, and then I'll direct you out."

Within five minutes, Kindra found Walnut Avenue and gunned it down the straightaway. At the end of the road was a company-emblazoned pickup with a bed cap in the otherwise empty parking lot. It was an old model but obviously well maintained.

Perfect.

Kindra parked next to the truck and broke into the cab in under thirty seconds. After tossing her gear in, she grabbed cable ties and went to transfer her prisoner.

He started talking when she opened the trunk, his breath forming clouds of panic in front of his face. "Don't do this. Please! You don't know—"

Kindra backhanded him, then tore his scarf off his neck and used it to gag him. "You stay quiet until I ask you a question. Get me?"

He nodded as Kindra tightened the cable ties on his wrists. Pulling him out of the trunk, she kept him upright by force as she dragged him to the truck and shoved him into the windowless back. Once he was inside, she looped another set of cable-tie cuffs around his ankles before shutting the gate. She jumped into the driver's seat and ducked to pop open the steering column and jump-start the car.

Kindra was moving again. "Where am I headed?"

Odira was ready. "A railroad track runs through the parking lot. Follow the track north until you can merge onto a service road. You may have to bust through a gate at the end of the service road to get out to Longwood Ave."

After acknowledging the order, Kindra bumped along the railroad track about fifteen miles per hour faster than was safe. Probably. It wasn't like there were posted limits here. Soon, Longwood was in sight. She crushed the gate under the oversize wheels of her truck and merged onto the momentarily empty street.

Stroking the steering wheel, she smiled. This was a much better choice than the Civic.

"We're running interference for you, trying to keep everyone off your six." Amett grunted. Something on his end of the line crunched, like the hood of a car against a solid wall. Whatever had made the noise, it didn't seem to be the car Amett was driving. "We can't back you up until the heat dies down."

"Understood." She drove carefully, obeying every major traffic law and replacing the mask with a baseball cap and the hood of her black jacket. The mask would've hidden her features better, but nothing said "I'm doing something illegal" like a solid black, full-face ski mask. "Where am I headed from here?"

Odira gave Kindra an address in New Jersey. "It's been empty for a few months."

"It's more than probable there's a tracker somewhere on Bernard." Amett panted slightly between words. In the background, Sera laughed. Something farther away exploded. "But if you turn on your scrambler, we'll lose you on comms."

It only took a second for Kindra to decide. "Give me my orders now. I'm not risking more unwanted company."

There was only a slight hesitation, but she read paragraphs in that moment.

Is there another option? A perfect imitation of Odira's voice rang in Kindra's head. *Can we get there in time to interrogate him ourselves? Shit. He should have been in the car* Amett *was tracking. No choice now. We're going to have to let her do it.*

"Interrogation," Odira said. "There is a list of questions at the bottom of your bag. Ask only those questions, and do *not* kill him before we have what we need."

"Lima Charlie." Odira and Amett didn't have to know Kindra had questions of her own for Bernard Gasper. "Going dark."

"Atropos bless," Sera muttered. A curse or her sister's version of wishing good luck? She chose to take it as the latter as the scrambler went to work and everything went quiet.

Kindra was on her own.

Traffic on the Alexander Hamilton Bridge was a little heavier, even this early in the morning, but it kept moving smoothly as Kindra eased her way into New Jersey. It lengthened the drive a little, but she stayed off River Road, keeping to the back streets until she pulled into the parking lot of a warehouse complex.

On the west end of the central building, right where Odira had said it'd be, she spotted a wide delivery door left open about six inches. She stopped in front of it and jumped out, sticking her fingers under and then lifting the heavy metal until it rolled upward on its own. Most of these kinds of doors were light—aluminum or thin wood. Not this one. It was thick and made her wonder what this warehouse had been used for that demanded reinforced doors.

Inside, it was obvious someone had been here before her. A metal chair had been bolted to the cement in the middle of the otherwise empty room.

At least something *is going right tonight.* If Odira or Amett had been here to bolt the chair down, she trusted that she'd be secure in the building as soon as she closed and locked the delivery door. At the moment, it was one of the few things she trusted where they were concerned. She was safe here. As safe as she ever was anywhere.

Getting back in the truck, she drove into the building and parked before getting out to close the rolling door and lock it in place.

She grabbed her bag from the cab and placed it in the corner of the room. There were some tools of the interrogator's trade inside, but she took only the list of questions and the tape and ties she'd need to strap him to the chair. She preferred her own weapons. There was plenty of controlled, painful, nonlethal damage she could do with a set of combat knives and a well-maintained Colt.

Once the stage was set, she walked to the back of the truck. She made sure her gun would be in view, and then unlatched the gate.

He sputtered around the gag when he saw her.

Effing hell. Odira would skin me if she saw this. Of all the amateur mistakes she could have made tonight, she wished it hadn't been forgetting to put the mask back on.

I hope he doesn't recognize me . . .

She'd so rarely faced a target while wearing her own identity. There was always a character to hide behind. The masks, literal or metaphorical, gave her free rein to raise hell and then retreat with hands as clean as someone's in this line of work could ever be.

Whatever. Not like it matters. Either he's going to die soon, or you are.

Settling herself into the moment, she blanked the expression from her face and stared down at Bernard with something scarier than hatred—indifference. "Make a move I don't like, and I might pull the trigger whether I mean to or not."

Kindra grabbed his wrist and pulled him out of the truck. Bernard's knees buckled. It was somewhat impressive that he kept his feet, enough so that she gave him a second before she tugged him toward the chair. He had to hop along behind her, his feet still bound with her cable-tie cuffs, but he made it without hurting himself unnecessarily. She strapped him to the chair.

While she worked, the knot she'd tied in the scarf-gag loosened enough for it to fall out of his mouth.

"Please." His voice was rough. "For the children of Echemorro, *please*, don't—"

Kindra jammed the scarf back into his mouth and tied the knot tighter. She couldn't handle the unedited rush that Bernard had been about to spill. She *needed* to control the flow of details to make sure she saw every single facet of this bloodstained mess.

"I'm going to ask you questions, and you're going to tell me what I need to know. Nothing more, nothing less. If you don't, I'll hurt you. If you lie, I'll hurt you longer." She held his brown eyes with hers. "Do you understand, Mr. Gasper?"

He nodded. Kindra tried to figure out what she needed to ask first, how best to use this perfect opportunity she'd been handed. Who was this man, and what did he have to do with Redwell and Garret Hadley? And what did any of it have to do with the dead children of Echemorro?

No matter what she found out, she was probably still going to have to kill him. There weren't many other ways out of this night for her.

Shit.

She couldn't blank her mind the way she usually did on a job. She couldn't erase images of those kids lying in the street in front of their schoolhouse. She couldn't make it untrue. Off-balance and out of focus, Kindra, for the first time in her life, wondered if finishing this mission and watching the life drain out of Bernard's eyes was the *right thing to do.*

She had silently laughed when she'd heard preachers and politicians moralizing on what was "right." Like such a thing existed. Like they'd really be worried about anything more than survival if the trappings of society were stripped away from them.

But here she was. Questioning.

She took a slow, quiet breath, stood up, drew her KA-BAR Tanto, and flipped it.

Her mind spun end over end just as quickly as her knife.

Is he worth risking my life to save?

Yes, she'd daydreamed about finding a way out of her life, but what would she do with herself? Odira and Amett had taught her how to hide, where to go, and who to get false documents from. The only escape route that didn't involve someone dying was running, and running wasn't a real choice. There was nowhere she could run that they wouldn't find her. Once she started running, she'd never *ever* be able to stop.

Becoming some kind of twisted, soul-blackened martyr hadn't been part of her life plan. Plans could change, though, if Bernard Gasper gave her the answers she needed.

The possibility struck her with the force of a concussion grenade a microsecond before the hilt of her knife landed in her hand. Her grip on the moment slipped.

Free. I could be free.

For the first time since she was ten, she almost dropped her knife.

Jacksonville, Florida

Garret Hadley opened his front door in a powder-blue bathrobe, a steaming mug of coffee in his hand. When he saw who was standing on the other side, his eyes narrowed and his grip on the mug tightened. For a second it seemed as though he might toss the scalding contents on his early-morning visitor.

"Matthew." He grunted and then stepped aside. "It is never a good day when you show up on my doorstep unannounced."

"You need to see this." Matthew strode across the foyer and into the living room as though familiar with the expansive house. Picking up the remote from the antique wood coffee table, he turned on the TV and flipped to CNN.

". . . and the fire on East Nineteenth is still raging, though it does seem the teams of firefighters have finally stopped the blaze from spreading." The same reporter Garret had watched the day Bernard Gasper *hadn't* died stood at the end of a street in Manhattan, flames and chaos behind her.

"Thank you, Anna." The muscle in the anchorman's jaw jumped as he straightened the papers on his desk. "Gunfire and severe car accidents are being called in from all over Manhattan, and the latest, albeit very brief, police statement has suggested that the outbreak of violence may be connected to a local terror cell that authorities have been trying to track down and eliminate. In addition, we have just received word of a massive explosion in a New Jersey warehouse. Firefighters and investigators are on their way, so we don't yet know if there's any connection between this latest incident and the violence still happening in the city. Police officials have asked everyone to please stay inside and—"

Matthew shut off the TV and faced Garret. "On top of *that*"—he waved his hand toward the dark screen—"I got word that Isaac Marks will be landing at a New York–area airport tomorrow morning. The two guys I sent after him down in Echemorro turned up dead."

"Vicious for a Fed, isn't he?" Garret sipped his coffee, only the whiteness of his knuckles giving away his tension. "We need to make sure he doesn't have time to check in with anyone, and Odira is otherwise occupied at the moment, so we'll redirect Javier. It seems as though his purpose as a fire under Odira's ass has been rendered moot."

"You want it public again?" Matthew's tone was even, but the slight curl to his upper lip spoke of distaste.

If Garret saw that, he ignored it. "Hell, no. The FBI will be crawling all over it if one of their own is murdered." He shook his head. "Accident. As soon after he lands as possible."

"They'll still look into it."

"Then Javier better be sure he doesn't leave any evidence behind."

Matthew nodded once and strode toward the front door. His hand was on the doorknob when Garret called, "Matthew?"

Slowly and with studied nonchalance, he turned toward Garret and waited.

"Javier had better be as good as you said, or he won't be the only one in trouble."

Matthew's dark eyes narrowed, but he didn't say a word as he opened the door and walked out.

Chapter Nine

Before anything else, Kindra remembered fire. She remembered the flames eating the wall like a mythological monster. Now it was too warm here. The flames must be getting closer. She had to move, or she'd fall to the fire's insatiable cravings.

Pulling herself further into reality, her right ear ringing with the aftereffects of the explosion, she tried to roll. Nothing but her head moved, and not in the direction she expected. She'd landed on her back, hadn't she? But her head lolled and hit her shoulder. She was sitting up. Somehow.

Surprise wrenched her into consciousness just enough to blink too-heavy eyelids but not enough to keep them open. She caught a brief glimpse of a blur of light and dark. None of it was the color of fire. There was no smoke in the air. Her mouth and throat were so dry, it felt like she'd been breathing through an open mouth for hours. Concentrating past the high-pitched whine in her right ear—the one that hadn't been protected by the comm—wasn't easy, especially since, wherever she was, it was quiet. There was a consistent thrum in the background. An engine, maybe. There wasn't much else to prepare her for the moment she had to open her eyes.

"Wakey, wakey." The voice sounded like Tenor: Calver team member and rescuer/kidnapper.

Her eyes popped open. Headlights glaring through the windows sent white and red spots flashing across her vision. Squinting only made them brighter. Head throbbing, Kindra tried to catalog her other injuries. They had to be there. Why else would her body ache like she'd been blown through a wall?

Oh, right . . . because I was almost blown through a wall.

Groaning through gritted teeth, Kindra kept blinking to clear her eyes and swallowing to moisten her throat. Neither worked well. And neither did a damn thing to ease the throbbing-stabbing-aching pains scattered across her body. She looked down, needing to make sure she wasn't leaking blood from anywhere— Oh.

That's why she felt overheated. Someone had added a thick pair of black pants and a black jacket reminiscent of motorcycle armor over her other clothes.

"Are you conscious yet?"

"No." Kindra's voice sounded like the croak of a dying frog.

"Okay. Good."

Kindra wanted to rub her eyes, but though she felt her arm *try* to move, it couldn't. Her legs couldn't either. Her limbs twitched and jerked, straining to respond to the electrical signals her brain shot at them, but they couldn't do more than that. She was strapped to the backseat of the car with no more than an inch of wiggle room in any direction.

At least the ringing in her right ear was beginning to fade.

"Sorry about the layers, but there's RFID blockers in those clothes."

To disrupt trackers. Kindra's heart sank into her stomach. She wasn't wearing a tracker, but the fact that Tenor knew how to block one wasn't a good sign.

An angry stream of demands bubbled up Kindra's throat, but set her coughing before a single one could be hurled at the pretty liar driving the car.

"Here." Eyes on the road, Tenor picked up a water bottle with a straw sticking out the top and held it back. Kindra was desperate enough to drink, even knowing it was probably laced with sedatives.

Tenor pulled it away before Kindra's lips closed around the straw.

Deprivation rather than pain as a form of torture? Haven't dealt with that in a while. At least Kindra knew now how to handle— *Wait, what?*

The girl brought the straw to her own lips and took a sip.

Kindra blinked. *Okay. Maybe not contaminated. Next play, what? Bribing me with water for information?*

Again the bottle appeared in front of Kindra, and Tenor's gaze met hers. Moss-green eyes in the face of a girl with shoulder-length, dyed-black hair. Eyes Kindra had first seen in the face of a boy named Dru.

"Knock this over or try to bite me, and I don't give you another one," Dru warned. Though Dru probably wasn't her name.

No demands or questions followed. That was it—an offer and a warning far milder than anything Kindra would've threatened if the situation had been reversed.

The coughing was less frequent now, each bark bursting out with less force, but Kindra's throat was still too dry and raw to respond in words. She nodded, and that was apparently enough. The bottle moved closer until she could finally—*finally*—grab the straw with her tongue and guide it into her mouth.

Once she'd drained half the bottle, the ache in her throat and in her head started to dull. Other pains and injuries jockeyed for attention, but she pushed them aside. The pain wasn't that bad, measured against other times she'd been laid up, battered and bruised and almost broken. Figuring out why she was here, with *Dru* of all people, was what mattered.

She was centered on the backseat of an economy sedan, a seat belt strapped across her body and somehow locked in place; it had none of the give belts normally had. Nylon rope wrapped around Kindra's ankles and slid under the seats in front of her, her right leg tied under the passenger's seat and her left leg attached to the driver's. Her arms were extended and held at a downward angle away from her body, more rope tied tightly around each wrist and attached to the doors. Dru had given her just enough slack to shift her weight and tense her muscles, but not enough to build momentum to free herself. Plus, with her hands on display like this, any movement in any direction was going to catch Dru's eye.

It was kind of brilliant. Dru obviously knew what she was doing and who she was dealing with, which scared Kindra more than waking up in bondage. Dru wasn't going to make assumptions because Kindra was a slim, cute, teenage girl. Her captor knew—or guessed—what Kindra was capable of and would treat her accordingly. In another situation, it might have been flattering. Right now, it effing sucked.

"You remember what happened?"

She wished she could finish off that water bottle to soothe her raw throat. Vague bits of memory reassembled themselves. She remembered threatening Bernard, the explosion, and her impact with the floor. She remembered being hauled into the car, but not being tied up. It was enough to feel honest when she said, "Yes."

"Hmmm. You *might* be lying, but it doesn't matter." Dru met Kindra's eyes in the rearview and smirked. "And don't worry. You weren't out for long, and you didn't give away any secrets."

"Like you'd tell me if I did." Kindra looked out the window and tried to figure out where they were. And where they were headed.

"I would."

"Right." They were still in New Jersey, and heading southwest according to the small markers on the rural highway, and while the sky wasn't the black of full night, the sun hadn't yet appeared on the horizon. Kindra couldn't have been out for even a full hour. "I should just trust you on that?"

"Yup."

Kindra met Dru's eyes in the rearview, allowing her skepticism to show on her face. "I should trust the person who has me strapped down in the backseat of her car?"

"Well, I guess not when you put it like that . . ." Dru laughed. "Ready to talk to me?"

"About *what*?"

"Pick a topic. I have a feeling that we have more than enough to choose from."

She wanted conversation? Fine. Kindra wanted information. "You work for the Calvers."

"Baby, I *am* a Calver." Dru grinned. "Dru Calver—and, yes, my name really is Dru. Eldest child and best thing my parents have ever done. My little brother is a close second, though, pyromaniacal bugger that he is."

The Calvers had kids. How had not only she, but Odira and Amett not known that Hugo and Cassidy had kids? "How old are you?"

"A year and two months older than you." Dru shot Kindra a quick glance. "Why?"

"I never knew Cassidy and Hugo had kids." Every time they'd joined Odira and Amett for jobs, it had only been the two of them.

Dru's expression grew grim, and her hands tightened on the wheel. Kindra expected to be told something along the lines of "piss off."

"No one connected to the business knew. The couple they fostered us with? We thought they were our uncles, but they were just a couple who'd been having trouble adopting. Mom and Dad only visited a few times a year. Probably would've stayed that way for the rest of our lives if someone they'd crossed hadn't figured out where we were and killed Uncle Tom and Uncle Dale." With a sigh, Dru unclenched her hands. "We wanted to know what had really happened—threatened to run away and investigate ourselves— so Mom and Dad gave us a choice: join them or head off to some exclusive, secure boarding school."

"I guess you joined up."

"I guess so."

Kindra wanted to know more—like why even a revenge kick would make someone *choose* this kind of life—but she also knew that those weren't the important points at that moment. The more crucial question was, "Why aren't I dead?"

"Do you want to be?" Dru asked, eyebrows arched.

"Not particularly." Though it *would* solve a lot of problems. Or at least make them inconsequential.

"Then why question it?"

"If I know why you saved me, then I can work out what you want from me."

Dru's eyes met Kindra's in the rearview mirror. "I figured you'd be cynical, but damn." She shook her head and returned her attention to the road. "FYI, when someone saves your life, the first thing to say is usually 'Wow! Thanks!'"

"Wow. Thanks." Kindra coughed, her throat still raw and the ache in her head getting worse. Not bad enough for it to be a concussion, but it was close. Luckily—*luckily?*—Kindra was used to pain and forcing her mind to think through it. "Now why the hell am I here instead of in a pool of blood and ash back at the warehouse?"

"Because, unlike you, I don't kill everyone I meet."

"Neither do I," Kindra shot back. "Or I would've shoved my knife in your heart on Friday."

Dru snorted. "You don't translate sarcasm or hyperbole well, do you?"

Before Kindra could say a word, Dru muttered a curse. The car swerved, cutting across two lanes of traffic to turn left. The turn happened so fast that Kindra's head snapped to the right, washing her vision out for a second and sending a sharp stab of pain through her head. Honks followed them as they careened down the highway.

"Are you *trying* to grab a police tail?" Kindra swallowed the bile climbing up her throat, and somehow kept from sounding as ill as she felt. The vision whiteout had only lasted a moment. *Thank Atropos.* Kindra did *not* want to spend any more time blacked out in the presence of someone who should, by all rights, want to kill her. "Cops don't take kindly to kidnapping."

"Please. Like you want to be in the crosshairs of a cop any more than I do." Dru's tone was so preoccupied that the retort came off like an automatic response.

"It'd be better than where I am." The cops would be easier to get away from.

"Baby, relax." Dru sighed, the sound exasperated. "If I wanted you dead, I could've let the fire have you. Why would I bother bringing you along?"

"That's a good question." The ache in her head throbbed. She gritted her teeth and forced herself to focus. "I'd kind of like to know the answer."

Dru rolled her eyes. "Because you're hot, and I wanted a bargaining chip. That good enough for you?"

Eyeing the reflection in the rearview carefully, Kindra tried to decide if Dru was being serious this time. Dru didn't wield her sarcasm in the same way as Sera, which meant Kindra wasn't sure how to respond. "It's only good enough if it's true."

"It's not *all* of the truth," Dru said with a shrug. "But it is true."

Taking a breath, Kindra shifted her weight, testing the knots of her bonds. They didn't budge. Minutes passed, and Dru just kept driving, silent and mostly still except for the moments her eyes flicked down to something on the passenger seat.

What should she be doing here? Dru had saved her, but then tied her up. Now Dru wasn't making demands or threatening Kindra's life or *anything*. Everything Kindra knew about dealing with being held hostage or captive didn't seem to apply here. Dru knew who she actually was, so no other personality would work.

She was floundering in new territory, and she didn't like it. "Are you just going to leave me tied up back here the whole time or what?"

"As temptingly kinky as that sounds, no." Dru paused and then tilted her head slightly, a sideways not-quite-nod. "Well, I don't *want* to, but I also don't want you slitting my throat or shooting me as soon as I give you an opening. And I *will* eventually give you an opening. I'm tired and stressed as hell and definitely not on my A game."

Kindra stared at the back of Dru's head. "Why would you tell me any of that?"

"Didn't your parents ever teach you that honesty is the best policy?"

"In our line of work?" Kindra snorted.

"Yeah. Never mind. Forgot who your parents were for a second." Dru shook her head and glanced back at Kindra. "They probably taught you to lie as soon as you started talking."

"It's saved my life more than once." And that *was* the truth.

There'd been that time in Mexico when she lied her way out of jail. And then the day she'd come face-to-face with another hit squad in Italy—they'd been coming after the target Kindra had been about to kill. She'd managed to kill the guy in front of them and *still* convince them she was just an innocent bystander. In Kindra's life, lies were as valuable as gold, and a good liar as prized as diamonds.

Kindra shifted slightly. The rope pulled on her right wrist, jarring her arm. Pain in her shoulder compounded the renewed ache in her head. She hissed and tried to settle into a less painful position. There didn't seem to be one.

"You're gonna have to hold on a little longer," Dru said, turning with a small frown on her lips. "I can't stop until he does."

"Who?" Kindra kept shifting, trying to find an angle that didn't aggravate her shoulder. "Where the hell are you dragging me?"

"We're going after the guy who stole Bernard and almost blew you up."

That caught Kindra's attention. "You know who it was?"

"Michael Ealy's doppelgänger."

The guy lurking around Bernard's building last Friday wasn't part of Javier's team? She'd thought . . . But no. Probably not, if Bernard wasn't dead yet.

"He wasn't—" she bit off the mention of Javier, John, or the Umarovs, finishing instead with "—one of yours?"

"No. We thought he was yours until I talked to you Friday. Then we figured he was working with Javier and John—first job, obviously. After this morning, though?"

"You're reevaluating?" Kindra asked dryly.

"To say the least."

Despite her yearning for a bottle of painkillers, she needed intel more, and Dru seemed willing to give it to her. "Did you ID him?"

"Nope. He may not have done much undercover work, but the guy knows a hell of a lot about keeping his face off cameras. And every time someone approached him, he bolted. In a purposefully nonchalant kind of way."

"How are we following him?" Kindra couldn't spot a car that Dru might be tailing, but every few minutes Dru took a seemingly random detour off the highway or slowed down and pulled into the right lane to stare at something on the passenger seat. Something like a GPS unit. "If you don't know who he is, how'd you get a tracker on him?"

"It's not on *him*. It's on Bernard. An implant." She said it almost like she was chiding Kindra. "The guy threw Bernard's watch and everything else potentially tracker-laden out the window, but he didn't check for under-the-skin trackers."

Who would? Kindra wasn't sure she would check for those automatically either. But she wasn't going to tell *Dru* that.

"How in the hell did this guy get the drop on *both* of our families *and* Javier's crew?"

"Because we each thought he was working for one of the other teams, and no one considered that he might be a whole new variable in this rather volatile equation."

"And you still don't know who he's working for?" Kindra asked.

"No. We don't have enough to go on, not even a face to run through a facial rec program." Another glance at the passenger seat and Dru swerved across three lanes to take the next exit—a long, tight circle that threw Kindra's balance off-center and gave her nausea new, acid-dipped claws.

"And you still think you're going to be able to keep Bernard alive?" Kindra somehow didn't throw up as she said it.

"We're sure as hell going to try. And you're going to help as long as you're with me."

Kindra wanted to laugh—was about to, actually—but then Dru took a sharp right. Kindra's head snapped left even though she struggled to keep herself still. A sharp, insistent pain bit into her head. Vision going black, Kindra fought back the bile. This time, she lost.

Leaning forward as much as her restraints allowed, she vomited onto the floor of the car.

"Shit," Dru muttered, glancing back.

Pain and a pulsing, multihued darkness flooded her mind. This time, she let it drag her into unconsciousness.

Chapter Ten

1308 : TUESDAY, FEBRUARY 16

K indra's blackout had been short-lived, but it did drive home a rather important point: if she was going to get any sleep, now was the time to do it. Dru had admitted to being deep into sleeplessness, so if Kindra forced sleep now, she'd be one up on her captor. Doing it while Dru was solidly occupied by driving and keeping Bernard within tracking range meant Dru wasn't likely to have the time to beat Kindra black and blue or get rid of her completely.

So she slept. Uncomfortably and fitfully, yes, but she slept.

The pinch of a needle driving into her neck jolted her awake.

Shit. I may have miscalculated.

"I'd say sorry, but I'm not." Dru looked grim when she pulled her hand back. Kindra almost laughed when she recognized the reusable auto-injector of a ketamine cocktail that Odira preferred, the one Dru had probably taken from Kindra's own bag. "We need to stop for a while, and I don't feel like being shanked when I get you out of the car."

The light-headedness hit first, the combination of swooning and spinning that this particular drug combination always had on her. Kindra fought it—her natural resistance enough to give her a few more minutes of control than usual—and stayed coherent while Dru pulled the car into the parking lot of a small motel. She held on long enough for Dru to come back from getting a room, but escape was impossible by the time she was finally unbound. Her limbs felt weighted, her mind spun without a single thought taking hold, and it was all she could do to stumble alongside Dru into the run-down room.

She fell into unconsciousness before she hit the mattress.

Kindra half woke up once; realized she'd been thoroughly tied down spread eagle on the motel bed; thought, *I'm not dealing with this shit right now*; and intentionally slid into actual sleep.

The escape couldn't last forever.

When she woke for good, she was alone, hungry, far too warm, strapped in so tightly she could barely fill her lungs, and in desperate need of a pee.

The heater barely clinging to the window clanked and groaned, and through the wall she heard what she thought was a TV, but Kindra couldn't sense another presence in the room. Light shone through the cracks in the grimy-looking curtains. Not enough time had passed for the sun to have set, obviously, but that didn't give her much to go on.

Carefully, she tested the bonds. Her left ankle had the most room to move, but freeing it wouldn't do her much good. If she could get a *hand* free, that would be something. Ryce had been the escape artist, idolizing magicians like Houdini as much as he'd respected the covert agents—both government sanctioned and freelance—who only ever got recognition by code names. Her brother would've known how to get out of here in seconds. Hell, Ryce never would've gotten into this disaster in the first place.

Before Kindra could figure out if it would be worth it to free her foot, the door opened and Dru entered with a gust of chilly air. She dropped two plastic bags on the second bed—one rumpled with use—and then shed her thick coat to reveal the body armor and shoulder-holstered gun beneath.

"My parents are *not* thrilled I brought you along."

"Mine probably aren't overjoyed either." If Kindra had been in trouble *before*, she was absolutely fucked now.

"They seem like they'd be against joy on principle alone." Dru strode across the small room and sat on the edge of Kindra's bed so cautiously that the mattress barely moved. "I'm glad you're awake."

Did she think I wouldn't *wake up?* Kindra should've been able to read someone else in the same line of work, watch similar training and habits give off clues to those who knew how to look for them. Dru had so few of the markers Kindra was familiar with—the stillness under stress, the carefully blank expression, the habit of silence. Dru didn't match the mold she should have, and Kindra didn't know what rules applied.

Dru made it even worse. "I'm going to untie you."

"And then what?" Kindra asked once she'd stopped blinking stupidly. "You want me to pinky swear to keep my knives to myself?"

"After I explain why it's in your best interests that you do, yes." Dru reached forward.

Although Kindra tried to inch away from her fingers, there was nowhere to go. Soft pressure tugged at something, and she noticed a detail she should have cataloged the moment her eyes opened.

There was something locked around her throat.

"What is it?" she asked, not sure she actually wanted to know.

"My brother cooked it up a while back." Dru's eyes were locked on Kindra's neck with an intensity that made her shiver. "It's something like a proximity fuse plus a dead man's trigger, and it means you're going to do your damnedest to make sure I don't stop breathing."

Every muscle in Kindra's body coiled, tense to the point of snapping. Except for her heart, which beat so quickly that her blood roared under her skin.

"You tied a fucking *bomb* around my neck? And you think *my* family is psychotic?"

Dru flinched. "Baby, if I could trust you not to run away or shoot me in the head first chance you got, this wouldn't be necessary. But I can't. So it is."

"Stop calling me 'baby.' I'm not your baby. My name is Alice."

"Bullshit," Dru said. "Your name is Kindra Adalia Weston, and I'm pretty sure my parents spent more time with you than me before you were eight."

"Whatever." Kindra resisted the urge to shake her head, pulling from Sera's repertoire of expressions instead and rolling her eyes. "Fine. You're Dru, I'm Kindra, our families have an effed-up history, and there's a bomb around my neck. Anything else I should know?"

"Yeah. That bomb will go off if you tamper with it, if you move more than a hundred yards away from me, or if I die. Or I can press a button I have somewhere on my person." She paused to take a breath, but spoke again before Kindra could. "And, no, I won't tell you where that button is, because I'm not stupid. Just know that I can get to it faster than you can get to me." For once, there was no smile on Dru's face. "Like I said, my brother is a pyromaniacal freakazoid. He's also more than a little bit of a genius."

"Lucky me," Kindra muttered.

Dru nodded, expression still serious. "Now I'll untie you, and you won't run or try to kill me, and then we'll get the hell out of here. Michael Ealy is on the move again."

Dru didn't move until Kindra grudgingly nodded agreement, but the shift of her head focused her attention on the bite of plastic and possibly leather around her throat. It felt thin, probably no wider than her thumb, but it wouldn't take much of a boom to do a whole lot of damage.

"Isn't this device of yours going to set off alarm bells when people see it?" she asked as Dru untied her feet.

"No. My brother made the whole thing look like a leather collar. It's a Goth fashion statement." Her words and her hands paused for a moment. She lifted one shoulder and started again. "Or bondage gear. Depends on who we run into."

"Fantastic. Because I'm *so* the submissive type."

The rope around her right leg loosened. Kindra almost hissed when blood rushed back into the limb, pins and needles eating away at her control. It had been so numb she hadn't noticed the lack of blood flow until her entire leg was shaking with it.

"Sorry, I was in a hurry when I did this." Dru's fingers dug into Kindra's calf, massaging to stimulate the circulation. The touch only lasted a second before Dru shook her head and moved to undo the next knot. "You're gonna have to make do. We're already lagging."

"You wouldn't be if I wasn't here." Kindra wouldn't have had to deal with any of this. Or the consequences that might be rocketing toward them out of the barrel of someone's gun. She'd be free of all this bullshit already if Dru had just left her in that warehouse.

Dru's smile finally came back. "But where would the fun in that be? Road trips are always better with a buddy."

Her right arm freed, Kindra clenched her fist and fought muscles that wanted to cramp. "Right. Buddies with bomb-shaped leashes."

That comment Dru ignored. "C'mon. The gear is already packed."

With Dru's help, Kindra tried to stand. Her legs buckled. Only Dru's arm sliding around her waist kept her from collapsing to the threadbare, floral-print carpet. Dru allowed her a pit stop in the bathroom—though she demanded the door stay open—then steered Kindra toward the parking lot. Kindra tripped over her own lagging feet several times on the short trip to the car, a brown sedan that Kindra thought might be a late-model Ford Taurus.

Looking at the options, Kindra expected to be shoved into the backseat and strapped down again. That didn't happen. Dru opened the passenger door and helped Kindra ease herself into the seat, instead. The only restraint Dru insisted on was the seat belt before she dropped the two plastic bags onto Kindra's lap and closed the door.

Kindra peeked inside the bags as Dru jogged around the car. There was a sensible mix of foodstuffs—snack packages of carrots and ranch dressing, a bag of cheese sticks, a box of cookies, a large bag of salty-sweet kettle corn, and a few bottles of sports drinks. Her stomach rumbled, and she had the popcorn bag open before she consciously decided to start there.

They were out of the parking lot thirty seconds after Dru dropped into the driver's seat and closed her door.

As they headed southwest on Pennsylvania's back roads, Dru was silent but not distant. Kindra was very aware of the periodic glances Dru sent her way. She saw how Dru tensed whenever Kindra moved unexpectedly, and noticed the seven different times the muscles in Dru's jaw moved like she was about to speak. She never said a word. Obviously she had questions, though—wanted information—so Kindra waited. Silently passed Dru three cookies and a cheese stick. Waited some more.

If Kindra breathed too deeply, the collar shifted around her throat, a tangible reminder of why she couldn't break Dru's neck and steal the car. Despite the thrum of the car's engine and the quiet, consistent beeps from the GPS system, the silence stretched thinner with each additional minute. Being incapacitated without actually being incapacitated grated on Kindra's self-control.

How the hell did I end up getting kidnapped by someone who is just as sadistically controlling as Odira?

The irony of it almost made her laugh. She'd thought about what it would be like to be kidnapped, whisked away from the life she'd been born into. Having seen a fair amount of what the underbelly of the world looked like, she figured there wouldn't be too many people she'd have a harder time dealing with than Odira.

Apparently she'd been wrong.

Though she held her tongue for as long as she could manage, eventually Kindra had to ask. "How'd you follow me to the warehouse? I had a signal blocker running before I crossed into New Jersey."

"I used my eyes," Dru said, her voice dry. "I was on my way in as backup. Got there just after you grabbed Bernard. I almost tried to move in when you switched cars, but I'd noticed Mr. Ealy tailing you by then and didn't fancy dancing in the crossfire."

So you waited until he tried to blow me up instead?

"Impressive, especially coming from the girl brain-dead enough to use the same recognizable bag twice on the same job."

"You say that as though I didn't do it on purpose. I played a hunch when I saw you window-shopping. If you'd been a local, you wouldn't have noticed me or the bag." She smirked. "And this is what happens when you underestimate people."

Kindra snapped the baby carrot in her hands in half, imagining it was Dru's neck. It might be a bad idea to physically hurt Dru while Kindra was trapped in the bomb collar, but weapons weren't the only ways to cause damage.

"Who did I kill when I took Bernard last night?"

"No one." Dru's knuckles turned white on the steering wheel, all amusement draining from her face. "It was my mother. And she's not dead."

"Really? She looked pretty dead when I left her in the car." Kindra infused the words with as much ice as she could and glued her features into a mask of indifference.

"Consarn it!" Growling, Dru twisted her hands, the movement almost convulsive. "You really do want me to kill you, don't you?"

"You will eventually." Kindra flicked a popcorn kernel at Dru's cheek. "I'd rather get it over with."

Even though her parents had survived into their early forties, Kindra had never been able to picture living past twenty. The possibility of dying on a job had always been real. Especially after Ryce's death. She'd had lengthy, philosophical conversations with Charon on two occasions and had long ago grown accustomed to death.

Shrugging at the inevitability was normal by now, but this emptiness in her gut and the lack of panic or plots at the threat of death? Seeing it as an intriguing change of pace?

That made Kindra blink.

Was it because of this job, or had it happened before? Maybe it didn't matter. Either way, death was a more attractive option than this limbo she was stuck in now.

"I don't want to kill you," Dru said after a moment of silence and a few deep, calming breaths. "I don't want to kill *anyone* most days, and I won't even pull a hair from your head unless you give me a reason to."

Kindra opened her mouth, but closed it again when she met Dru's gaze. Her mottled-green eyes were piercing with that little flare of anger brightening them.

"And no, I don't expect you to believe me yet," Dru said. "Not with the life you've lived. And not while you're wearing that . . ."

"Bomb? I think the word you're looking for is '*bomb*.'"

Dru rolled her eyes, but before she could say anything, the GPS fixed to the dashboard beeped. At the next intersection, they turned right to follow the route Michael Ealy had taken.

"Where is everyone else?"

"You mean your family and Javier's crew?" Dru asked. "They're playing a really vicious game of hide-and-seek with my family."

"Any casualties yet?"

"Two dead and a few injuries in the apartments above Amour. Plus, Bashir Umarov. He died after you shot up his car—not from the gunshots, though. He drove himself straight into a pole. Apparently broke his neck on impact, according to the report my brother dug up." Dru took a breath that Kindra couldn't hear, but she saw her shoulders rise and watched the body armor over her lungs shift. "As far as our families go, it seems like everyone but Bashir and Mom is only collecting cuts and bruises. The NYPD is sure it's a terrorist attack."

A knot in the center of Kindra's chest, one she hadn't previously allowed herself to acknowledge was there, loosened. For now, Sera was safe. It was hard to tell if she should be happy about Odira and Amett being alive or not, but there was no question about Sera.

For a couple of miles of rural highways, neither of them spoke. The road signs said they were heading south more often than not as they traveled through Virginia. Eyes on the road, Kindra let her mind ponder possible destinations. South, but not along the coast, where most of the major cities were. Atlanta, maybe?

Then Dru broke the silence. "What did your parents tell you about your client?"

"Nothing." Kindra shrugged, barely keeping the wince off her face when the movement nudged the collar around her throat. The bomb didn't *seem* motion sensitive, but figuring that out didn't do much to soothe Kindra's frayed nerves.

"Answering my questions honestly would really be in your best interest, baby."

"I *am*." Kindra almost choked holding back another protest of the stupid endearment. There was a strong chance that annoying Kindra was exactly why Dru kept using it. "I don't need to know anything about the client to do the job."

"Uh, yeah. I guess." Dru's eyebrows pulled together when she glanced at Kindra. "He said that, but I thought he was exaggerating. I mean . . . *Really*? You didn't know anything about *why* you tried to kill Bernard?"

"I *never* know. I don't need to." Maybe, if Dru had asked these questions a month ago, she might've lied. Habit and training and self-preservation would've demanded at least a little prevarication. Now . . . it was as though breaking *one* of Odira's rules had snowballed out of control, loosening the stranglehold of the old rules and expectations. "Odira and Amett make the decisions, we help with the work, everyone gets paid. That's it. I don't usually even know the client's *name*."

Dru had turned her attention back to the street, but at this her head snapped toward Kindra, her eyes sharp. "You *usually* don't. But you did this time?"

All the truth or part of it? Kindra wondered. *Might as well go for broke, right?* There wasn't much Dru could do with the information to hurt her, not any more than Odira would if Kindra ever made it back to the team alive. Nothing in what she told her would help the Calvers find or harm Sera.

"Only by chance." Shifting in her seat, Kindra glanced in the side mirror, automatically scanning for a tail. The traffic patterns seemed normal. "I was there when Odira got the call."

Dru kept her eyes on the road, but Kindra felt her attention like a low-level electropulse in the air, brushing against her skin and making it vibrate. Or maybe that was the effing bomb around her throat. Who knew what kind of signals it was emitting?

It took a hell of a lot of willpower to shake the shivers off her skin at *that* thought.

There were a couple of beats of silence before Dru asked, "When you go out on a job—a normal one, not this clusterfuck—what *do* you know?"

"About what?"

"The client, the target, the job, whatever. Anything."

"I *told* you—nearly nothing. I only ever know the minimum necessary in order to get the job done."

"And nothing about *why* that job needs doing." It wasn't a question.

"Why doesn't matter." It was a rote explanation Kindra had heard more than once in her life. "Someone is going to make money off the job, so it might as well be us."

"Right. Money. Because you spend all that money on such fun things. Beach vacations and fine art and big-screen TVs and diamonds and whatever the hell else." Dru glanced at Kindra, a lopsided frown marring her full lips and a sardonic gleam in her eyes. "But, no. You don't get any of that, do you? You just get more guns and better tech and another job."

Yes. That was exactly what they got. That was *all* they ever got. Kindra had no idea what Odira was chasing or trying to prove, but she was relentless in her pursuit of . . . whatever it was.

"Haven't you ever wanted something *more* than that?"

"More than *what*?" Kindra infused her words with scorn. Reality didn't allow enough headspace for daydreaming—why bother when it only made her pay attention to how utterly effed up her life was? Instead, she pretended her life was just wonderful, thank you. By now the proof was all lined up and ready to use. "How many sixteen-year-olds have seen as much of the world as I have? There isn't much on the planet I haven't experienced or eaten or enjoyed or ended. I mean, come on. In a single month, I spent a week at Windsor Castle as a guest of the royal family and two weeks in the favelas of Brazil. I've gotten to know what it's like to *live*."

. . . and I've seen so much death.

"Hmmm. And so just because you get to travel, that makes everything else worth it?" Dru pinned her with a skeptical stare. "You've really never thought of leaving it behind? Doing something else with your life?"

"No." *Yes.* But she'd never been the same person long enough to figure out what she might do or where she would go. Even if she could.

There were only three ways she saw it playing out:

A) She ran, used her skills to keep running, and never stopped.

B) Odira and Amett both died in some catastrophe or another, leaving her (and hopefully Sera) free to live the lives they *wanted* to live.

C) Kindra died.

Those were the only possibilities that seemed realistic, and Kindra couldn't find it in herself to truly *want* any of them—not even Odira's death.

"Well, you may not ever want a different life, but I do." Dru checked the side mirrors and switched lanes, easing to the right side of the highway. "I've done the small-town-slash-suburb thing, and I don't think I want to do it again. One day I'm moving to a big city, getting a degree in something happy—like cooking or etymology or music theory or something—and teaching self-defense classes on the weekends."

"Okay. Good luck with that."

But even as she tried to brush off Dru's words, an image appeared in Kindra's mind. A penthouse condo in a major city—Europe somewhere, New Zealand, or maybe Japan—with high ceilings and huge walls filled with classic and contemporary art, a personal gallery of her curation. Not that she *owned* any art. It would've ended up in storage, and what was the point of that? Art was meant to be seen, not hidden away in a climate-controlled storage unit.

Silently laughing at herself, Kindra shook her head and wiped the image away. If she left behind everything being a Weston entailed, she'd have nothing. No past, no home, no family, no friends, no money—it all went through Odira—no job history, and no formal education.

"C'mon. Just think about it. A normal life with a predictable schedule where you could travel just because you wanted to visit a place and not because you had to go there to kill someone." Dru threw her right hand up high enough that it hit the roof of the car. "The perks are many! Like weekends! And days off. And not checking your six for tails. And sleeping in. You can't tell me that *none* of the bonuses of civilian life appeal."

Civilian life . . . Few of her skills would be marketable in civilian life. She couldn't imagine having meaningful conversations with her "peer group," and she didn't think she could get away with swapping war stories with veterans. She didn't know who she was outside of the job.

"You know what they say." Shrugging, Kindra scanned the cars behind them again. For the tails that civilians apparently never needed to worry about. "You can sleep when you're dead."

"Plan on dying anytime soon?"

Kindra glanced down, even though she couldn't see the collar. "I guess we'll see how the day goes, won't we?"

Chapter Eleven

2013 : TUESDAY, FEBRUARY 16

"**H**e's stopping." Dru's eyes darted between the road and the location on the GPS tracker, at the now-stationary red dot they'd been following all day. Night had settled around them as they drove, and the Taurus was illuminated only by the headlights of passing cars and the dashboard lights. "I don't know why. It's too early."

"But they didn't stay long at the last spot." Stiff from being stuck in a car for hours, Kindra was glad of a possible chance to move. "If it's only the one guy with Bernard, he's *got* to be running on fumes. Can we take him out?"

Dru huffed a sharp breath. "Not everyone needs to die, Kindra."

"This guy probably does."

"Before we know who he works for or what he wants from Bernard?"

"Hey. *You're* the ones who want to play bodyguard." She still didn't know what any of the information she'd stolen from Bernard meant, still wasn't sure if it was worth dying for. "Alive or dead doesn't matter to me. I just really want this week from Tartarus to end."

Am I talking about Bernard or me?

She didn't know, and she also didn't know what would happen if she was alive when this fiasco came to a close. Could she go back to Odira and Amett? There was a chance that she'd be able to track them down through one of their networks after Bernard was dead, but . . . did she want to? They were probably working on the assumption that she'd been kidnapped and would be used against them. If she went back, the debriefing would look more like an interrogation.

Dru grunted. "It matters. We're going to scope out the location and plan a grab for both of them. *Alive.* All of us."

"Yes, mistress." Kindra stretched, slowly testing each limb and muscle to search for cramps and loss of blood flow.

"You wish," Dru retorted, a small smile curving her full lips.

"No, I don't. I already have too many people giving me orders, thanks. I don't need to add another." *But I wouldn't mind you calling me that for a night.*

"Not everyone who tells you what to do is evil." Dru's assessing gaze cut to Kindra for a second. "He's gone, but what about Ryce? Wasn't he—"

"If you say one more word about him, I will end you and *damn* the consequences."

The words were out before Kindra could stop them. Only after they'd spilled from her lips did she notice her clenched hands and her pounding heart. Only after she'd spoken did she realize how true that statement was.

Kindra felt her expression fall into practiced blankness. "Understand?"

Eyes wide, it was a couple of seconds before Dru cleared her throat and nodded slowly. "Lima Charlie."

Twenty minutes later, Kindra still hadn't calmed down. She hadn't heard Ryce's name in years. Dru shouldn't have even known that Ryce had died. No one outside her family and the Calvers knew he'd ever been alive, and *no one* had been there when he died. They'd never found his body on the banks of the river in Switzerland. Just blood on the cliff above it. Lots of blood.

How the hell did Dru know he'd died?

"They're just ahead," Dru said ten minutes later, her voice much softer than before. Almost like a wordless apology. "At that campground, I think."

They'd left the main road a couple of miles ago. Trees and shadows stretched out on either side of the road, broken only by one-lane roads leading into the forest. Through the trees, Kindra could make out lights, and sometimes she spotted small cabins and cottages, but mostly there were only shadows. Concentrating on the darkness, Kindra shoved the questions and memories of Ryce into the small, dark corner of her mind he now occupied, the place Kindra hid everything she didn't want—or wasn't supposed—to think about.

Although the GPS indicated that Bernard was about two hundred yards northwest of their position, Dru turned down a road leading in the opposite direction, toward a completely dark cabin. Kindra didn't have to ask why. Especially without knowing what Ealy's endgame was, driving straight up to his cabin would be as stupid as knocking on his front door and expecting him to let them in without question.

Dru parked near the seemingly unoccupied cabin and shut the car off. "Here." She offered Kindra an earpiece.

It wasn't the invisible earpiece Kindra had used for most of this job. It was a Bluetooth-looking single-ear set, and Dru explained that it had been rigged to work as an always-open, hands-free walkie-talkie system. It was pretty damn cool, actually.

Dru watched Kindra closely as she hooked the device over her ear, almost as though she didn't trust Kindra to do it right. "We need to split up and check the perimeter. It seems like Ealy is working alone— or *maybe* with a long-distance team—and taking no chances. We also need to make sure Bernard is still alive."

"Right." Kindra scrutinized the cabin they'd parked near as she stretched again, trying to prepare her body for the change of pace, movement after so many hours trapped in the car. The perimeter seemed to be well within the hundred-yard limit of Dru's electronic leash—the cabin itself couldn't be more than thirty feet wide and the tree line was only another ten feet from that. As long as Ealy's cabin wasn't much bigger, she should be safe. Still . . . "Be careful where you step. I don't want my head to explode just 'cause you can't keep yourself from tripping over a rock and breaking your neck."

"Your concern is touching. Truly."

"Whatever, Bomb Squad."

Dru's head tilted as she considered Kindra. "Even if we get to the point where I trust you enough to take that off, I'm never living this down, am I?"

"Nope." Kindra got out of the car.

The temperature had dropped since sunset, settling somewhere around fifteen degrees. Kindra was glad of her multiple layers of clothing and even happier that all of those clothes were black. This kind of work wasn't easy at the best of times, but it was stupidly hard when you weren't camouflaged right.

Despite the distance between them and Ealy, Kindra and Dru stayed quiet, closing the car doors with a *click* and keeping to the road's cracked pavement as much as possible when they moved toward Ealy's cabin.

"There." Dru nodded toward a faint light filtering through the trees. Ealy's cabin was set deeper into the woods than most of the others, and although some lights were on inside, the curtains were drawn across every window. Only thin slants of light escaped. The narrow strip of glass set into the door didn't seem to be blocked, but Kindra was not about to offer to peer in *that* particular gap in his defenses. This guy didn't seem stupid enough to leave something that obvious open. Not without reason.

For almost half an hour, they watched the house, moving slowly and silently around the perimeter while checking for any way to figure out what was going on inside. Their Ealy doppelgänger was good. He hadn't left them a single peephole. They'd have to approach the house to get anything.

"Head for the north wall and let me know what you hear," Dru whispered. "We need positions and condition. And intel."

Something cool pressed into Kindra's hand—a microphone specially designed to pick up speech vibrations through walls or windows. It was similar enough to a model that Sera had modified that Kindra knew how to operate it. There were no headphones attached to this unit. She understood why when she flicked the switch that activated the mic, and quiet static buzzed through the earpiece Dru had given her.

Whoa. It's all linked to the same system? Cool.

Hiding her tech envy from Dru, she checked the settings on the small battery pack that controlled the unit and muttered, "It's not the first time I've done this."

"Maybe not," Dru agreed. "But it is the first time you've done it with *me.*"

"Oh, go swallow a gun barrel." Kindra moved to the right, staying hidden in the trees as she circled the house until she could approach at an angle that kept her away from the windows.

"Report." Dru's voice was just loud enough in Kindra's ear to make her jump.

"I've got jack-shit. It's been less than sixty seconds since I saw you." Kindra gripped the device harder, wishing it were a gun. "My own mother doesn't pester me this often."

"Yeah, well, your mother doesn't have to worry about you defecting."

Kindra opened her mouth, but the words died on her tongue. That might have been true once . . . but that was before last week, before the moment she'd realized how little she knew about what was happening in her own life and finally said no.

Even if she hadn't said it aloud.

Swallowing, Kindra forced herself to say, "That's because my mother—"

"Tsst!"

The sound was sharp through the earpiece. Kindra froze, recognizing what it meant. Movement or noise detected. Or gut instinct flaring to life.

"Clear," Dru whispered over the comm. "Go."

Settling into the headspace where she concentrated best, Kindra checked her surroundings and crossed the remaining twenty feet to the cabin. She kept low and moved slowly, limiting the chances that her movements would attract attention from inside. In moments, Kindra was plastered against the exterior wall, head cocked for any sound and eyes jumping between the windows and the ground for any signs of a trip wire or a trap. Nothing. But then, Ealy hadn't had a lot of time to set them up. Dru had only been about five minutes behind him.

Keeping herself below the sight line of the window, Kindra fixed the small, round microphone to the bottom corner of a glass panel and then flicked the switch to activate it.

Low-level static filtered through the earbud, but under that were distant voices, the words muddled. No one in this room.

Gently removing the device, she shifted to the second window on this wall. This time, when she pressed the mic against the corner of the glass, voices came through sharp and loud.

"—remember? This doesn't give us anything!" It wasn't quite a shout, but it was close. "What the hell am I supposed to do with this?"

"I didn't think they knew I had the information, Aaron." Bernard. He sounded hoarse and weary, but he wasn't gagged and he wasn't dead. "I didn't think to memorize it on sight."

Damn it, he's alive. Nothing can ever be easy.

Ealy's voice—*I guess Ealy's name is Aaron?*—spoke again. "This is really about drugs? Hadley took out a hit on you just because of *drugs?*"

"And because I wasn't going to sell him my company, not after what I'd learned," Bernard said. "He wanted the export rights we hold and land we control in Echemorro. He was willing to kill half of a community to gain the land deeds he wanted. Taking a hit out would've been nothing for him."

Kindra hoped that her current partner could hear what was being said, because she didn't dare even whisper this close to the targets.

"The deaths aren't just in Echemorro," Aaron said. "Jenna lived in *Florida.*"

"I know, but I can't—" Bernard stopped, the words lost in coughing. "Did you have to blow the building up?"

"Yes. Or that Catwoman-wannabe would've gutted you." Clinks and shuffling, and then Aaron—*is that his first or last name?*—said, "Drink this. The last of the smoke inhalation should clear by the end of the night."

"So he doesn't want Bernard dead," Dru said through the comm. "Good. That'll help."

Won't help me *any.*

The curtains above her head shifted, and light spilled into the darkness.

She couldn't detach the mic without risking the movement catching his eye. Her clothes and her hair were dark, and her hands and face were as hidden as they could be. Holding her breath, she hoped she blended into the shadows.

"Warm up some water on the stove, Bernard," Aaron said. The words seemed normal, but the tone was off. Too stressed. Too clipped. An order.

"What?"

Aaron grunted, and the curtain dropped back into place. "The steam will help your throat."

"Wha— Um." The pause was brief, but it was there. And when Bernard talked again, the speech pattern was off. Forced calm, his words flowing too evenly compared to a moment before. "Okay. If you say so. I'll try it."

Soft thuds. Footsteps retreating. One set and then two, heading out of the room.

"Kindra?"

Ignoring Dru, Kindra waited another ten seconds before pushing herself up, detaching the mic, and moving away from the house.

"If you don't answer, I swear to Audrey Hepburn I'll—"

Only when she reached the tree line did she respond to Dru's increasingly frantic whisper.

"What? Kidnap me and strap a bomb to my neck? Oh, wait."

"Stop it. Where are you?"

"North of the house." Kindra settled behind a tree, her back pressed against the rough bark and her breath curling in the air in front of her. "Did you get that? Because I'm not going back."

"You think he saw you?"

"He suspected *something*. That last bit was definitely code for 'get the eff out.'"

"Stay there. I'm coming to you."

Kindra was still too close to the cabin for comfort, so—mindful of the hundred-yard limit—she inched deeper into the shadows. Ten feet into the woods, she was able to tuck herself into a natural alcove between two wide trees. The space was almost entirely lost in darkness. It was as good a hiding spot as she was going to find in the dark and with no knowledge of the landscape.

"Call your friend out, or I'll shoot you here."

And apparently it wasn't good enough.

She felt the cold metal of a gun barrel press against the top of her spine, mere inches above Dru's proximity leash. That as much as the sudden words spoken out of the dark silence sent chills down Kindra's spine. No one had sneaked up on her in a long time, but Aaron was effing stealthy. She'd never heard him.

Atropos bless it, this is not *my week.*

"Shoot me and I might take you out with me," she told him. "I'm wired with C-4. Just, you know, FYI."

"Bullshit."

Kindra snorted. "Yeah, I wish."

"If you wanted to play, all you had to do was say please." *Dru.*

Relief bloomed in her chest. She hadn't thought she would ever be this happy to hear Dru, even though, if she hadn't known better, she wouldn't have recognized Dru's voice at all. The slow, slithering, seductive drawl didn't sound like Dru.

"You shoot me, I shoot her."

"And then we all go kaboom," Dru said. "She wasn't lyin' about the C-4, ya know. And that ain't the way I plan on goin' out, Aaron."

As soon as she felt the gun leave her skin, Kindra dropped, rolling to the side and standing up on the other side of the tree. Dru still had Aaron in her sights, the customized and well-loved Nighthawk T4 Kindra had seen holstered on her earlier pressed to the base of his skull.

Out of his bullets' immediate path, Kindra crossed her arms and leaned against the trunk, studying the face in front of her as best as she could. Bad lighting and all, it was a better look than she'd gotten all week.

He *did* resemble Michael Ealy, especially the shape of his face and the tone of his skin. The features were a little different, his eyes wider and, from what she could see in the limited light, not blue. The left side of his face was marred by a dark-pink scar that ran from half an inch past his hairline to just under his eye. Even with Dru's gun digging into his head, Aaron managed to glare across the two feet that divided him from Kindra. She smiled and held out her hand. "Give it over, or I take it from you."

The movement was fast. Aaron chucked the gun at Kindra's head and ducked in the opposite direction, slamming his elbow into Dru's gut as he moved.

Dru fired. The bullet lodged in the tree.

Kindra grabbed Aaron's gun just before it hit her face, careful of the trigger, and then flipped it, aiming for the space Aaron had been standing in a second before.

He was already behind a tree and getting farther away.

"Con*sarn* it, that bastard is quick!" Dru ran after Aaron, Kindra close on her heels.

"*Corre!*" Aaron yelled. Spanish. "*Abra la puerta y corre! Sube al coche!*"

"What the shit did he just say?" Dru hissed.

"Spanish," Kindra huffed. "He told Bernard to open the door and run to the car."

"You speak Spanish?"

"You don't?"

Instead of chasing Aaron through the house and possibly running straight into the barrel of whatever firearm he managed to grab inside, Dru and Kindra headed toward the front, where his SUV was parked.

"Did you disable the car?" Kindra asked.

"No. But I slapped a tracker on the damn thing."

"What *is* it with you and trackers?"

They rounded the house and skidded to a halt as something sailed through the air near their heads.

"Grenade!" Kindra grabbed Dru and hightailed it *away* from where it looked like that thing was going to land.

They made it behind a huge tree. Kindra pushed Dru face-first to the forest floor, falling on top of her and covering her own ears with her hands, mouth open slightly to equalize the pressure she knew was coming. Less than two seconds later, the grenade exploded.

The blast rolled over her, compression of air building until she wanted to scream. Heat flashed next, the lick of fire burning far too hot in the cold night. In the warped, sizzling stillness that settled once the blast passed over, Kindra thought she heard a car door slam and an engine turn over. It seemed far off, but she knew the effects of a grenade blast too well to put much stock in that guesstimate. Two explosions in twenty-four hours? Her hearing probably wouldn't be right for hours. If she was lucky.

Kindra pushed to her feet and ran toward the road, dodging small fires and falling embers. She reached the paved path just as the slightly beat-up tan Explorer flew past at around forty. The car peeled away, burning a streak of rubber into the asphalt. Kindra raised Aaron's gun. Dru knocked it aside before she could fire a single shot.

"I told you that we're not killing them!"

For once, Kindra had been aiming at the tires. She doubted that Dru would believe it, so they watched as Aaron and Bernard got away. Again.

When the taillights disappeared, Kindra glanced at Dru. "I think it's safe to say he knows we're following them now."

Dru didn't respond. She was staring at Kindra, eyes slightly narrowed. "Do you realize you might have just saved my life?"

"Uh, yeah? I thought that was the whole point of the bomb thing."

"It was." Dru nodded slowly, her gaze remaining steady on Kindra's face. "But that doesn't mean I expected you to play along."

"Great." Kindra stuffed Aaron's gun in the pocket of her RFID-disrupting coat and headed in the direction of the Taurus. No way had that explosion escaped official attention. They'd be converging *soon*. "I'll keep that in mind next time."

Dru caught up before Kindra had moved more than a few feet away, a smile spreading across her face. "Admit it. You're getting used to me, baby. You'd miss me if I was dead."

"Want to test that theory and see if you're right?" Kindra asked.

Dru laughed. "Not particularly."

"You are in a scary-good mood for someone who just lost their client," Kindra grumbled as they moved quicker through the trees.

"'Cause you're grumpy enough for both of us, darlin.'" That seductive drawl was back, and Kindra shivered.

She planned to die before ever admitting she found that sleepy accent ridiculously sexy.

Good thing it was looking more and more certain that this job would kill her.

Chapter Twelve

Dru took Aaron's Beretta away as they fled the campground, but Kindra didn't care as long as Dru didn't fight her about stopping at a CVS on the way out of town. Compliance seemed to come more from confused curiosity than anything else.

The bag Kindra brought back to the car was filled with art supplies. Dru raised one eyebrow. "And we needed to do this because . . ."

"Because we need to ID this guy, and we didn't get a picture."

"Which means you need a hundred colored pencils?"

"Shut up and drive, Dru. Unless you're scared I'll stab you with my goldenrod?" Kindra held up the golden-yellow pencil.

"Only if you've got a death wish, baby."

Kindra rolled her eyes. "Who doesn't in our line of work?"

"I don't."

Snorting her disbelief, Kindra flipped open the sketchbook she'd bought, turned on the overhead light, and got to work. It took about an hour to get all of the details right—or as right as they'd ever be when she was working with colored pencils in a moving car.

She tossed the sketchbook on Dru's lap. "Pull over and send that to whoever you send things to."

"Whoa." Dru's eyes widened. She eased the car toward the shoulder of the road, then picked up the portrait of Aaron, staring at it. "This is amazing."

"It's good enough for now." Kindra shrugged. "You might be able to get a match off it at least, if you run it through the right database."

"No, seriously. This is *fantastic*." Dru's index finger traced the pinkish scar on Aaron's face. "I didn't get a good look at him, so I thought we still had nothing, but with this?"

Dru grabbed her bag from the backseat and extracted a portable scanner. She plugged it into her phone, scanned the image, and told her phone to "Call Holly Golightly."

"Does your mother think she *is* Audrey Hepburn or something?"

"No, but she wishes she was." When she spoke again, it obviously wasn't meant for Kindra. "Bernard called him Aaron. Don't know if it's a first name or a last name. We didn't get a photo, but we have a sketch."

A pause.

"No, of course I didn't do it. I think everyone remembers my last artistic masterpiece." This time when she paused she rolled her eyes. "Obviously, yes. If I'm calling you, I'm still alive. So is she, by the way."

Another beat of silence and Dru shook her head. "If he is private sector now, he wasn't always. Guy's got 'military' written all over him in huge red, white, and blue letters. Start with their database and move out from there. That'd be my best guess."

Without a good-bye, Dru ended the call and merged back into traffic. The silence between them didn't last long this time. "So, you're an artist?"

"No," Kindra scoffed. Artists had visions of beautiful and terrible things that they somehow transferred to colors on canvas. She just happened to know how to produce facsimiles.

"But you can draw."

"So can several million other people."

"Yet you don't consider yourself an artist."

"Sketching something I've seen makes me a human photocopier, not an artist. I've never created a piece of art in my life."

Dru hummed, the sound something between acknowledgment and disbelief, but she didn't say anything.

With nothing to distract her but the thrum of the motor and the periodic buzz of passing cars in the background, Kindra calculated the hours since the warehouse explosion. Everything had exploded just before six this morning, and now it was nearing midnight. Her fingers twitched as she fought the urge to trace the collar around her neck.

It had been an extraordinarily effed-up eighteen hours.

"You were there the day of the first attempt, right?" Dru asked apropos of nothing.

"Same as you." That was the day she'd seen the photographer who became "Dru," who became her kidnapper, who became a Calver.

Dru glanced over, a small nod her only admission. "Bernard had a packet of papers on him. You were the one who took them?"

"Yes." She absolutely did *not* look at her bag. "Odira wanted them."

"What did they say?"

Kindra blinked. "Bernard didn't tell you?"

"He told us what he remembered, but it's not like the guy has a photographic memory."

Right. That's what he'd been telling Aaron: that he couldn't remember all the details. He'd mentioned Redwell, Garret Hadley, and drugs. Maybe that was in the spreadsheet of numbers Kindra hadn't had time to focus on?

"Now I want to know what *you* remember," Dru said.

There was one question written across Kindra's mind in large neon lights and surrounded by glowing, blinking arrows: should she tell Dru that she *had* the papers? Unless . . . Had Dru found them when she searched Kindra's bag? This might be a test of Kindra's loyalties and how willing she was to do what was momentarily necessary to survive.

Kindra met Dru's eyes for a moment, looking over just as a flash from oncoming headlights lit up her face. Dru's expression was strange, expectant in a way that didn't seem to fit the conversation. If Kindra assumed that Dru *didn't* know the documents were in the car, there were only three ways she could answer without pissing Dru off and maybe getting blown up:

One: Tell the story the way it *should* have happened. All client information was need to know, and Kindra had never yet needed to know.

Two: Tell the almost truth and give Dru the details Kindra could remember.

Three: Tell the actual truth and hand over the copies stuffed in the lining of her bag.

Keeping silent wouldn't protect Kindra, and it wouldn't get them any closer to ending this drawn-out waking nightmare. And, hell, it wasn't like the chances of Dru reporting back to Odira were higher than zero point zero two percent. For all Odira knew, Bernard had already given the Calvers a new copy of the reports.

"Will the details help us track down Bernard?" Kindra needed to be sure of her choice before she made it.

Dru's eyes widened ever so slightly, as though she was surprised by the answer. She cleared her throat. "Even if they don't, they might help us figure out why Aaron wants him. And we might be able to figure out how to get him off of Redwell's shit list."

Kindra closed her eyes and pressed her forehead against the window, enjoying the soothing chill of the glass against her skin.

To truth or not to truth? Right now, that was the question.

If the information helped them find Bernard, that was a good thing. Kindra could always figure out how and when to kill him later. If she wanted to.

"There were pictures of the school massacre, but not a lot. Pages of coded information—letters and numbers in columns, but I have no clue what it was for."

Dru waited a second, as if checking to see if Kindra had more to say. "That's it?"

"No," Kindra admitted, her head still resting against the cold window. "There were death certificates and land deeds. All of the deeds sold land that once belonged to the dead people, and all of them turned control over to Rose Water Farms. At least seventeen different plots of land. And seventeen death certificates to go with them."

"Do you remember the names?"

"Only a few. Someone named Maria de Abaroa Abreu died, and then a few days later her husband Vasco Espinosa Abreu signed papers selling their land. Same kind of thing happened with Carlos Barros de la Cruze, Hernán Mata Merlo, Zamora Silva Rios Toset, and Lino Vargas Paredes."

"There should be a notebook in the glove compartment," Dru said, tension in her voice. "Write down those names. Please."

Kindra blinked and sat up, more than a little startled by the "please," even if it had been tacked on like an afterthought. "Please" was something she only heard from strangers. The people in her world rarely bothered with polite turns of phrase. Courtesy was a waste of air and time.

Apparently not to Dru.

Oddly, that made it a little easier for Kindra to say, "I'll do you one better."

Moving quickly, she twisted to grab her bag from the back. Dru tensed but didn't try to stop her. She dragged the bag into her lap and plopped back into the seat. The first blade she found was the small one she sometimes hid in her bra on jobs. She cut into the lining of the pocket. It took a little rooting around to find the papers—they'd shifted each time the bag got tossed—but she pulled them free and held them up.

"You *have* them?" Dru's tone was sharp and her voice rose several decibels. Shock or anger? "Why didn't you say so before?"

"You didn't ask if I *had* them," she said evenly. "You asked what I *remembered*."

"You take things *way* too literally sometimes." Dru's jaw was tense. "Did you see Bible passages in there?"

"Yeah. I remember them too, just to be clear." Kindra almost smiled when Dru rolled her eyes. "The ones I saw were Psalms 2:8, 'Ask of me, and I shall give thee the heathen for thine inheritance, and the uttermost parts of the earth for thy possession,' and Hebrews 9:22, 'And almost all things are by the law purged with blood; and without shedding of blood is no remission.'"

"Jesus," Dru breathed. "Well, *those* make sense."

"You broke the code?"

Dru gave her a strange look. "You didn't see the investigator's notes? Bernard couldn't remember the passages but he said that Isa—that the guy investigating made notes about what they meant."

Kindra opened her mouth and then shut it, shaking her head and refusing to explain *why* she hadn't gotten that far.

"All righty. Well, it's not a code, not in the way things are usually coded. Do you know about the connection between Rose Water and Garret Hadley?"

Kindra hadn't dared research Garret Hadley or Redwell on any device linked to Odira's system, so she still knew next to nothing about the client who'd ordered Bernard's assassination. When Dru glanced over, Kindra shook her head and said, "Only that there *is* a connection."

"There definitely is. Rose Water is based out of Balama, and it's the parent company of Hadley's holdings in Echemorro."

Wait . . . Rose Water? R. W. How did I not catch that earlier? Kindra had connected Garret Hadley to the *G. H.* in the note scrawled on the photo of the schoolyard massacre, but not Rose Water Farms to the *R. W.* listed on the same note. *B caved to R. W. (R's E business partner) 2 days later*, it had said. She'd thought that the *B* meant Bernard, but maybe it referred to the city of Balama instead?

"What does Hadley want in Balama? Why bother with Rose Water?"

"Rose Water exports crops and textiles for Garret, but it's a cover for drug running—mainly cocaine, but not exclusively." Dru drummed her fingers on the steering wheel as she spoke, tapping out a rhythm Kindra couldn't follow. "The letters always end with a Bible passage. It took a while for the investigator to pinpoint it, but every so often the first and third letter of the Bible book are written in cursive instead of print. Apparently *those* passages were orders from Hadley to Rose Water. Bernard remembered the translation that the investigator had suggested, but not which passages had been used."

It was like someone had finally handed Kindra the picture to the puzzle she'd been trying to finish, each new tidbit slotting itself easily into her memory.

"For the last six months or so, Rose Water has been trying to buy up as much coastal land as possible, but they ran into trouble in the town of Balama," Dru explained. "It's a small city, but control of that port is crucial if you're trying to get things in or out of the country without attracting official attention. Gasper Exports' government contracts give him primary control of the port, and a lot of the other parcels in the area have been passed down for generations. No one wanted to sell. Rose Water's president, Eduardo Melo Santos, sent the Psalms passage after he ran out of legal ways to obtain the land."

"'Ask of me, and I shall give thee the heathen for thine inheritance, and the uttermost parts of the earth for thy possession.'" Kindra filtered the words through the information Dru had bestowed. "If you want me to, I'll get you the land the villagers own."

"Yeah. Exactly."

Kindra swallowed. "And Hadley ordered a slaughter. 'Without blood there is no remission.'"

"Pretty fucking much." Dru's voice was heavy and thick, but she didn't stop talking. "As soon as that note reached Rose Water, a group of mercenaries masquerading as members of the southern rebels ran over Balama with guns. Dozens of people died that day. A lot of the dead were children."

It had been obvious when she'd seen the dates on the deeds and the death certificates that the two were connected, but hearing the rest made the whole thing so much dirtier. Rose Water had bought that land from decimated families and grieving mothers.

"The coast is tightly controlled, but the rest of the region is becoming a war zone. It can't go on much longer before people who have no business fighting anyone try to start a revolution that is going to turn bloody *fast*." There were five seconds of leaden silence—Kindra counted, too out of her depth to do anything else—before Dru spoke again. "*That's* Garret Hadley. *That's* the guy who hired your family to kill Bernard Gasper."

Keeping her face perfectly blank, Kindra shrugged. Inside, she trembled.

Atropos bless.

Kindra had never been under the illusion that what they did was good, helpful, or even necessary in the quest-for-global-peace sense of the word. It had been about survival for her. She'd never thought her family might be playing a major role in the destabilization of nations.

Dru shook her head, her lips pursed. "Why'd Odira let you keep all that?"

"I'm the one who stole them, remember?" *Please leave it at that.*

"So? You probably have standing orders to ignore anything you pick off a target."

She twisted to face Dru, her eyes narrow. "How the hell would you know anything about my standing orders?"

"I don't, but your parents seem like exactly that kind of control freak."

Shit. Kindra hadn't thought this through to the admission of *how* she'd collected these copies, and now Dru was watching her expectantly. Almost *too* expectantly, as though Dru already knew everything and was just waiting for confirmation.

"They don't know I have these," Kindra grudgingly admitted. "I kept an extra set of copies."

"Why?"

Because I wanted to know if Bernard killed those kids. She held those words back, but let her temper surface. "Because Amett had just *missed* a shot for the first time in my life, and I thought an insurance policy might not be a bad idea if everything else started going to hell. Which, obviously, it has! And look how much good *that* decision has done me."

For some strange reason, Dru's lips curved into a smile. "You know, you're crazy cute when you lose your temper."

"This isn't even close to losing my temper." Kindra held Dru's gaze for a second, refusing to acknowledge the warmth spreading in her chest. A stupid, and probably fake, compliment from Dru should *not* feel this nice. "If you think this is cute, you should see me when I'm *actually* pissed. I must be freaking adorable."

Dru laughed. "I don't doubt it, baby. Not even for a second."

What is wrong *with this girl?* If Dru didn't stop oscillating between flirting and threatening death, Kindra was going to do something drastic.

Like kiss her.

Just to freak her out and shut her up, of course. Not because Dru's lips looked tantalizingly soft, or because her in-need-of-a-touchup, black-dyed hair gleamed in the shafts of light coming through the window, or because her twistedly morbid sense of humor meshed beautifully with Kindra's. Definitely not because Kindra wanted a reason to slide her hands under Dru's layers and find out if she was as lithe and toned and *warm* as she looked.

No. Kindra only wanted to kiss Dru to shut her up, and that wasn't an option while the girl was driving, not unless Kindra actually did have a death wish.

Kindra settled down and shut up instead.

The problem with silence was that it left nothing to hide her thoughts behind. The longer the stillness stretched, the more questions gathered in Kindra's head until, finally, she couldn't beat them all back anymore.

At least one *had* to be asked. "Did the warehouse burn down?"

Dru barely startled at the sudden break in the silence. "Not everything. Dad said fire and rescue got there before too long, but C-4 is gonna do some serious damage when it's used right."

"And Aaron knows how to use it." Kindra absently rubbed her shoulder. Her body was a little bruised and battered from the warehouse explosion. The ringing in her ears hadn't faded entirely, either. The grenade hadn't helped any. Still, she'd dealt with worse. "Do they think I'm dead?"

Dru's eyes pinched a little, deep lines appearing. "I, uh... Honestly, I don't know. It's not like we can call them up and ask."

The fire and rescue teams wouldn't have found a body. Since she had never checked in, Kindra's family would assume that one of two things had happened: she'd been kidnapped, or killed and disposed of elsewhere.

If they found Bernard, eventually they'd find Kindra too. Whatever Odira would do to Kindra—for failing, for betrayal, or for whatever other offenses she'd committed in Odira's eyes—had to be easier to deal with. It was also probably a lot less deadly than an effing bomb collar.

I hope.

She swallowed, and the collar seemed to tighten around her throat. Needing to *do* something, she set up the portable scanner and followed Dru's instructions to send scans of Bernard's documents to Cassidy and Hugo, wherever they were.

Hopefully Kindra would still be alive when the cavalry arrived. Hopefully the cavalry wouldn't be the ones to put a bullet in her brain for turning traitor.

New York City, New York

Isaac Marks climbed onto the shuttle for the rental car lot and dropped into the seat closest to the driver.

Something heavy *thunked* against the side of the shuttle.

"Oh, hell."

Isaac jolted up, his hand falling to his hip, though no weapon sat there. He eyed the door as though he were a general and it was a breach in his defenses. When he saw the woman with a long curtain of mahogany hair trying to haul a suitcase over the first step of the shuttle, the tension—or some of it—seemed to ease out of his shoulders.

"Would you like some help, ma'am?" he asked, peering over the low partition.

The woman swept her hair over her shoulder and smiled; her accent hinted at Norway. "Yes, *please.*"

She sat across from Isaac once her bag was stowed and told him her name was Ingrid. They talked about restaurants and weather and how complicated air travel had become over the years.

Although Isaac's initial tension never left him, and he easily sidestepped questions like "What do you do?" with vaguely truthful answers like "Oh, I'm just a government peon," he never turned his watchfulness on her.

He didn't notice the way her startlingly blue eyes periodically studied him with the intensity of a mathematician working out a complex equation. He didn't notice the texts she sent periodically while they spoke. He didn't notice the tracking device she placed under the collar of his coat when she patted his back to say good-bye.

Instead, Isaac Marks checked in with the rental agent, begging them to find him anything that ran despite his lack of reservation, and later breathed a sigh of relief when he slid into his compact sedan. He smiled when he turned his personal cell phone on and saw the influx of texts, nodding when he saw the latest message from his kid, Blake, which read, *Dad, you've been gone so long I don't even know why I keep sending you these every morning, but it's a "she" day.*

He plugged in his headset and called his child, not looking surprised when he ended up hearing the voice mail message instead of Blake's usual grumpy morning greeting.

"Morning, sweetheart. Just wanted to let you know that I'm back stateside, but it might be a while longer before I'm home. You'll probably be with Uncle Altair this weekend. And don't worry too much if my phone is off for a while, okay? I still have some things to take care of." Isaac took a long breath and smiled. "I love you, Blake. I'll see you soon."

He ended the call, pulled the earbuds out, and powered off the phone.

Twenty minutes later, Isaac's steering column locked, his brakes failed, and he slammed into the support column of an overpass at fifty miles an hour.

He never heard the cheery message Blake left on his voice mail while she was at lunch.

He was dead before a young man rushed toward the smoking wreck and grabbed Isaac's wallet, phones, and messenger bag, before removing the tracker from his coat and the device under the steering column—the one that had turned his car into a coffin.

Chapter Thirteen

The fifth time Dru rolled her shoulder like she was fighting a massive muscle cramp, Kindra spat out the question she'd been holding back for two hours.

"Let me drive already!" *Okay, maybe you should've phrased that more like a question and less like an accusation. She still does hold the key to the bomb around your throat, Kindra.*

"So you can take us straight back to your psychotic family?" Dru scoffed. "Uh, no, thanks. I'm fine."

"You're *not* fine. Besides, I couldn't take us back there even if I wanted to. I've been with *you* for the past twenty-four hours." Kindra twisted to face Dru. "How would I know where they are now? Gonna let me call?"

Dru's eyes narrowed. "No."

"Then pull the hell over and let me drive. I can follow a GPS signal as well as you can."

Although she hesitated, Dru caved. "Fine. Whatever. Make a wrong turn and I will make you regret it, baby."

"I already regret everything."

Dru pulled into a twenty-four-hour gas station on the edge of Savannah and stopped at one of the pumps. After the shit-show in middle-of-nowhere North Carolina, Aaron had made his way southeast, apparently willing to sacrifice stealth for the speed of the major highways. Kindra looked around as Dru set up the pump, but there wasn't much to see from this part of the city. "I don't think I've ever been anywhere in Georgia except the Atlanta airport."

"You're not missing much." Dru pulled her dark hair out of its ponytail, shook her head, and then restrained the strands once again. "I need caffeine. Want? I promise not to poison it."

Her lip quirked up into a teasing smile that made Kindra want to either kiss her or punch her. Not able to do either without consequences she wasn't prepared to face, Kindra nodded. "Cream and four raw sugars if they have it."

Dru's eyebrows arched. "*Four*? Sweet tooth much?"

"There are worse vices." That and it covered the taste of the actual coffee. Kindra wanted the caffeine, not the bitter flavor.

Eyes narrow, Dru looked between Kindra and the store before slowly stretching out her arm and touching the skin above Kindra's collar. "One hundred yards. I'm trusting you to remember that."

The brush of Dru's fingertip against her neck sent amazingly pleasant warmth across her shoulders and down her spine, but she'd already given up too much control to Dru; no way would she give Dru this too. She forced the reaction down as she knocked Dru's hand away. "Like I'm about to forget?"

Still seeming reluctant, Dru headed inside the store.

Out of sight of her captor—*captor, Kindra; remember that part*—she gave in to the temptation to run her fingers along the edge of the collar. She flipped down the visor and opened the mirror, tilting her chin up to examine the device. Dru had been right when she said it would look more like a BDSM statement than a bomb. A cheap statement, but still. The only sign of its true purpose was a tiny, barely visible green light almost directly under Kindra's right ear.

Grunting, Kindra slapped the visor shut and rested her head against the headrest, closing her eyes. She knew well how fast the entire world could shift, rearranging itself into something almost unidentifiable, but the past week it'd been like the ground kept getting sucked out from under her feet. Every time she thought she'd adjusted enough to function, everything changed.

Like Dru agreeing to let her drive.

Would Dru take the collar off eventually? If that happened, could Kindra kill her? That's what Amett and Odira would order. But Dru had saved Kindra's life—apparently against her own parents' orders, or at least against their better judgment. She'd been almost funny at times and somewhat . . . sweet, when she wasn't being unquantifiable, unclassifiable, and impossible. At times, Dru almost seemed normal.

Not that it mattered if Dru took off the collar. Kindra had somehow managed to trade Odira's metaphorical leash for an actual one. Being with Dru was simply more entertaining.

Not "being with." Don't you dare start thinking like that. You're not "with" her. She's using you just like Odira did.

Slipping out of the car, Kindra pulled her arms over her head and then folded in half, grabbing her ankles until her forehead touched her knees. Straightening, she brought one knee up to her chest, wincing when her hip popped. It hadn't been the same ever since she dislocated it in Italy last year. The way this job was going, she'd be surprised if she didn't end up with another chronic injury.

Hell, she'd be lucky to get through this job alive.

Or maybe it'd be luckier if I didn't.

The tracker pinged.

Kindra dropped onto the seat and glanced at the device. An alert had popped up at the top of the screen: *TARGET STATIONARY.*

"Shit." Kindra laid on the horn twice in quick succession.

Dru appeared in the door of the station with two paper cups and wide eyes, running toward the passenger side. Kindra leaned over to open the door so Dru could climb in.

"What happened?" Dru set the coffee in the cup holders.

"They've stopped. Not far from here." The pump automatically shut off as Kindra got out and rounded the car. She slammed the pump back in place, slapped the gas cover closed, and then slipped back into the driver's seat. Dru already had the keys in the ignition, so they were out of the station in seconds.

Eyes jumping between the GPS and the road, Kindra wove through the minimal early-morning traffic with practiced ease. It was almost stupid how much simply being in the driver's seat made her feel in control. Nothing had changed, but that didn't matter when Kindra had her foot on the gas pedal and her fingers wrapped around the wheel. For the first time since Amett and Odira's plans had flown off the rails, Kindra felt like she could breathe.

Aaron's battered SUV was sitting almost dead center in the quiet parking lot of a small shopping plaza. The hairs on her arms rose. It was too easy. Too obvious. Far too exposed.

"The car looks empty." Dru scanned the area.

The car *was* empty, but Bernard was, according to the GPS, within a hundred yards of that car. Kindra eyed the screen, trying to figure out which store they should search first.

Bernard's signal disappeared. Another alert pop up with a quiet *ping.*

SIGNAL LOST.

Kindra's heart thumped quadruple time, propelling the sudden excess of adrenaline through her bloodstream. More pieces of this messed-up puzzle clicked into place. "We've gotta move."

"We don't know where they went! Bernard could be—"

"Working *with* the guy we're chasing!" Kindra shoved the gearshift into reverse and burned rubber leaving the parking lot.

"Where are you going?" Dru demanded.

"Far the hell away from here! This is a setup, you fucking moron!"

Dru opened her mouth, but the buzz of her cell phone cut her off.

"It looks like they dumped the car," Dru growled as soon as she answered the call. "Now Kindra's driving like a bat outta hell when we *should* be looking for—"

Her mouth snapped shut, and her eyes narrowed.

"What? Are you serious?" Dru smashed her fist on the dashboard. "Aaron called the fucking cops and reported us for kidnapping a little girl."

"You still want them both alive, don't you?"

Dru pressed the Bluetooth earpiece against her ear. Whatever the other person said, Dru didn't say another word before she hung up.

"Did Bernard know about the tracker you had on him?" Kindra asked.

"Of course he did! We had to cut him open to put it in."

Kindra turned into a neighborhood, hoping for fewer traffic cameras and an easily stealable car. "How likely is it that he didn't spill *that* little detail?"

"What the hell do you want me to do about that *now*? Shut up and drive!"

Slamming the car into a sharp right, Kindra smiled when Dru's head *thunked* against the window. Her smile only grew when Dru glared. "What? You told me to drive."

For the space of time between two blinks, it seemed like Dru was going to laugh. Then her head tilted like a dog catching a far-off whistle. "Are those sirens?"

Kindra listened. "Yes. A lot of them. And moving in our direction, I think."

The Taurus's headlights lit up a black Civic coupe. Newer model. Kindra calculated how long it'd take to jump-start that car and then guesstimated how long they had before the cops found them. "Not enough time to switch rides. We're gonna have to run for it if they find us."

"Run for it," Dru said. "They found us."

In the rearview, the first cop car clumsily swerved onto the street. From the club-like strobing happening behind him, his buddies weren't far off.

"Atropos bless it!" A sharp left and a block later, Kindra spun the car onto a main road. It had more room to maneuver. And more damn traffic cameras. "If you'd let me shoot out the tires last night, this wouldn't be happening!"

"I didn't know you were aiming for tires! I thought you were going to kill them!"

"And risk you triggering my slave collar?" She wasn't *that* suicidal.

"Oh. Right." Dru cleared her throat. "Get on the highway. They think we have a kid. They're not giving this chase up until we're stopped or dead."

Dru dragged a black duffel bag from the backseat, unzipped it, and pulled out extra magazines, a Kevlar vest, and Aaron's gun. The gun landed in Kindra's lap.

"Use that in less than a life-or-death emergency, and you won't like the consequences."

"Are you serious?" One-handed, Kindra picked up the gun, checked the safety, and made sure it was loaded. "Between you and the bomb, how much worse can it really get?"

"Don't be a brat, baby. I did save your life, you know." With quick, practiced motions, Dru strapped into the body armor and adjusted her seat, sliding it forward a few notches.

They'd almost reached the highway, but the cops had gotten closer. Glancing at Dru, Kindra considered surrender for a second.

If she cried kidnapping and gave one of her false identities, Seraphina might catch the alert when news of the "rescue" hit law enforcement channels. Her family *might* come find her, but it'd be a death sentence for Dru, and Kindra would be in for a long time in Tartarus herself. She'd be giving up her best shot at finally getting *out* of everything. This life, these jobs, her family.

Oh, I hope I don't regret this.

Kindra took the on-ramp to northbound I-95, a trail of cop cars following like ducklings. Screaming ducklings with flashing lights implanted in their heads.

"Are you going to use that gun, or is it just for show?" Kindra asked after the first half mile. A few cars had tried and failed to bump her off the road, and Dru hadn't fired a single shot.

"I didn't want to have to do this." Dru frowned, but she turned in her seat, bringing her knees underneath her and staying low. Bracing her back against the dashboard and using what little cover the cushioning could offer, she fired off several rounds through the rear windshield.

Not a single car dropped out of the chase.

They did start firing back, though.

Bullets shot past their heads. They ducked as low as possible, shielding themselves from bullets and glass. Dru popped up and fired five more rounds. Kindra watched the rearview, hoping at least one of those shots found a useful target. Like the drivers.

Hoods, windows, and tires all gained bullet holes, but not one car fell away.

"Atropos bless, your aim is shitty." Kindra swerved when the rear window of the car completely shattered and a bullet lodged in their dashboard.

"Fuck you!" Dru reloaded and fired several more rounds. "I'm not going to shoot cops."

"Then *you* drive, and *I'll* shoot them!"

"Damn it." Dru adjusted her aim. "I need to buy you a cricket."

Kindra swerved around a slow-moving, beat-up Corolla. "A *cricket?*"

"Yes!" Another three rounds wasted. "You need a freaking conscience. A cricket worked for Pinocchio. Mulan had one too."

"What the *hell* are you talking about?"

Dru snorted and fired again. "Let me guess, your crazy-ass parents never let you watch Disney movies either."

"Does it *matter*? I'm kinda trying not to turn us into pavement art right now. Can we discuss the inadequacies of my childhood—" One of the cops got close enough to ram the side of the car, shattering what was left of the driver's side window. She winced to protect her eyes and then fired three well-placed shots into the cruiser's engine block. It started to burn even before she slammed on the gas and got the hell out of the way. "—later? Or, you know, never?"

"Hell no, baby." Dru reloaded and fired another three rounds. She so consistently missed the occupants of the cars in favor of the cars themselves that Kindra was impressed. Her aim and her control of that gun had to be *damn* good. "If we survive this, you and I are going to have a nice *long* conversation."

"Oh, joy. Something to live for." Kindra wanted to be aggravated at this whole situation. She should be fuming. She should hate Dru and everything she'd subjected Kindra to. So why in all that Atropos held holy was she having *fun*? She almost felt like *laughing*.

Analyze your idiocy later. Find a way out now.

As long as they were in the cops' sight line, they couldn't switch cars. This chase needed a finale. "Please tell me you can reach my bag."

"Why?" Dru asked even as she slithered into the backseat, keeping as low as she could.

"I should have some C-4."

"Because *that's* something everyone just happens to have." She grabbed Kindra's duffel and opened the main zipper pocket, pulling out a block of explosive. "What the shit am I supposed to do with a block of C-4 and no ignition?"

"We're surrounded by cars on fire! You can shoot C-4, and you can throw it in a fire . . ." Kindra waited for recognition to set in.

"But never do both at the same time." Dru grinned and lobbed it into the flames jetting from the closest car. Taking aim, she fired one perfect shot, confirming everything Kindra had guessed about her skill with that Nighthawk.

Boom.

The car flipped, slamming upside down on another car. Two more cops swerved to avoid the wreck, crashing into civilians who'd tried to flee but couldn't get farther than the tree line along the road. The wreckage blocked the whole highway. The cars behind couldn't get past. Dru grinned as the sirens faded into the distance.

"I'm *really* curious to know how blowing cops up is better than shooting them," Kindra said as they raced away from the fiery mess.

Dru paled, and her mouth snapped shut. She stared back at the crash, her eyes wide.

Kindra bit back a sigh. It wasn't that she *liked* killing cops—she didn't like killing anyone who wasn't a target—but those who chased after armed suspects were asking to get shot.

The guilty devastation on Dru's face hurt, reminding her far too much of all the times she'd watched the collateral damage pile up.

"I'm sure they're fine," she muttered. "Their buddies probably pulled them out. And they'll get them to a hospital or . . ." *The morgue.* "Or, you know, whatever."

Dru nodded as she turned around and buckled her seat belt; her hands shook badly enough that she missed the first time.

Kindra looked away. The tremor reminded her too much of Amett and why everything in her life had gone even more wrong than it already had been. *That* was the reason she reached over and took Dru's hand. To stop the trembling. Not to offer comfort. They were killers. They didn't need comfort. To give it or get it. Right?

"It's over." Kindra's words were quiet but firm, and she kept hold of Dru's hand, gently brushing her thumb along Dru's knuckles. "We need a new car, and we need it now. And you need to get your head together fast or this is going to happen again. Get it?"

"They're probably dead." Dru's voice was almost sad.

"Maybe. And maybe not." She squeezed Dru's hand and then made herself release it. "Have you really never killed anyone?"

"I have. More than a few. But it's different when . . ." Dru swallowed and dropped her chin to her chest. "It doesn't matter as much when they deserve it, but I don't like taking lives that don't need to end. People who haven't done anything wrong. *Those* guys didn't do anything wrong. They probably had families, and they were just doing their jobs, and now they're dead."

"We don't know that they're dead, and we can't do anything about it either way. We're still on the run, in case you haven't noticed."

Dru took a deep breath, seemingly staring at her hands in her lap. Then, with a shudder, she rolled her shoulders back and looked up. "Even if we grab a car, we'll be screwed as soon as it's reported stolen."

"There's a set of clean New York license plates in my bag. Unless you tossed them."

"Right." Dru seemed to pull herself together a little bit more. "Then I guess we should go car shopping." Another deep breath, but this time Dru's attention locked on Kindra. "We're going to need to split up. I'll find us a new ride while you clean this mess out so we can get the hell out of this city before they track us down."

"No, thanks. I like my neck where it is."

Silently, Dru watched Kindra for a long, weighted moment. "If I remove the collar, will you stay with me instead of trying to run back to Odira? And *not* try to kill me first chance you get? I want to be able to trust you, baby."

"I'm not your baby." The words had no venom, though. Not even any real expectation of being listened to. Kindra's mind was too busy spinning out on that offer.

It had only been a day. A really long day during which they'd saved each other's life, but still barely more than twenty-four hours. How could Dru trust Kindra that much? If their positions were reversed, Kindra wouldn't even consider taking off the collar yet, but Dru was more than considering it.

"So? Deal?" Dru asked.

Kindra wasn't sure if she'd stick to their agreement or not, but she definitely knew which answer was in her best interest.

"Sure. I'll play nice."

Chapter Fourteen

After a quick argument about the division of labor and Dru's seemingly reluctant removal of the bomb collar, Kindra dropped Dru near a large apartment complex and drove off, dumping the car a couple of miles from the vehicle Dru was about to steal. Soon, the Taurus was half-buried in the woods on an empty stretch of road.

Once it was hidden, Kindra pulled everything out of the car and scrubbed the dashboard, the steering wheel, the doors, and anything else they'd touched or sweat on. She dumped half a bottle of ammonia-based cleaning solution on the spot where she'd thrown up yesterday—and then sat on the closed trunk, waiting for their new ride to appear.

It only took about ten more minutes for Dru to show up. In a forest-green minivan.

"Are you serious?" Kindra asked when Dru got out.

"The cops'll think the same thing." Dru grabbed one of the bags by Kindra's feet and carried it to the van. "We're trying to throw them off, remember?"

"Yeah, but it's still supposed to be a *getaway* car. What the fuck is this supposed to get us away from? Little League practice?"

"Don't be so judgmental. These things have more power than you think." She smirked and nodded toward the Taurus. "Did you wipe it down?"

Kindra could've just said yes, but Dru had gotten so indignant every time she heard about Kindra's effed-up childhood that the urge to mess with her was too strong to resist.

"Why bother? I don't have any fingerprints." She held up her hand to show the almost unnoticeable scars on her fingertips and across her palms.

Dru winced. "Your parents really are psychotic. Jesus. Chemical burns? How old were you when *this* happened?"

Eight. She looked at her hands, and suddenly it wasn't funny anymore. *Nine. Ten. Twelve. Thirteen . . .*

The first time was two weeks before her first job. It'd almost become a ritual for the family over the years to gather around the sink and concentrate on not letting even an eyelid twitch as Odira dabbed acid on their fingertips and across their palms. Their hands still had identifying scars and ridges, but they changed so often that there was little chance of anyone using them as a positive ID.

She bit the inside of her lip and tried to hate the pity she saw in Dru's eyes.

"Well, *you* may not have fingerprints, but I do. And you *know* fingerprints aren't the only way they can find you." Dru pulled a rag and a bottle of cleaning solution out of a duffel. "Help me wipe this down. We need to get out of here."

"Shit, stop." Kindra grabbed Dru's wrist. "I'm not a moron, Dru. It's done. I was the one whose DNA was all over the backseat, remember?"

Dru shoved the cleaning supplies back into her bag. "Get in the fucking van, then."

They tossed their bags into the middle row of the van and climbed in. Kindra ended up driving again, and had to admit—at least in her own head—that Dru had a point: the van had more pickup than she'd expected.

"You know, you may call it psychotic, but fingerprintlessness is simple efficiency." Why was she defending the practice she hated so much that even the memories of each rescouring made her hands burn and her eyes water? "How much time in your life do you think you've wasted wiping down something you barely touched?"

"Days. Weeks. Doesn't matter. I'm keeping my skin the way it is."

Good. It's nice skin. Kindra kept her lips locked tight. Her head was in a damn weird place right now. Maybe the sudden lack of a bomb collar had made her light-headed and stupid.

"So what now?" she asked, pushing everything else aside. "No trackers, no ID, and no effing clue where Aaron is going."

"Yes, thanks for pointing out everything we *don't* have. You really need to look on the bright side once in a while, baby. How about you start with 'we're alive'?"

"Yay. We're alive." Kindra wiggled one hand with obviously false enthusiasm. "Now what the fuck is the plan? Because if you don't give me a direction, guess where I'm going?"

"Back to the people who burned the skin off your fingertips and deprived you of Disney movies?"

Kindra rolled her eyes. "Really? Chemical burns and a Disney-less childhood rank as equal abuses in your book?"

"You underestimate the power of a good musical cartoon," Dru said, nodding slowly.

"Oh, Atropos bless it." Kindra groaned. "I forgot they're all musicals." She could get behind the animation, though. As an art form, it seemed sort of underappreciated. "You're never making me watch those. Ever."

Dru laughed. "Never say 'never ever.'"

Kindra got back on the highway, headed south, and smiled when three cop cars went screaming in the opposite direction. The expression didn't last long, though. She slammed the heel of her hand into the steering wheel. "If you don't give me a damned destination, I'm heading the hell—"

The buzz of Dru's cell stopped Kindra's words in her throat.

Atropos, please let that be something useful.

"Give me something good or I'm up a class-six rapid without a consarn raft." Dru paused and rubbed her forehead. "Oh, come on, Mother. I. Answered. The. Phone! The fact that I'm alive should not be a question."

Whatever Cassidy said made Dru's cheeks tinge pink.

"Yeah, I know. I'm sorry. I love you too."

Kindra raised an eyebrow in the slight pause after those words.

Dru glanced her way and cleared her throat. "*Now* will you tell me what you found out?"

After a pause, Dru started repeating the information Cassidy relayed.

"Aaron Tanvers. Sergeant in the marines." Dru's eyebrows rose. "And currently AWOL. Well, *that's* useful."

"Only if the military bugged his ass, and we can tap into their signal," Kindra muttered.

Dru ignored her and continued to repeat the information Cassidy spilled into her ear.

"His sister Jenna Tanvers was a student at Florida State University in Tallahassee, but she was working an internship at Genesis Financial in Jacksonville when she committed suicide. No one had reported any warning signs, but there was a note in her handwriting and no signs of foul play. After Aaron disappeared, his boyfriend Geo—ex-marine, medical discharge—and a couple of his friends in the Corps reported that he refused to believe his sister had done it. He was *convinced* someone had staged the whole thing. It's in his military file as a mental breakdown due to emotional trauma and stress."

"What the hell does any of this have to do with Bernard?" Kindra asked.

"The company Jenna was working for?" Dru glanced over. "Burn through some shell corporations and a bunch of red tape, and Genesis is owned by Garret Hadley."

Kindra stilled for a split second before she made herself shrug. "So, he's got more fingers in more pies than you realized. Why'd Aaron kidnap Bernard and drag him down the Eastern Seaboard?"

Another pause while Dru listened to the voice coming through her headset. "Dunno, but Mom thinks they're headed for Jacksonville."

"What? Why?"

"Because that's where Genesis is based. That's where Jenna died." Dru sighed. "And that's where Redwell's headquarters are too."

"Jacksonville? Really? Not, like, Los Angeles or, hell, Miami if they really wanted to hang out in Florida?" What kind of power-hungry CEO planted himself somewhere like Jacksonville?

"You wanted a destination, and I gave you one. Jacksonville."

Luckily, they were already headed south on I-95.

"How far is Savannah from Jacksonville?"

"Four hours? Five, maybe?" Dru shrugged and pulled the GPS out of her bag and plugged the city into the device. "Huh. Only a little more than two on the highway."

"So, if they left as soon as Aaron narced on us, they could be halfway there."

"Possibly."

"And we're hoping to stumble across them in a city that probably has about half a million people."

"Something like that."

"Fantastic." Kindra barely contained the urge to smack her forehead against the steering wheel. "So good to know we have a plan."

Atropos bless it, she thought. *This is so going to suck.*

The executive floor of Redwell's main headquarters was nearly empty, but Garret Hadley had already been at work for an hour. At work, but not working. The breaking news broadcast out of Savannah had commandeered his attention.

A kidnapping report, a high-speed chase, multiple explosions, several police fatalities . . .

"How in the hell did my week turn into *that*?" Garret asked the screen, running a hand over his thin, graying hair.

Someone knocked on the office door, and Garret glanced at the dark wood as though considering ignoring the summons. He didn't.

Matthew was standing in the hallway when Garret opened the door, top several buttons of his shirt undone and sleeves rolled to his elbows. His normally golden-brown skin was oddly pale, and his dark eyes had the bleary look of someone who hadn't slept in far too long. Although he nodded a hello to Garret, his gaze shifted farther into the room—to the TV on the wall. "You saw that, then."

Garret stepped back to let him in. "Are we sure this is connected?"

"As much as we can be." Matthew moved to the computer on Garret's desk and typed *explosions North Carolina* into Google. He clicked on one of the first links that came up and gestured for Garret to come closer.

"What does a charred cabin in the backwoods have to do with anything?"

"Because when we arrange the incidents on a map with time stamps, we get this." Matthew grabbed the keyboard again, and with a series of commands, brought up a file he'd shared between their computers.

The map of the East Coast had several red markers, each labeled with a military time stamp, and the series showed an inexorable march south. Toward Jacksonville.

Garret closed his eyes and ground his teeth. "I want security tightened on this building, on the warehouses in use this season, and at home." He opened his eyes and glared at Matthew. "Reports every six hours from everyone. I want you riding Odira and Javier so closely that you're practically using their eyes as goggles."

Matthew nodded. His hand lifted to the back of his neck, fingers digging into the knots there. "No one can connect any of this to us."

"Not now, but they'll do it fast enough if Bernard Gasper finds a new contact at your old stomping ground."

"Our people will warn us if that happens." Even as Matthew said it, his gaze flitted to the TV, where the news showed an aerial view of the carnage on I-95.

"You better hope so, or *that* is going to start hitting us a lot closer to home." Garret stared at the twisted wrecks as Matthew left, shaking his head, nose wrinkled in disgust. "If all the time and money we poured into getting a leash around Odira's neck goes to waste, I'm going to fucking kill someone."

Chapter Fifteen

By the time they reached Jacksonville, Cassidy had emailed Dru a list of addresses—the bases of operations for Genesis and Redwell, as well as six likely motels in places Aaron might set up camp while he prepared for the next step. Whatever the "next step" was in his mind.

A quick drive-by eliminated two of the motels. Checking the computer system of one other crossed that off. Then they hit a break. Next on the list was a Motel 6 about ten minutes away from Genesis, but this time Kindra saw what she was looking for in the computer: a man had checked in not long ago and asked for a corner room.

Kindra heard the van's engine roar back to life. Time to leave. Ducking out of the office, she hid behind a plant as the clerk passed, and then strolled through the lobby. She didn't shut off the device she'd been using to scramble the security cameras until she was nearly at the van.

"Verdict?" Dru asked when Kindra jumped into the passenger seat.

"The guy in room three-fourteen checked in without a reservation this morning."

"These buildings are only one story. Where's three-fourteen?"

Kindra unfolded the map she'd picked up from the reception desk. "It's the building in the far southeastern end of the lot." Looking between the map and the actual lot, Kindra could see the appeal of the location for a short-term hideout. "He picked well. Trees on two sides, so any sign of life back there would be worth checking out. And worse comes to worst, he could jump out a window and get to the highway. Probably cause enough of a ruckus to get someone on 95 to call the cops."

"What?" Dru squinted at the map. "Isn't 95 . . . Oh. Shit. The on-ramp is right behind this place, isn't it? Damn. He did pick well."

"So. Storm the barricade or sneak attack?"

Dru wrinkled her nose. "Neither?"

"There isn't a third option."

"Uh, yeah there is, baby. Didn't anyone ever teach you how to use your words?" Dru shook her head and drove around the lot, stopping on the north side of building three.

"You think he's actually going to *talk* to us?"

She parked and huffed. "He may not talk to *us*, but I think I can get him to talk to *me*."

"Every hour I spend with you makes it clearer that you are absolutely out of your mind." In very appealing ways most of the time, but not right now. Dru going in trying to wave a truce flag was stupid. And would probably end with her getting shot.

"Don't argue with me on this." Dru crawled between the front seats and opened the bag stuffed between the two second-row seats, grabbing something out of it before shoving the rest aside and sitting down.

And then Dru started stripping.

Kindra's tongue practically stuck to the roof of her suddenly dry mouth as layer after layer of clothing fell to the floor of the van. Dru stopped when she was wearing a white tank top so thin that the lean lines of muscle were obvious. All she wore on the bottom was a pair of black, boy-cut underwear.

She looked like she could walk straight onto the set of slumber-party fantasy porn.

"What are you doing?" Kindra managed to ask without sounding strangled.

"I'm changing." Dru dived over the last row of seats, her feet using the second row's armrest to keep her from falling. "I thought that'd be obvious."

"Yeah, but *why*?"

"I need something . . . something . . ." Dru lunged deeper, and Kindra heard her rummaging through the bags, shifting and digging until, finally, "Aha!"

A pile of black cloth came sailing over the seat, followed quickly by a bundle of lemon yellow and another swath of black. Leaning closer, Kindra grabbed the clothes. Black leggings and a miniscule black skirt with a tight yellow long-sleeve shirt. The outfit wouldn't show much skin, yet everything would be on display.

"The only way Aaron will talk to me even through a window is if I'm unarmed." Dru settled into the second row of seats, taking the leggings from Kindra and wiggling into them. Kindra watched for a second, vaguely hypnotized by the motion, before forcing herself to look away. Dru grunted. When Kindra looked again, the leggings were in place, completely encasing Dru's muscular legs. "Can't hide much more than a tiny flat blade in these."

"Are we seriously going up there unarmed?"

"You weren't listening, were you?" She pulled the yellow shirt over her head. "There is no 'we.' Me. I'm going up there alone."

Kindra raised an eyebrow. "And you think *I'm* the suicidal one?"

"Hey. When *I* tell Aaron that I don't want to kill him or Bernard, it'll actually be the truth." Dru adjusted the seam of the tight sleeves. "Besides, I know how to handle myself."

"Yeah, because unarmed combat always works wonders against a bullet."

"Aw, I didn't realize you'd care." Smirking, Dru snatched the skirt and slithered into it. "Besides, you stole his gun, remember?"

"You think he only had *one*?" Kindra glanced at the bags scattered around the car. They had several guns, more than a few mags of ammo, a dozen or so knives, a couple more bricks of C-4, and some tech that would be ten kinds of illegal on the commercial market. Deluding themselves into thinking that Aaron came into this mess with only his service weapon would be idiotic.

"Oh, hell. You *really* don't know wishful thinking when you hear it." Dru groaned and dropped her head back, staring at the ceiling. "It's like you're not even human!"

Kindra's body went cold. "This is news to you? I was pretty sure you already knew that."

Turning, Kindra sat down and stared into the parking lot. They were in the shade of a huge tree—some kind of oak. Its branches cast dappled shadows over this corner, and Kindra concentrated on creating patterns in those shadows, wiping her mind of anything else.

Why had that comment even bothered her? "Human" was so far away from where Kindra's mind lived that the curvature of the Earth would prevent line of sight.

You're still thinking about it. Stop. It won't get better with time.

"Hey." Dru's soft voice was so close to Kindra's ear, it startled her.

She hid her flinch, but couldn't hide the sharpness of her breath when she turned to find Dru's face less than six inches from hers. It was unfairly mesmerizing how the filtered sunlight slanting through the window highlighted Dru's moss-green eyes.

"I didn't mean it. It was a bad joke, okay?"

"Like it matters?" Kindra huffed and shook her head. "We're not exactly friends, Dru. When this job is over, I'll either be dead or we'll go back to opposite sides of the fence. I don't care what you think."

Something almost like hurt flashed across Dru's face. "Right." She shifted back, her eyes averted, and dropped into the seat behind her. "I'm sure you miss your family. I know I miss mine."

"Yeah." *No.* Aside from being relieved to hear that Sera seemed to be alive, how much had she thought about her family? Hardly at all. And missing them? Please.

Being away for the first time in *years* made everything so much clearer. Kindra finally saw how draining it had all been—the constant question of how much information Odira and Amett had been holding back; the ever-present threat if even the smallest order was poorly carried out or, Atropos help her, disobeyed; the wondering *why* about everything they'd done while pretending, even to herself, that she didn't care.

Honestly, the only family member she missed was Ryce, but he wouldn't be there waiting for her when she found them again. *If* she ever went back.

It had to say something that the nonstop insanity of the last thirty or so hours with Dru had been less stressful than the last three years with her family.

Hell, by now they probably assumed Kindra was dead. Burned to ash at the warehouse or dumped in the Hudson River somewhere.

Stop effing thinking about it. "Are you just going to go knock? We're not even sure it's Aaron."

"How many people check into a hotel without a reservation in the early morning?"

"Long-haul truckers do that a lot."

"Do you see a big rig anywhere?" Dru asked.

"It's a possibility. That's all." Kindra closed her eyes, pressing them shut until Dru's hand rested gently on her shoulder.

"Look, if it's not Aaron, then I giggle, apologize profusely for knocking on the wrong room, and stumble away like a drunk go-go girl." Dru picked up a pair of black stilettos Kindra hadn't noticed. "If it's the wrong room, it's not a problem."

It was only a problem if it was the *right* room.

Dru opened the door of the van and stepped out. Kindra almost let her go. Then, hand rising to her throat, Kindra reconsidered. No collar anymore. Dru trusted her enough to take it off. Dru *trusted* her. It was a stupid thing for anyone to do, really, but the farther away Dru got, the more an itch spread across the back of Kindra's neck. The more Kindra fidgeted in her seat.

Shit.

Grabbing Dru's gun, Kindra stuffed it under the RFID-blocking jacket Dru still insisted she wear. The glint of metal caught her eye, and Kindra saw one of her own beautifully sharp Boker blades in the bag Dru had left between the seats. Palming that, Kindra grabbed the keys, locked the van, and ran after Dru, her footfalls nearly silent on the pavement.

Despite Kindra's stealth, Dru glanced back when she approached. "I told you I was going alone."

"Bite me, Bomb Squad," Kindra said. "You die, and I lose any chance of living through this mess. I'll stay out of sight, but I'm going as backup. Deal."

Dru stopped walking, staring at Kindra with wide eyes that belied the furrows between her eyebrows. Shock? Confusion? Distrust? It looked like Dru couldn't decide. Whatever was happening behind those eyes, it stayed mostly hidden. In seconds, those small signs disappeared, and Dru shrugged. "You *better* stay out of sight, or we're done before we start."

Kindra stayed with Dru until they hit the southern side of building three. There was a narrow parking lot on this side and then trees. Not a forest or anything, but the line of foliage was thick enough to block out the next hotel. Thick enough to hide Kindra.

Tilting her head toward the trees, Kindra waited until Dru acknowledged the motion before she scanned the area and darted across the open lot. Once she'd concealed herself, Dru stepped onto the walkway, singing. Kindra couldn't hear the words, but the tone of her voice carried across the distance. She was no Aretha Franklin, but she didn't suck.

Moving ahead of Dru, Kindra kept her eyes on the end of the row. The daylight made it hard to tell which of the curtained rooms were occupied, but no one except the guy in 3-14 was worth worrying about.

Dru wove her way closer, carrying her heels like a party girl finally making it home after a night out. She was singing something vaguely familiar. Kindra barely stifled a snort of laughter when recognition hit. The girl was stumbling into danger with obscenely sexy confidence, and she was singing. Not just singing. She was singing Journey.

She is so *effing adorable.* The thought popped out of nowhere. She deleted it just as fast. *Stay focused, Kindra. No crushing on Bomb Squad, damn it.*

Dru walked past the last door—probably to try to look through the crack in the curtains—before backtracking. Kindra was almost positive the off-white fabric twitched when Dru knocked.

"Bernie? Bernard, sweetheart, let me in, okay?" Her voice, only slightly higher pitched than usual, was strangely loud in the early morning silence. "It's Dru! I just want to talk. Please?"

Was that . . . Did she just give them her real name? Atropos bless it, does the girl not have any survival instincts at all?

But then, Dru wasn't working this job from the same angle as Kindra, was she? Dru had risked her life getting Bernard Gasper to safety the day the Westons had almost shot him. Using her name wasn't brainless, it was brilliant, but Kindra would screw it up for both of them if Bernard or Aaron spotted her before Dru explained.

She tucked herself deeper into the shifting shadows, her gun trained over Dru's shoulder.

"Bernie, I know you and Aaron are in there. Jenna told me, okay? I just want to talk."

Oh, shit. If this guy loved his sister enough to abandon a career-military track just to hunt down a hunch, taunting him with her death would be the fastest way to bring out his bad side.

The door slammed open. Aaron's glower—and the glint of the gun pointed at Dru—was perfectly highlighted by a thin shaft of sunlight.

Dru shifted her stance. To a normal pair of eyes, it might look like she was still drunkenly tilting, trying to keep her balance, but Kindra saw how Dru's weight was now spread more evenly, centered over the balls of her feet, and noticed how she gripped those stupid heels like she was getting ready to jam the stiletto into someone's eye. Dru wasn't tilting; she was preparing to run, duck, or fight.

Aaron spoke. It seemed Dru responded, but Kindra couldn't hear. This was why she hated going without comms. How the eff was she supposed to know if tensions were nearing the flashpoint if she couldn't hear what anyone was saying?

Maybe I should end it here. Aaron was in her sight line, and Bernard stood just off his shoulder, barely visible in the dimly lit room. A very small shift of her aim would bring Bernard's head into her crosshairs. Two quick shots and this would be over. She could run to 95 and hitch. Or steal a car and drive. She might be able to track down Odira. Or she could let everyone assume she'd died, and disappear.

Or Dru might move and end up in a puddle of blood on the floor.

Maybe that was for the best. Amett and Odira planned on killing the Calvers. Dru's family. Dru. If Kindra pulled the trigger, death would be fast. Nearly painless.

The safety was off. Kindra's finger was on the trigger. Three twitches of her finger and there would be blood staining the concrete sidewalk for days. Ghosts lingering for years.

Kindra shifted her weight, exhaled, and steadied her hands.

Fucking hell. Can I really kill the girl with her own effing gun?

Dru turned, giving Kindra a profile view. Tension gathered around Dru's mouth when her eyes flicked toward the tree line, and the hand half-hidden behind her back twitched. Two fingers curled, then flattened, her wrist shifting her hand right and then left.

Kindra blinked. Those were her family's old signals. They hadn't used them in years—since a year after Ryce died—but Kindra remembered them. Dru had just told Kindra to approach unarmed.

Fuck that! Kindra snorted to herself. Aaron was well trained and pissed off, Bernard knew Kindra wanted to kill him, and Dru was confusing.

Dru repeated the signal. She didn't glance at Kindra, but the tension in her body ramped higher. The third repetition was sharp.

Atropos save me. I'm either going to have to kill her or listen to her.

Groaning, Kindra stuffed Dru's Nighthawk into one boot, made sure the blade was well concealed in the other, and stepped away from the trees.

Immediately, Aaron's weapon shifted, the sights of the gun now aimed for Kindra's head. She itched to duck behind the closest car, draw her own weapon, and execute, but Aaron had already proven to be damn quick. No way was she going to test his accuracy like that.

Keeping her motions slow and steady, and her hands held slightly away from her body, Kindra crossed the narrow lot, but no hand signal in the world could make her step within arm's reach of that room before she got a better feel for what kind of mess she was walking into.

"Not dead, huh?" Aaron said when Kindra stopped.

"Nope."

"It's like you're a fucking cat," he muttered.

Kindra grinned, broad and toothy. "I've gone through way more than nine lives already."

He glanced up the row of rooms, his eyes lingering on the camera at the end of the building. "Get inside. Now."

Kindra shook her head. "I'm not going—"

"Yes." Dru glared back at her. "You are."

Any more of this shit and it'll take the goddess of strategy herself to get me out of here.

Aaron backed up a step, and Dru moved forward. The gun stayed on Kindra, but Aaron's eyes followed Dru. Lips pressed tight, Kindra strode into the dim room behind Dru, kicking the door shut. As soon as they were all closed inside, someone flicked the lights on, casting clarity on a very strange scene.

Bernard was standing near the bathroom like he was on the verge of ducking inside if things went bad. Aaron stood braced for battle a few feet away from the wall opposite the door. Kindra stayed close to the door, very aware of Aaron's gun aimed between her eyes. In the middle of it all stood Dru, dressed up like a club girl and looking completely at ease—the only one who did.

Aaron scanned Kindra, his gaze lingering on her throat. "No collar anymore, kitty?"

"Kindra earned a reprieve." Dru shifted backward a step, moving just a little closer to Kindra. "Saved my life. I decided that explosives weren't necessary."

"Explosives?" Aaron's eyes narrowed. "The C-4 bullshit you tried last time?"

"Wasn't bullshit," Kindra said. "Bomb Squad over there thought it was the only way to keep me from killing her."

"Was she wrong?" Aaron asked.

"Not really."

"And now?" This time, it was Bernard who asked the question.

"Now I want to know what the fuck is going on here." Kindra met their eyes, refusing to be cowed. "I'll decide who to kill later."

Aaron's eyebrows shot up. "I really can't tell if you're serious or not."

Dru sighed. "Serious as a fucking knife to the intestines."

"And you *trust* her?" The furrow between Aaron's eyebrows was so severe it looked permanent.

Her expression was a little reserved, but Dru nodded. "Yeah. I do. For now."

Aaron scanned Kindra again, then jerked his chin in her direction. "The layers. Take them off."

Kindra crossed her arms. "I'm not stripping for you, asshole."

"And I'm not giving you the chance to break my arms when I try to search you." He nodded toward Dru. "You should've done what she did. I wouldn't be asking for a peep show."

The room was too warm for the layers Kindra was wearing. She should've gladly freed herself from the outerwear Dru had been so insistent on, but she didn't take anything off.

"Bomb Squad gave me these threads." Kindra held firm. "I've grown attached. Especially to keeping my head attached to my neck."

"I will very rarely be opposed to Kindra wearing less clothing, but this is one of those times." The surprised, breathy laugh that escaped Kindra brought the tiniest of smiles to Dru's lips, but she didn't look away from Aaron. "That outer layer has RFID blockers in the lining."

"You're being tracked?" Aaron asked.

"No." Kindra shrugged. "Tried to tell her that yesterday, but she won't believe it."

Aaron waited, glowering at her. It was amusing. Kindra wanted to pat him on the head and explain that he didn't rank anywhere in the top twenty scariest people to ever have had her at gunpoint.

Dru mumbled something incomprehensible before she groaned and relented. "Baby, do what he says. But she can only be out of them long enough to prove she's clear. They're going back on, or we're all fucked, all right?"

"I am so not anywhere close to being your baby," Kindra shot back, stripping the heavy jacket and tossing it to Dru. The thick pants zipped up each leg, letting Kindra rip them off without having to remove her boots and reveal the weapons stashed there. She almost shivered, the air cold after the heat of her layers. Her black jeans weren't skintight, but they were very fitted. Same with the long-sleeve black shirt. She lifted the hem of the shirt, folding it to just under her breasts, and turned around, showing Aaron there was no gun or knife hidden underneath. "I'm not taking anything else off."

"Boots." Aaron's tone made the word an order.

Dru held out her hand. "Just hand them to me."

"Whatever. They're yours anyway. I didn't want to toss it into the woods." Rolling her eyes, Kindra bent to retrieve the weapons. She placed the Nighthawk and the blade in Dru's hand. "Figured you actually would kill me if I lost that gun."

And I didn't want to be anywhere near this mess unarmed! What the actual fuck am I still doing here?

"Good call." Dru clicked the safety on and glanced at Aaron, waiting until he nodded to slide the gun into her waistband at the center of her back. The bumpy outline under her second-skin outfit shouldn't have been hot, but *damn*. Kindra had to force herself to look away as soon as Dru handed her the outer layers again and gestured for her to put them back on.

Instead of watching Dru, Kindra studied Sergeant Aaron Tanvers. Slightly crooked nose, scarred temple, thin top lip and plush bottom one, close-cropped hair, angular chin. She cataloged it all, coming back to his eyes more than once. His eyes were cartoonishly huge for his face, but their startlingly light golden-brown color and their intensity made them captivating. Separately, none of his features were particularly nice—except those eyes. They made him interesting, though. And sexy. In different circumstances, Kindra wouldn't have minded seducing him to the dark side. Now . . .

Now Kindra felt Dru standing nearby and any potential interest evaporated. Aaron was intriguing, but Dru was magnetic. The effing Tesla Hybrid Magnet. Cross-dressed, staring at Kindra from the shadows, or threatening her with bombs—it didn't seem to matter. Under every single interaction Kindra had with Dru was the undercurrent of *want, want, want.*

And Odira is probably going to kill everyone bearing the Calver name.

Forcibly wiping her mind, Kindra finished zipping up the pants and then straightened. Aaron was still watching her. She rolled her eyes and put her hands on her hips. "Is this a staring contest, or is there an actual purpose to this shindig?"

"We can help you." Dru's words pulled Aaron's attention toward her. "We have resources you don't have access to, and we can help you do things you won't be able to accomplish alone."

"Why the hell would you get involved in this?" The guy looked almost painfully confused. "This isn't your mess."

"Not true. My family has been investigating Garret Hadley for years, but we didn't have enough to pull in the Feds, or be sure we were taking out the entire chain of black ops command he has hidden inside Redwell. The puppet master knows who we are, so we can't get too close without putting him on high alert. Every time we do, codes and routes and plans completely change."

"And then they send a hit squad after you?" Aaron asked.

Dru nodded. "It's happened more than once. But that's the point. We need to get somewhere more secure if we're going to start something that might make an impact."

Kindra eased closer to the door, and the gun in Aaron's hand followed.

Aaron's eyes stayed on Dru. "Lemme guess. You know the perfect place?"

"'Perfect' may be stretching it," Dru acknowledged. "But I guarantee it's better than this."

"In exchange for what?" Aaron wasn't going to let go of his suspicion easily, apparently.

"Working *with* us. Not trying to kill us. *Any* of us." Dru's eyes flicked meaningfully toward Kindra. "Sharing information. Generally pretending you trust us."

Aaron made a sound somewhere between a snort and a laugh. Gun still aimed in Kindra's general direction, he looked over his shoulder at Bernard. The man who'd started all of this had stayed silent and nearly hidden in the dark doorway to the bathroom this entire time.

"You really trust them?" Aaron asked Bernard.

Bernard's mouth opened, but he had to swallow several times before more than a rasping breath emerged. "Dru. I trust Dru. The Calvers were protecting me, but . . . Kindra?" His dark eyes widened enough that white showed all the way around. More than slightly bloodshot white. He shook his head, closing his eyes and shuddering. "I don't know her. Our last meeting was . . . It wouldn't have ended well for me if you hadn't shown up, Aaron."

"Not a ringing endorsement." Aaron rolled his eyes toward Kindra.

Was there more amusement or disgust in the curl of his lips? Kindra didn't know. She *did* know that the stress of the last week had them all on edge, and the little bit of sleep they'd gotten in the past two days couldn't possibly lend itself to clear heads. Add in a few guns and several people who knew how to use them, and this room could end up painted red in a split second if she said the wrong thing. And she'd go out first.

"My family was hired to do a job," Kindra said after a few seconds. "I have nothing against Bernard personally, but the client isn't going to stop just because the hit failed. If anything, it's going to make Garret more desperate to see Bernard's heart stop beating."

The outside edge of Aaron's right eye crinkled. "That supposed to make me trust you?"

"Would you trust me if I cried and begged you to believe that I'd never hurt anyone?" Kindra asked, exhaustion seeping into her voice.

"No."

"Then why the fuck shouldn't I tell you how it is? None of you are brain-dead. You all know how much of a shit storm this mess has turned into."

"So you want me to follow you to some undisclosed location to meet a family who exists solidly in the moral gray-zone with a girl who's likely gonna kill us all as soon as she get away with it?" Aaron shook his head. "I don't think so."

Dru laughed once. The sound grated. "Fine. Stay. Stage a *coup* or what the fuck ever you were planning on doing to get yourself killed." She stepped closer to Aaron, intimidating despite being about four inches shorter than him. "Don't drag Bernard to his death, though. Not for your overdeveloped sense of justice. Let him come with me if he wants."

Aaron's reaction only lasted a second—wide eyes, a prolonged blink, and then the already deep furrow between his eyebrows etching deeper. Sure, he'd saved Bernard from Kindra back in New York, but it seemed he hadn't considered what it would mean to drag a civilian into the lion's den like this.

"Bernard? Do you want to go with them?"

Inching into the room, Bernard nodded slowly. "The Calvers were working on getting what we knew to the FBI, Aaron. I may not trust Kindra—and I definitely intend to stay as far away from her family as possible—but if we can reach a place the Calvers have fortified, we'll be a lot safer with them than we are alone."

Aaron sagged, his body drooping like someone had tied a weighted noose around his neck. He tucked his gun into the holster on his hip. "Let's move out, then."

More than ready to do exactly that, Kindra opened the door. For just a second, she put her back to the room, trusting Dru not to stab her with that Boker blade.

She stepped onto the sidewalk.

Something cracked against her ankles. She nearly toppled. Less than a blink of time later, Kindra heard the *zing-thud* of a bullet striking the wall, and she dropped to the ground.

Who the hell is shooting at me?

Kindra rolled toward the room. Hands wrapped around her upper arms and yanked. The weather stripping on the floor scraped against her jacket. Someone masked and shrouded in black jumped over her and darted into the room.

"Get in here!" Dru hissed.

"Shut the fucking door," he growled back.

I know that voice.

Another silenced shot, this one narrowly missing Kindra's thigh. The door slammed shut. One more shot embedded itself in the metal.

Kindra collapsed against the door and scanned the room. Bernard must have dived into the bathroom, because Aaron was guarding the doorway, gun drawn and eyes on the black-clad stranger. Dru was a few feet away, crouched under the window with the new addition; both of them had their guns out. Kindra's body thrummed with adrenaline, and her fingers twitched, itching to curl around the grip of a gun or even an effing Molotov cocktail she could chuck into the trees.

"What are you doing here?" Dru demanded as she rose and fired through the window. "Who is it? Weston or Martinez?"

"Of course it was Weston!" The stranger shot twice and then ducked as another round blasted into the room. Kneeling on the floor, he twisted to check something on his right sleeve. "Shit. She fucking winged me when I came in."

I know that voice. Why do I know that voice? Kindra replayed the conversation she'd overheard in Bernard's home office, but this voice didn't come from that memory. It came from something else. Something older. The voice had changed since the last time she heard it.

More shots fired in both directions, but gunshots she could handle.

"She would've done a lot more than wing you if she'd seen your face." Dru crawl-ran into the bathroom and came back with a folded washcloth that she stuffed under the stranger's sleeve to put pressure on the wound. "What are you doing here? This is a stupid idea!"

He took precious seconds to aim, firing twice before ducking for cover again. "What was I supposed to do? I wasn't about to watch either of you die!"

Dru's eyes flicked to Kindra and away. "Yeah. That would've sucked."

Kindra's hands shook, and her head spun. Too little sleep, too little food, too many near-death experiences. Her ability to cope had reached the breaking point. "What the *fuck* is going on? Who are you?"

Dru emptied the rest of her magazine into the trees. On the floor near her feet, the stranger shook his head. "It's better you don't know who I am. Just know I work for her family."

I know that voice. I should know who this is. Kindra's mind spun like a tornado, pulling in random details and trying to force them into a coherent picture. It wasn't working. She needed more. There was still some crucial detail missing that would turn the mystery into an obvious answer. "Work for them. But you're not a Calver?"

"I wish." He rose just enough to peer out the window, but no more shots were fired.

Dru swatted him on the back of the head, her eyes scanning the trees. "No, you don't."

"Right now I do," he muttered.

"Take off the mask." Kindra's voice was far hoarser than she would've liked.

"Not a good idea." Dru moved closer to Kindra, staying as low as she could.

"Take off the mask." The shaking in Kindra's hands spread. Up her arms. Into her chest.

Dru's face looked like it was locked into a forced calm as she reached for Kindra's hand. "I promise we can trust him."

"No." She shoved Dru away. "No! This is *bullshit*. You kidnapped me and trapped me here, and someone is out there trying to shoot us, and I swear to Atropos I know his voice, so *take off your fucking mask!*"

Her throat felt raw, and the room seemed too quiet. Only then did she realize she'd been yelling. Screaming at the stranger with the familiar voice.

When his eyes met Dru's, she shrugged, the gesture almost helpless. Sighing, the stranger pulled off the black mask.

An impossible face appeared in front of Kindra. A face she hadn't seen in years.

A face that belonged to a dead man.

Ryce smiled, the expression ruined by the hesitance in his light-brown eyes. "Hey, Kinny. Miss me?"

For the first time in her life, Kindra fainted.

Chapter Sixteen

K indra slipped away each time memory and consciousness began to return. A few sharp gunshots and a burst of motion that felt like flying brought her closer to reality. Multiple voices shouting unintelligible words, the clank and slide of a van door, and then Kindra was jostled even more. Before she could pull herself completely into the waking world, the van door closed and tires squealed.

"I can't believe she's still out. Did she really faint?" Deep, gravelly, sharply enunciated words. Aaron Tanvers. Doppelgänger. Marine. AWOL.

"Does she *look* conscious?" That voice needed no processing. Dru Calver. Enemy. Hotshot. Kidnapper. Bomb Squad. Sexy as hell.

"It's just such a movie cliché. She *swooned.*" Aaron again. "Are we sure she didn't get hit?"

"I checked. I don't see any blood." *That* voice sent shudders through Kindra and a jolt of icy shock that almost sent her back to unconsciousness. The can't-possibly-be-Ryce audibly swallowed. "It's my fault. I shouldn't have shocked her like that."

"Yeah, seriously. That," Aaron said. "What the hell was that reaction about?"

The pause in the conversation felt loaded. Heavy. Explosive.

Ryce huffed. "I'm her brother. She thought I died a few years ago."

"Shit." There was a quiet thud, like someone sitting down too quickly. "Yeah, never mind. I think you're fucking lucky she passed out instead of trying to kill you."

No way are they having this conversation without me. Kindra's head lolled when she shifted. She tried to sit up; something across her chest held her in place.

Atropos bless it! If Dru tied me up again, I'm going to strangle her.

A rush of frustrated anger was just enough to shove Kindra—blinking, disoriented, and struggling—into the world.

"Easy." Ryce's voice spoke low into her ear. "You're not tied down. That's the seat belt."

Seat belt? Kindra blinked, and the last of the haze cleared from her vision. They were in the middle row of a three-row, bench-seat passenger van. Looking down, she saw the gray nylon strap of the seat belt that had kept her from moving.

That and her supposedly dead brother's hands locked around her biceps.

"I'm sorry. Atropos bless it, Kinny, I'm *sorry*. But you need to stay calm and listen."

Betrayal and relief and fury crashed together in Kindra's chest, creating an icy detachment that protected her, kept her from feeling anything, and gave her the strength to strike.

Kindra latched on to one of the pressure points in Ryce's wrist. He winced and released her, but didn't move away fast enough to escape her other hand wrapping around his throat.

"You fucking liar! We thought you were dead, you asshole!"

Arms locked around Kindra's chest, pulling her away from Ryce.

"Breathe." Dru tightened her grip when Kindra tried to pull away. "I know you're pissed, and I'm sorry, but killing your brother will only make things worse."

I'm sorry? From Ryce, those words were understandable. From Dru, those two words flash-reassembled a series of clues, and then handed Kindra a realization on a silver platter.

Dru had known Ryce's name. She said he was gone, but never said he was dead. She knew too much about Kindra's childhood. She knew the Westons' old hand signals, signals that they hadn't started using until after Hugo and Cassidy left. Dru had known far too much and made far too little out of her knowledge—like she'd been intentionally trying to gloss over it. Downplay it. Because she had always known Ryce was alive, and she'd guessed exactly how Kindra would react to that fact.

And she'd been right.

"Let me go, or I swear to Atropos I will break your arms and use your own bones to end you," Kindra growled.

Behind her, Dru froze. In front of her, Ryce paled and backed away another six inches. As far as he could go without falling off the bench. Ryce glanced over Kindra's shoulder and nodded once. Only then did Dru's grip loosen.

Kindra ripped free, unbuckled the belt, and slipped past them to sit in the last row of seats. Her mind threw every emotion Kindra had a name for into a ball in the center of her chest, because it couldn't seem to decide what she should feel. It felt like everyone should be able to see the way her breath shook in her lungs, but her movements were sure and steady.

Distantly she noted the leather interior and the high ceilings of the van. Probably a Mercedes model. Seating for twelve or so. Bernard and Aaron sat in the first row of passenger seats, both of them watching Kindra cautiously. Two more people sat up front. She didn't recognize the driver or the passenger, but she cataloged all of it and put it away to think about later. She couldn't handle anything but the new flashing lights on the merry-go-round of thoughts that had been spinning in her head for days.

Ryce is alive.

Because he *faked* his death.

Ryce is alive.

Because he *left*. He left Kindra behind.

Ryce is alive.

And then he joined the Calvers.

But Ryce is alive. Living and breathing and sitting in this van.

Kindra almost cried.

She closed her eyes and breathed slowly, centering herself as much as she could with the continuing whispers floating around her. Blocking them out, Kindra paid more attention to the whispers inside her head.

You really trust them enough to let your guard down like this? a small voice asked.

Dru would have killed me by now if she really wanted to. She's had plenty of chances.

What about Ryce? the voice countered.

He would never hurt me.

He left.

But he'd never kill *me.*

Then you trust him too? the voice asked.

Kindra took another deep breath. *Yes. Kind of. In some ways. Eventually.*

Another breath and Kindra opened her eyes, her gaze immediately meeting Aaron's. It looked like weariness was slowly winning the fight against adrenaline, because his blinks were slightly too long and his movements a little too careful. His mind seemed to be alert as ever.

"For a second back there, I thought you were dead," Aaron said. Then he almost smiled. "It was a good second."

Kindra relaxed a little. "Sorry to disappoint."

"Life is pain." Aaron smirked and shrugged. "Anyone who says different is selling something."

"That movie *never* gets old," a voice from the front quipped. The guy—kid?—in the passenger seat turned. He looked younger than Kindra, maybe around fourteen or fifteen, with loosely curled, dark-brown hair, dark eyes, and olive skin a couple shades darker than Kindra's. The construction of his facial features reminded Kindra of a combination of Dru and what she remembered of Hugo Calver.

"What movie?" Kindra asked.

"*Princess Bride.*" Aaron said the name like it should've been obvious.

"You really did have a deprived childhood," Dru muttered.

"Shut up." Ryce issued the order before Kindra could.

The sound of his voice made her flinch.

In the silence that settled over the van, Kindra rested her head against the seat. Ryce wasn't the only thing she had to figure out how to handle, he was just the problem that was literally staring her in the face. The other problem was still at the distance of a sniper rifle. She spoke to the ceiling. "Was that Sera or Odira behind the scope?"

Ryce cleared his throat. "Sera. I've been tracking her for the last day or so."

"How did she find us?" Kindra asked.

"They picked up your trail after Savannah—that car chase wasn't exactly discreet. Even before the C-4." The leather seat creaked, and

Kindra could almost picture her brother shifting uneasily. Ryce had always had a hard time staying still, especially when he was trying to hide what he was feeling.

Her voice was toneless, as dry as bones scattered across the Sahara. "Just them?"

"Javier's team split off after Manhattan," Ryce said, still hesitant. "We lost track of them after that. The mission was Bernard, so we had to focus on finding him and keeping him away from . . ."

Away from the Westons. Their family. Kindra closed her eyes. "How'd they get to the motel so fast?"

"They were already in Jacksonville when they picked up your tracker." This Ryce delivered quietly, like he was trying to pass the information solely to Kindra despite the five other people listening. "It didn't take Sera long after that. I barely kept up."

Kindra's heart stalled. Lifting her head off the seat, she pinned her brother with a razor-edged glare, anger crackling through her voice. "*What* tracker?"

"The tracker you didn't think you had," Dru said evenly.

Ryce jabbed Dru in the side with an elbow, even though his eyes stayed on Kindra. The movement was so reminiscent of a decade earlier—eleven-year-old Ryce and six-year-old Kindra fighting in the backseat of the van and desperately trying to hide that fact from Amett and Odira—that it sent a wave of something like nostalgia through Kindra's chest.

Don't go there. Not yet. If she fell down that hole now, she didn't know how long it would take her to climb out again. The tracker, though . . .

There had only been, what? Two minutes when she hadn't been wearing Dru's anti-RFID layers? Three? Not long, but long enough to pinpoint a signal.

Ryce kept talking. "I guessed that after I . . ."

"*Died*?" Kindra supplied when Ryce hesitated, her voice as sharp as her glare.

Shifting uneasily, Ryce nodded. "Yeah. I figured Odira would overcompensate. I went off alone, and bad things happened. She'd never allow something like that to happen again. She'd want to know where her entire crew was every second of the day."

She never implanted a tracker, Kindra wanted to insist. She couldn't; it was so obviously a lie. Unless Ryce had led Sera to the motel, or Amett had uncovered Aaron Tanvers's identity *and* managed to track him down, there was really no other way the Westons could've found them in that motel. And definitely not that quickly.

"She makes it pretty obvious that if anything bad happens, it's gonna be because she ordered it." Ryce huffed and wrinkled his nose in disgust. Then he took a deep breath. When he spoke again, his voice was quiet and almost solemn. Regretful. "I'm guessing she placed it when she was stitching you up after a job. That way there wouldn't be a new scar to question."

Shit. It made sense. Odira never asked permission or forgiveness. If she felt as though she needed to tag her team to keep track of them, she'd do it. It probably wouldn't even occur to her to let Kindra know, because when had she ever filled Kindra in on anything? Everything in their lives had been need to know. This was one more thing Kindra had apparently never needed to know.

And one more reason escape has never been an option. She had always known they'd find her if she tried to run, but with this? She wouldn't have lasted a day.

"Why did they try to take me out?" Kindra voiced the question before she even realized she was thinking it.

Creases appeared around Ryce's eyes even as his shoulders pulled back, as though he was preparing himself to deliver bad news. "Did you really think that Odira would do anything other than shoot first and sort everything else out later?"

Kindra's blood reached the boiling point in an instant. The new wave of rage and betrayal collided with everything already swirling in her chest, and she barely won against the instinct to scream and punch her hand through the window. She couldn't stop the words, though.

"They weren't even going to *ask?*" The speed of it gutted Kindra. The dearth of evidence against her made it so much worse. Her *family* had not only wholly abandoned her but actually tried to end her life, and for—what? Convenience? Security? "I woke up tied up in the backseat of a car after Aaron blew the fucking building up. The target was gone, I had a *bomb* strapped around my neck, and all I had were shit choices! What was I supposed to do?"

Ryce's eyes popped open wide. "You had a *what* around your neck?" He glared at Dru, his eyes cold. "Are you fucking kidding me?"

It was stupid in the midst of everything else, but Ryce's shock and obvious anger on Kindra's behalf calmed her somewhat. She was still pissed at him—beyond pissed—but that reaction was enough to prove that the brother she remembered really was alive and well, and that his loyalty to the Calvers was neither unquestioning nor absolute.

"There was never a bomb, Kindra." Dru's voice was so quiet, it was nearly inaudible over the thrum of the engine, but the words snagged in Kindra's ear. Dru's dark-green eyes locked on Kindra, watching carefully, like she was trying to predict Kindra's reaction. "What I locked around your throat? I improvised. That was just a belt I cut up and an LED."

Kindra forced her face to go blank. From Ryce's muttered curse and Dru's quiet intake of breath, Kindra was pretty sure she'd taken it a step past blank and straight into I'm-about-to-commit-murder territory.

"I didn't know how else to convince you to play nice long enough to get you to listen!" Dru's voice rose in pitch, becoming almost pleading as her words tumbled out faster. "We needed to work together. I just wanted to get through this job with everyone still alive, and then I hoped that by the end of it you'd think about your answer for more than a half a second if I asked you not to go back to them!"

"Well, I fucking can't now, can I?" Kindra's eyes narrowed slightly—ever so slightly. It was enough to cut off the stream of Dru's babbling.

It wasn't that she honestly wanted to go back, it was just . . . having the option ripped away from her. Again. One more choice she wasn't allowed to make. One more person deciding that she knew what Kindra needed to know, and fuck whatever Kindra thought.

She was just as pissed at Odira as she was at Dru, but Dru was the one sitting in front of her now. Dru was the focus of the hurt and the rage roaring through her blood.

"In the last day, you have kidnapped me, threatened me, mocked me, and *lied* to me. Now, I find out that you've not only been part of why I've spent the last four years thinking my older brother was *dead*, you've also put me in position to get assassinated by my own family because they think I've betrayed them." Which she had in a lot of ways, but fuck them all if they thought she'd admit that now. "Have I *missed* anything?"

Except for the drone of the engine and Kindra's harsh breaths, silence descended on the van. All six of the occupants were watching her like she was an explosive they were trying to figure out how to defuse.

Ryce's voice broke through her thoughts. "Kindra, we can't—"

"Shut the hell up and let me think." Kindra knew she had to calm down before she hurt something—some*one*—but the same merry-go-round was spinning in her head. The horses were different colors now. Same chaos, different song.

I can't ever go back.

Kindra didn't want to kill Bernard anyway.

Sera tried to shoot me!

A lot of people had already died because of this. Including a school full of kids.

I can't ever go back.

Why would she want to?

Because I have nowhere else to go. The Calvers are never going to let me stay.

The Calvers had let Ryce stay.

Ryce had probably never tried to kill one of them!

The van moved east into a district that looked industrial, traveling deserted streets that ran between huge buildings with hundreds of shadowy corners that Kindra watched carefully, hunting for the telltale glint of a sniper's scope or the quick flash of gunfire. There was nothing. The shadows surrounding them contained nothing but shadows.

Apparently her demand for silence worked. No one said a word until they pulled into a warehouse and a reinforced rolling door slid shut behind them with a clang. Despite the silence, Kindra hadn't come up with a single solution. Without a better alternative, she had to stay put and do her best not to kill her brother or any of the other people on her new . . . team.

She'd decide later if she actually trusted any of them.

"Home again, home again, jiggity jig," the kid in the front seat sang as he jumped out.

That's probably Daelan. She'd heard the name the night the Calvers took out the bugs in Bernard's condo. It was the only one that didn't have a face yet.

Two cargo vans, a classic Dodge Challenger, and a Ducati Diavel were parked in the cavernous space. Along the far wall, three folding tables set end to end were covered with computers and electronics. Nearby, several aluminum trunks, each big enough to stuff two full grown men inside, were stacked. One of them was open, and Kindra spotted the familiar barrel of an L115 rifle sticking out.

A woman with pin-straight, medium-brown hair stood up from a folding chair in front of the computers as soon as Aaron opened the van's sliding door. Aaron moved stiffly, tension in every muscle and every twitch of his expression, but he didn't reach for his gun. Kindra pushed past Ryce and Dru to step out behind him, her body itching for motion. The woman's back straightened when her eyes met Kindra's, but otherwise she didn't move. The slightly scoop-necked collar of her black shirt revealed heavy layers of bandages covering her right shoulder and wrapping around her chest, the lumps under the fabric of her shirt stretching down to just above her belly button.

Aunt Cassidy.

Which meant that the driver—the man walking around the front of the van and the only person whose face she hadn't yet seen—had to be Hugo. He'd seemed like such a giant when she was a kid, but he was maybe five ten. He had close-cut, dark-brown hair, pale-green eyes, and skin a few shades darker than his children—somewhere between olive and bronze. His nose was crooked and an inch-long scar marred his chin, a scar that hadn't been there when Kindra was a kid. Also missing was the smile that had so imprinted itself on her memories of this man. When he looked at Kindra as he passed, she saw only caution and exhaustion.

There'd be no happy reunion here. Not for Kindra.

I can't go home, and I shouldn't stay here . . .

Hugo put a gentle hand on Cassidy's unbandaged shoulder and leaned in, whispering something in her ear. His words didn't carry, and his face was turned away from Kindra; lip-reading wasn't an option. She'd have to wait to see what fresh hell awaited her here.

When Hugo stepped away, Cassidy took a deep breath, only the tiniest of flinches hinting at how much the motion hurt her. "Well. I honestly wasn't sure you'd make it here alive."

"Are you talking to me or Aaron?" Kindra asked. "Because I almost didn't make it here alive, and I definitely tried more than once to take him out. One thing I'll say for the marines is they must beat amazing survival instincts into their men."

"Oorah," Aaron muttered, his body still taut and his eyes scanning everything.

Cassidy's eyes lingered on Aaron before she looked at Hugo. "Is she still bugged?"

Hugo nodded. "Didn't have the time or tools to dig it out on the way here."

A beat of tense silence passed before Cassidy's hazel eyes locked on Kindra again. "Are you going to volunteer for this, or should I sedate you?"

"Volunteer? To let you make me bleed?" Kindra crossed her arms. "Sure. Why not. Should be the cap on a fucking *fantastic* day."

Cassidy's lip twitched. "You're just as sarcastic as I thought you'd grow up to be."

Kindra barely had time to blink at that comment before Cassidy nodded toward the third table along the electronics wall. Its metal surface gleamed under the fluorescent lights, like the operating table of some mad scientist. The image didn't make Kindra any keener to hop on up, but she doubted Cassidy's mention of sedation had been an idle threat.

"They won't do anything more than find the tracker and remove it." Ryce's unexpected whisper near her ear should've made her jump, but it felt like she didn't have the capacity for surprise anymore. "They *won't* do anything else. I won't let them."

Several responses occurred to Kindra. Sniping back with something sarcastic or purposely hurtful, for one. Or turning around and breaking his nose, maybe. She didn't do either. "It's fine. I got this."

"You can take off those layers now," Cassidy said before Kindra sat on the table.

Kindra's eyes flicked up as though she would spot Odira and Amett watching. "Isn't that a bad idea?"

Cassidy shook her head. "No signals that aren't part of my network can leave this room."

"Selective blocking, huh? How'd you manage that?" Kindra looked around, her eyes lingering on the wires running from the computers, up the wall, and out through a tiny hole near the ceiling. Just from listening to Sera bitch, Kindra knew it was nearly impossible to block *all* outside signals without disrupting your own.

"Maybe I'll tell you one day." Cassidy held out a hand, and Kindra shrugged off her slightly malodorous jacket. She really needed a shower. It felt like her skin and her teeth were starting to grow things.

Despite the slight chill in the room and the seven pairs of eyes watching her, Kindra followed Cassidy's instructions and stripped down to her underwear: a black bra and black boxer-briefs. She couldn't bite back the gasp when her bare skin touched the cool metal table. Goose bumps erupted across her body. She had to grit her teeth to make herself lie down on her back when Cassidy told her to.

From the next table, Cassidy picked up a device that looked like a tiny metal wand. With methodical sweeps of her uninjured arm, Cassidy ran the scanner over Kindra's body, lingering over her few scars. Odira knew the value of a good plastic surgeon. Scars became memorable identifying marks, and those were bad in their line of work.

When Cassidy didn't find anything on Kindra's front side, Kindra flipped onto her stomach and the process began again. At least this time the table had soaked up some of her body heat, so she didn't feel like she'd been sprayed with liquid nitrogen.

"What is this one?" Ryce lightly traced a scar Kindra knew was there but had rarely seen. It was thin but long—six inches—and it ran in a diagonal stripe across her back: a memento from one time Kindra had been captured by an enemy team. Captured and tortured for information. Not the only time she'd ever been captured, but it *was* the only time the people demanding answers had been specially trained to extract them.

"Whip." Kindra closed her eyes, glad her face was already hidden in the crook of her arm. "Couple of years ago. The doc managed to erase most of the stripes, but that one was too wide to get rid of entirely."

Ryce's touch quivered before his palm flattened against Kindra's skin. The touch was solid, but not strong enough to be meant as a restraining force. It felt almost like reassurance, like a promise that it wouldn't happen again. Which would be a stupid thing to promise. Who could possibly keep a promise like that?

The pressure of Ryce's touch released, and the scan resumed. They scanned her whole body, but the wand only beeped while hovering over Kindra's right shoulder.

"Just the one, it looks like. Hold still," Cassidy warned as someone rubbed something into Kindra's skin. Antiseptic *and* anesthetic, Kindra hoped. She relaxed a little more when she felt the familiar pinch of a needle. Her tolerance was pretty high; unless they overdosed her, the anesthetic might not do much.

While they waited a few minutes for the drugs to take effect, Kindra pressed her forehead into the cool surface of the table and gripped the edges, preparing for the worst and hoping for better.

"Breathe and relax as much as you can." Hugo's voice was soft, but the slight scrape of metal against metal destroyed any reassurance in the words. "We'll try to make this quick."

Someone's hands restrained Kindra's calves. Another set of hands gripped her hips. Body heat from those surrounding her seeped into her skin. It only made her more aware of how exposed and cold she was.

Something sliced into Kindra's shoulder just inside the shoulder blade. She shouldn't have felt it, but she did. She tensed even though she knew it'd make the pain worse. The pressure on her legs and hips increased, keeping her locked to the table when she would have willingly rolled off the side to escape Hugo's tiny blade.

"Forceps," Hugo demanded. A clink of metal. The pain in Kindra's shoulder rose as Hugo dug into the muscles. Each millimetric shift of the forceps felt like a foot, and each second it lasted felt like an hour. Finally, Hugo tugged something free. "Sorry. The muscles grew over the stupid thing."

Kindra took a long breath, her eyes squeezed shut. Something cool sprayed over her shoulder. Pain flared. Pressing against the table, she tried to free herself. Someone's hand left her back and rested on her head.

"Breathe," Dru whispered. "He needs to stitch you up. Breathe, and it'll be over soon."

She felt the first stitch close her skin before Dru had finished talking. Kindra breathed into the pain, let it wash over her and fall away. It didn't hurt much compared to the day she picked up the whip scar, or the day she broke her leg parkouring over a ten-foot wall. It had been the unexpectedness of it, the shock, that hurt.

Once Kindra relaxed against the table, Dru's hands became more comfort than restraint. Her fingers traced Kindra's hairline on the back of her neck and stroked her unmarred shoulder softly, the motion unceasing until Kindra heard the snip of scissors cutting thread. A bandage was taped on, and someone patted her lower back.

"You're good," Cassidy said. "Get up and get dressed before you catch pneumonia. This may be Florida, but it's still cold in here."

The hands all left her, only one pair lingering, and Kindra shivered again without that slight bit of heat to warm her. When she moved, the stitches in her shoulder pulled, but the pain had dulled to the equivalent of a deep paper cut.

After she sat up, Hugo dropped clothes in her lap. The same ones she'd been wearing since the god-awful-early hours of Tuesday morning. Obviously they weren't giving her a fresh set.

"You don't happen to have a shower in this place, do you?" Even putting on that dirty, smelly outfit would be okay if she could clean herself up first.

"Locker room thataway," Daelan said from his chair near the computer, pointing to a door on what she thought was the west wall.

"Get dressed for now." Cassidy nodded toward one of the vans. "We'll need to dig clean things out for you and Dru, and I don't want you freezing in the meantime."

As Kindra slid from the table, she thought about her bag of clothes in the van. They'd be easy to get to, but she put on her grimy black pants and shirt anyway, not wanting to push her luck too far too fast. As soon as she had a layer of cloth on, she held out her hand. "Can I see it?"

Cassidy picked up a small glass cylinder from the towel on the table and handed it over. Kindra wiped a spot of her own blood away and stared at the tiny device that had, apparently, been hiding in her shoulder. It was small, maybe two centimeters long and maybe three millimeters in diameter, and inside were wires, several microchips, and a thin battery. Odira never used any stock tech, and she'd trained Seraphina into the same compulsion. The workmanship in her hand was oh-so-familiar.

The batteries couldn't have lasted more than a few weeks at a time, which meant that Odira had managed to charge or replace it. More than once. Often. Like those nights Kindra had slept so deeply that she'd woken up confused and—

No. Stop. Don't think about it now. It won't change anything.

A little numbly, she handed it back to Cassidy. Everyone was already gathered, so Cassidy stepped into the center of the loose circle and held up the device.

"Thanks to this and what happened at the motel, the Westons know we're in town. That means that Garret will too, and probably Javier's team, if he's still using them."

"We have three options from here." Hugo stood just off his wife's shoulder, his pale-green eyes lingering on Kindra longest. "We can run and concentrate on surviving. We can stay, but keep to the shadows and run the same long game we've been playing for years. Or . . ."

When Hugo paused, Cassidy picked it up. "Or we can try to take him out before he takes us down."

"Whatever you guys do, I'm walking through door three," Aaron said. "I'm not just running from Hadley, I'm running from the military and her family." He jerked his head toward Kindra. "I have shit I need to see done before someone takes me out or locks me down."

Cassidy and Hugo nodded and turned toward Kindra.

What was this? An audition? A short-term partnership? A way to keep their enemy close? Kindra's presence—and that effing tracker— had brought a raft of shit floating straight into the Calvers' lives. How long would they be willing to put up with her when it meant that Odira would only be gunning for their family that much harder?

But, really, where else was Kindra going to go? This whole thing was still such a mess; she hadn't had the time to mentally untangle any of it yet.

"Whatever." She wrinkled her nose, pretending indifference. "I figure there's a ninety percent chance I'm dead at the end of this no matter what door I pick."

Cassidy glanced at Hugo and then Dru. There seemed to be a question in her eyes, one Dru answered with an expression Odira had always described as a "facial shrug."

"Welcome to the Citadel," Cassidy said. "Rest, eat, heal. We've got a lot of work to do, and we need everyone on this if any of us are going to have a chance of coming out the other side intact."

Garret Hadley hadn't left his office at Redwell until after midnight last night and had been back around sunrise. The first half of the day had been so hectic that it wasn't until after eleven that he reached for the couriered parcel from South America. He pushed aside several soil samples and plant cuttings, attention focused on the hand-addressed letter on top of the stack of documents.

15 February
To: Redwell, Inc.
Attn: Mr. Garret Hadley

The initial suggestions made by your research team have already created statistically significant results. We will continue to implement the changes per the schedule previously outlined. Hopefully the enclosed samples will be sufficient to adjust that timeline if necessary.

God bless,
Alejo Crespo Franco-Ferro
Isaiah 26:3

He picked up the leather-bound, gilt-edged, personalized Bible on his desk and expertly flipped through the pages until he found the passage he needed.

"'Thou wilt keep him in perfect peace, whose mind is stayed on thee: because he trusteth in thee.'" Garret snorted and slammed the book shut before tossing it carelessly back to the corner of his desk.

"As long as you keep thinking that, Alejo, that's all that matters. Shit, at least something is going right this week."

Leaning to his right, he hit the button on his phone's intercom.

"Yes, sir?" the voice on the other side asked.

"In here, Charles."

"On my way."

The intercom clicked off, and Garret stood. He kept the letter from Alejo aside, but placed the other samples and documents back into the manila folder. A moment later, there was a knock at the door. Garret pressed the button to unlock it and let them in.

"Hurry up, Charles. I'm running late."

"Of course." Charles's blond hair was side-parted and brushed back. His deep-blue eyes swept the room before landing on Garret and staying there. "What can I do for you, sir?"

"Run this down to the team and take a message on all my calls until I say otherwise." He handed Charles the parcel and then picked his jacket up off the back of his chair. "I have a lunch that might run long."

"It usually does with Lillian, sir," Charles said, a wry smile on his face.

Garret chuckled as he left. "Kid, you have no idea."

Chapter Seventeen

The trees grew so close together here that Kindra had to turn sideways to walk between them, something that wouldn't bother her so much if the motion didn't always disrupt the piles of snow clinging to the branches above, dropping handfuls of it on top of her head. Shivering, she kept walking.

Ryce better hurry the hell up. I might never get warm again at this rate.

The Swiss Alps in winter were a tourist destination, but people came for the skiing and the cozy lodges, not hiking up snow-covered mountains in the dead of the night. Kindra wanted them to kill this guy, finish the job, and go back to their nice, warm base camp.

"I've got the target in sight," Ryce murmured over the comms. "Moving in."

"No, hold! Wait until someone is there to watch your six." Odira's words crackled over the comm, the distance and the mountains creating interference. "We don't know he's alone."

"We're closest," Kindra said. With a glance at Amett for confirmation, she quickened her pace in the direction her brother had been searching. "We can be there in five."

"I've got a shot. I'm moving to take it. Going dark." Ryce's comm cut off, empty silence replacing the ambient noises that had been traveling through his mic.

"No! Report!" No answer came to Odira's demand. "I swear to Atropos I will beat some sense into that boy one day."

Amett grunted at that, then said, "Pick it up, Kindra. We need to get there before his stupidity gets him in trouble."

Moving as quickly as they could through thick snowdrifts and closely packed trees, Kindra and Amett ran toward Ryce's last known position on the ridge overlooking the river. Odira had thought it more likely that their target would stay to the lowlands, heading for a cabin he could hide in for a while, but even Odira had to be wrong sometimes.

They climbed quickly once they broke free of the trees, following the path Ryce had taken. Someone besides Ryce had passed this way—there were too many footprints in the snow—and that confirmation of the target's presence kicked more adrenaline into Kindra's bloodstream.

Crack-boom.

A gunshot, its echoes reverberating through the rocky landscape, growing louder with each cycle until it rattled Kindra's bones like a powerful roll of thunder.

A scream followed it. A scream that cut off far too quickly.

"Report!" Odira demanded.

Kindra didn't answer. She sprinted the rest of the way up the mountain, her Colt in her hands. Vaguely she registered Amett answering Odira's demands for information, but her mind focused on calculating the quickest possible route to Ryce. Ryce, who might be in trouble. Ryce, who had gone off alone. Ryce, whom Kindra couldn't bear to lose.

Ryce, who wasn't there when Kindra and Amett reached the ridge.

Two days of searching and all they found was blood—so much blood—and footsteps, too small to be Ryce's, leading down the other side of the mountain.

Kindra woke up with a jerk and a rush of adrenaline, snorting a breath that tickled the back of her throat. That dream hadn't plagued her in two years.

You're not in Switzerland. Not even close.

She was in a small room with cement walls and a window that looked into a larger warehouse. The lights in the room weren't on, but the fluorescents in the warehouse provided just enough glow to outline several cots and the people sleeping on them: Dru, Bernard, and Ryce. The brother whose blood she could still smell, mixed with the thin, icy air of the Swiss Alps. The brother whose body they'd searched for. Two days and nights spent on the freezing banks of the river below that cliff, and they never found a thing. The arrival of a military team drove them away.

That had been the first time Kindra had ever stabbed a target and been glad when the knife found an artery. She'd been *happy* to take the life of the man who'd taken her brother.

Only that wasn't what she'd done, was it? Because Ryce hadn't died that day.

Knowing she wouldn't be going back to sleep anytime soon, Kindra folded the cot's thin blanket back and left the room. She wasn't ready to face Ryce. If she did it now, the odds weren't good that he'd still be alive at the end of the conversation.

Luckily, she had a *lot* of practice stuffing this particular memory into a lead-lined box and burying it so deep it was practically gone.

"Garret has been business as usual today, excepting his long lunch with Lillian French," Daelan reported as Kindra closed the door to the office/dorm with a soft *click*. He and Cassidy sat in front of the wide bank of monitors, while Hugo leaned against the back of their chairs, eyes locked on the screens.

For a moment, Kindra debated the benefits of a silent approach. Then she remembered that she was the only person in the room without access to a weapon. Probably not best to startle anyone. She made her next footstep deliberately audible. Daelan was the first to look up.

"Oh, thank the Easter bunny! There's a free bed." He pressed a few keys and clicked something on the screen before jumping out of his chair. "Please try not to wake me up for at least six hours."

"I promise nothing," Hugo said as he sat in the chair Daelan had vacated.

"Then I don't promise to be anywhere close to cheerful if you wake me up early."

Hugo and Cassidy both smiled as he stepped into the office.

"He got that mouth from you," Hugo said.

"I know." Cassidy chuckled. "It's fantastic."

Instead of stepping up behind them, Kindra stayed off to the right, deliberately placing herself within their peripheral vision. She watched Cassidy, her eyes lingering on the bandages, and wondered if they expected her to apologize for the bullets that had left those wounds. Kindra didn't feel sorry for it. For the aftermath and the pain it was pretty obvious Cassidy was still in, sure. Not for the shooting. Kindra was eighty-three percent sure that Cassidy would've done the same thing if the situation had been reversed.

Deciding that not talking about it at all was the best option, Kindra picked something else to focus on.

"This warehouse is pretty well fortified." The walls were solid concrete and extra thick. The steel doors slid open on a reinforced track, and they looked almost vacuum sealed once shut. Even the window to the office was, if Kindra had to guess, bulletproof. "Is it yours?"

Cassidy grinned, more than a little mischief in her hazel eyes. "It is for now, but that's because the owner of record has only used it between March and December for the past five years."

Kindra looked at the warehouse again, and at the smile on Cassidy's face. If they'd been watching this place for five years, then that had to mean . . . "This belongs to Hadley?"

"One of Redwell's import/export subsidiaries, technically," Hugo clarified.

"And you guys are using it as a base of operations in some grand plan to take him out at the knees?" Kindra had a whole new appreciation for the place. "That's practically poetic."

"Daelan's plans usually are," Cassidy said. "When they're workable at all."

"He dreams big, that boy." Hugo's words were teasing, but Kindra thought there was some pride hovering right beneath the surface.

Which was another reminder that although Dru had given Kindra the general background on the relationship between Redwell and Rose Water, she still wasn't sure what Redwell actually did. She knew someone in the company was pretty good at killing people and running drugs, but that couldn't possibly be what they made their taxable income doing.

"I know Garret Hadley is dirty, but what does Redwell do?" With anyone but the Calvers, she would've hidden the depth of her ignorance, but Hugo and Cassidy knew how much Odira and Amett kept to themselves.

"They put a lot of money into agricultural development and research," Hugo said. "Disease- and drought-resistant crops, forest- and resource-management methods, and human-safe pesticides too. They do medical research, pharmaceutical development and testing—drugs to fight antibiotic-resistant bacteria and new viral immunizations without the same side-effect rates."

"A separate division works on technology, and they cover everything from network security to physical security systems." Cassidy clicked an icon and typed something into the web browser she had pulled up. An image search showed a slew of what Kindra thought might be power cells. "They're also working on alternative energy concepts."

"And then there are their military contracts." Hugo rubbed the back of his neck, his expression grim.

"Right. They do some development through their tech arm, but mostly their contracts are for manufacturing other people's designs," Cassidy explained. "Everything from small arms and body armor to transportation and temporary base housing."

"But it's not just that, right?" Kindra couldn't quite mesh what she'd experienced of Garret Hadley and what Hugo and Cassidy were telling her about his company. "These guys kind of sound like saints."

"That's the point. They *are*. Both in the eyes of the public and in reality, more or less. It's what makes them a perfect shield for a corrupt CEO to hide behind." Cassidy's nose wrinkled as she said it, like the whole concept disgusted her. "The agricultural, technological, medical, and military branches are where most of the focus goes and where most of Redwell's money comes from. And what this warehouse is usually used for."

"Okay, but if the company is that big, Garret can't be the only one working the black market from the inside. Will taking him out do any good?" Kindra shook her head. "Seems like chopping the head off the hydra."

"Your parents are still obsessed with ancient Greece, huh?" Hugo said.

Kindra ground her teeth. "And you guys still fall back on classic movies, huh?"

He didn't move his head, but his eyes flicked toward Cassidy. "Pretty much. Even 'the Citadel' is a movie reference."

"Fitting, too," Cassidy quipped. "Especially given the circumstances."

"I've never seen it."

"Most people haven't," Hugo said with a shrug. "It was released in 1938."

Atropos bless it. 1938? How long did it take her to track down that *one?* And then she shook herself away from that train of thought. "We were talking about targets, not movies."

They shared another quick, speaking glance, something deeper than the way Amett and Odira communicated. It was like they were reading each other's minds, not just guessing.

"People aren't mythical monsters, Kindra," Cassidy said. "They're not interchangeable parts, either. If the right people are taken out and new ones put in place, Redwell will become as clean as it looks on paper. You heard some of the work they do. This company has helped a hell of a lot more people than they've hurt."

"It's the people working in the shadows we need to worry about." Hugo brought up another folder and quickly scrolled through the images it contained. Burned-out homes. Articles in Spanish about a string of unsolved murders. Funerals. Civil unrest. Grief. Loss. Rage. "It's not the only country affected, but Echemorro is the one about to hit the tipping point if we don't do something to stop what's happening down there."

"Right." In addition to the information on the screen Hugo was using, there were three additional screens displaying feeds from sixteen different cameras—some hidden in offices and homes, others in more public areas. It was all so reminiscent of the setup for Odira's jobs . . . "One question first."

"Yes?" Hugo drew the word out slightly, clearly wary.

"How in the hell is this different from what Amett and Odira do? Because 'taken out' doesn't sound like it means anything different to you than it does to them."

Cassidy closed her eyes. Hugo's wariness transformed to weariness as he shook his head. "There's still a very strong need for the sharp end of the stick today. Bad people exist, people who won't ever quail under threats of 'justice' or 'prosecution.' The system has escape hatches, and the ones who exploit them most often are the ones who don't deserve the forgiveness. We saw it and kept wishing those loopholes would become nooses around their necks."

"We aren't saints," Cassidy said. "There's a reason we worked with Amett and Odira for all those years. We saw the need for it, and we saw that no one else was going to sully themselves with the cleanup."

"At first it was fine. Bad men ordering hits on worse men." Hugo's lip curled. "We were working for scum, but we were taking out scummier."

Kindra leaned against the edge of the table, shifting to see their faces better. "What changed?"

"Odira took a job from Garret Hadley." Cassidy moved her right hand toward her head, but winced and quickly lowered the arm.

Well, that didn't take long. Kindra had guessed he'd played a part in the split between her family and Dru's, but somehow the fact that it started *and* ended with him surprised her.

"We should've checked, but we'd fallen into habit. Odira handled the clients." Hugo's lips pressed into a thin line. "It was a rush job on top of that. We barely had time to locate the target before we had to move in."

Cassidy sighed and brought up a photo of a college-age girl with ebony skin, long hair, and a brilliant smile. "Norah Whittaker. It's been twelve years, and we still don't have a consarn clue why they wanted her dead. Norah was intelligent, motivated, and generous. In the article about her death, her sorority sisters called her 'the counselor.'" Cassidy practically growled. "She was going to be an elementary school teacher, for Chrissake."

Norah Whittaker wanted to teach kids. Garret Hadley had no qualms about killing them. Her loss for his gain definitely didn't seem like an even trade.

"We didn't know any of this until after she was dead." The regret was clear in Hugo's voice. Even for something that happened over a decade ago. "It was too late for Norah. We made anonymous donations to her family and to the school that she'd been hired at but never got to set foot in as a teacher."

"We swore we wouldn't be that careless again," Cassidy added. "And that we'd never take a job from Garret unless we knew *exactly* who we were after and why."

"It wasn't an issue for a couple of years, but then Redwell popped up again. Odira agreed to take the job before they'd even named a target." Hugo stared at Kindra, searching her expression. For whether or not Kindra believed him, maybe. "Garret paid exceptionally well for an extraordinarily soft, easy job the last time."

"As long as we get paid." Kindra spoke the words by rote. It was practically Odira's catchphrase.

"As long as we get paid, the why isn't important."

"As long as we get paid, the target doesn't matter."

"Shut up because it doesn't matter. We're getting paid at the end of this."

"Guess that much hasn't changed," Hugo said.

Cassidy laughed, a dry, humorless sound. "Did you think it would?"

"I hoped."

"Optimistic fool," Cassidy said with a soft smile, turning the slight into an endearment.

Kindra didn't think she'd ever seen her parents look at each other with that much tender affection in their eyes. It almost felt intrusive to be sharing the same air.

Luckily, they broke their own moment before Kindra had to do it.

With a couple clicks, Cassidy brought up another picture, this one of a family. A blond couple, maybe in their thirties, and two towheaded boys under the age of eight.

"It was supposed to be him," Hugo said, indicating the father figure. "Lee Michaels seemed just as clean as Norah. The only hitch was that he worked for a company that, after a few parent companies and a little digital wizardry, was owned by Garret."

"We told Odira we wanted out." Cassidy stared at the photo on the screen. "No way were we going after someone else like Norah."

"She said Garret would hire someone else the next day if we didn't do it." Hugo's face was blank. "Then she reminded us that the team had already taken the job. If we backed out now, Garret would add *us* to his shit list."

"You backed out." Kindra remembered Odira and Amett's fights—literal knock-down-drag-outs a couple of times—she'd just never known the *why*.

"Bet your ass we did," Cassidy muttered. "Tried to warn Lee, but he wouldn't listen. He bunkered down in his house. So Odira lit the whole thing on fire."

When Cassidy reached out and almost touched the faces of those two boys, Kindra felt like she'd been punched in the kidney. "They were *all* in the house?"

The older one must have been almost the same age I was that year. That realization was like an aluminum bat to the side of the head, and those fuckers *hurt*. Kindra couldn't find any way to rationalize the necessity of killing kids. Kids young enough to play with your own children. Where and how was that *ever* okay?

"She pumped the place with a sedative gas first." Hugo's lips thinned again. "It's one of the few markers of compassion I have ever seen that woman display."

"I don't think they ever realized they were burning." Sighing quietly, Cassidy clicked another picture open. This one showed three houses in a solidly middle-class neighborhood somewhere in the Northeast. The center house was a burned-out, blackened shell. "Odira and Amett made it look like the gas line exploded."

Kindra knew that, just like the schoolchildren of Echemorro, Norah and the Michaels family would stay with her a long time. "What did you do after you left? Obviously you didn't start running the straight, narrow, and legal."

"Obviously not," Hugo agreed with a breathy laugh. "We've diversified a little—custom security systems, short-term bodyguards, data collection of one sort or another, and the odd assassination or two if the target was right."

Cassidy nodded, trying and failing to swallow a yawn before she spoke. "We got to pick our own jobs, and that helped."

"With what?"

"The guilt." Cassidy gestured at the picture of the burned-out Michaels home. "Feeling like we were actually contributing somehow to making the world a little *better* instead of just making money."

Kindra remembered the moment in the car with Dru when she realized that taking out Bernard would be helping Garret Hadley continue destabilizing Echemorro . . . and then she cleared her throat and changed the subject. "So taking out Garret is actually going to take care of this Redwell disaster?"

Cassidy nodded. "Redwell isn't a hydra; it's a body infected by cancer. Every single illegal operation we've found traces back to him."

With a couple taps of the keyboard from Hugo, the pictures on the screen cleared. A few more clicks and he had a new picture loaded. The cancer inside Redwell finally had a face.

The man was on the upper end of the "middle-aged" spectrum, his brown hair heavily streaked with silver, and his pale skin roughened by the sun and age. His expression was solemn and his suit subdued—charcoal-gray jacket, silver tie, white shirt—and his angular nose was definitely the most prominent feature on his face. The rest of him was amazingly unremarkable.

Cassidy nodded toward the picture. "That is Garret Hadley, the CEO."

"He's the one Rose Water has been dealing with," Kindra said.

"Exactly. Redwell has an executive committee, a board of directors and other major players involved in the running of the company, but for all of the black market shit?" Hugo waved his hand at the screen. "It's all him."

"But never in a way that can be proven in court," Cassidy said, bitterness seeping into her tone. "Isaac told Bernard there hasn't ever been enough to prosecute."

"Who's Isaac?" Kindra asked, just as the word "prosecute" clicked in her brain. "Wait, Isaac Marks? The FBI guy?"

Cassidy blinked, but it was Hugo who asked, "How'd you know that?"

"The night you guys debugged Bernard's condo, Odira and Sera managed to get the signal blocker out of the way before you disabled the camera in his office." Kindra shrugged at Cassidy's affronted expression.

"Well, shit." Hugo seemed vaguely impressed.

"You mentioned something about Isaac Marks landing on Wednesday." Despite everything, Kindra couldn't help feeling a tad smug revealing knowledge that the Calvers hadn't expected her to have. "Didn't take Odira and Amett long to figure out who he was."

"Oh, I'm sure it didn't. He was the one who got Bernard the information you saw." Cassidy gently rubbed her wounded shoulder and then looked at Hugo. "Have we actually *spoken* to Isaac since then? He was supposed to get in yesterday. Are we sure he's still alive?"

"I'll find out." Face grim, Hugo moved toward one of the vans, pulling out a cheap, disposable cell phone. He dialed a number from memory, but the pause between the beginning of the call and the moment his lips moved hinted that no one had answered. When he hung up, he slid the phone into his pocket instead of tossing it.

"He'll call back if he can," Hugo said when he returned to the computers. It seemed more like a reminder for himself than a statement for everyone else in the room.

Cassidy nodded, swallowing another yawn. She was shifting stiffly on the chair, and lines of concern radiated from Hugo's eyes as he picked up a prescription bottle and placed it in front of her.

"Don't argue," he said as soon as she opened her mouth. "You take one, kick Dru out of bed, and lie down."

Cassidy cringed. "Bossy bastard."

"Yes." He held her chin and planted a kiss on her lips. "Now listen to me for once."

Odira would've punched, argued with, or ignored Amett, but Cassidy swallowed the pill dry and stalked off, grumbling to herself the whole time she followed the orders.

Kindra couldn't make herself apologize and mean it, but she had to ask. "Is she okay?"

Hugo's eyes were guarded as he nodded. "She was lucky. The center-mass shot caught her vest, but the shoulder . . . You missed anything vital by millimeters."

"Good." She could tell him that she'd purposefully *not* taken the head shot. It might help. He might even see it as some sort of apology. But then Dru shuffled out of the makeshift bedroom, a thin blanket around her shoulders and her hair sticking out at odd angles where it had tried to pull free of her braid. She looked soft and effing adorable.

Before, Kindra had warned herself not to crush on the enemy, but the Calvers weren't the enemy now; they were sanctuary, and she really wasn't sure how long this dysfunctional truce could last once the job was done.

Protecting Kindra for now was one thing, but no way would they want to put up with her forever. A team of five was already a little big for the kind of jobs they took. Six was pushing it. Right now they'd ballooned up to eight if you counted Bernard, which Kindra wasn't sure she should—all she'd seen the guy do so far was cower. Aaron definitely counted. He had the training, the motivation, and, just like Kindra, nowhere else to go, since he wasn't a current favorite with the Marine Corps.

Just like Kindra, Aaron Tanvers had claimed sanctuary at the Citadel.

"Fill me in." Dru's voice was still rough with sleep as she plopped into the seat her mother had vacated.

With only a quick glance at Kindra, Hugo gave Dru a rundown of everything they'd told Kindra. It wasn't surprising that none of it seemed to be news to Dru except when Hugo mentioned the conversation Kindra and her family had caught the tail end of.

"Really? What'd you hear?" It was hard to tell for sure, but Kindra was almost positive that Dru was nervous as she waited for an answer.

"That you think my family is the stuff of children's nightmares. You said you'd be meeting Isaac Marks on Wednesday, and you dropped the 'Tiffany' clue that led us to Amour." Kindra crossed her arms. "You should really be more careful about where you have super-secret-spy-mission planning sessions."

Dru huffed and rolled her eyes. "I'll keep that in mind." Her nerves seemed to settle a little as she scanned the screens, eyes flicking between small squares of information and codes and videos with practiced ease. "Have we decided what we're going for yet? Shock and awe? Divide and conquer? Antagonize and annoy?"

"You're probably an expert in that last one, aren't you?"

Dru stuck her tongue out at Kindra. Hugo shook his head, barely hiding a smile. "Recon first. This one is going to take a whole lot of finesse."

"Recon," Dru muttered. "Otherwise known as 'how long can you manage to pretend to be someone else, or sit staring at a computer, and not let anyone see how consarn bored you are.'"

"What does that word even *mean*?" Kindra finally had to ask.

"Consarn?" Dru grinned. "It's an old-timey replacement curse for goddamn. Mom picked it up from one of her movies."

"It's weird."

Dru laughed. "Weirder than swearing to the Greek goddess of scissors and string?"

"Atropos is fate. Death. The end of the line. Not scissors and string." Kindra shrugged. "Makes sense in our line of work."

"*Obviously* you both need something to keep you busy." Hugo typed in a keyword and clicked an icon that turned up in the search. "We haven't finished cataloging what Kindra scanned and sent us while you guys were on the road. We have a backlog of Redwell footage to go through too. We kind of got sidetracked by . . . whatever." He waved a careless hand, dismissing the chaos of the last week.

"Oh, come on," Dru moaned. "Don't make me do the footage review. *Please?*"

Hugo ignored his daughter, and so did Kindra. Strangely stated or not, those had clearly been orders, and orders were supposed to be obeyed.

Kindra sat next to Dru, her eyes already tracking patterns of movement in the video taking over one of the screens. "What are we looking for?"

"Garret Hadley or any one of them," Hugo said, indicating several pictures popping up on the screen to their right, including a woman with a bright smile, elegantly graying hair, dark mahogany skin, and a conservative black pantsuit. The name on the picture was Lillian French. "Look for anything out of place. Hidden security. Anything that looks clandestine. Info drops or pickups. The usual."

Dru sighed as she grudgingly moved closer to the computers. "The usual. In other words, *everything*."

Chapter Eighteen
1017 : FRIDAY, FEBRUARY 19

Kindra had been taking out her boredom and frustration on a sparring dummy for the past half hour, and sweat dripped into her eyes. Wiping it away with the sleeve of a shirt she'd borrowed from Dru, Kindra adjusted her grip on her borrowed blade.

My entire life *is borrowed right now.* She absently flipped the knife as she cast an eye over the room.

Cassidy and Ryce were sleeping, Daelan was tinkering with his latest explosive experiment, Bernard was using one of the disposable phones in an attempt to reach Special Agent Isaac Marks again, and Aaron stood behind Dru and Hugo as they worked on hacking their way into Redwell's apparently impenetrable security system.

Unless she was taking her turn at the computers, monitoring current footage while cataloging recorded video—and contemplating unnecessarily complex patterns revolving around a single rose tattoo—she found it hard to sit still. Or keep from twitching when she didn't have her back to a wall. Not that she thought anyone in the warehouse was likely to sneak up from behind and garrote her, but the tingles that ran down her spine every time she felt someone approaching couldn't be stopped.

And after the chaos of the past week, spending twenty-four hours in the same place felt wrong.

So she kept busy. And kept avoiding Ryce, too. If she wasn't sleeping or sitting at the computers, Kindra trained. In one corner of the room, mats lined the concrete floor, three pairs of weights sat against the wall, and a freestanding striking dummy waited for opponents. The Calvers had even given her a blade. It wasn't one of hers—she wasn't entirely sure where her bag had ended up and thought searching for it would look too much like snooping—but the KA-BAR Tanto was good enough.

"I think something has happened to Isaac." Bernard stared at the phone in his hand, his lips pursed and the lines around his eyes deepening. He'd looked stressed the day Amett missed, but that was nothing compared to the strain ingrained in every line of his body now. "His voice mail is full."

Hugo looked up, frowning. "He hasn't returned my call yet either."

"I know." Bernard's hand tightened around the cell phone. "He could have been delayed coming back from Echemorro—it's a long way to travel—but if he was headed for New York to meet me, then . . ."

Then someone else might've been waiting for him. After all, Javier, John, and Nuura hadn't been seen since Tuesday, had they? If Garret had redirected them . . .

It would be so easy. Hack the passenger manifests, track his arrival at the airport, follow him home, make it look like a robbery gone wrong. At least, that was how Odira had organized it last time they pulled a job like that.

"As far as we've heard, no one has asked after you or left anything at your offices." Hugo typed in a command and his screen switched to an image of Bernard's office. "The investigation and your disappearance are still making news. Your face has been getting a lot of screen time."

"Not for the right reasons." Bernard placed the phone on the table near Hugo's computer and then ran his fingers through his hair, disarraying the thick gray-smattered strands. "It won't exactly help me keep a low profile."

"Isaac is a smart guy, and he knew the dangers going in." Hugo looked up at Bernard, his expression calm but his knuckles white on the edge of his chair. "He probably decided to lie low."

Bernard nodded, but he didn't seem to buy the lie any more than Hugo did. They pretended anyway. Trying to make each other feel better? Maybe. It wasn't a habit Amett or Odira had ever indulged in. Hope distorted truth.

"You miss what's there when you only look for what you hope *to find."*

Kindra shook her head and shifted her grip on the knife, returning to her mock battle with the dummy.

Ding.

Everyone stilled.

"Bernard, it's from Isaac," Hugo said.

Sheathing her knife and then picking up the towel she'd tossed on the edge of the mat, Kindra wiped her skin dry and jogged across the warehouse. She wasn't the only one. Ryce had rushed out of the office-bedroom. Daelan and Aaron were already there, staring intently at the screen displaying the disappointingly brief email.

B. G.,

Worse than we thought. The octopus has a thousand tentacles, and each one is wrapped around another creature's throat.

Information requested is attached.

Your sister says hello.

I. M.

"Well, *that* doesn't sound good," Daelan muttered as Dru downloaded the linked, password-protected file. Kindra noticed Dru's motions, but her attention was mostly on Bernard.

His copper skin had gone paler than usual. His hands were shaking, his eyes were shut tight, and although his mouth opened several times, he said nothing. Not until he swallowed twice. "He's dead. Isaac is dead."

Hugo jerked around, his eyes narrow. "How do you know?"

"My sister died when I was fifteen," Bernard said. "That last line, the closing? We chose that as a code I'd recognize if the worst happened. Mentioning my sister means he was sure he was about to die."

"He must've thought the danger was imminent, at least," Hugo said softly. "It reads like a dead man's trigger, something that wouldn't send unless he wasn't around to delay it."

"So he might have just got caught somewhere he couldn't access his computer, right?" The hope in Bernard's voice made Kindra wince.

Hugo closed his eyes for a moment. "It's possible, but . . . I think it's far safer if we assume otherwise."

Aaron closed his eyes, dropped his chin, and sighed, his lips moving in what Kindra thought might have been a prayer.

"This file is hellishly encrypted." Dru squinted at the screen and shook her head. "We need Mom for this one."

Dru rose from the chair, but Hugo put his hand on her shoulder. "Stay. I'll go wake her up."

"You want in, Dae?" Dru plopped back down into the metal chair. Her brother's only answer was to slide into the chair their father had vacated.

"Were there any other recipients on the email?" Bernard leaned closer to peer at the screen.

Dru shook her head. "No, doesn't look like it."

He stepped back. "I think that, for him to send all of the information he collected to *only* me, he must have suspected someone else betrayed him."

"It's a strong possibility," Dru said. "Garret has had ties to the FBI for years, specifically a couple of people who were suspected of treason. And that person might be why we haven't heard anything about his death yet."

"It isn't necessarily a person," Kindra said. "Redwell specializes in network security, right? *And* they have active military contracts. There's no guarantee that Garret didn't have someone plant spyware in the Feds' system somewhere, but it's likely that Isaac was traveling under false documents to keep himself off Garret's radar. It'd leave him as a John Doe in the morgue while the local PD looked for a real identification."

"Now there's a fun thought," Daelan muttered as he typed codes and commands faster than Kindra could follow, but she *did* recognize the data tag.

Her eyebrows rose. "It's a Tru3 v4ult encryption? Hellish is right. Is Cassidy going to be able to crack that without a key?"

"Eventually." Dru's smile was small and slightly crooked—a smile that held secrets. "If the woman who created the encryption can't break it, no one can."

"Cassidy designed Tru3 v4ult? No wonder Odira talked about her like she'd been born inside the internet."

Daelan laughed. "Half our cash is from her freelance network security work. It's all her legal computer shit that lets us finance the unpaid black-ops work we do sometimes."

"And hopefully one day the *legal* work will be *all* this family is involved in," Cassidy grumbled behind them. "Scooch, Dru."

"You'd be bored in a week," Dru said as she stood.

"No." Cassidy glanced meaningfully at her bandaged shoulder. "I really wouldn't. Sometimes enough is too much."

Dru bit her lip and ran her hand over her mother's hair, pressing a kiss to the top of her head. There was more than a little reproach in Dru's eyes when she looked up at Kindra.

Kindra ignored her.

After a minute or so, everyone else wandered off. Kindra watched Daelan and Cassidy work, listening to them speak in computer code and attempting to decipher what they were telling the computer as their fingers flew across the keys. It would've taken Sera and Odira most of a day. In three hours, Cassidy sat back and sighed as the files populated the screen.

"We're in," Daelan called out.

Everyone rushed back to the computers as spreadsheets, scans, photographed notebook pages, and text files opened on the screens. The folders seemed to contain everything Isaac Marks had compiled against Garret Hadley.

The first folder Cassidy opened was labeled *Correspondence*.

Photographs of handwritten letters filled the folder, each of them labeled with two dates. Date the letter arrived and date the picture was taken, if Kindra had to guess. Lips pressed thin, Cassidy opened the most recent file.

January 15
To: Rose Water Farms
Attn: Mr. Alejo Crespo Franco-Ferro

Rose Water's work of late has been exemplary, and Redwell looks forward to joining forces on more significant projects in the future. When you can, please forward the information I requested the last time we spoke.

I hope to hear from you on this soon, Alejo.
Garret Hadley
Joel 3:8

The *J* and the *E* were both cursive. This passage was an order, not just a Biblical signoff.

Cassidy's expression turned grim. "Dru, grab the Bible."

"Joel 3:8," Dru muttered, flipping through the pages. "'And I will sell your sons and your daughters into the hand of the children of Judah, and they shall sell them to the Sabeans, to a people far off: for the Lord hath spoken.'"

"Threat?" Hugo asked.

"Maybe." Cassidy's forehead furrowed, and when she spoke, she seemed to still be trying to work out the angles. "A local would have plenty of reasons to become noncompliant after what's happened down there. It'd be a death sentence, but they'd have reasons."

"It could be instructions," Dru said, staring at the Bible in her hands.

"Instructions *against* someone noncompliant?" Hugo suggested. "It's directed to Alejo Franco-Ferro instead of Eduardo Melo Santos. Change of power due to insubordination?"

Cassidy shook her head. "Pointless to speculate based on the information we have here."

"Work backward." Kindra pointed at the next file. "We might be able to piece things together with things we already know have happened."

"Which isn't much." But Cassidy still clicked on the next file. There were three letters open side by side on a desk, all correspondence between Garret and Alejo.

January 4
To: Rose Water Farms
Attn: Mr. Alejo Crespo Franco-Ferro

Let me take this chance to congratulate you on your position and welcome you to the Rose Water family. Through our dealings, I have gotten to know Eduardo very well. I feel you will make a valuable addition to the team.

Congratulations and God bless.
Garret Hadley
James 2:10

7 January
To: Redwell, Inc.
Attn: Mr. Garret Hadley

Enclosed, please find the requested climate and agricultural data for our area over the last five years. Eduardo may have overestimated the damage erosion has wrought. I hope this will assure you and the Redwell board that the investments we have spoken of will not be made in error.

Many blessings.
Alejo Crespo Franco-Ferro
Psalm 119:60 / Revelation 14:12

January 10
To: Rose Water Farms
Attn: Mr. Alejo Crespo Franco-Ferro

While I am glad to see that the erosion isn't as dangerous as Eduardo thought, the initial review by my team has raised some lingering concerns. Attached is a list of those reservations as well as suggestions and possible solutions.

I appreciate your cooperation with us on this project.
Garret Hadley
Acts 20:7

"Dru?" Cassidy didn't look up from the screen, but she didn't need to. Dru already had the Bible open in her hands, quickly flipping through the pages.

"Consarn it," Dru muttered. "Where the hell is the book of James?"

Bernard took the book from her, expertly sifting through the pages to the section they needed. His skin was still too pale, but his jaw was clenched and his entire face set. Determined. In that moment, practically glaring at the Bible in his hands, Bernard seemed almost capable. Completely unlike the stressed, cowering man Kindra had seen until now.

"James 2:10," Bernard read, his voice raspy but steady. "'For whosoever shall keep the whole law, and yet offend in one point, he is guilty of all.'"

"That doesn't sound good," Aaron muttered beside Kindra.

Ryce lifted one shoulder, an almost helpless shrug. "Nothing I've seen this guy say or do sounds good."

"What did Alejo respond with?" Hugo asked.

"The psalm is . . ." Bernard flipped through the book again, clearing his throat before reading, "'I made haste, and delayed not to keep thy commandments.'"

Cassidy typed Eduardo Melo Santos's name into the search engine.

"What about Revelation 14:12?" Ryce asked while Cassidy searched through the results for anything relevant.

It didn't take Bernard long to find the right page. "'Here is the patience of the saints: here are they that keep the commandments of God, and the faith of Jesus.'"

Then Cassidy opened an article in Spanish, posted over a month ago, the headline huge and bold across the top of the page: *Balama Mourns Eduardo Melo Santos*.

Before Kindra could offer to translate the rest, Cassidy clicked an auto-translate option and the text shifted, the readable Spanish switching to broken English that Cassidy summarized for everyone.

"On January 11, Eduardo Melo Santos was found dead in his apartment by his sixteen-year-old daughter, Beatriz." Cassidy winced.

Her hesitation was slight but noticeable before she announced, "It was apparently a heart attack."

Ryce shook his head. "I'd bet against bad odds that we're missing one piece of that chain, the one where either Alejo blows the whistle or Eduardo says no for the first time."

"Garret doesn't like hearing no." Cassidy's left hand rose. Kindra stared, wondering what the signal meant, until Hugo slid his hand into hers and squeezed. Oh. Not a signal, then. "When police went back to question the girl, Beatriz, no one could find her. She vanished."

"'And I will sell your sons and your daughters into the hand of the children of Judah,'" Bernard whispered.

The silence that settled was almost tangible—a weighted reminder of the kind of person they were up against and the power he wielded. Willingly and often. The kind of person who thought the only lives that mattered were the ones that affected the bottom line.

Hugo broke the stillness. "What's the last message?"

"Acts 20:7." Bernard took a long, slow breath. Other than that sigh of air, the only sound in the warehouse was the soft *shoosh* of the Bible's thin pages shifting against each other. "'And upon the first day of the week, when the disciples came together to break bread, Paul preached unto them, ready to depart on the morrow; and continued his speech until midnight.'"

"Wonder what happened at midnight on the seventeenth." Daelan's question ran on a strange tangent. Everyone looked at him, waiting for more. He seemed confused that no one else had jumped on his train of thought. "What? On most calendars in the US, the first day of the week is Sunday, right? So that passage was obviously setting up some kind of meeting for midnight on a Sunday. It was written on the tenth, which was a Sunday, but because it was mailed, there's no way the meeting happened that day. The seventeenth was the closest Sunday to when Alejo would've gotten the message, so . . ."

Kindra wasn't sure why anyone else was staring at him, but she was impressed he'd known which date the Sunday fell on. "Do you have the entire calendar memorized?"

"Is *that* why you're looking at me like I'm an alien?" Daelan shrugged. "I'm good with dates."

Dru snorted. "'Good with dates,' says the boy with the practically eidetic memory."

"It's not eidetic—that's basically impossible . . . but I do have a very good memory." The grin that spread across Daelan's face was sly bordering on smug. "It's just less like bragging if someone else says it first."

"Humble isn't a good look on you, Dae. Don't try." Ryce reached over and mussed Daelan's hair. Kindra closed her eyes, mentally flinching away from the familiarity of the gesture—another stinging reminder of everything she'd missed about his life for the past four years. Like the fact that he was *alive*.

Laughing, Daelan opened a new document and began transcribing the correspondence into one file, all of it dated and decoded, the actual Bible passages typed out next to the book, chapter, and verse notation that Garret Hadley, and Rose Water on his behalf, employed. It was laid out almost exactly the way Odira would've wanted it organized.

Because Cassidy and Odira ran things together years ago, Kindra reminded herself. *They used the same systems and worked from the same playbook.*

Kindra had known that, but seeing this systematically employed proof unsettled her. She almost stepped closer to Dru just for the physical contact, something to anchor her to this new reality she found herself drifting in.

"Well, if Eduardo was already dead when Alejo got the letter about selling sons and daughters, was that about Beatriz or was that threat intended for someone else?" Aaron asked.

If they made Eduardo's daughter vanish . . . "Did Isaac Marks have kids?"

Cassidy and Hugo looked at Kindra, their faces drawn. Their eyes shifted to Bernard and then each other, each transfer of attention adding another layer of bleak to their expressions.

"Does he?" Hugo asked Bernard.

"I don't know. I never actually . . ." Bernard shook his head and rubbed one shaking hand over his face, his eyes squeezed shut. "I didn't know the man."

"You weren't supposed to, Bernard." Ryce laid a hand on Bernard's shoulder. "He was doing his job. Isaac knew exactly what risks he'd face down there."

Dropping his hand, Bernard sucked in a slow, shaky breath. "I feel like the man died because I sent him up against a god with a pocketknife."

"Garret isn't a god," Aaron insisted. "I don't care how strong he seems; he is *not* a god. He's mortal, and I guarantee he'll bleed before this is done."

Daelan raised one eyebrow. "Oorah, Sergeant."

Aaron's eyes narrowed at Daelan, like he was trying to decide if Daelan was mocking or not. For once, the expression on Daelan's face seemed more serious than sardonic. Aaron nodded and left it at that.

"Do we contact the Feebs, then?" Kindra wasn't fond of any communication with the alphabet agencies—not when versions of her face were wanted on four continents for a rather impressive collection of crimes—but she also wasn't keen on the idea of Marks's kids, if he even had any, getting murdered . . . or worse.

"Yes." Cassidy turned to the computer and shifted back to the main folder Marks had sent them. "We have a contact—we met while playing bodyguard for someone the Marshals couldn't protect. It should be possible for us to get him a message about the threat against Isaac's family."

"Do you think he'll actually listen?" Kindra asked.

"We have to hope he will," Hugo said, his voice heavy with concern and frustration. "It's all we can do for now."

"No." Cassidy typed a coded message and clicked Send. "*All* we can do is get this information transferred to someone we can trust at the FBI."

"'Someone we can trust at the FBI' seems oxymoronic to me," Kindra muttered. Only Ryce laughed.

Dru blinked at the screen. "That folder has over ten thousand files in it, Mother."

"That we were going to have to decipher and categorize anyway," Cassidy reminded her. "We're just shifting the timeline a little. And keeping our eyes open for a hidden message for Marks's family.

If . . ." Her hands paused on the keyboard. "If it had been me, I would've tried to leave something behind."

"So we're looking for a possibly embedded, probably hidden, most likely heavily encoded message inside a mountain of embedded, hidden, heavily encoded information." Dru shook her head. "This is worse than looking for a needle in a haystack. This is looking for *hay* in a haystack."

"Then we better get started, don't you think?" Hugo asked.

Kindra wanted to bang her head against the metal table. She didn't, but she wanted to.

Chapter Nineteen

2035 : MONDAY, FEBRUARY 22

Cassidy, Daelan, Hugo, Bernard, and Aaron had dived into deciphering the mass of information Isaac Marks had sent. It seemed to include everything that Kindra had stolen from Bernard last week and a whole lot more. Thousands of files more.

That had left Dru, Ryce, and Kindra with a backlog of security footage to review, current footage to monitor, and a distinct lack of interaction with anyone else. The cycles shifted incessantly—sleep, training, computers, repeat—and if not for the voices of other people in the other section of the warehouse, Kindra might have believed she was alone.

Kindra blinked, wincing at the burn of her eyes. How long had she been staring at the screens, watching strangers come and go? How long had it been since she blinked? Her eyes felt bloodshot and so dry they were almost sticky.

She glanced at the clock in the corner of the screen and bit back a groan. Four hours. It had been four hours since she got out of this effing uncomfortable, uncushioned folding chair. Looking down at her annotations on the legal pad in front of her, Kindra mentally shrugged. She'd finally found the pattern.

"You know, you *can* ask for breaks." Ryce pulled up a chair, close enough for quiet conversation, far enough away to jump out of range if Kindra decided to take a swing at him. "Cassidy and Hugo aren't slave drivers."

Like Amett and Odira. Ryce had left the words unsaid, but Kindra was positive they'd both heard the silent end of that sentence.

"I prefer being busy." She wasn't ready to talk about their family with Ryce. She couldn't even look at him yet without an impossibly complex tangle of emotion rising in her throat and a thousand angry questions dancing on her tongue. She nudged the legal pad at him instead. "Check it out."

"Shit. It's been years since I had to read this code," Ryce muttered, rubbing his eyes before picking up the pad and studying the page.

Kindra's eyebrows furrowed. She hadn't even thought about the fact that she'd written everything in the Westons' shorthand. It was habit. Forcibly ingrained habit.

"Am I reading this right?" Ryce sat up straighter, his eyes narrowed. "Three different limos and three different cars in rotation every weekday and switching between . . . four different clients?" He shook his head. "The math on this is insane. How the hell did you even spot this kind of a pattern? I barely want to call it a pattern. It's too consarn random."

Hearing the Calvers' curse out of Ryce's mouth made Kindra mentally wince. *Don't think about it. If you strangle him, they'll kill you. Or at least kick you out of here.*

"This guy was the key." Kindra pushed aside the stinging reminder that Ryce had spent years becoming part of someone *else's* family and found the still frame she'd pulled from the video. The drivers looked like a matching set while in uniform, but one of them had a rose tattooed on the right side of his neck, just above his shirt collar. "Once I had his schedule worked out, the rest was easy."

"Easy. Right. Spotting a quad-pronged cyclic permutation in real time is always easy." Ryce studied the picture on the screen, then glanced at Kindra with a smirk in his eyes.

"Sera would've spotted it faster." The steel running under her tone turned the words into a pointed jab at how little he knew his own family. A needle-sharp prod Kindra couldn't help making.

The smile in his eyes faded. "Would she?"

"That girl is like a walking computer. With a really vulgar mouth and a dark sense of humor."

"She always had a dark sense of humor." Ryce turned his attention toward the notes again. "Seraphina was a lot like Odira. Too much like."

Kindra should have had something to say in the silence that followed, either agreement or argument. She couldn't make herself do either, feeling lost in no-man's-land between the two. Like a civilian wandering accidentally through a war zone.

Ryce was alive. Odira and Amett had blacklisted her. Sera had tried to kill her. Only emotional and mental distance kept her brain from overloading and shutting down. Kindra knew that, like ignoring a debt to a hit squad, it wouldn't work for long. The debt was always there, and one day someone would come to collect.

"Who's that?"

Kindra almost turned around and kissed Dru for appearing before Ryce could say anything else. Dru leaned over them, one hand on Kindra's shoulder for balance. "Not my type, but he's still kinda cute for a suit."

"He's the key to this." Ryce held up the pad of notes. "Kindra found a quad-prong cyclic permutation in the rotation of the drivers."

"A what? Seriously?" Dru's hand dropped from Kindra's shoulder as she straightened. "Hey!" she yelled across the room. "We've got a key."

Cassidy and Hugo immediately abandoned their inspection of possible disguises, Daelan his latest explosive invention, and Bernard his self-defense lesson with Aaron.

"You guys are getting *way* too excited." Kindra shook her head. "This pattern alone isn't going to give us much."

"It's more than we had this morning," Dru said.

Ryce got up so Cassidy could take the second seat at the computer. Everyone else gathered behind, silently waiting for an update. That apparently Dru and Ryce expected *Kindra* to give.

She cleared her throat and quickly explained about the tattoo. "Once I created a calendar and filled in the days he drove either Hadley or the other three superparanoid majordomos, I spotted a trend in how the drivers appeared." She brought up an Excel file with dates in the far left column, and four other columns with strings of numbers one through six. "I gave each driver a number and tracked the days they showed up. The guys look a lot alike, on purpose, I'm sure—harder to tell apart and track the pattern—but the same crew of six is working for each client."

"It's really only six guys?" Daelan asked.

Kindra nodded. "Garret Hadley is far too careful and controlled to use a slew of random people for something as close-quarters as a driver. This guy demands background checks that look into second cousins." Kindra raised an eyebrow. "And that's for a secretarial position. Think about what he'd demand for someone who has access to his home and his schedule."

"Who does the checks again?" Hugo asked.

"In-house," Cassidy said. "The ex-G-man."

"Right." Hugo shook his head, nose slightly crunched like he was berating himself for forgetting.

"They have a Feeb?" Kindra asked.

"Matthew Nevarez," Cassidy said. "He wasn't ever charged, but he resigned from the FBI eight years ago under a haze of suspicion. Everything from tampering with evidence to selling state secrets. They didn't have enough to charge him with anything, but no way was he innocent." Kindra opened her mouth, but Cassidy cut her off. "And before you ask, no, there's not a connection between him and Isaac Marks. They were working out of different states during the overlap of their employment, and never even worked the same case from a distance."

"All right. And Garret picked him up after he resigned."

"Maybe," Cassidy said. "Garret might've been one of his outside bosses all along."

"Atropos bless it, that's . . . that's good." Kindra nodded. Cassidy wasn't the only one who stared at her for that comment. It didn't get any better when Kindra added, "The pattern alone didn't give us anything, but with this? It's perfect."

Cassidy was the one who finally asked, "Why?"

"Because he's a traitor willing to sell his bosses out for money. They've seen him do it. Hell, they probably exploited the fact for years." Kindra shrugged. "Once people know you're capable of that kind of treachery, it's easy to convince them you've done it again."

"Okay. Great. So we paint him with tar, feather him, and hang him like a consarn piñata," Daelan said. "That will get us what, exactly? They'll just hire someone else."

Dru figured it out first. "It'll give us a window. A day, maybe two if we time it right."

"To do *what*?" Aaron asked.

Kindra watched the light go on in Daelan's face. Cassidy and Hugo were only a second behind. Daelan laughed as he filled in the blanks for Aaron and Bernard. "Switch out a driver."

"The companies run their own security checks, but they're easier to cheat." Hugo smirked as he talked. "We can insert our own driver in the rotation."

Cassidy glanced at her husband before her eyes returned to the screens. It was only a few seconds before she blinked, brought up Garret's picture, and turned to face the group gathered behind her. "If we place someone on this rotation, we'll expose ourselves more than we have since the beginning of this. Staying out of sight hasn't given us all of the information we need, but it's kept us alive to look for more. We do this, and there's a chance someone won't make it." Her wounded shoulder shifted slightly. "Garret pays well for very good, very *persistent* bodyguards."

Bodyguards, even persistent ones, could be dealt with, especially with a team this big. The more pressing problem, and the one no one seemed to want to talk about much around Kindra, wasn't the bodyguards—it was the Westons and Javier Martinez's team. Only six people, but those six people could rip an unpatchable hole in the Calvers' team. In their *family*.

Hugo rolled his neck and released a breath. "So the question becomes, is it worth the risk?"

Like she suspected, they were moving on without mentioning the lingering threat. Fine, then. Kindra wasn't ready to force the issue into the open either.

"You all *do* realize that grabbing Garret will send anyone else involved in the black-market business into deep, *deep* hiding. Like secret-fortress-buried-in-the-Mariana-Trench hiding." Daelan pointed down for extra emphasis. "Or maybe they'll just hire global-peace-summit-level security details. Either way, it won't be good for us if we don't get what we need the first time around."

Cassidy nodded. "So we need to make the most of the opportunity, and we need to have multiple backups and contingencies in place. It means getting Bernard to safety, with a copy of everything we have, *before* we make a move."

"Have we worked out how much control Garret has over the Redwell low-orbit satellites?" Daelan asked.

"I don't think it's much, but even a small amount of influence could be dangerous for us," Hugo said. "The low-orbit military satellites could be hell if they manage to locate us."

Kindra wanted to laugh. The chances of surviving this mission were getting smaller by the minute. She didn't even have a real reason to be here except that she had nowhere else to go and a professional hit team was trying to kill her. The enemy of her enemy was her friend. And now Kindra would be risking her life on a mission that only mattered to her frenemy. And her should-be-dead brother.

Not that Garret doesn't deserve to perish in a pile of smoldering rubble, but am I really willing to die to make it happen?

Even contemplating it seemed insane. But here she was. Contemplating.

"Isn't the primary liaison for their military contracts an exec who uses this ridiculous driver schedule?" Cassidy asked.

"Yes," Daelan confirmed, his eyes shifting like he was reading something in his head. "Lillian French is ex-navy. Retired as Lieutenant Commander French, but never saw service in a war zone. She's held the liaison position since 1999."

"Does she have anything to do with Garret's side projects?" Kindra asked. "If she does, we should grab both of them at the same time."

"Not everyone has to die, baby," Dru murmured, a reminder of their conversation the day of her . . . kidnapping? Rescue?

"I'm just making sure I have all the relevant information."

"We don't think she's involved." Cassidy turned slightly, shooting Kindra and Dru a vaguely amused half smile. "Lillian French and Garret Hadley came up the company ranks together, so we've kept an eye on her. There's no chance of her qualifying for sainthood, and she *is* closer to Garret than most of the other executives, but we don't think she's got anything to do with the drug running."

"I'd like to call attention to the fact that we're also kind of persistently ignoring two major factors while making this plan." Ryce had his imperiously precise voice on, one he only ever used when he was getting annoyed. It was both strangely relieving and horrendously painful to still be able to pinpoint his tones. "There are two rather notorious snipers aiming in our direction."

"Amett can't shoot anymore." The words burst out of Kindra the moment she realized that Ryce didn't know. Her brother didn't know that their father had been diagnosed with a debilitating neurological condition.

Every one of the Calvers spun to look at her, but Ryce was the one who stutter-screamed, "Wh-what?"

"We didn't find out until the day he missed . . ." Kindra didn't say his name, but she couldn't keep herself from glancing in Bernard's direction. Swallowing, she dragged her gaze back to Ryce. "He's been diagnosed with—well, it's either essential tremor or Parkinson's. Doc J wasn't sure because apparently there isn't any real way to *be* sure? It'll depend on the progression and his other symptoms, but . . . yeah."

It took every ounce of willpower to keep her eyes on Ryce and not on the concrete floor of the warehouse. "He can't guarantee accuracy anymore because of the tremor, so Odira moved him to logistics. I was supposed to switch off on the wet work with Odira, but . . . that'll probably be split between her and Sera now."

Kindra had tried for carelessness to mask the uncomfortable curl of betrayal settling in her stomach; she wasn't sure it worked. She shouldn't care—she *shouldn't*—considering the people she'd sometimes called family would quite literally kill her the next time they saw her, but it was hard to lay aside sixteen years of conditioning in a few days.

Cassidy's gaze flicked from Kindra to Ryce to Hugo in quick succession. "That is . . . good to be aware of. Thank you, Kindra. I know that—"

Beroop! Beroop!

A red alert flashed on one of the computers. Aaron and Kindra jumped back as the Calvers and Ryce dived into motion. Bernard wasn't fast enough and ended up on his ass when Dru ran for the office door.

Ryce locked the gun trunks and hefted them into one of the cargo vans. Hugo met Dru at the office door, grabbing two folded cots and a pile of blankets from her. He yelled over his shoulder, "Is it them?"

"Almost definitely." Cassidy's focus on the multiple warnings popping up on the screens was intense and complete. "We have motion in the northeast quadrant, but nothing visible on camera. And an SUV we logged this morning is back. South edge of the property."

Hugo placed the cots into the van and raced back to the office for more. Ryce had moved on to the tables of tech, packing up everything not in immediate use by Cassidy. The tension in the air made Kindra itch. She went to help Dru, needing something to do.

And you do not want to be here if the Westons are about to blow this place to Hades.

"Who left today?" Hugo demanded.

They hadn't given Kindra any tasks that took her out of the warehouse—and she hadn't asked—but the others went into the world at least once a day. Picking up food, checking on surveillance equipment, dropping notes in the mail, or whatever else needed doing.

"Aaron, Mom, and me." Daelan's eyes were on the one active screen even as his hands disassembled another computer. The SUV had pulled up alongside the west gate. From the shape of the shadow in the driver's seat, Kindra guessed that it was Amett. Amett and, most likely, a really big gun and a shit-ton of explosives, weapons for which accuracy wouldn't matter because brute force did more than enough damage.

"Is there a chance you were spotted?" Hugo asked as Dru and Kindra finished clearing out the office. Dru moved to the free weights and mats in the far corner, but Hugo stopped at the computers, placing one hand on Cassidy's good shoulder and one on Daelan's. "Something must have given us away. Neither of you saw *anything*?"

Daelan shook his head. Cassidy looked up, her expression anxious and strained. "I'm not at my best, though, Hugo," she said, her voice low. "I can't say I didn't miss something."

Hugo squeezed her shoulder. "Done is gone, love." Releasing his wife and son, he turned and speared Aaron with a steady stare. "Aaron?"

Aaron halted in the middle of folding a training mat. "If they saw me, I never saw them."

"Well, they sure as shit saw something," Hugo muttered.

Ryce grunted as he hefted a crate of tech. "The bogeymen have come."

"You were one of those bogeymen once," Kindra reminded him as she dropped a crate into the van.

His glare stopped her dead. "Only by birth."

Ryce slammed his crate into the van and pushed past Kindra to fill the next one. She wanted to grab the first solid object she could find and pitch it at the back of his head.

"Retreat plan Juliet," Cassidy ordered. "Departure in less than six minutes. Essentials-only if we can't pack everything."

"We've got movement along the northern perimeter." Daelan's eyes were glued to a large tablet. "Two, as far as I can tell."

"Exploratory or explosive?" Hugo asked Cassidy.

"A breath of the latter and a lot of the former, probably," Cassidy said. "And we only get that reprieve because this place is owned by Garret. Odira won't cause damage to the client's property unless she has to."

Atropos bless. It's eerie how well she knows Odira. Kindra lobbed a duffel bag of clothes into one of the vans.

Hugo helped Aaron load the collapsible sparring dummy. "Let's just make sure they don't find anything worthwhile."

Everyone moved in silence after that except for Bernard, who silently stayed out of the way. The room was clear less than five minutes after the alarms.

Then Cassidy started issuing orders. "Dru, you're with Kindra. Aaron, you drive, I'll direct—Bernard, you'll ride with us."

They abandoned the passenger van Dru and Kindra had arrived in days ago, and split between the two cargo vans, the Challenger, and the Ducati. Dru grabbed Kindra's hand and led her to the second van; Cassidy took Aaron and Bernard to the first. Glancing back, Kindra watched Ryce swing his leg over the Ducati. Daelan slid into the passenger seat of the Challenger his father had already brought to life.

Dru shoved Kindra into the van and shut the door behind her, running around to the driver's side. In less than ten seconds, they were belted in, the engine was on, and the van was in gear. Though everything so far had been impressively well coordinated, it had also been predictable, all of it very much like what Odira and Amett would've done.

Then things skewed.

Along one wall, there were six doors wide enough for a van, but their cavalcade turned to face a wall of solid concrete. A thick, steel-reinforced wall of solid concrete.

Kindra glanced at Dru. "This seems like the opposite of a good idea."

"Presto." Something heavy and solid *thunked*, and Dru smirked. "Chango."

The wall in front of them shifted, but instead of rolling aside or up as Kindra might've expected, it moved *down*. The whole thing dropped like a drawbridge, shifting to create a steep ramp that disappeared into darkness.

"Okay. *That* I wasn't expecting."

Dru huffed a half laugh. "If we're lucky, neither will the bogeymen."

"They're working for Garret. You think they won't know about a huge secret tunnel in a Redwell-owned warehouse?" They passed under the main entrance and began to descend. Kindra had to fight the urge to duck. The ceiling was inches away from the roof of the van.

"Yes, but Garret likes his secrets. Whatever information she got about this warehouse probably came from the official records—and this tunnel isn't on those records. We're betting he won't have told her about it either."

"And if you're wrong?" Kindra asked.

Dru shrugged. "Then get ready to run."

The door whirred as the wall lifted back into place. Even though the van's windows were closed, Kindra heard the unmistakable *thud-hiss* of a hermetic seal. Garret hadn't been messing around when he built this. That door was meant to keep everything and everyone out of this tunnel. Even light.

Excepting small LED strips along the floor, the tunnel was pitch-black. No one turned their lights on. They navigated by the glowing panels and saw only by the dashboard lights, which were a far more vibrant red than should've been possible.

"How long is this thing?" Kindra kept her voice quiet, almost a whisper. It seemed wrong to talk louder than that in such darkness.

"A couple of miles." Dru's voice wasn't much louder. "It goes under the St. Johns River and comes out near an industrial park north of us."

"Owned by Garret, I assume." Kindra waited until the shadow that was Dru nodded. "What makes you think Odira isn't watching that one too?"

"She is. But it's easy to avoid a camera when you know it's there."

"And you know where they are?"

She heard Dru shift. "Because of the tunnel exit, we've had our own cameras there. We watched her install hers yesterday."

And no one had said a word to Kindra about the sighting.

It's always need to know. And no one ever thinks I need to effing know.

"Whatever you're thinking, you're wrong." Dru's voice was loud. Strong.

The words jolted Kindra enough that her thoughts started tumbling from her mouth. "I'm wrong that you guys saw what was happening, decided to keep it need-to-know, and then put me on the wrong side of that equation?"

"No, that part's right."

Kindra grunted. "So where'd I get it wrong?"

"The why."

"*Why* doesn't matter."

"Bullshit. The why *always* matters. Or . . ." Dru tilted her head; the red light playing across her face made her look almost demonic. "Well, I'd say the why matters about 82.3 percent of the time."

"That's ridiculously specific."

"Invented statistics usually are."

It took the beat of silence that followed for Kindra to realize that Dru wouldn't say anything else. Not unless Kindra asked for more. Biting back a groan, she gave in. "Why did they do it, then?"

"Not they. Me."

Kindra blinked, an icy, leaden weight settling solidly in her chest. "What?"

"My parents didn't make the call. I did."

The weight shifted lower, dropping into Kindra's stomach with a *thud.* Why was it so much worse to contemplate that *Dru* had been the one to cut Kindra out of the loop?

Maybe because you thought she was the only one of this fucked-up family who seemed to trust you.

"It wasn't because I don't trust you."

Kindra stopped breathing. *Shit. Did I just say that aloud?*

"I just . . . There are some things we're better off not knowing, okay?"

"No." Kindra shook her head and forced herself to start breathing again. "It's not okay. What in Tartarus are you talking about?"

Dru sighed, the sound carrying more exhaustion than Kindra had heard since their endless hours chasing Aaron down the East Coast. "Odira is in clear shot almost the whole time, and she's talking to someone, probably Sera, on the other side of the comm. If you can read lips, you get her half of the conversation."

Scoffing—not avoiding the real subject or anything like that—Kindra asked, "Who in our line of work can't read lips?"

"My dad," Dru said immediately. "He'll catch one word in ten if he's lucky."

Kindra couldn't think of anything to say after that. *Get it over with. They already tried to kill you. It's not like you don't know what's coming.*

"What'd she say?"

"Sera must've been reporting that they still hadn't picked up your signal." Dru shifted. "Odira said that the signal didn't matter because you were dead, or you would be as soon as they found you."

This wasn't news, and it shouldn't have hurt, but it *did*. Not in the way she'd seen betrayal metaphorically slice people open from navel to nose, no. Instead, this reminder of how little her parents and her sister cared stung and ached and nagged like an old wound reawakened. Worse, she knew it only hurt because she had a comparison now that hadn't existed before.

Kindra had seen almost every kind of family. Poverty stricken, strung out, and struggling; poor but gracefully holding it together; rich, loving, and happy; so consumed by power and wealth, they forgot they had a family; contently married after a few decades; married and divorced so many times they'd lost count. Kindra had seen examples of it all, but she hadn't ever been able to compare those families to her own. It would've made as much sense as comparing grapes and grenades.

Then came the Calvers. In the past few days, she'd seen the obvious love Hugo and Cassidy had for each other, a love they willingly and unstintingly shared with their children—the biological ones and the adopted one. She'd also seen how that didn't change the way they worked, didn't make them weak or inefficient or inept. If anything, it made them stronger. They were a team *and* a family, and they did both well.

Kindra had never been part of a family, only a member of a team. Now, seeing what it could've been like, she felt robbed. She wished Hugo and Cassidy had kidnapped her when they left.

Or that Ryce had included her in his plans.

He'd been the one she leaned on emotionally, the only one she ever *could* lean on without feeling weak. When he vanished—*died*—she'd cut that part of herself off. It felt like it was trying to regrow now, but she wasn't sure she should let it. She didn't know if she could handle losing it a second time.

"You don't have to protect me from Odira. Not like that, anyway," Kindra finally said. Her voice sounded reassuringly steady to her own ears. "I lived with her for sixteen years. I know what she is."

"She's your mother."

Kindra shrugged. "Maybe. But she's never been my mom."

The subject dropped, and Kindra was glad because she had nothing else to say.

She flinched but didn't pull away when Dru slid her fingers down Kindra's bare arm. Their fingers intertwined, and Kindra stared at the shape they made in the eerie red light. She wanted to tell Dru that she didn't need the comfort—and she didn't—but it felt nice. Purposeless touch wasn't something Kindra had experienced much of, but she'd seen it, and she'd always thought it looked warm.

She'd been right.

Honestly, eff it. Kindra was taking the comfort. Their linked hands heated and the oddity of the connection made her fingers feel strange, but accepting this from Dru didn't hollow her out. Didn't weaken her. It almost made her feel as though, whatever she was losing, it wasn't anything when measured against what she gained. Like the chance to keep the Calvers, even if only for the length of this one job. Even if she had to move on at the end of this.

Even if she died before it was over.

She tightened her fingers around Dru's and traced a path back and forth across her index finger. They spent the rest of the short drive in silence.

Holding hands, of all the stupid things.

Chapter Twenty

On the third level of a mostly empty parking garage, the Calvers and Aaron Tanvers said good-bye to Bernard Gasper. It was only going to get more difficult—more dangerous—from here on out. They couldn't hand him off to the Marshals; the risk of a leak or a hack was too high. Lucky for Bernard, the Marshals weren't the only people in the country with a mission to protect those who couldn't protect themselves. Cassidy and Hugo apparently had ties to a private organization whose members' loyalty wasn't called into question quite as often as government employees'.

The exchange must've been in the works for a while, but Kindra had been left completely out of this loop. She didn't ask where Bernard was going or who the eerily nondescript white guy driving the windowless van was, and none of the Calvers told her. If she didn't know, she couldn't pass the information to Odira or anyone else. Easy. She swallowed the resentment, told herself it wasn't the same as Odira keeping her in the dark, and shut her mouth.

What she *did* know was that these people could get a copy of the flash drive Bernard had in his pocket into the right hands at the FBI—Isaac Marks's onetime training partner, Special Agent in Charge Altair Ameen Zaman. The transfer might even take some of the heat off Bernard. If the Feds already had the data, the damage Bernard could do was done. He became a far lower priority for elimination. Or that was the hope.

Kindra hung back for the entire five-minute production, watching Bernard hug Cassidy and Dru, gently tousle Daelan's hair, clap Ryce on the shoulder, and warmly shake Hugo's and Aaron's hands. Then he met Kindra's eyes and excused himself from the group, steadily crossing the ten feet or so that separated them. Unsure what to say to the man she'd tried to torture and kill, Kindra evened her stance, kept her hands in plain sight, and waited.

Bernard stopped two feet away, his hands in the pockets of his jeans and his head tilted as he considered Kindra. "I don't know what to make of you."

"Neither does anyone else." Right now, she didn't know what to make of herself either.

"If you have any compassion at all, help the Calvers finish this." Not a plea or an order. It was like he was making sure she knew the option existed, that there was a choice to make.

"Avoid windows and stay out of sight for a while," Kindra said. "Just in case the people coming after you are smarter than whoever will be protecting you."

He studied her face for a moment, then nodded once and walked straight to the open door of the van. After he climbed inside, the door closed and the van drove off, turning down the exit ramp and disappearing from view.

Kindra hoped she never saw that man again.

Setup always took longer than teardown. Moving the Citadel was no exception.

The house they ended up at was small, but it bordered another industrial section of Jacksonville and came with a two-car garage that meant the motorcycle, the coupe, and one of the vans could be hidden when not in use. Another bonus? Of the eight houses on this block, five were for sale or rent, and all of those were currently vacant.

The Calvers were obviously masters of urban black ops hide-and-go-seek.

Six hours after they arrived at their non-Garret-owned, and therefore somewhat less fortified hideout, Kindra pulled the last cot from a van and carried it to the south bedroom.

"That gives us, what?" Ryce was asking as she neared the living room. "A week? Ten days, tops. This is a lot to pull off in ten days."

"I know." Cassidy stood by the sliding glass door that led to a small backyard surrounded by an eight-foot fence. "We need to find the right trigger."

Kindra spotted Dru leaning against the wall and moved in that direction. She didn't look at Dru or touch her or get close enough for their arms to "accidentally" brush, but as she settled an arm's length away, Kindra cursed herself six ways from Sunday for giving in even this much to her ill-advised infatuation.

"There might be something useful in Isaac's information, but we haven't finished analyzing it yet," Daelan reminded Cassidy.

Cassidy tilted her head, a somewhat sardonic smile on her face. "Then I suppose everyone knows what they're doing tonight, don't they?"

"Oh, fuck a fucking duck." Hugo ran a hand over his short hair. "Please tell me the coffeemaker made it into one of the vans."

"You curse more than you used to," Kindra observed.

"You're older than you used to be." Hugo smirked. "I figure that, by now, there's not much I can say that you haven't already heard."

"True enough." Kindra's eyes lingered on the screen that showed Lillian French—*the military liaison*—climbing out of her limo in front of Redwell, Inc.'s global headquarters. She glanced up at the building, and the camera caught her bright smile, but Kindra was pretty sure that expression was a lie. Her movements were too stiff. "So, what do we only have seven to ten days to pull off? And why ten? What happens in ten days?"

Hugo glanced at Kindra. "You mean besides giving a couple of expert trackers and an ex-Fed that much time to find us?" He returned his attention to the screens. "Garret Hadley leaves the country in two weeks, and he'll be gone for an undetermined length of time."

"That means we have ten days to pull off your plan." The look on Dru's face when she met Kindra's eyes was somewhere between expectant and proud.

"*My* plan? You mean the thing with framing the Fed and switching drivers?" Kindra raised an eyebrow and glanced at the Calvers. "We're actually doing that? And you guys want it to happen in *ten days*?"

Cassidy nodded. "We already set up several bank accounts that track back to Nevarez, accounts that show steady deposits from untraceable locations. We need to deepen the surveillance on him, but we have the beginnings in place."

The trigger. "You need someone to find something incriminating so Garret goes looking for the accounts and blacklists him. Or kills him, depending on the mood."

"Not like he'd be a big loss to humanity," Ryce muttered.

Kindra shrugged, not caring one way or the other. Dru and Daelan glanced at each other, and there was judgment in their eyes: condemnation of Ryce for essentially dismissing a human life. Kindra almost laughed. Apparently some of Odira and Amett remained ingrained in Ryce's head despite his best effort to erase them. She was glad Dru and Daelan would likely never meet Seraphina. That girl could get positively gleeful planning a job. They'd hate her.

"So we find the right bit of information, something valuable and harmful, and make sure Mr. Matthew Nevarez is caught with it at the wrong time in the wrong place." Cassidy seemed to be thinking out loud, working through the problem.

Kindra couldn't keep herself from shaking her head and saying, "It won't be enough."

"It's what we have," Hugo said.

Ryce sighed. "She's right."

"Unless what we plant on him is nearly catastrophic for Garret, it won't be enough without doubt already in place," Daelan said.

There was a beat of silence. Cassidy and Hugo did that silent communication thing again, their expressions shifting slightly, like they actually were talking telepathically. Finally, Cassidy simply asked, "Whisper campaign?"

"And who's gonna run that?" Dru huffed. "The Westons have pictures of me in a couple of different disguises, and they know exactly what you two look like. They'll have told Garret about us, and he probably passed it along to Javier's team. Dae might be able to sneak in undetected, but he doesn't do characters well. Ryce is supposed to be dead, and he *could* play it, but he does intimidation better than infiltration. Plus, if Odira spots him, we lose four years of holding on to the element of surprise."

Ryce looked a little pleased by the statement, and seemed to shrug off the reminder of what would probably happen if Odira ever realized he was alive.

"Garret won't know Aaron," Cassidy said. "Or Kindra."

"Odira and Amett most definitely gave up everything they had on Cassidy and me," Hugo said, nodding slowly. "No way did they reveal the fact that their own daughter defected. It makes them look weak."

"They wouldn't have had to say I was their daughter." Kindra worked hard to keep her voice low and steady. "They could've made me look like *your* daughter."

"Would they have gone that way?" Hugo asked Cassidy.

"I don't know. If Odira was pissed enough, she might've." Cassidy sighed and gently rubbed her bandaged shoulder. "I still think Aaron and Kindra are our best bets."

Dru's arms tensed. "I don't like it."

"I'm sure you don't, but it's not your call." Cassidy almost smiled, a softness that changed everything about the statement it accompanied. Coming from Odira, that reprimand would've bitten like a whip. Cassidy said it like a gentle reminder that they couldn't control other people's lives.

Kindra shifted against the wall, weighing the chance to get out of this house against the very real possibility that Redwell's security might flag her as soon as she walked through the door. *Whatever.* "I'll do it if we've got what I'll need to get in."

"What about you? You're in, right, Sergeant?" Daelan asked with a grin.

"Oorah," Aaron agreed.

Daelan's head cocked. "You know where that came from?"

"What? 'Oorah'?" Aaron shrugged slightly. "Back in boot, they told me it translates to 'kill' in Turkish or something."

"Yeah, I've heard that story too. It's completely wrong, but I've heard it." Daelan grinned. "What if I told you it has more to do with submarines than kill shots?"

Aaron snorted. "I'd call bullshit."

"Seriously. Look it up. There's a story that back in '53, a team in the First Amphibious Reconnaissance Company traveled by sub a lot while they were stationed in Korea. That noise the alarms make when the sub dives? *Aarugha*," Daelan mimicked. "They started using that as their war cry. It caught on, and then it morphed into 'oorah' over the years."

Aaron stared at Daelan for a second. Then he blinked and nodded once. "Makes sense. Boredom and circumstance, man. Right up there with necessity as the mother of invention."

"It's messed up that he can keep so much random trivia locked in that tiny head of his," Ryce said, a playful smile on his face when he looked at Daelan.

Dru grunted and absently stroked the end of her black braid. "This *job* is messed up."

"Everything Garret Hadley is involved in is," Hugo said. Behind him, Daelan and Aaron had launched into an in-depth discussion of the etymology of military slang. Hugo smiled and slid his hand around Dru's shoulder, pulling her off the wall and into a one-armed hug. "C'mon, Drury Lane. If you're so worried about our volunteers, you can help me set up their identities."

Kindra watched them leave, stiffening when Ryce stepped into the spot Dru had occupied. With the exception of the morning when she explained the cyclic permutation, she'd managed to avoid spending time alone with him. It couldn't possibly last forever, but would it be better to get it over with now or walk away before he had a chance to say anything?

It's not like it's going to get any easier . . . ever.

"She likes you, you know."

He cannot be serious. That *is what he wants to talk about?* "Ryce, we are *not* going to gossip about girls."

Her brother smiled and didn't relent. "She does."

"Picked up on that, thanks." Kindra slid her hands into the pockets of her jeans—because otherwise she might wrap them around his throat and demand answers to questions almost half a decade old. "Poor judgment on her part."

"It's probably my fault. At least partially." He ran his fingers through his dark hair, barely disarranging his thick, short curls.

A lot of things are your fault. The words were on the tip of her tongue, but Kindra bit them back, managing to ask, "How's that?" instead.

"She's been listening to me tell stories about you and Sera for years now." His broad, muscled shoulders somehow looked small as he curved them inward. In that moment, with that stance, it was eerie how closely he resembled Amett the day their father came back from Doc J. "I missed you. I may have made you into a cross between a fairy-tale princess and the knight who rescued her."

"That explains a lot." About Dru's opinion of her, but not about Ryce. Kindra tried to imagine what kind of fairy tale she could ever play a role in. It would have to be a dark, effed-up story. On the plus side, Ryce's explanation deflated a small amount of air from the balloon of anger that had been filling in her chest. "She always seemed to have too much backstory on me and a whole shitload of unrealistic expectations."

Ryce shook his head, his eyes never leaving Kindra's. "She has hopes, not expectations. There's a difference."

"Is there? They seem pretty similar to me." And they both seemed unrealistic. Hopes got dashed and destroyed, ground into dust under the heel of someone's boot. Expectations were impossible to meet in the first place.

"Expectations can't usually be lived up to," Ryce said. "Hopes are mutable. They shift as the situation does. They can be realized a lot of the time." He paused for a breath and shrugged. "As long as the person doing the hoping isn't completely delusional."

"That vote is still out on Dru."

Ryce chuckled. "Smart-ass. Don't try to tell me you don't like her. She seems like she'd be just your type."

"What? She's not *your* type?" Kindra shot back. "Or maybe Mr. Rose Tattoo is more your speed?"

"Neither of them. Not even a little."

"No?" She made herself leer. "I liked Rose Tattoo. I'd do him."

"You'd do anyone."

Her nose wrinkled. "Not *anyone*." Not if she was the one picking her partners. "I'm bi, not a nympho." Then the conversation really registered. "And how the hell would you know what my type is, anyway? They'd only sent me out on a couple of those jobs before you *died*."

He shrugged, refused to meet her eyes, and then avoided the question entirely. "You were lucky. You know how hard it is to fake your way through that shit every time?" Ryce shuddered. "Hated it when Odira made me do that."

Kindra blinked, a little more of her anger fading as memories realigned in her head. The briefings when Ryce's eyes would go distant and empty, or the early mornings when he'd return to their base of operations and take a shower that lasted over an hour. She'd never considered that the command seductions were what had caused that bleak discomfort in her brother.

"Was it the guys or the girls?" Kindra wasn't sure she wanted to know the answer. If Ryce had hated it that much, then . . .

"Neither was all that great, but it was a little easier with some—a very few—of the girls." Ryce still wouldn't look at her. "Even then . . . Whatever. It doesn't matter. Even if I'd told Odira when I realized I was asexual, it wouldn't have changed anything."

The sexual side of things had rarely bothered her. It was a physical skill, something that needed to be done, and most of the time— unless the mark was wholly disgusting—she hadn't *hated* it. They did what the job needed, and that was that. Obedience was expected and enforced. Kindra resisted the urge to touch her left wrist—Odira had almost broken it two years ago when Kindra had resisted a mission-necessary task.

Seraphina's skill with the technical side of the jobs had mostly kept her away from those moments, but if placed in those same situations, would Sera be more like Kindra or Ryce? Would she find the concept appealing at all, even if the individuals were sometimes straight out of Tartarus, or would she have to close her eyes and wish herself somewhere else to get through each encounter? Kindra didn't know the answer because the question hadn't come up. Suddenly she was glad of that.

"But that's not what we're talking about here, Kinny. This isn't one of Odira's seductions. What Dru wants is different."

There wasn't any way to deny that. Instead, she shrugged and told him a version of the truth. "Doesn't matter. A hookup is a horrible idea, and anything more than that is impossible."

"Why?" His forehead creased, and his nose wrinkled.

"Because at the end of this I'll either be dead or on the run."

Ryce's eyes widened. "You really think those are your only options?"

"In all probability, yes." She hoped for a third option—the same option Ryce had found—but it didn't feel possible enough to trust yet.

For a moment, Ryce studied her face like her thoughts were transcribed on her skin. Then he swallowed and blinked heavily. "I'm sorry."

Dread dropped onto Kindra's chest. "For what?"

"Leaving you behind with them."

All of the anger rushed back into her chest, filling the balloon almost to bursting in seconds. She barely kept her temper in check. "I was twelve, Ryce, and you were sixteen. What could you possibly have done?"

"I could've lied to you and taken you with me that day. Or gone back to pull you out even though Hugo and Cassidy told me it'd be a suicide mission."

"Why didn't you, then? What *happened*?" The words came out sharper and louder than Kindra had intended. *Shit.*

Ryce released a short, sharp breath that made his upper body shake. The bleak, guilt-ridden look in his light-brown eyes made her pause.

Atropos bless it. Has this been eating at him this much for the last four years?

She could only guess that, yes, it had been. This much tension did not build up in a night. Or even in a week.

Kindra wanted to scream at him with all the rage of her twelve-year-old brokenhearted self. She wanted to wrap her arms around his neck and say something that might ease Ryce's remorse. Stuck between the two, she could only watch the myriad of expressions on his face and try to remember how to breathe.

"C'mon," Ryce said after a minute of strained silence, tilting his head toward the sliding glass door. "Let's get some air."

He walked out of the house, shoulders hunched. It looked like he was battling the biting winter wind in Chicago, but both the breeze and the temperature outside were mild. This was *Florida*.

The door had been left open in an attempt to rid the house of the musty, stale, unused smell that had permeated the air. Kindra wanted something solid between her and the Calvers for the duration of this conversation, so she forced the wide door—an ancient thing that was impossible to move silently—shut.

They walked to the center of the yard, each step as methodical as if they were walking through a minefield. Kindra watched Ryce, but Ryce wouldn't look at her. His eyes went everywhere else, landing most often on the crystal-clear sky.

"I spotted Cassidy and Hugo while we were on that job in Belarus—the one before Switzerland—and I . . . I begged them to take me with them." Ryce rubbed the back of his head, and Kindra knew he was tracing the inch-long scar mostly hidden by his hair. "I would've just left then, but Odira would never have stopped looking for me unless she thought I was dead."

Kindra couldn't argue. Odira was not the "live and let live" sort.

Ryce met her eyes, but looked away too quickly for Kindra to read him. "They arranged the whole thing, even set up the Alps job for us. It was Cassidy we tracked up that mountain. The blood and the gunshot and all of it, they . . ."

Four years hadn't dimmed the memory at all. "They helped you make it look like you'd been shot, had bled on the rocks, and been pushed into the river." She crossed her arms and glared at her brother. "I know what it looked like. I'm the one who fucking got there first, you asshole."

Ryce flinched as though Kindra had struck him.

"I saw the blood, and I heard the scream, but— Atropos bless it, Ryce! Why didn't you take me *with* you?"

"There wasn't time! We did all of that in a week, Kindra!" Ryce stalked closer, his hands linked behind his neck. "A week and . . . you guys fled the country two days later."

"Then why didn't you come back?" Kindra hated how young and broken her voice sounded, but she couldn't have forced the words out any other way. Not even if someone had a gun to her head.

"We did. *I* did. It just . . . It took us a while to find you guys again." Dropping his hands to Kindra's shoulders, Ryce stared down the few inches that separated them. "But if you think for one second that I didn't spend every day looking for a way to get you out of there, you don't know me anymore."

"It's been *four years*, Ryce. Of course I don't know you anymore."

He took a deep breath and held it before releasing his thoughts in one gust. "When we found you, it was . . . it was that job in Baku, Azerbaijan." His hands tightened on her shoulders. "I got there just in time to watch you seduce that guy into the alleyway, stab him, and run off laughing."

There were a lot of jobs that Kindra had mostly forgotten, because she'd forcibly erased the experience or because it wasn't worth remembering.

The Baku job had been impossible to erase.

The target had been one of the rare ones whose eyes were so cold and twisted that they gave *Kindra* the creeps. Her laughter? That had been because of the curses he'd thrown at her head after she'd sliced through *both* of his wrists before drawing her two small blades across the arteries in his throat. That laughter had been because, the day before Kindra killed him, Odira had threatened her with something very similar if she didn't pull this job off without a flaw.

Cursed ten ways to Tartarus if she failed *and* when she succeeded. The irony had been hysterical at the time.

"Who doesn't know who?" Kindra knocked his hands off and stepped back, needing the distance to keep from smacking him or wrapping her arms around his neck and crying. "It's adapt or die, remember? You weren't there, so I did what I had to do to survive."

"You just— You looked exactly like Odira, the same way that Sera has always reminded us of her, and I didn't know if you'd *want* to come with us." Ryce rubbed his hand over his face and muttered something Kindra couldn't hear. "We couldn't try to talk to you—*I* couldn't try to talk to you—unless we knew you'd listen."

"Then why'd Dru kidnap me back in New Jersey?"

"Crime of opportunity?" Ryce said it like a question, his voice sounding a little lost.

They stared at each other in the dim light of the backyard for a long, silent moment, one that was somehow both four years and only four minutes long. It stretched for miles, and those miles were littered with betrayals and dead bodies and missed opportunities and secrets and losses and spilled blood and so many things that hadn't yet been said. That might never be said.

Then Ryce tilted his head back to look at the early-morning stars.

"The Calvers have been watching Odira since the families split." Ryce's declaration was made to the sky, apropos of nothing. And he wasn't finished. "Cassidy and Hugo have done what they could to hide targets that didn't deserve to die—they've faked more than a few deaths over the years—but mostly they wanted to make sure they were ready the next time Odira took a contract from Garret Hadley."

Hands shoved wrist-deep in his pockets, Ryce met Kindra's eyes. "Okay."

He blinked. "Okay?"

"I don't know what kind of reaction you expected, but I'd kinda figured that part out already." Kindra shrugged, pretending more indifference than she felt. "Compared to the story of how you *faked your death*, this isn't really a blip on the radar, brother mine."

"I followed you guys sometimes too," Ryce said, his voice quiet and slightly hesitant.

This time his words sent a flutter through Kindra's chest. Pain? Regret? Relief? She wasn't sure what to call it.

"You remember that job in Helsinki a year ago?" Ryce asked.

"The artist-assassin." Kindra nodded. "I want one of those freaky paintbrush/blow-dart things."

Ryce huffed a laugh, and his shoulders relaxed a little. "That was kind of ingenious."

Her eyes narrowed. That job had been well after Ryce left. He shouldn't have known anything about it. "I'm guessing weapon envy wasn't why you brought that up?"

"No." His shoulders tensed again, but they didn't climb to his ears like they had earlier. "The day you found him in Market Square? I . . . There was a kid on a skateboard and . . ."

Kindra sucked in a breath, her heart beating faster and her eyes widening. "And he almost knocked me on my ass because he came out of effing *nowhere*." She swallowed and took a step closer. "That was *you*?"

Ryce nodded slowly, watching Kindra's face like it held the PIN to a Swiss bank account with unlimited funds. "There was an undocumented accomplice. That's why some of his kills seemed so impossible: he wasn't working alone." His eyes flicked down as he planted his feet wider in the slightly brown grass. "She'd spotted you, and she was about to . . . You never saw her, Kinny. You wouldn't have made it out of that square if I hadn't taken you down so Hugo could take her out."

Kindra remembered everything from that afternoon. The clear, pale-blue sky and the intensity of the sun that had made her regret not adding sunglasses to her disguise; the vibrant orange tents and stall shades; and the savory scent of *karjalanpiirakka* pastries in the air. Kindra had logged it all, but her attention had focused on the seemingly frail old man painting landscapes. The wind had carried the first bite of winter; Odira had been issuing a constant stream of instructions; tourists had flowed around her like they were a river and she was a misplaced stone; and the target had never seemed to blink as she approached.

And then a kid in a black beanie with five piercings in his lip and a tattoo covering half his face had caught the wheel of his skateboard on a loose stone and down they'd both gone. Kindra had finished the job, stabbing the artist with a needle that delivered a lethal dose of the same mixture of chemicals he used, but she'd seethed for months over not spotting Beanie Boy.

Beanie Boy was Ryce. Ryce saved my life.

Part of Kindra still wanted to punch him and rail at him, demand to know why he'd let her suffer for years thinking he'd died alone. The rest of her wanted to hug him and thank him for not forgetting about her.

Ryce grabbed her wrist and tugged her forward. She stumbled, landing with a solid *thud* against her brother's chest, his arms wrapped tight around her shoulders.

"I worked so hard to keep you alive all these years, and I just got you back," he whispered into her hair. "I don't want to lose you again."

Closing her eyes, Kindra let herself return the gesture, patting Ryce on the back and leaning into his embrace. She still didn't think she'd get to keep the Calvers if she survived this job, but . . .

"Maybe I'm wrong and we'll all make it out alive. I've been wrong before, you know." Kindra pulled away, glaring into his eyes. "Like when I thought you were dead."

Ryce grunted. "I guess I deserve that."

That and more, if Kindra was being honest. "If Dru isn't ever outliving that stupid bomb-collar trick, you're *definitely* never getting out of that."

"Know what?" For the first time since they stepped into the backyard, Ryce smiled. "As long as you're alive to give me shit about it, I do not care."

The sliding glass door rattled and groaned as someone shoved it open. Kindra stepped back from Ryce as Dru poked her head through a space barely as wide as her shoulders.

"You guys okay?" Concern was etched in the lines crossing her forehead.

Ryce subtly nudged Kindra's shoulder with his own, and she bit back a sigh. In a different world where they were different people with different families, and had met under *way* different circumstances, she might've chased Dru to the ends of the earth to seduce her. Now she only reminded herself, again, that getting involved would be a really bad idea.

A bad idea. It'd be a very bad idea . . . Wouldn't it?

Kindra cleared her throat. "You need us for something?"

"Yeah, you're up." Dru stepped back from the door, tilting her head toward the computers set up in the living room. "After that catch with the cyclic permutation, Mom wants you to take a look at what they've managed to catalog so far of Isaac's files."

"They're going to be pissed when they realize the driver schedule was a fluke," Kindra muttered under her breath to Ryce, keeping her lips turned away from Dru.

"No, they won't, Kinny. Seriously. They're not like that. Cassidy isn't like Odira." Ryce's lips pursed when Kindra raised an eyebrow at him. "They took me in, didn't they?"

A snippet of the conversation the Westons had overheard last week popped back into Kindra's head.

"She's a bogeyman in training," Hugo had warned. *"If she figures out who you are, she'll slit your throat first and question why later. Or never, maybe."*

Dru had tried to protest. *"But R—"*

"Not the same, and you know it." Hugo's voice had been sharp when he cut her off. *"That was voluntary, not forced."*

The situation hadn't changed. She hadn't come voluntarily, and a team couldn't afford to pick up any stray that wandered across its path. If the Calvers couldn't trust her not to betray them—to Garret, to Javier, to *Odira* especially—then they had no reason to let her stay . . . and every reason to kill her.

She met Dru's eyes as she passed, though, and felt more than a pang of regret. Dru's lips were full, her hands were soft except for a few calluses in the right places, and Kindra thought it'd be really nice to have someone like Dru watching her back.

Maybe I can pretend. She sat down at the tech table with Ryce and listened to Cassidy explain the bass-ackwards categorization she and Daelan had set up for the latest set of observations. Kindra was good at pretending, had survived this long because of it, but when she met Dru's eyes again, she knew pretending wouldn't make her life easier this time around. Now, pretending would only make it hurt worse when she had to let the lie shatter.

Dru smiled. *Shit.* She had to make a choice before they got any deeper into this job.

Blinking at Dru, Kindra carefully kept her expression away from practiced blankness. Dru would recognize that look as a lie too easily. Instead, she let her eyebrows furrow and her nose wrinkle slightly before deliberately turning away.

In her peripheral vision, she saw a flutter of confusion cross Dru's face before her lips pressed into a thin line. Dru stood there watching for another ten minutes, listening as Cassidy and Daelan tossed out wild conjectures and valid theories on where the information Isaac collected had come from. Kindra never met her eyes. Not once.

Resignation finally settled, and Dru walked out of the room.

Ryce's hand gripped her shoulder, and he bent low, his voice a breath in her ear. "It doesn't have to be like that, you know."

"Yeah." Kindra glanced at him without moving her head. "It does."

"I hope you know what you're doing," Ryce said, a sigh in his voice.

Kindra almost laughed. Of course she didn't know what she was doing. Her entire life had been lived under a very strict set of rules, but the past few weeks had shot, frayed, torn, burned, melted, stabbed, and drowned her playbook. She had absolutely no effing clue what she was doing. All she knew was that she'd have some choices to make when this was over. And that, maybe, she'd have a chance to make a life somewhere hidden. A real one.

"It'll depend on when and how we get into his life," Cassidy told Daelan as Kindra came into the room that afternoon. "Having more than one method ready to go is only prudent."

"But paper?" Daelan scoffed. "Who uses paper anymore? Honestly."

Cassidy smirked at her son. "Paper can't be hacked."

"No, but it can be lost, dropped, misplaced, stolen, burned, ripped, and eaten by dogs," Daelan countered. "How is that any safer?" He noticed Kindra and reached out with one hand, drawing her into the conversation. "Will you tell her that hacking is not justification enough for a security official to use paper notes and messages?"

"I've seen more than a few agents use paper." Kindra shrugged at Daelan's disgruntled expression. "But most of them do seem to rely on technology these days. Speed and accuracy over caution. Why does that matter now?"

Daelan held up a black flash drive. "I designed spyware based off the FBI's most commonly used program, with a few tweaks of my own. If we can get this onto a Redwell computer with high-level access— Garret Hadley's, preferably—we'll be able to get a much better look at everything they're running. If anyone discovers it, it'll look like it traces back to the Feds. Specifically, Matthew Nevarez's ex-partner."

If whatever was on the flash could manage all that, it'd be perfect. Only one kind of huge problem. "How are we supposed to get it onto one of their computers? We can't do it when we grab Garret. It'll be too late by then."

"Yeah." Daelan scratched the back of his head. "Um, that's the part I'm still trying to work out."

"You don't want me to take it with me?"

Cassidy shook her head sharply. "Your goal that day is to get intel on the employees, get a look at the internal security, and plant suspicion within the ranks. I'd lay good money against them letting you anywhere near a computer while you're there. Especially not alone."

"Shouldn't I have it with me anyway?" Overprepared had to be better than under.

"And give them something to crucify you with if they search you?" Cassidy huffed and crossed her arms. "Single-person ops fail when there are too many goals and too many ways for the agent to get caught. I'm not sending you in there without backup *and* carrying incriminating evidence."

Kindra glanced at Daelan, expecting him to argue the point, but he sighed and tossed the drive onto the desk. "Pragmatism sucks sometimes."

"If you're sure." Kindra looked at the drive, slim and innocuous and far more capable of wreaking havoc than anything she could whisper into anyone's ear. "Seems like a wasted opportunity."

"We have our mission, and you have your focus." There was a warning in Cassidy's voice. She had made her decision, and woe to those who chose to disobey. "We'll take this in when we infiltrate later. All we need now is for you to find us a way in. *That's* your job."

"That and to sow the seeds of discord." Daelan grinned, looking far too pleased with the idea.

Kindra let the conversation drop, but later she palmed the drive and cloned it during her next shift on the surveillance computers. She also snatched one of the Calvers tiny wireless cameras. Cassidy might not think the risk was worth it, but Kindra had seen the specs for Redwell's security system and read the dossiers on all of their upper-level personnel. Being on Garret's most-wanted list had kept Cassidy and Hugo out of the building for years. What if she *couldn't* find them an after-hours way in? When would any of them get another shot at this?

Maybe the Calvers weren't going to tempt fate, but Kindra wanted this job done.

Maybe, if she played it all the right way, she'd feel like she had earned—that she deserved—a place with this family.

Maybe, if she got them what they needed but were afraid to ask for, they'd trust her enough to let her stay when Garret was no longer the unifying threat.

Baltimore, Maryland

"In here, Blake." The head of the school ushered the new arrival into her office and then tried to shut the door. She couldn't. Blake Marks had stopped a foot inside the room, staring at the two besuited men waiting inside.

"What happened?" Blake's dark eyes jumped from one face to the other. "Where's Dad?"

The two men glanced at each other before the shorter, sharp-featured Hispanic man spoke. "Some threats have been made against your father and you—threats we believe to be credible."

"We've made arrangements to move you to a secure location." The taller, scruffy-haired man glanced at his watch. "We have to leave now, though."

Blake's large eyes narrowed as they spoke, and he rocked back on his heels, running a hand over his short hair. The other he shoved into the pocket of his jeans, where he wrapped his fingers around his cell phone. "You didn't answer my question. Where is my father?"

"We don't have a fix on his location yet," the taller one said, his rosy cheeks flushing and his dark-blue eyes shifting to the left. "We're working on it."

Blake worried his plush lower lip with his teeth, but then words spilled out of his mouth, spoken in the cadence of a poem. "'In nature there's no blemish but the mind.'"

Both men blinked.

Blake turned and *ran*.

He sprinted through the halls with the ease of familiarity, only the heavy *thump* of his backpack slowing him down. Pulling out his cell phone, he tried to access his contacts, but fumbled entering the passcode on the lock screen. Grunting, he stopped trying, gripping the phone tight and putting on another burst of speed. He propelled himself through the side door, almost tripping down the staircase a few feet away, but he caught the railing and descended.

A hand grabbed his arm. Another covered his mouth before he could scream.

"'None can be called deformed but the unkind,'" the man who held Blake captive said, finishing the quote the men in the office hadn't known.

Blake sagged, tears welling in his eyes.

"We have to go, Blake. Will you come?" When Blake nodded, the man released his mouth, but not the grip he had on Blake's arm. "C'mon. I don't think they're far behind."

He pulled Blake toward the street, where a black van was waiting, its door already open.

Blake hesitated at the door, warily eyeing the van and the man sitting inside. Then the two fake agents burst out of the school, guns drawn and deadly determination on their faces. Uncertainty gone, Blake jumped in the van, and the driver peeled out of the parking lot.

In addition to the driver and the man who'd pulled Blake away from the school—Max and Scott, according to their harried introductions—there was a man with copper skin, silver-streaked dark hair, and an almost tangible aura of exhaustion.

"Are you all right?" he asked as the van rocketed toward northwestern Baltimore.

"I don't know yet." Blake's hands shook, and he kept blinking as though he couldn't get his eyes to focus. "Who are you?"

"My name is Bernard Gasper. The same people who want me dead are after you, and . . ." He looked away, his expression pinched and his body tense.

"Dad is dead, isn't he?"

Bernard shuddered and seemed to have to force his eyes open. "I am so sorry."

A sob escaped Blake's lips. His hands clenched into fists on his thighs, and his shoulders stiffened when he asked, "How?"

"We don't know yet." Bernard's voice was hoarse, nearly raw. "Isaac was working with me on an investigation, but the last message he got out to me was . . . there was a phrase in it that we'd agreed he would use if the worst happened."

Blake collapsed. His hands came up to cover his face, and he folded over his legs, sobs racking his frame until Bernard's hand tentatively pressed to the center of his back and rubbed in small circles.

"I am so sorry, Blake," Bernard whispered. "Your father was a great man, and I owe him more than I can possibly repay. I promise I will do everything in my power to keep you safe."

Blake didn't respond, but neither did he move away from the comfort.

It was a long time after that before either of them spoke again.

Chapter Twenty-One

1515 : FRIDAY, FEBRUARY 26

Kindra's heels clicked against the marble floor. The charcoal-gray pencil skirt hugged her thighs, forcing her to walk in the seductive swish of "Chanda Dhillon." Hugo and Ryce had darkened her hair last night from deep brown to black and helped her apply a tanning cream that darkened her skin about three shades. Daelan had laughed when he saw her this morning and claimed she looked "like Business Barbie meets Princess Jasmine."

Kindra let this persona sink into her skin and mold itself to her bones. Chanda had spent the first ten years of her life in England before her father's business moved her family to the United States. She graduated with honors from Berkeley, and then completed her master's in sustainability at Wake Forest. In this moment, and only inside Kindra's mind, Chanda had a family, a history, and a life. She relaxed and felt almost serene as she enveloped herself in the comfort of a lie.

She approached the security desk, eyeing the two guards covering this shift. Twenty-year veteran Thomas Wilson sat to her left, his steel-gray hair cut short and his slightly tubby middle section offset by surprisingly attentive eyes. Guard number two had only been on the job for a year. Gregory Jones was twenty-three and overzealous in his protection of the company. Understandable given that his salary was enough to provide full-time home care for his mother. Luckily for Kindra, the kid was currently giving the UPS delivery guy—Aaron in heavy disguise—the fifth degree.

Unclipping her ID badge from her beaded lanyard, she handed it to Wilson with a vaguely polite smile. "My name is Chanda Dhillon. I'm an EPA liaison to the United Nations Environmental Programme."

Wilson's thick eyebrows rose a notch, but the rest of his expression remained neutral. He took the badge and scanned the barcode at the bottom, typing in her information. "Who is your appointment with?"

"No appointment. Surprise visit." She added a few more teeth to the smile, letting it seem forced. She had to indicate trouble without explaining what that trouble was and then hope that rumors of strife spread in her wake. "I'll be visiting your research, legal, and regulatory departments. And I may need to speak to the executive committee."

"Hmm." Speculation danced behind his hazel eyes as soon as she mentioned the directors. His system beeped once, and he looked away—seeing the confirmation of Kindra's fake identity if Cassidy, Hugo, and Dru had done their parts right. "It'll be a few minutes for us to verify, and then you'll need an escort."

"Of course." She leaned on the high counter and smiled down at him with more genuine warmth. "Want to get out of that chair for a while?"

He laughed, exactly as she'd hoped he would, and then shook his head. "I don't have the clearance you'll need for some of those areas. Someone should be down shortly."

"Thank you, Thomas. I appreciate your help." Kindra took her ID back, clipped it in place on her lanyard, and then added the visitor's badge he passed her. Pulling a tablet out of her briefcase, she scrolled through some of the documents she'd downloaded. Normally for a cover like this, Kindra would've spent a week or more studying the information someone in Chanda's position would know. This time she'd had a couple of days.

Ten minutes later, Kindra heard Chanda's name being called.

"Ms. Dhillon?" A tall, sharp-featured Vietnamese woman in a pantsuit that made her look like an FBI stereotype stood on the other side of the turnstile, a tight smile on her face. As the head of Redwell's security, she worked closely with Garret. Chances were very high that she was one of those who knew about his black-market deals.

Kindra smiled her most engaging smile and strode toward the gate.

"I'm Susan Phan. Our head of operations is out sick today, so I'll be accompanying you." She held out a hand and sounded pleasant enough, but she was eyeing Kindra warily.

Smile never faltering, Kindra shook her hand. "Chanda, please. I appreciate the assistance. It's always easier to maneuver when I have someone who knows the building as well as I'm sure you do."

Susan's head tilted slightly, and her shoulders relaxed just a touch. "Thank you. You said you needed to start in one of the research departments?"

"Yes, please, specifically the group managing the agricultural development initiatives in South America." Kindra kept up a stream of relevant chatter as they entered the elevator.

The control panel inside required a key card before the floor numbers appeared on the display. Another employee had entered the elevator seconds before them, and only a third of the floors were lit. When Phan swiped her card, every number became available.

"We need a copy of that card," Cassidy said softly, her voice coming through the tiny comm embedded in Kindra's inner canal—hidden from all but the closest exams.

"Do you mind if I take a look at that tablet?" Susan asked. "Just a security precaution."

"Of course. I understand." Kindra unlocked the tablet and handed it over. The program Cassidy had installed to record Kindra's visit and transmit the information to the Citadel was impossible to find in a cursory search. When the elevator *dinged* a minute later, Susan handed the device back with a smile.

Within the confines of each conversation Kindra had over the next hour, she dropped hints that her visit was the beginning of a larger investigation, or that the company was in financial trouble, or that the executives no longer had their employees', or the world's, best interests at heart. It was important, but it was also incredibly *boring*. To keep herself entertained, Kindra memorized the faces and descriptions of the scientists, lawyers, and administrators, and what fields they specialized in. She calculated the likelihood that their involvement in the company delved beyond the surface. Better, she also searched out the many and varied ways she could cause explosions within these rooms.

The camera in her tablet recorded everything.

Two hours in, Cassidy's voice in her ear had only interrupted her thoughts twice, and only to provide information Kindra hadn't known.

Even though Cassidy and Hugo had told her what Redwell did, it was still somewhat shocking to see precisely how harmless—even significantly beneficial—the operation was. Maybe taking out Garret Hadley *would* be the same as excising a tumor.

"Just one more stop." Kindra followed Phan to the elevator after a mind-numbing thirty minutes spent with a regulatory agent. "I need to speak to the executives, please."

Susan shook her head. "I'm afraid that might not be possible."

"We'll have to make it happen." Kindra gave the woman a firm but understanding smile. "I have several questions that I need to address directly with the committee."

Although she'd lost most of her wariness over the last several hours, Susan hesitated now. "Only a third of the execs are on-site today."

"A video conference with the remaining members would be fine, but I *do* need to speak with them."

Lips pressed tight, Susan nodded and swiped her card in front of the elevator's reader. Kindra shifted her weight too far to the right, let her ankle buckle as she took the next step, and toppled herself into Phan.

"Oh, shoot!" Kindra dropped her tablet and grabbed for Susan, pulling the woman off-kilter with one hand and using the other to swipe the all-access pass she needed.

Susan smacked one hand against the wall to keep them on their feet.

"I am *so* sorry!" Kindra crouched to reclaim her tablet, her back to the elevator's camera.

"It's why I stopped wearing heels."

With a quick sleight of hand, Kindra pressed the card against the reader Cassidy had installed in the tablet, and then straightened, back still facing the camera, laughing. "I keep telling myself I'll learn to walk in them, but it never seems to happen." Still smiling and holding Susan's eye, Kindra slid the card into the woman's pocket. "I should give up, but it's a weakness of mine." Looking down at the floor, she lifted her foot to better display the Louboutin knockoffs. "Designer copies. They're gorgeous, aren't they?"

"Probably not environmentally friendly," Susan said, her smile wry.

"No, but I drive electric, eat organic, recycle, and campaign for better environmental oversight." She glanced at Susan and winked. "I'm allowed one little vice, right?"

Susan nodded. "As vices go, it's not that bad."

"Good work," Cassidy whispered through the comm.

The comment jolted Kindra straight out of character. She blinked, confusion fluttering in her chest like a trapped bird, and offered thanks to Atropos that Susan wasn't watching her face. Odira never would've offered praise for something she was *supposed* to do. It warmed her in a way she wasn't familiar with, and set her off-balance in a way she didn't like.

The elevator chimed, and the doors opened silently, releasing them into an expansive foyer with floor-to-ceiling windows behind the wide desk. A guy in his midtwenties, who looked like the poster child for the "all-American boy" stereotype, stood and gave her a politician's smile. Charles Upton, Garret's personal assistant.

"Welcome to Redwell, Ms. Dhillon. I'm afraid Mr. Hadley was called off-premises not long before you arrived." Charles's head cocked, his expression taking on a vaguely apologetic look. "An emergency at a local factory."

Otherwise known as a desperate bid to get rid of evidence? Kindra took a quick look at the room and wondered what they had stored here or nearby that the EPA might take offense at. Or maybe, possibly, something with Odira had demanded his attention. The timing was too coincidental to be anything else.

"We're working on locating him," Cassidy whispered as Kindra shook the apple-cheeked boy's hand.

"Sometimes that can't be avoided," Kindra said. "It would be helpful if I could speak to the rest of the committee, however. A video conference would be fine. There are just a few concerns I need to address with them directly."

"Some of the members are international," Charles informed her. As though someone in her position wouldn't know. "It may be a while before we can get them all connected."

Kindra put a little steel into her smile. "I have time."

Charles never faltered. "Well, if you'll wait here, I'll see where we're at."

Susan stepped closer to Charles, murmuring something Kindra didn't catch. Kindra looked around the room again, her movements casual and her attention anything but. Something about the space nagged at her, but she couldn't place her finger on what. After a few seconds, Charles nodded and left.

"I hope you don't mind if I leave you here," Susan said.

"I won't need an escort on this floor?" Kindra let her actual surprise show. Never had she thought they'd willingly give her a second alone.

"Every door on this floor is key card-access only, including the elevator and the stairwell." Susan looked smug. "Charles will let me know when you've finished and are ready to leave. I'll be back to escort you out."

"I apologize for keeping you from your work this long, but I do appreciate your help."

"It's not a problem. It was nice to meet you." Susan offered her hand, and Kindra shook it.

"Would there possibly be a restroom on this floor?"

"Down the hall and to your left," Susan said.

Kindra tilted her head. "Do I need a key card to access it?"

"No." Susan smiled just a bit, acknowledging the joke. "It's the one exception. I'll let Charles know in case he gets back before you do."

"Thank you again, Susan."

Then, with a sharp nod, she left, and Kindra was stuck waiting.

She found the restroom just off the foyer and went in, using the moment alone to regroup. Taking out her tablet, she scrolled through her reference sheets one more time, preparing for the conference call. Only a small portion of her mind focused on that, though. The rest was itching to somehow make the most of this opportunity she'd been handed. Odira would've been barking orders and demanding information from filing cabinets and secure computers, but the comm in her ear was silent.

The silence was somehow worse.

Perfection had always been expected. Perfect aim and perfect obedience in perfect silence. Kindra had lived up to those standards her entire life, but the Calvers seemed to allow for mistakes and missed opportunities. What she couldn't understand was why the leeway to watch this moment pass by only made her urge to *do something* that much stronger.

"Take a deep breath, head back out, and sit tight," Cassidy whispered through the comm. "We still don't have a location on Hadley."

Sit tight. Sure.

Biting back an impatient sigh, Kindra took one last moment to enjoy being in one of the only rooms in this entire building *not* on security camera, and— *Oh.*

The thought sparked a realization so sharp and vivid Kindra almost gasped. Cameras. *That's* what had been off about this floor. Not an addition, but a lack. She hadn't spotted a single camera in the lobby or the hallway. Once she stepped off the elevator, she had essentially become invisible.

Atropos bless it.

Kindra slipped out of her heels and, after making sure her way was clear, padded through the hall. The offices didn't have windows that looked into the hallway, so her movements wouldn't be noticed. A door marked Emergency Exit: Alarm Will Sound stood out in the northeast corner of the building—she didn't remember seeing this stairwell on the map. She made a mental note and moved on.

She scanned doorways and tested locks until she struck gold: a slightly ajar office belonging to the unexpectedly absent CEO. He must have been in such a rush to leave that he hadn't noticed the corner of a tapestry hanging near the door had gotten caught in the frame and kept the latch from securing the room behind him.

No time for second-guessing.

The USB drive she'd copied was stashed in her heavily padded bra. She pulled it out as she entered the office and reset the door exactly as it had been.

"I'm in Garret's office." She ran to the desk and plugged the USB drive into the computer. "Drive is in place. Upload now."

"What the hell are you thinking?" Cassidy sounded pissed—and panicked. Dru cursed in the background. "This was *not* the plan. Where did you even get that drive?"

"I copied it! Now help me or listen to me die," Kindra hissed. "We need this."

She searched through the pictures and papers on his desk, looking for anything useful that might have been left in the open during Garret's obvious rush to depart. Cassidy cursed for a solid minute, but Kindra could hear her fingers flying on the keyboard, and she saw Garret's computer come to life as Cassidy took control of the system.

The Calvers had cracked Redwell.

As Kindra searched, she watched Cassidy work out of the corner of her eye. Windows and programs and files opened and closed, command prompts were entered and run, spyware was installed, and then the whole thing went in reverse, deleting its tracks and putting the computer back to sleep.

"Done," Cassidy muttered in Kindra's ear. "Now get *out*."

Retrieving the drive, Kindra slipped it back into her bra, made sure the office was exactly as it had been when she entered, and jogged to the door. Out of a pocket hidden in the waistband of her skirt, Kindra pulled the tiny wireless camera she'd taken from the Citadel and stuck it to the top of the doorframe. The battery would only last a few days, but a few days should be all they needed.

Opening the door a crack, she listened first, waiting for footsteps against the hardwood. Hearing nothing, she opened it farther, enough to peer into the hallway. Still nothing. Kindra slid through the half-open door and pulled it mostly shut behind her, leaving it at exactly the same angle it had been when she entered.

"Clear," Kindra mumbled just loud enough for Cassidy to hear her. In the hall, she replaced her heels and strode back to the lobby. Her pulse picked up as she prayed to Atropos for luck. She'd been gone several minutes. The bathroom excuse might not hold up if Charles had been waiting for her.

Luck was with her. She settled back into her chair in the waiting room across from Charles's desk seconds before the man returned.

"Sorry for the delay," he said. "It'll be just a while longer."

Kindra made a noncommittal noise and nodded, keeping her attention on her tablet. Across from her, Charles sat down and went back to work. The phone on his desk rang a few minutes later, and he answered it with the Bluetooth earpiece hooked around his left ear. When he hung up, he rolled his shoulders. It was the only crack in his serene facade.

"If you'll follow me, Ms. Dhillon?" Charles walked in the opposite direction of Garret's office, and Kindra kept close to his side.

"How long have you worked for Redwell?" she asked, though she already knew the answer.

"I did the internship for my MBA here, and they hired me straight out of grad school two years ago." Upton smiled a very press-friendly mask of a smile. "They've given me some fantastic opportunities."

"I don't doubt it." Kindra turned her head toward the conference room—the only glass-walled room on this floor—but kept Charles in her peripheral vision. "You must've worked on some very diverse projects, considering how widely spread Redwell's interests are."

He didn't flinch. "Yes. It's completely dynamic from day to day. I'm *never* bored."

"Hmm." Kindra tapped her fingernails on the aluminum casing of her tablet, pleased when Charles twitched at the sound. She feigned reluctance before she leaned closer and whispered, "It's not my department, but there are rumors that the company is under investigation for more than just environmental issues. The allegations I've heard would turn your hair white."

Charles met her eyes, his lips tight and his jaw clenched. Fear or anger? If Kindra was reading him right, he was on the borderline between the two.

"I shouldn't say anything, I know, but . . ." Kindra bit her lip as though debating whether to say more. "Just, be careful, Charles."

"We're ready for you, Ms. Dhillon," someone called from the open conference room door.

Kindra cast a meaningful look at Charles. "Thank you so much for your help. I wish you all the best."

Finally, he looked a little flustered. His hand was clammy when he shook Kindra's. "It's been a pleasure, Chanda. Please let me know if I can assist you with anything else."

"I certainly will." Kindra turned a brilliant smile on her new escort and strode into the conference room. It was a risk meeting with them like this, but if she'd dropped the right bread crumbs throughout the day and could whisper the right hints into the ears of the executives, there was a chance—if only a *chance*—that someone inside Redwell would finally discover some of the bloody deeds being carried out under the cover of their name. "Let's get this started, shall we? I think I've taken up more than enough of everyone's time this afternoon."

Jacksonville, Florida

"Shall we try this again?" Garret Hadley took two steps forward, the heels of his oxford leather shoes clicking on the concrete floor. "Why are you here?"

The man tied to the chair in the center of the ten-by-ten room spat blood on the plastic sheeting protecting the floor and muttered something indistinct in Spanish.

Standing behind the man, looming over him like a bird of prey, Odira pressed the tip of her knife under his ear and leaned down to whisper in the same language, "I can make this so much worse."

"Beatriz . . . I *said*—" The man broke off and groaned. When Odira cut deeper with the knife, he continued in heavily accented English. "That *desgraciado* killed my brother and took my niece! I want— I . . . I want to bring her *home*." His voice cracked, and tears ran down his cheeks in streams thick enough to cut through the sweat, dirt, and blood caked there. "*Madre de Dios, por favor*! She is the only family I have left. *Por favor*. Just let me see her again."

Garret surveyed the man and the entire bloody scene with badly concealed disgust. When the heavy door behind him opened, Garret turned to watch Amett approach. "And?"

Amett barely spared the man suffering Odira's attention a glance. "He is who he says he is, from what I could pull up. Guillermo Melo Santos, Eduardo's older brother. Beatriz would be his only living relative. Acting alone here *and* in Echemorro, I think."

Garret nodded once. "Good. Then it'll end here. I don't have time for this shit."

He strode toward the rolling cart of tools Odira had been using, picked up her gun, and shot Guillermo twice in the chest.

Odira barely jumped out of the way in time to avoid the through-and-through shot that would've embedded itself in her thigh.

Rolling his shoulders as though adjusting the fit of his suit jacket, Garret wiped the gun down with a handkerchief and then set it back on the cart.

"Clean this up quick," he said as he left, never casting another glance at the man who hadn't quite finished dying yet, or at either of the Westons watching him with surprise in their eyes. "You've still got a lot of work to do, Odira, and not much time left before I start making calls you *really* won't like."

When the door closed behind Garret, Odira looked at Amett and opened her mouth as though to speak. She closed it without making a sound, grimaced, and turned to Guillermo. She and Amett stood close enough for their arms to brush, watching the man take his last breaths.

For the next hour they worked in near silence, cleaning up the bloody mess that Garret Hadley had left behind.

Kindra got into the passenger seat of the sedan driven by Hugo. His makeup made him look thirty years older.

"I'm not sure if you're brilliant or bat-shit," Hugo muttered as he pulled away from the curb.

"I got it done, didn't I?" Kindra shrugged and kept her eyes on the window, watching for possible tails or undue attention. "I'm leaning toward brilliant."

Hugo snorted. "I don't think you get to make that call." He turned onto a side street, his eyes on the rearview mirror. "Cassidy wanted to reach through the comm and throttle you, and I thought Dru was going to drive up to Redwell and drag you out by your hair."

"She could *try.*" Kindra glanced over her shoulder again. They were a mile from Redwell, and she didn't spot anything behind them. But Redwell—and therefore, by extension, Garret Hadley—had access to satellites. They might not need a car to track people.

Hugo pulled in to the Hilton parking garage ten minutes later. Once inside, they moved upstairs to the floor where Chanda Dhillon and her companion George Wilson had adjoining rooms. As they walked, they chatted about the meeting and their next move— exactly the conversation one would expect two EPA agents to have. They entered Chanda's room, but inside Hugo veered off through the connecting door and into the next room's bathroom.

Showering off the heavy makeup and changing into new disguises took them a solid forty minutes, but at the end of it, Kindra had morphed into a sullen teenage boy and Hugo had become the boy's slightly annoyed uncle.

"Ready?" Hugo asked.

Kindra adjusted her hat over her wig of scruffy dark-blond hair and nodded. Someone paying *very* close attention to the single security camera in the hallway would notice that the teenage boy and the late-twenties man had never entered room 1224, the room technically registered to George Wilson, but by the time they figured that out, Kindra and Hugo would be long gone and the disguises would be buried in the trunks of supplies at the Citadel.

The trip back was quick and silent, but it felt like that moment between an earthquake and the aftershock—when the world held its breath, waiting for the next tremor, the one that might send everything crashing down.

Kindra wasn't sure if the stronger aftershock would come from facing Ryce, Cassidy, or Dru. She still wasn't sure when she walked into the house and found Ryce and Cassidy waiting for her.

Biting back a sigh, she closed the garage door behind her and stepped into the room. She'd barely gotten a few feet inside before Ryce grabbed her, hugged her so tight that her spine popped, then let go and walked away.

Left facing Cassidy without the buffer of her brother, she did the only other thing she could think of—slid her hand down her shirt to retrieve the flash drive trapped between her breasts. It was harder to get it out from under the binding of her current disguise, but a couple more seconds of wiggling freed it. She held it up and then tossed the drive to Cassidy.

"Thanks." Cassidy contemplated the drive for a moment before she looked up at Kindra. "I can't deny that you did good work." Her lips were too tight for that to be it.

"But?" She pulled off her wig and wig cap and then shook her damp, matted hair out.

"*But* if you go off-task like that again, we won't ever let you go in alone."

"It was cost versus payout." Kindra ran her fingers through the knotted strands of her hair and then pulled it back into a braid to get it out of her face. "I had a chance, and we needed to plant the bug sooner rather than later. Probable payout outweighed the possible cost."

Cassidy tensed, her body so taut that it *had* to hurt her shoulder. "Your life is never an acceptable possible cost, Kindra. That's something you can't ever get back."

If the temperate praise during the Redwell mission had thrown her off-balance, those words were like a battering ram to the side of the head. With the faint ringing in her ears came the reverse echo of words from months ago.

"I don't care if you have to throw yourself in front of a bus with *the target, Kindra! You get the fucking job done!"*

One of these things is not like the other . . .

"It'll be *all* our lives if we don't end this soon." Kindra clenched her fists, anger burning under her skin and no one to vent its fire on—no one who deserved it.

Cassidy's lips went so tight they almost disappeared, and Kindra took advantage of the moment of silence. She didn't regret what she'd done, and Cassidy was still mad at her for it. Nothing either of them could say from this point would be productive, so Kindra left, walking into the bedrooms where they'd stored the spare clothing.

She stripped off the too-big clothing of her disguise and grabbed a set that fit. Just when she buttoned her jeans, the door clicked shut. She tensed. Only one person would've closed the door like that.

Closing her eyes, she took a breath and waited.

"Why do I feel like you've been avoiding me?" Dru finally asked.

That answers the tremor question—the stronger shake-up is definitely coming from Dru.

Kindra exhaled, pulling her shirt on and turning around. "Because you're not an idiot, and I've been going out of my way to avoid you."

"Okay." Dru huffed. "Well, at least you're honest about it."

"Why lie?" Kindra crossed her arms and leaned against the wall. "Like I said, you're not an idiot."

"I'm just someone you've decided to ignore since we moved the Citadel." Dru's hands were on her hips, but her face was unreadable. "Feel like telling me why?"

"Not really."

"Do it anyway."

Kindra's lip twitched, a smile almost breaking free. Atropos bless it, Dru was cute when she got all huffy and tough. That was exactly why

Kindra had been avoiding her. She was too damn adorable to resist. But if avoiding her made Dru get all determined and confrontational like this, maybe it wasn't the best long-term plan. "I'll stop if it bugs you this much."

"That'd be great." Dru's voice was Sahara-dry, and Kindra could practically see her fighting the urge to roll her eyes. "What would be even better would be you explaining why you started doing it in the first place, baby."

Kindra's stomach jumped hearing that term of annoyment trip off Dru's tongue. It only made an appearance when she was trying to drive Kindra up a wall. When she stopped, and only after she stopped, Kindra had finally admitted to herself she kind of liked it. That word was a sign Dru was paying attention, that she wouldn't let Kindra get away with being Odira's mindlessly obedient soldier.

Clearing her throat—and hating that obvious sign of discomfort—Kindra shook her head. "Why doesn't matter."

"Oh my God." This time, Dru did roll her eyes. "We already had this conversation! The why almost *always* matters."

"Not this time." Kindra stepped away from the wall, her hands dropping to her sides. "I already said I'd stop, so unless you have some other complaint to lodge, I'm going to get back to work."

She tried to leave the room, but Dru blocked the door.

Kindra raised an eyebrow. "You going to move or what?"

"When I'm ready." They stared at each other across the space dividing them. Dru looked scarily resolute. "You armed?"

She had a small knife tucked in a sheath inside her bra, a slightly longer one along her hip inside her jeans, and the ring from her Chanda costume—one with a cool little poison-tipped needle hidden inside—on her right hand. "Yes."

In two long strides, Dru closed the space between them, her arms outstretched. For a second, Kindra thought Dru was going for her throat. Then her fingers slid into Kindra's hair, gripped the back of her head, and pulled her in for a bruising kiss.

There was no seduction in Dru's hold or softness in the way their lips met. This was fear and anger and why-the-fuck-did-you-stay-away-for-so-long. This was a kiss that felt *real*. There was no agenda and no target. All of that, everything this kiss was, was exactly why Kindra had been avoiding Dru. Avoiding this. Because she'd known that as soon as she had it, she'd want more.

Kindra had never been sure there would be a difference between on-the-job kissing and just-because kissing, but holy shit, had she been wrong. Deliciously, amazingly wrong.

Oh, I am so effing screwed.

Kindra sank into the kiss.

The itch to slide her hands under Dru's shirt was intense, but Kindra resisted. Barely. The internal battle made her clutch Dru tighter than she meant to. Dru didn't seem to mind. She moaned and pressed herself closer, using her hold on the back of Kindra's head to tilt her at a better angle. The heat Dru's touch generated in Kindra's body could have kept her warm in the middle of a Siberian winter.

Then Dru's lips broke away from hers.

"I could've *killed* you when you went into that office." Dru's voice against her ear was whisper-quiet and hoarse, like Dru's throat was clogged with something thicker than air. Like tears. "If someone had found you, we wouldn't have been able to get you out."

Kindra swallowed and pressed her hands against Dru's shoulders, forcing space between them. "Yeah, well, wasn't your call. I saw an opening, and I got something we needed."

Dru's eyes narrowed when Kindra stepped back. "You're going to pretend you didn't want that, aren't you?"

"Want what?" Kindra forced disinterest into her voice. "You mauling me out of nowhere?"

"Please," Dru scoffed. "Why do you think I asked if you were armed? You would've sliced me open if you hadn't wanted me to touch you."

"And risked pissing your family off by making you bleed?" Kindra thought about the fast-acting poison in the ring, her blood chilling at what might have happened if that had accidentally scratched Dru. "Or killing you?"

Dru smiled. "We may be on the wrong side of the law most days, but my parents are still very big proponents of 'no means no.' Death would've been a little excessive for a kiss, but they would've told me I deserved it if you'd made me bleed."

"I can still make you bleed," Kindra muttered. "Maybe it'll snap you out of this idiocy."

"What idiocy is that?"

"Thinking you know me." Kindra's voice was quiet but sharp. Harsher even than she meant it to be. "And thinking that this is ever going to be a good idea."

"Why?"

"Because I'm one of the bogeymen, Dru." Kindra stepped closer, almost nose to nose with a girl she would love to kiss again. The girl she had to push away. She knew she might regret this if she got the chance to stay, but this time the cost-payout analysis wasn't so clear. She couldn't be sure of anything and couldn't seem to keep the cruel words from tumbling out of her mouth. "I don't belong here, I don't *want* to be here, and once this job is over, I'm gone."

"To where?" Dru's eyes tightened, but her breath smelled like wintergreen, and it tickled Kindra's lips. "Unless they die in the crossfire, you'll still have Odira and Amett after you."

"I know how to hide."

The idea of doing that, of disappearing into the crowd and finally, actually becoming someone else, was simultaneously the most beautiful and most horrifying idea Kindra had ever had. She'd do it, though. She'd run and hide in the middle of a forest somewhere for the remainder of her life if it meant keeping Ryce, Dru, and the rest of them safe. She'd step off the top floor of Redwell's business tower right now if it would keep them all safe.

All she said to Dru was, "I can take care of myself."

"Right. And *I'm* the one who's an idiot?"

"No. You're just acting like one right now. And you're not hearing me. I'm out of here as soon as this job is done, Dru. Gone." And then she spoke the words she was pretty sure would make Dru back off fast. "There's no reason for me to stay."

"Right." Hurt flashed in those green eyes, and Dru pulled back. When she crossed her arms over her chest, the gesture looked more defensive than angry. Kindra almost wanted to apologize, but she couldn't. Wouldn't.

"No reason to stay. Not even your brother, right? And because the same kind of person who has no reason to stay would also step away from someone offering sex?" Dru shook her head, and Kindra had absolutely nothing to say. "I can't tell if you're only lying to *me*, or if you actually believe your own bullshit. When you figure it out, come find me."

She thought Dru would leave then, turn on her heel and stalk out of the room.

Instead, Dru closed the space between them. This time when her hands slid into Kindra's hair, the touch was gentle. This time when their lips met, the kiss was soft. A promise. A blessing. A seduction.

Then she turned on her heel and stalked out of the room, leaving Kindra with kiss-puffy lips, a spinning head, and a nearly insurmountable urge to chase after Dru, pin her to the wall, and pick things up where they'd left off.

She couldn't. Kindra didn't trust the safety of the Calvers. Didn't trust the situation. Didn't trust *herself*. Letting her guard down now, only to lose everything when this mission ended? No. Unbearable. Kindra would rather walk away than be shoved, half-broken, out the door.

But, Atropos bless it, none of that meant Kindra didn't want to rip off Dru's fitted gray T-shirt and see what her skin tasted like.

Yep. I am completely effing screwed.

Chapter Twenty-Three
1100 : MONDAY, FEBRUARY 29

It was either reverse psychology or Dru was more pissed than Kindra thought, because for the last few days, Dru had been the one avoiding Kindra. And Kindra wasn't the only one who'd noticed.

"So what'd you do to piss my sister off?" Daelan sat cross-legged on a closed toilet, laptop balanced across his knees. They were tucked into the bathroom of an empty apartment across the street from the Redwell complex, watching as Aaron's UPS truck rolled up, his sixth day making deliveries to the company. He was starting to become part of the scenery for them.

"She wanted something, and I said no." From her perch on the stool in the middle of the bathtub, Kindra snapped a couple of pictures of the plainclothes security guard in Redwell's courtyard. He was good. The only reason Kindra had spotted him was because of how closely he tracked Aaron's movements. No one not being paid for it was that interested in a delivery guy. "Apparently your sister doesn't like being denied."

"It doesn't happen often."

"That explains a lot," Kindra muttered.

"Because she never asks for anything."

Kindra blinked and looked away from the window. "What?"

"She's not the type. Dru always just kind of makes do with what she has. She doesn't ask for much, so, yeah. She's used to getting what she asks for." Daelan shrugged, his eyes flicking between the window and the laptop screen, where he was watching the feed from Garret's office. They had to be close to the building to pick up the short-range camera's signal. Yes, they could've left the laptop here and just bounced the signal to the Citadel, but they needed in-person surveillance in case Garret did anything that required immediate intervention.

"She's good people, you know."

"I never said she wasn't." Kindra lifted the camera to take a picture of another plainclothes guard leaving the building behind Aaron.

"Just figured you should know. She—" His mouth clamped shut, and he frowned down at the screen. "We've got something here."

He unplugged the headphones he'd been wearing. Garret's voice echoed off the bathroom's cream-colored tile as Daelan turned the laptop for Kindra to see.

"Charles, get IT in here *now*. I'm not dealing with this anymore." He shut off the phone's speaker with an unnecessarily forceful jab, muttering to himself.

"He noticed the spyware." Daelan looked positively gleeful.

Since they were working on a limited timeline, Daelan had engineered the program to not only spy on the system, but also cause it to run slower than usual. The Calvers *wanted* Garret to discover it. After Cassidy had downloaded everything of importance, of course.

Once someone who knew what they were doing started poking around, it shouldn't be hard for them to track the "source" of the spyware. So far, it looked like things were going according to plan.

"The system has been glitchy all day," Garret told the tech guy who jogged into the office. "I don't have time for this. We pay you to keep these systems running *without* issues."

"Sir, no system in the world exists without issues." The guy sat down at the computer, never taking his eyes off the screen. "I'm not sure God himself could pull that off."

"Shut up and fix it," Garret growled. "I have a meeting, but I expect this issue to be resolved by the time I get back in an hour."

"I'll do what I can, sir." To his credit, the guy barely spared Garret a glance.

Kindra returned her attention to the courtyard when Garret strode out of the office, buttoning his suit jacket and settling his face into a pleasantly neutral expression. When Daelan poked her shoulder an hour and a half later, the screen showed Tech Guy still hard at work. His fingers flew over the keyboard, but the lines around his eyes and the pinch to his mouth had gotten deeper. As she watched, Tech Guy's lips formed soundless words. She thought that he'd just muttered, "What the fuck?"

"C'mon, put it together!" Daelan practically yelled at the screen. "It's not rocket surgery!"

Kindra smiled. "Do you even know what you're saying half the time?"

"Every word." Daelan smirked. "Haven't you heard? I'm a genius."

The door to the office beeped, and Garret walked in. "You're still here?"

"Uh, yes, sir. I think we have a problem here," Tech Guy said. "This isn't a system glitch. This is spyware."

"I stayed off those sites you sent out warnings about!" Garret ran his fingers through his hair, disarranging the thin, graying strands. "And isn't that what those fucking antivirus programs are supposed to keep *off* our computers?"

The guy was already shaking his head. "Not that kind of spyware, Mr. Hadley. With the depth of the problem and how long it's managed to keep itself hidden in the system, it had to have been directly downloaded onto the computer sometime last month." Tech Guy's expression turned hesitant. He glanced again at the screen and then up at Garret. "Sir, I . . . Well, it looks like the program has been sending information straight to the FBI."

There was a question in the guy's tone and confusion on his face. The confusion turned to outright fear when Garret shouted, "*What?*"

"Jackpot!" Daelan cackled as Garret started screaming profanities at the hapless techie.

"Sir? Sir!" Tech Guy had to scream it to get through Garret's stunned rage.

Kindra watched Garret take a deep breath. It was fascinating to see him slowly tamp down his burning fury, compressing it into a deeper sort of anger. The kind that burned cold and lasted longer. The far more dangerous kind.

"*How* did this happen?" Garret's voice was level and deadly calm.

"That's what I was trying to tell you, sir." Tech Guy swallowed, and Kindra could see his hands trembling ever so slightly on the keyboard. "In order to get past the security and the firewalls built into this system without alerting anyone to the hack, they had to have loaded it in person. Which means they were in this office."

"So you're suggesting that either someone from the outside got past Matt and Susan, or someone with high-level clearance to this building uploaded this software." When Tech Guy nodded, Hadley closed his eyes for a solid second, somehow maintaining his mask of control when he opened them again. "How much has it gotten?"

"It's been here for over a month, according to what I see." Tech Guy bit his lip and double-checked something on the screen. "It's got a keylogger and a subroutine to copy all files whether you save them to the main drive or delete them and . . . Sir, it has everything. Anything you worked on here."

All of the blood that had rushed to Garret's face flooded back out, leaving his skin gray-tinged. Once again, he seemed to shove whatever he was feeling away fast, because he regrouped and began issuing orders.

"I want a new unit installed within the hour, and then I want you to dig through every single bit of that virus and figure out how far it's spread and who put it there, when they installed it, and exactly what communications have been going back to the FBI." Garret's back was to the camera, but whatever Tech Guy saw on his face made him quiver. "Every. Single. Bit. Am I clear?"

"Yes, sir." Tech Guy shut down the system and started unplugging everything. "I'll email you a report as soon as I find anything."

"No." Garret shook his head, the motion slow and considering. "Handwritten notes only on this. I don't want anything else being tracked or hacked."

"Of course." Tech Guy awkwardly hefted the computer's tower into his arms, his enthusiasm to be *gone* obvious. "I'll let you know as soon as I have something concrete, Mr. Hadley."

Garret nodded, but most of his attention was on his cell phone. Tech Guy—clearly intelligent enough to take the opportunity when he saw it—left in a hurry.

As soon as the door closed, Garret pulled a small flip phone out of his pocket, an older style that companies only sold for prepaid programs. Growling curses under his breath, Garret punched the buttons. Texting, Kindra guessed. Even short messages were frustrating as fuck on those old phones, something Kindra knew from personal experience. There wasn't a huge chance that anyone but the Westons or Martinez—possibly both—were on the other end of that connection.

Then he dialed a number from memory.

"We have a problem." Garret bit the words out, seemingly a hairsbreadth away from completely losing his cool again.

"Fuck it all," Cassidy muttered over the open comm. "I wish we had a clone of that phone. Who's he talking to?"

"No one we have tabs on." Hugo cursed, his line faintly staticky.

"I am going to ignore the implications of that statement—I did not *do* anything!" Garret almost slammed his fist on his desk, stopping himself less than six inches from the hardwood surface. "We have more pressing problems. The director of the IT department has my computer so that he can do an in-depth scan and try to explain to me how FBI-sanctioned spyware ended up on my personal system."

The pause in the conversation was short this time, just long enough to allow Garret to regain a little bit of control.

"Apparently, someone got past our entire security team, every camera in the building, and all of our key-card doors in order to sneak into my office and install spyware on my computer that essentially sent copies of the entire system to the FBI." Garret took a long breath and then exhaled it in a sharp burst. "Either someone from the outside managed to pull all of that off, or someone with high-level clearance, someone we *trust*, did it."

The response from the other side of the connection was brief, and Garret rolled his eyes.

"Of *course* Nevarez! I *told* you it was a mistake bringing him into this." He sat down behind his desk and almost immediately got up again. "Matthew Nevarez turned traitor. How can we ever trust a person who so easily abandoned everything they believed in?"

Garret moved to the ornate sideboard and poured himself a triple shot of something honey-gold from a crystal decanter. Scotch, maybe. He downed a third of it in one gulp and then thumped it down on the sideboard.

"'Prays to the dollar and worships at the altar of survivalism'? Really? Where do you come up with this shit?" Garret ran a hand over his hair and shifted his weight like he was fighting the urge to pace. "But, fine. Maybe someone made him a better offer. Or he decided his chances of survival looked better with someone else's backing."

While he listened, he fingered the etching on the tumbler. Then he nodded once before he took another, smaller sip of the liquor.

"I'm glad you agree. I've already got both teams on standby for the order." Garret pulled the flip phone away from his ear and glanced at its screen. After he read whatever was there, he returned to the conversation. "They'll move on Matthew tonight. I'll apprise Martinez of the situation, and if Odira fails again, he'll eliminate the issue."

Garret flushed with obvious anger. Rage, even. His hand gripped the phone so tight Kindra thought he was a breath away from chucking it at a wall. Somehow he stuffed the anger down and ended the call without breaking the phone. After it was back in his pocket, he downed the remainder of his drink, refilled it from the decanter, and then carried the tumbler back to his desk.

Kindra blinked at the screen, a little shocked that the plan seemed to be going according to . . . well, to plan.

"So I guess the driver switch is a go." Kindra focused on her digital camera's small display screen, scrolling through the last half hour of pictures. "We've got twenty-four hours to get me hired and placed on that rotation."

"Where is Matthew now?" Daelan asked Cassidy over the open comm.

"Out of the building." The first time he had been in almost a week. They'd waited until he was gone because they had to make sure Garret was the one to find the evidence they planted, not Matthew. The spyware implicated Matthew, but it would be better if Garret found evidence to back it up. "We followed him a couple miles when he left, enough to guess that he's heading to one of their subsidiaries. He goes to most of the local ones monthly to check in. Surprise inspection." They heard keys click before Cassidy added one last detail. "Looks like his visits average about four hours. He's been gone for one and a half."

"Now or never?" Aaron's words were slightly muffled over the comm.

"Are you in position to make the drop?" Hugo asked. "You don't have to do this if you're not comfortable with the risk, Aaron."

Aaron snorted. "I knew when I went AWOL that this would be a suicide mission of one sort or another. Either I die, or I go back to the military and my career is FUBAR BUNDY." He grunted, and the engine of his delivery truck rumbled to life. "I can make the drop in twenty minutes, but if I die doing this, I'm comin' back to haunt all y'all's asses until the job is done. I hope you know that."

"Shut up and drive, Soldier Boy," Daelan taunted.

"Call me 'soldier' one more time, and I'm going to sedate you and tattoo 'Property of the USMC' on your forehead."

Cassidy snorted back laughter, but Daelan didn't bother, cackling merrily. Eyes on the courtyard below, Kindra shook her head and let herself smile.

Twenty minutes later, Aaron's truck rolled to a stop in front of the building, and he hopped down carrying a thin manila envelope.

"Again?" Thomas Wilson's voice rang over Aaron's comm channel.

"Somehow this ended up behind my seat." Aaron's voice conveyed both frustration and sheepish embarrassment. "Didn't find it until I was almost all the way back to the distribution center, man."

Thomas chuckled. "I hate those days."

A pause—for Aaron to collect a signature, Kindra guessed. "Hey, man, you mind if I use the bathroom? Thought I'd make it back to the office, but that was before I had to come back here again. Wilson, lunch is *not* agreeing with me, ya know what I mean?"

"Ouch." Thomas's sympathy was clear. "Yeah sure, kid. Show the guard at the elevator this. First floor and to your left. Can't miss it."

"Lifesaver. Swear to God." There was a thump, like Aaron had slapped his hand against the security counter, and then nothing but the ambient noises of the lobby level.

They listened as Aaron got on the elevator, rode up one floor, and went in to the men's room nearby. With the program Kindra had loaded onto Garret's computer, Cassidy had gained limited access to the security cameras and systems. Now, she looped five seconds of empty hallway so that Aaron could walk to the supposedly alarmed northeastern stairwell.

It was a complicated system, one Kindra appreciated the design of. In the event of a fire alarm, doors in that stairwell would open and allow access to an additional escape route. The rest of the time, the only people who could gain entry were those with unrestricted access to the building. Like Susan Phan, Garret Hadley, and Charles Upton. It was a useful trick if you ever needed to get out of the building without being seen. Or get someone else in.

Luckily, Aaron had a copy of Susan's card. Cassidy's team was the only one with the real feed, so they were able to watch him wave the key card Kindra had made in front of the camouflaged sensor and sneak inside.

"In," was all he said to confirm.

"Do we care that Odira and Amett are probably going to kill Matthew tonight?" Daelan asked as they listened to Aaron's steady breathing, seeming genuinely confused. It was as though he thought he *should* care, but couldn't quite manage it.

"No." Kindra adjusted her hold on the large camera and checked the courtyard again. "We need him out of the picture anyway. Dead works."

Daelan hesitated, and that caught Kindra's attention. He wasn't the type for hesitation.

"Do we . . . do we care that Javier might be after Odira and Amett?" Daelan asked quietly.

Kindra only held his eyes for a second before she looked away. "They know. We spotted Javier that day in Columbus Circle. If Odira and Amett can't keep themselves alive against a threat they *know* is coming, well . . ."

"Fifth floor," Aaron huffed.

"You really don't care if your parents die?" Daelan watched Kindra as though the answer—and the *way* she answered—mattered.

Biting back an impatient sigh, Kindra lowered the camera. "They're not my parents like Hugo and Cassidy are your parents. They were my drill sergeants when I was a kid, and they've been my bosses for the past six years."

"Hmm." Daelan shook his head as he plugged the headphones back into the laptop. Garret's muttered ranting cut off midcurse.

"Ryce pretty much said the same thing when he came to stay with us, but . . . I don't know. I guess I didn't really get it then."

It still didn't seem like he really got it. "Plus, they *did* recently try to kill me."

He blinked at that. "Right. Okay, good point."

"Ninth floor." Aaron's breathing had become more labored.

Unmuting the comm, Daelan taunted, "Just be glad you're not carrying a fifty-pound pack."

"Fuck you too, asshole." A couple more minutes of heavy but even exhales and Aaron said, "Twelfth floor."

"The stairwell is tucked in a corner." Kindra closed her eyes and tried to picture that hallway. She'd reported this already—they even had pictures thanks to her tablet cam—but the reminder couldn't be amiss. "If you open the door slowly, you should be able to check for occupancy before you head into the hall."

It felt like everyone on the comm line was holding their breaths.

This was where it could all go wrong in an instant. Aaron's delivery uniform marked him as out of place immediately, and Cassidy's limited influence over the security system was no help here. No cameras meant no way to watch out for Aaron or warn him of trouble approaching. If anyone spotted him on this floor, there was no way in any level of Tartarus or any parallel universe that he was getting out of the building as a free, unharmed man.

A click as the door opened. A slight creak as it eased a little wider. An obviously relieved exhale. "I'm clear."

Six simultaneous sighs rattled across the comm. Hurdle one was behind them. Now they just had to leap over the next dozen.

"Are you okay?"

Daelan's question almost startled Kindra into dropping her camera. "What?"

He had his hand on the mute button of their comm and concern lined his face. "The pulse point in your neck is jumping like crazy, and you just missed one of the security personnel arriving. Are you okay?"

It wasn't until his words filtered into her head that Kindra noticed her own erratic heartbeat or the numerous changes to the population of the courtyard, changes she should've been tracking. Something Kindra couldn't call anything but anxiety crawled up her spine and nested in the back of her mind, its focus on the slightly labored breathing coming through the speaker and the ever-growing odds that Aaron wouldn't leave that building under his own power.

Holy shit, I care. *What in everything Atropos holds holy is* wrong *with me?*

Adjusting her grip on her camera, Kindra took a very deep breath and turned to watch the courtyard below. "I'm fine. Just want this shift to be over with."

Behind her, Daelan hummed, the noise more than a little doubting, but he didn't say anything else. Worse? Kindra knew that he was right to doubt.

She couldn't focus on what she was supposed to be doing. Her attention drifted to Aaron's hushed conversation with Cassidy as he installed hints of subterfuge on Matthew Nevarez's computer and placed a camera in the office—the same model Kindra had left to watch Garret. Once that signal came through, Ryce and Hugo guided Aaron through a quick search of the office, telling him what to risk taking out of the building, what to take pictures of, and what to ignore.

Why did Kindra *care* if Aaron made it out or not? It wasn't solely because of what failure would do to the rest of the job . . . . *Oh.*

Kindra straightened as she remembered exactly *when* she'd felt this anxious waiting for someone to finish their part of a job.

The night Ryce supposedly died.

Now, for some reason, it mattered that Aaron Tanvers made it out. Not because his capture would destroy the work he was doing right now, but because she didn't want him to get hurt. Because he'd managed to earn her grudging and rare respect. And—fuck it all—she almost liked the patriotic bastard.

How much worse would it be if Dru was the one inside?

The thought made her hands tremble so much that the picture she snapped was unusably blurry.

Shit.

In thirteen days, she'd come to care more about the fates of the Calvers and Aaron Tanvers than she'd cared about anyone since she'd lost Ryce. Disconnected from emotions for so long, though, Kindra had no idea what to do with the frankly fucking useless tangle of them in her chest.

Taking more pictures than they needed gave Kindra something tangible to focus on, but she couldn't really concentrate until Aaron stepped into the stairwell, down to the first floor, and into an empty elevator.

"Man, I would highly recommend not visiting the first-floor john for at *least* an hour," Aaron joked as he passed security and returned the borrowed badge.

"Good God, yeah." Thomas laughed. "If you're just leaving, then *whew*. Thanks for the warning!"

Kindra held her breath until the front door opened and she saw him walk out of the building safe and whole.

"He's out," Kindra announced. Only then did she feel like she could breathe deep without risking hyperventilation.

Daelan was watching her, studying her reflection in the window. Could he see the tension in her shoulders and the quivering pulse point in her neck? It took more effort than she wanted to acknowledge to keep her hand from rising to cover the telltale flutter. Thankfully, whatever he guessed from observing her like she was their next target, he kept it to himself.

In fact, he didn't say a word until Hugo and Ryce showed up half an hour later, when he mentioned the Weston situation again, asking Ryce the same question he'd asked Kindra.

The only comment Ryce had on the possibility of their family's deaths was, "I wish we could've gotten Sera out of there."

But Sera was *definitely* Odira's daughter. Even if Kindra and Ryce could have pulled her away, there was no guarantee she'd come. She'd be just as likely to stab them and escape as she was to cheerfully join Cassidy's merry band of renegade bodyguard-assassins.

Watching Daelan walk out of the cramped bathroom, Kindra couldn't help wondering if Ryce would be as unaffected about leaving Daelan behind. Or Dru. She was beginning to wonder if *she* would be.

She met Ryce's eyes, and she knew those thoughts were coming through loud and clear in her expression. Ryce sighed and said, "Yeah, I know."

It was a relief when neither of the Calvers asked what, exactly, either of them knew. Hugo sat on the closed toilet, picking up the laptop from the vanity where Daelan had left it and covering both ears with the headphones, effectively blocking all of them out.

"Well, this looks like it should be an entertaining shift," Ryce said as he plugged a new SD card into the camera to replace the one Kindra was carrying back to Cassidy for analysis.

"Yeah. Good luck." Daelan slapped Ryce's shoulder and then followed Kindra out of the apartment.

The whole way back to the Citadel, Kindra pretended not to notice Daelan watching her. Pretended not to hear his quickly aborted attempts at conversation. She definitely pretended she couldn't see the concern on his face or the questions he wanted to ask. He left her alone, and she pretended everything was fine.

When they reached the Citadel twenty minutes later, it was almost true.

"**S**hould've known it'd come to this." Matthew Nevarez laughed, the sound more than a little broken, and checked the rearview mirror again. The same blue sedan had been following him several cars back for the last hour, ever since he left the Genesis Financial offices. "I mean, damn, Garret. You're not even trying for some fucking subtlety here. I *hired* that asshole!"

At a red light, he took a long breath and then pulled a legal pad out of his briefcase, penning a quick note.

If I'm going down, I intend to take them with me.
Gracelyn Bedford
Mutual Liberty Bank and Trust, Atlanta
129 36

He tore the sheet off as the light turned green. It took him a second red light to find a blank envelope in his case and press a stamp to the corner. It took a third to write an address in the center. At a fourth light, he wrote his name with the address of the Miami FBI field office as the return address.

The fifth light was when his tactics changed.

Matthew cut through the next intersection just *after* the light turned red, trapping his tail behind a blockade of cars. Several quick turns and five minutes later, he pulled up next to a mailbox, took a small key off his key ring, dropped it into the envelope with the letter, sealed it, and shoved it into the mailbox.

For ten minutes he drove fast but aimlessly; it seemed more like an attempt to confuse his stalkers rather than evade them. Another ten minutes and Matthew pulled into the driveway of his house. The sun had set and so the interior was dark, but he didn't turn on many lights. Instead, he walked to the fireplace in the living room, started a fire with a stack of papers he collected from his home office, and then switched on his stereo. Jazz filled the room.

The hard drive from his desktop only took a couple of minutes to extract. He calmly smashed it to pieces, and then threw the remains into the cheerily burning blaze. Doing the same to his laptop took longer, but Matthew worked methodically until the spacious, well-appointed living room smelled like burning plastic and heated metal.

Moving through the house, he closed curtains, locked doors, and armed the security system before grabbing his gun out of the lockbox in his office. He poured himself a full tumbler of bourbon from the small bar along one wall. Easing himself into his armchair, he sipped the liquor, eyes trained on the door to the backyard as the music floated over the room. It was peaceful, until his breaths started wheezing through his throat.

Sitting up, one hand pressed to his chest, he tried to breathe deep and even. It didn't work.

The wheezing got worse.

Matthew held up the tumbler in his hand, staring at the amber liquid as though it had betrayed him. Then, barely able to breathe, he began to laugh. He laughed until the glass fell out of his hand and cracked on the stone floor.

He laughed until he couldn't anymore.

He laughed until he died.

Chapter Twenty-Four

0119 : TUESDAY, MARCH 1

It had been almost twelve hours since Kindra watched Aaron walk out of Redwell's headquarters, and she couldn't quite eliminate the knot of worry in the pit of her stomach.

How did anyone *do* a job like this when they cared about the people working with them? And the Calvers *did* care. About each other and Aaron. About Ryce, whom they'd essentially adopted years ago. About Kindra too, she supposed. They cared, and without losing their shit, they somehow managed to watch each other walk into situations they might not come back from. Every single time.

Maybe it was easier if you'd spent your entire life caring. Maybe if Kindra had time, if this job wasn't her last with the Calvers, she'd be able to figure out the answer.

Clearing her head was obviously a lost cause. She slumped in the metal folding chair, ignoring the look Daelan shot her. Halfway through trying to run her hand through her hair, Kindra winced. Her fingers caught in the knots, and she felt the sweat and oil that had built up over the last two days. Since the last time she'd had the chance to take a real shower. By design, she hadn't given herself enough downtime yet. Downtime gave her mind too much room to roam.

Can I blame this shit month on temporary insanity and start over?

Kindra needed to get clean and get some sleep, but only one of those would be possible with the way her mind was churning.

"Do you think that driver knows there's something off about a sudden six-figure job offer?" Daelan's fingers paused on the keyboard.

"If he doesn't question it, he's an idiot. But that doesn't mean taking the job is the wrong move." Kindra shrugged. "Even if these drivers don't know exactly what Garret is doing, they've got to know *something* isn't right. I'd jump on the chance to get away. Especially if an offer like this presented itself."

"Even to go to an only slightly lesser evil?"

The kid had a point. Full-time driver to a morally gray state senator was only a couple steps up from the type of corruption he worked with now.

"One of you is free to go if you want." Aaron's announcement broke into the conversation. "Dru should be here soon to relieve the other."

Daelan and Kindra shared a glance. Kindra nodded toward the door. "Go get some sleep."

"You probably need it more than I do." But Daelan's eyes were drooping, and he'd been sagging deeper and deeper into his seat over the last hour.

"I won't be far behind you." *And I won't be able to sleep yet anyway.*

Although he hesitated, Daelan did nod and relinquish his seat to Aaron. The rest of the changing of the guard happened in silence. Aaron sat, made a note on the activity ledger, and quickly skimmed everything he'd missed since his previous shift.

"When was the last time anyone spotted Nevarez?" he asked.

"Just before 1900 last night." Through the camera he'd placed in Matthew Nevarez's office, Kindra had watched Susan Phan and the same tech guy who discovered the software on Garret's computer scour the room. Susan scowled when she found the hints Aaron had left behind and looked nearly apoplectic when she discovered the hidden camera that, if she believed the software on his computer, downloaded straight to the Feebs. "Susan finished her search about twenty minutes before Matthew returned to the building. When he left for the night, an hour later, he was followed by one of their plainclothes security. A guy Hugo and I identified earlier."

"I thought they'd called your—uh . . ." He glanced at Kindra. "I thought the Westons were called in."

"The guard was there for confirmation." Kindra managed, somehow, to keep most of her own confused emotion off her face. "Dru and Ryce were watching from the street. They said it was hard to see much, but they're pretty sure it was poison of some sort. Don't know if it was airborne or laced food, but he was alive and alone for half an hour or so before he stopped moving. The guard who showed up later stayed for about twenty minutes—took some of Nevarez's shit too: papers and some tech—and then he left. Ryce and Dru didn't think it was worth the potential risk to check it out for themselves, so cause of death is speculation at this point. No one has reported it to officials yet."

"Good riddance, traitor." Aaron dropped the logbook to the desk and leaned back in his chair. "Javier's team wasn't there?"

Kindra pursed her lips. "If they were, we never saw them."

The intervening silence grew teeth. Not sharp ones that ripped and tore at Kindra; flat, omnivoric teeth that gnawed on her patience and control until she *had* to say something just to break the tension.

"Why are you here?" Kindra blinked when the words tumbled out of her mouth. Whatever she'd been expecting to say, it honestly hadn't been that.

Aaron turned, his eyes glowing gold in the light thrown by the monitors. "You guys have my entire personal and military file. You *know* why I'm here."

"Not really." Kindra focused on the screens, gaze flicking between the internal feeds of Redwell headquarters and the cameras they had on Garret's house. "All I know is the what: the chain of events that happened. The why is different. The why is what made you go AWOL when other people would've hired a private eye or harassed the police or ignored the entire situation and drowned themselves in alcohol. But you? You run from a solid, apparently meaningful life to track down a stranger and take on two hit squads and an internationally respected—and feared—corporation." Kindra forced herself to look at him and, meeting his eyes, ask what she really wanted to know. "Why? Why do any of this?"

"Left a boyfriend too," he admitted a little ruefully. "He's pissed enough that I think he might actually kill me if I make it back alive. Geo is a scary sonuvabitch sometimes."

"See, though? That's my point. You had a *life*. Why did you walk away from it?"

Aaron shook his head. It seemed as though he wouldn't answer, that he'd brush off the question with a joke or ignore it completely. Then he ran a finger along the scar on his face.

"Jenna was brilliant—borderline genius—but she never wielded it the way you see some people do, you know? Never thought anyone else was stupid just 'cause they couldn't connect the dots like she could." Aaron smiled, a sad, toothless smile. "She was brilliant enough that she could've gotten an internship anywhere, but she was so excited to work for Genesis Financial because it meant she got to go home. We grew up just outside of Jacksonville, on the other side of the Georgia border, and our whole extended family still lives around here. She thought Genesis would be perfect. She could turn this internship into a job and have everything—the career she wanted in a place near us and near a couple of bases I could maybe get myself stationed when my deployment ended."

He'd been staring down at his hands, fingertips and eyes tracing the numerous scars and calluses that marred his dark skin, but he looked at Kindra then, his gaze steady and intense. "She was excited, couldn't stop talking about it. And then she did."

"Suddenly or slowly?" Kindra adjusted the focus on one of the cameras, but most of her attention was on Aaron.

"I'd've paid more attention if it happened all at once," Aaron admitted. "It trickled off, and I was so wrapped up in my own shit that I didn't press. And then it was too late and my CO was sending me home on emergency leave to attend a fucking funeral."

Ryce never got a funeral.

The thought popped into her head, clogging up her mind and her throat with more stupid, pointless emotion. It didn't matter. He hadn't died. Besides, what good would a funeral have been? There wouldn't have been anyone but his family to mourn him. No one else knew he existed.

And wasn't that just a kick to the kidney?

"So that was it?" Kindra cleared her throat. "Because she stopped talking about her job, you decided to launch yourself out of a good career and onto a slew of hit lists?"

"Her last letter had . . ." He grunted and rubbed his hand over his hair, his throat moving like the words were physically lodged there.

"You don't have to tell me if you don't want to."

Apparently permission to stay silent was what Aaron needed in order to speak. He cleared his throat and managed words.

"I didn't see the hint at the time, not until after she'd died, but . . . in her last letter, she said, 'To see the honor, the courage, and the determination humanity is capable of and not do our damnedest to live up to our own potential is the worst kind of failure and the darkest of sins.' And then, after that, you know what she said?" His breath caught, almost shuddered. "She wrote, 'How could I not risk everything to live up to the example you've always set?' A week after I got the letter, my mother called to tell me she'd died."

Kindra hesitated. "That's not a lot to go on."

"No, but it was enough to make me at least *look*." The fierce determination in Aaron's face almost made Kindra shrink back. "I found a couple of other cases that looked an awful lot like Jenna's—sudden suicides with families left wondering what the fuck they'd missed—and then I found out the companies they worked for were all tied to Genesis Financial and Redwell."

This part she knew. When he found out, he'd followed the trail to Bernard Gasper and put himself in the crosshairs of Redwell to try to solve the mystery of Jenna's death. All of that to answer the call for help that he'd heard too late.

Would Kindra have done the same for Ryce? If she'd had any indication that his death was fake, would she have hunted down the truth?

No. Probably not. Before this job, Kindra didn't know how to question orders.

Staged suicides though? What the hell could Garret be covering up with that? Something worth killing over. Something worse than murdering a few—a dozen? a hundred?—employees.

"Why the sudden interest?" Aaron was watching Kindra, scrutinizing her face with something between curiosity and skepticism. "Why ask now?"

She considered ignoring the question, but that wouldn't fly. Not after she'd dug into his personal life. But that didn't mean she had to tell him the *whole* truth.

"Haven't had much of a chance until now," she said. "And the only people I've ever worked with were related. I don't like not being able to predict my team members. To some extent at least." Sera never was entirely predictable.

Aaron nodded, but the intensity as he searched her face hinted that he knew there were pieces missing from her answer.

"What'd I miss?" Dru yawned widely as she spoke, practically stumbling into the room. Her baggy pajama pants were shockingly yellow when everything and everyone else in the house was dressed in shades of beige, gray, and black. She was like an amazing, perfectly timed ray of sunshine, because her arrival meant Kindra could flee, leaving behind a conversation that was about to head into uncertain territory.

"We're waiting on a report from Cassidy about the car for tomorrow." Kindra signed out of the shift on the logbook and wrote one last note beside the entry. Because she *should*, not because it gave her a valid excuse to avoid looking at either Dru or Aaron. Of course not. "I'm going to shower and try to get some sleep while I can."

Before either of them could say anything to hold her there, Kindra left, heading straight for the bathroom and locking herself inside. Not hiding. No. Just . . . a strategic retreat. To give herself the space to calm the fuck down.

In the morning, she'd be driving straight into the lion's den to grab the enemy by the scruff of the neck and drag him in for justice. Or punishment. Anything that threw her brain off-kilter needed to go. She'd put people in danger if she wasn't on her A game.

Stripping quickly, Kindra dropped her clothes in a pile and stepped into the shower. The water hit her cold at first, the shocking chill enough to knock her out of the emotional spiral she'd been trapped in for the last day.

Kindra felt unmoored, but all she could do was let the slowly warming water wash away as much of the grime and stress as it could.

Everything else? Well . . .

Day by day. That's all you can do. Day by day.

Chapter Twenty-Five

The itch was going to drive her crazy before she even pulled up to Garret Hadley's pompous monstrosity of a mansion. It was a single bobby pin that had been badly placed, and it was tugging on a single hair underneath her short brown wig. That was it. A single bobby pin. It took far more concentration than she liked to admit to keep her fingers away from her hair.

Some careful interference in Garret's communication with the limo company meant that he was currently unaware his usual driver no longer worked for him. The stress of the apparent defection of Matthew Nevarez and the continued hunt for Bernard Gasper meant—they all hoped—that he wouldn't bother looking too closely at his driver and noticing the switch.

The Calvers had observed Garret interact with the drivers often enough to know that he barely remembered their names. It seemed like his chauffeurs were practically an extension of the car to him: a part as essential but interchangeable as the steering wheel. Today, Kindra and the Calvers were counting on that oversight.

Parking, but leaving the engine running, Kindra got out of the limo and walked around to stand by the rear passenger door. She'd had to practice moving in the lifted shoes and the padding that gave her a breadth her frame didn't usually carry. Hands clasped behind her, shoulders back, chin up, eyes down, and feet shoulder-width apart, Kindra sank into the role she was supposed to play. Valet-bodyguard. Servant-protector. And, eventually, kidnapper.

That was the part Kindra was looking forward to: the moment when realization dawned in his eyes and fear took over every thought and reaction. She *loved* that moment, thrilled when it happened.

Exactly how fucked up was her mind, that another person's fear could make her feel so in control of her own? Was it more or less fucked up to be glad she still looked forward to that thrill despite her apparent emotional growth?

Doesn't matter. Not now.

One side of the massive, dark wood double door opened, and Garret stepped out of his imitation-Mediterranean mansion, his attention on the tablet in his hand. His forehead was etched with furrows that hadn't been this deep or obvious last week.

"Run the red lights if you have to," Garret ordered when Kindra opened the door for him. He never even looked at her. "I need to be there in five minutes."

The drive took fifteen. At least. But it didn't matter because that wasn't where he would be heading this morning anyway.

"Yes, sir," Kindra murmured, lowering her voice enough not to set off subconscious alarm bells in Garret's brain.

He slid into the car, and Kindra closed the door behind him, smiling. Worry and distraction could be better than a disguise sometimes.

For the first few minutes, she followed the expected path. Then, as they reached the halfway point of their time on I-95, Kindra opened the center console and flicked on the signal disruptor she'd placed there this morning. Once she was sure the car's GPS and whatever tracking systems Garret was wearing wouldn't reveal their location, she eased off the highway.

Garret didn't notice until they were halfway through the tightly curved off-ramp. "What the hell? Where are you going, you moron?"

The off-ramp merged straight into traffic. Kindra made a sharp right one block from the highway. Ryce and Aaron, both wearing masks, were waiting in a narrow side street where the buildings had few windows and the city had no cameras. They dove into the car as soon as she slowed, both of them training guns on Garret.

"What is this?" Garret's voice was low-pitched but loud. Scared and angry. "Who are you?"

"I'd stop talking right now if I was you." Ryce made his voice almost gravelly, twisting the words into a South African accent. Kindra had always been better at disguises and characters—backstories and specific psychologies and in-depth knowledge of the person she created—but she'd never been able to mimic accents as well as Ryce.

"You have no idea what kind of hell you've just raised," Garret growled.

"Maybe. Maybe not. I guess we'll see whose day looks worse when we get to the end of it, hmm?" Ryce laughed and took a black strip of fabric out of his pocket. "Seems like you need help keepin' quiet, *chommie*."

With Aaron holding his gun six inches from Garret's head, Ryce gagged the man, knotting it behind Garret's head so tightly that it pressed his cheeks back in a ghastly mockery of a smile. Garret protested—the words turned into garbled moans by the gag—but he didn't struggle. Not while Aaron watched him with emotionless eyes and a steady aim.

Kindra watched all of it in the rearview mirror, relishing the glint of barely controlled terror in Garret's eyes, but didn't say a word as she drove the route with the fewest traffic cameras, through backstreets and neighborhoods. They stopped in a parking garage to switch to a small cargo truck before making their way to the rendezvous point.

On Sunday, Cassidy had pointed them toward an empty three-story warehouse looking out over the harbor. When their truck approached the door now, the wide aluminum entrance rolled up without a sign or signal from Kindra. Dru stood off to the side, automatic assault rifle at the ready and her hand on the rolling door's controls.

As Kindra eased the truck into the warehouse, Dru caught her eye, anxiety obvious. Kindra winked as she passed. Dru didn't respond, but Kindra saw her relax slightly as she returned her attention to the world outside the warehouse, covering their backs until the door that Dru and Hugo had reinforced with Kevlar panels could be closed.

When Kindra rapped the all-clear on the back of the van, Aaron opened the rear door and, still aiming his gun at Garret's forehead, jumped backward out of the vehicle. Ryce had Garret by the collar of his suit jacket, forcing him to follow Aaron with a rough shove. Kindra and Dru followed them up to the third floor.

Most of the windows had been covered, leaving only a few open for surveillance of the parking level. The vantage provided a much better view not only of the lower level but the surrounding buildings. It was a risk, but combined with the cameras Daelan and Aaron were monitoring downstairs, it gave them a better chance of spotting anyone on approach.

In the center of the almost empty room, Hugo and Cassidy were waiting. *Almost* empty—except for the metal chair and rolling medical tray with an array of shiny, viciously pointy instruments of pain.

Cassidy smiled—a smile cruelly cold enough to remind Kindra of Odira. "Hello, Garret."

He tried to speak around the gag, his bloodshot eyes widening. Kindra grinned at him, reaching up to tug out the bobby pin that had been irritating her since she left the Citadel early this morning. Once that one was gone, the rest quickly followed so she could pull off the wig cap and shake her hair free.

Ryce pushed Garret's shoulder so hard he struggled to stay on his feet. He gasped something unintelligible when he saw Kindra freeing herself from the disguise's padding, and she put a little more tooth in her smile. She couldn't dredge up even the smallest iota of guilt for what he would suffer in this room today. His decisions had spread pain and death across half the world. Maybe more. Nothing Cassidy and Hugo could do to him here would reap half of what he had sown.

For most of her life, Kindra had been a gun, loaded and aimed by someone else's hands for someone else's reasons. Today she got to be the hand holding the gun, and she was extraordinarily pleased with her aim.

Hugo and Ryce securely strapped Garret's ankles to the legs of the chair with duct tape, zip-tied *and* duct-taped his wrists to the arms, and looped more tape across his waist and around the back of the chair like a seat belt. Garret Hadley wasn't escaping until Cassidy and Hugo were ready to let him leave.

Only when they were done did they remove the gag.

"Do you know who we are, Garret?"

He coughed and swallowed before nodding, anger and fear battling for control of his expression. "Fucking zombies."

"We might as well be for as many times as you've tried to kill us," Hugo said.

"Which has obviously done you *so* much good." Cassidy held a finely honed blade in her left hand.

With a look from her, Hugo grabbed Garret's short hair and yanked his head back, allowing Cassidy to draw the tip of the blade across his throat. The pressure wasn't enough to break skin, but it left a red line, like a guide for later.

"You're going to die today, Garret," Cassidy said. "And you're going to do it knowing that everything you spent years hiding in the shadows and squirreling away in overseas bank accounts is in the hands of the FBI. You're going to die with *nothing*, not even the name you've tried so hard to keep clean. What you do in the next hour will determine exactly how fast that happens."

When Cassidy pulled the knife back, Hugo released Garret's head. She slapped him across the face, the open-palm *smack* loud in the empty room. Garret's head jerked back so hard Kindra could hear the bones in his neck protest. He hissed in pain, anger momentarily overwhelming fear as he glared at Cassidy.

"I'm going to give you something to make my job a little easier, but it'll dull things for you." Cassidy sounded resigned. Almost disappointed. "So before we get to that, I want to make sure you know exactly how bad I can make this experience."

Kindra shuddered as Cassidy picked up a thin blade and slammed it into Hadley's left side: under his ribs, over his kidney.

Someone had done that to Kindra once. It *hurt*. She'd hated the fiery slice, the agony that had radiated through her entire torso so strongly that she hadn't been able to pinpoint exactly where she'd been stabbed for minutes. She'd hated the way the pain had both sharpened her senses and dulled her mind. She'd *hated* suffering that torment at the hands of a warlord Amett had pissed off. But she grinned listening to Hadley scream.

"Sadist," Dru murmured.

Kindra glanced her way, just to make sure the teasing note in Dru's voice also showed up on her face. "Problem?" she shot back.

"Maybe." Dru almost smiled.

"Don't worry, Bomb Squad. I won't hurt you any more than you like."

"My safeword is 'Columbus,'" Dru deadpanned, a slight smirk on her lips, but her eyes studied the parking lot below.

Columbus? Circle? Where they'd spoken to each other for the first time. In disguise, yes, but the reminder was almost . . . sweet.

In the background, Garret's screams had dropped to moans, and those faded to helpless whimpers when Cassidy picked up a syringe of sodium thiopental—truth serum—and injected a dose into his arm. The clatter when Cassidy dropped the syringe onto the metal tray echoed off the cinderblock walls.

Garret flinched, and his breathing hitched unevenly. Panic. Or maybe he was on the verge of tears. Garret Hadley was ruthless, yes, but it seemed most of the blood he had on his hands had splattered on him from a distance. He wasn't used to pain, and he definitely wasn't used to this kind of pressure. Maybe this man could control a boardroom and a shadowy international empire and never feel a twinge of nerves or guilt, but here he was the weak link, and Kindra was pretty sure he knew it.

"No matter what you get out of me, it won't—it won't matter." Garret was beginning to slur, but he was obviously trying to fight the drugs. Sitting ramrod straight, his chin lifted, only his slower-than-normal blinks and the soft edges to his speech gave away that he was losing that battle. "They'll change all the codes as soon as they know I'm gone, and switch all the keys. You could pull every . . . every last memory out of my head and it wouldn't—it still wouldn't get you any closer to . . . anything."

He'd started his speech with purpose, but by the end he looked a little lost, a lot confused, and utterly drugged.

"I think it's time to see if you're right." Cassidy gave Garret a shark's smile and leaned closer. The blade in her hand, already stained with his blood, sliced easily through his expensive shirt and left a paper-thin trail of blood on the skin beneath. "Now tell me, Garret. What happened to Isaac Marks?"

Garret pressed his trembling lips together and shook his head. Tears leaked from the inside corners of his eyes. He was a man on the edge of cracking, and Kindra saw the moment he tumbled into helpless, babbling fear. It was the same instant Cassidy smiled and said, "All right then," as she pressed the blade to the skin over his heart.

Garret's voice broke when he screamed, but he forced words through his beleaguered vocal cords. "Fucking car accident! We paid—paid— Shit. Matt found him . . ." He trailed off, confusion and pain carved in the lines of his face. "To Martinez. He did it."

"The squad you have after the Westons?" Hugo walked behind the chair, and Garret's tension visibly rose. His head twitched and his red-rimmed eyes practically spun in his head trying to keep Cassidy *and* Hugo inside his field of vision.

"Trial—" he wheezed. "Pulled them off—off the Westons for— Marks was a trial run. New team. Hadn't worked with them. Before this."

Cassidy and Hugo shared a look over Garret's head, the same silent communication Kindra had seen from them a thousand times now.

"Watch the windows." Dru's free hand, the one not steadying her rifle, brushed Kindra's palm. Their fingers linked for a moment, and then Dru pulled away. "I'm going to walk the perimeter."

Kindra eased into Dru's position by the windows, hidden from sight but with a good view of the surrounding area. It had definitely been a good idea to have Daelan and Aaron on the ground floor. The interrogation was a distraction. They had holes in their surveillance net—unavoidable given their time constraints—and they had to be kept as small as possible. It helped that everyone was aware of the holes, and that they didn't plan on staying here once Garret lost his usefulness.

Despite the disturbingly interesting sounds coming from the center of the wide-open room, Kindra watched the parking lot and the buildings in the near distance instead of Cassidy's handiwork. From the sounds, Garret seemed lost to the pain and the drugs now, spilling information as fast as he was probably spilling blood.

"What about the ties to Burma?" Cassidy asked, her voice coaxingly soft. "You're using Redwell's work there to cover yourself like you did in Echemorro, aren't you?"

Garret started mumbling a broken answer. Ryce input notes into the laptop connected to Daelan's. Everything Garret told them would have to be verified before it could be trusted, but Kindra wasn't thinking about that now. Instead, she reveled in the anguish of a man partially responsible for ripping her life and her family apart—more than once—and kept an eye on the outside world, trying to make sure that the power he wielded didn't strike her down again. Kindra knew all too well how easy it was for disaster to sneak up on someone.

The faint *clack* of metal against plastic gave away Dru's approach and kept Kindra from jumping when Dru murmured, "What do you think?"

"About your mother's interrogation techniques?" Kindra glanced over her shoulder at Dru.

"About today. Getting him here." She shifted her weight, her eyes darting to the windows like she expected to see someone floating in midair, watching them. Her rifle was slung across her back and the Nighthawk was in her hand, her finger hovering very close to the trigger. "It feels too easy."

"Sometimes plans work, you know." But Dru wasn't wrong. They'd expected a tail. A rescue. An ambush. Something. It had been very quiet on all fronts, considering exactly who they'd kidnapped less than an hour ago.

Dru shook her head. "No. Daelan just told me that there's been *no* police contact or calls to Redwell's internal security team. The other execs just got an email, supposedly from Garret, claiming a stomach flu."

Atropos bless it. Daelan had been keeping an eye and an ear on Redwell's reaction so that Cassidy and Hugo would know when they had to move. This was bad. This meant Garret's second-in-command had probably decided to cut their losses rather than risk the press and possible exposure of rescuing him.

"Kindra, *nothing* with Garret Hadley is this easy." When Dru absently stroked her Nighthawk with her thumb, Kindra saw how hard she was fighting the urge to pace and fidget and triple-check the perimeter. "Something's not right."

Shifting her weight to the balls of her feet, Kindra scanned the windows of the building opposite them one more time. It was the only building of similar height in this complex. If Odira was coming for them, that's where she'd be. Setting up a strike from a distance to eliminate as many of the Calvers as possible before anyone could react.

"Should we interrupt?" Kindra asked when another agonized scream ripped through the room.

Dru nodded and stepped toward her parents. Kindra spotted a glint where there shouldn't have been one—the scope and barrel of a rifle where a second ago there hadn't been anything.

"*Get down!*" Kindra tackled Dru to the ground.

Glass shattered.

Two bullets.

They hadn't hit the floor yet.

Someone screamed.

A split second pause.

Two more bullets blasted through the window.

All Kindra knew was that she hadn't been hit. That Dru hadn't been hit.

Someone else had.

Staying low and small, Kindra scrambled along the floor toward the center of the room.

She didn't bother checking on Garret. The damage the high-powered round had done to the man's head was obvious and brutal.

Hugo lay on his back next to the dead hostage, stunned but not bleeding. Cassidy knelt over someone else, her breathing harsh and her movements frantic.

Blood. There was so much blood spilling out of that body.

Kindra knew who it was before she saw his face—she'd known who it was as soon as she realized Hugo wasn't the one who'd been hit. Her mind hadn't let her acknowledge it, though. Hadn't let her attach that name to the life bleeding out onto the cold floor.

"I can't—I can't stop it!" Cassidy's hands pressed against the wound in Ryce's abdomen, but it didn't matter. Blood bubbled up in the spaces between her fingers, and the cloth she'd pressed almost inside the wound was soaked through. The smell coming from her brother's body meant it wasn't only blood. The bullet had hit organs. Acids and bacteria were spilling into cavities not meant to contain them. Stopping the bleeding wasn't their sole concern: even a top-tier surgeon and a cargo ship of antibiotics might not be enough to save Ryce from the infection that was already setting in.

Kindra leaned over her brother, her eyes burning and her throat almost closed.

"You already died on me once. Don't you dare do it again!"

Shots echoed through the room. More glass shattered. Something in the distance exploded. Kindra didn't even glance up to see what was happening.

Ryce was coughing up blood.

"Don't, Ryce." Kindra's chest hurt like she was the one who'd been shot.

"Trying not to." Ryce coughed something that might have started as a laugh.

"Try harder!" She grabbed his shoulders and pressed him onto the floor as if she could keep him from dying just by holding him in place. The trained, logical, distant portion of her mind already knew how hopeless this fight was. The rest of her didn't care. She could barely stop herself from shaking him. "You're not dying on me again! You can't leave me alone!"

"You're—you're not alone. Stay with them, Kinny," Ryce gasped, blood pooling in his mouth. "Don't—" He cringed, his entire body tightening to protect himself from the pain. There was nowhere for him to go. This time, there was no escaping it. "Don't disappear. You need them. Stay . . ."

His eyes closed. Kindra watched him struggle like hell to get them open again. He'd lost too much blood. There was too much internal damage. Her brother was slipping away. Dying. Again. And this time she had to watch it happen.

"Promise, Kinny. Stay."

He died, eyes open and locked on hers, before Kindra could say a word.

Someone pulled on her arm, but Kindra didn't budge. She didn't know who was there, but it wasn't Ryce.

Ryce was gone.

Chapter Twenty-Six
0932: TUESDAY, MARCH 1

When the tug on Kindra's arm repeated, she couldn't resist the pull. It yanked her away from her brother's lifeless body and nearly sent her sprawling across the cold floor. A bullet hit the wall behind her. It had been a second away from passing right through her head.

She didn't care.

"He will never forgive you if you get yourself killed," Dru whispered, her voice trembling and thick. "Get up and *fight!*"

A hand grabbed the back of Kindra's shirt and hauled her to her feet. Training kicked in, helping her stumble forward without tripping under Dru's forced guidance. Years of practice compelled her to lock her emotions away in a triple-sealed box in her subconscious and concentrate only on the details. Only on the job.

Survive. Get through this. Break later.

Everyone was retreating, getting away from the exposure of the wide panels of visually obstructed but not bulletproof windows on this floor. They grabbed their gear and guns, and bolted toward the stairwell, leaving two dead behind.

Dru shoved a Kevlar jacket into Kindra's arms. She almost fumbled it, but her grip tightened and it stayed. Putting it on was another story. As soon as they were in the stairwell and behind a solid concrete wall, Kindra dropped her bags, wiped her bloody hands, and shrugged into the Kevlar, buckling it tight. Beside her, Dru did the same.

"Where are they?" Kindra watched the stairwell door, but no one appeared. Hugo and Cassidy were trapped inside by the bullets still blasting through the broken windows, or they were dead. Or, maybe, but not very likely, they'd found another way out.

"I saw them head toward the west stairs." Dru efficiently checked her guns as they raced down to the second floor.

Kindra looked back at the third floor. "I thought those were blocked off?"

"Then they unblocked it!" Dru, wrapped in as much Kevlar as she could be, stopped on the landing midway between the second and ground floor. She pressed against the wall next to the window, rifle at the ready, took a deep breath, and slowly peeked out, her gaze darting everywhere until she pulled back sharply, her eyes closed.

"One van and two cars on the ground level. I think I saw Javier. We're fucked if Odira decided to play nice with someone else for once." Dru swallowed and opened her eyes. "I saw what looked like a booby trap on the west door."

Kindra shifted around her to peek out the window. The building was L-shaped, which was the only reason they could spot the devices rigged to two of the doors on the perpendicular extension. It also gave them a decent shot at those two traps.

"Motion sensors with trip wires as backup, if it's Odira's work." She pulled Dru down the last half flight of stairs to where Aaron and Daelan were armed and waiting. "They can't have covered all of the exits, though, even if there are six on their crew."

"Can we disarm the traps? Or avoid them?" Daelan's attention locked on the closest exit, finger resting just off the trigger of his AK-47. Hell might be about to burst through that door.

Kindra grunted. "I could try, but there's no way they're using the same system. Sera would've altered it as soon as they declared me anathema."

"Shoot them." Aaron rolled his shoulders, his expression grim. "If we take out two of the traps at the same time, it may divide their attention enough to give us a chance to get out."

"Will that work?" Dru asked, looking to Kindra.

"Maybe. We'd have to split up." Kindra couldn't focus on exactly how Odira would react in this situation—or Amett or Sera—because the anger that overwhelmed her only made it harder to concentrate. And harder to push away the memory of Ryce's last, blood-clogged breath. "Best shot we have right now."

Dru glanced one more time at the stairs—the ones Hugo and Cassidy *hadn't* followed them down—then back at Kindra. Their comms were blocked or scrambled or broken. Maybe all three. Not a surprise with Odira and Sera working against them. They couldn't go looking. If they didn't keep moving, *all* of them would die here today. The more time they gave Odira and Amett to react, the harder it would be to outmaneuver them.

Dru nodded. "Move out."

As if they'd been working together for years instead of days, they ran in sync. Aaron took the lead, clearing the hallway and scouting the rooms, keeping their path away from windows. Daelan was behind him, eyes alert and movements sharp. Dru moved next, watching the sidelines but slightly distant, her mind probably working out the angles and paths of escape. Kindra walked mostly in reverse, making sure no one shot them in the back. Making sure her own *family* didn't shoot them in the back.

They paused in the middle of the warehouse, knowing this was their last second to plan.

"Escape and move to Quebec," Dru ordered. "If no one else is there within two hours of arrival, you run for your fucking life, and you don't stop for anything."

Dru grabbed Kindra and hauled her close for a kiss. It was more teeth than lips, more weapons than skin, and it felt more like a good-bye than an "I'll see you later." It didn't matter. The touch, the reminder of something other than loss and rage and too much blood, settled something in Kindra. It made it possible for her to *think*.

"Don't you *dare* die, baby, you hear me?" Dru spoke with the same voice she'd used to issue her orders. The determination and the glimmer of fear in her green eyes drew Kindra in. She rested her forehead against Dru's and breathed in the moment, opened her mouth, and—

The south wall exploded.

Kindra pushed Dru down, diving in the opposite direction and hoping to draw fire. Bullets smacked into the walls, the windows, the floor, shattering glass and cracking concrete. Kindra scrambled across the floor, almost colliding with Daelan. Shoving him onward, she stayed low and searched for cover. Looking back was impossible.

She had to hope Dru and Aaron had gone in the other direction, had found shelter or, better, a safe exit.

They were all trained and knew how to take care of themselves. If Kindra let herself focus on them—on Ryce, on *Dru*—she'd get herself killed.

Kindra practically lifted Daelan off the ground by his backpack as she helped him to get his feet underneath himself. They ran for a small side door, locked and dead-bolted. The chances of death on the other side were about fifty-fifty, but staying here kicked the odds up to about ninety.

Kindra aimed her Colt and fired until the handle of the door was obliterated. The next three shots went to the corner where the detonator—if there was one here—would be. Nothing exploded. She rammed the door with her shoulder and ran through first, tense and ready to cover Daelan if someone was lying in wait.

The coast seemed clear. Not for long. Bullets were getting closer, barely missing them. One passed so close to Kindra's head that she felt a heat welt rising on her cheek. Off to the left, another heavy *thud* like a door being slammed open far too hard. Dru and Aaron escaping the building? *Atropos bless it, I hope so.*

"Hold this!" Daelan thrust his bag into her hands, unzipping it and digging out a device that looked like four bricks of C-4 and an old cell phone. In his other hand, Daelan held another disposable phone. He tossed the bomb into the doorway they'd exited and then grabbed his backpack, jabbing at Kindra to get her to move.

They ran. Daelan hit a couple of buttons on his phone. A two-second delay.

Boom.

The fire behind them grew louder and brighter and hotter, fueled by the additional explosion. The fire would help hide their trail. It would help hide the evidence of their time in the warehouse. It was a good thing as long as Dru, Aaron, Cassidy, and Hugo had made it out in time.

There was no going back now, not for anything or anyone.

"We need transport! *Now!*" Kindra grabbed the wall to pull herself around the sharp corner without falling. Daelan followed, his boots thudding out of time with her steps.

They weren't moving fast enough. Based on the quickly widening column of smoke rising into the air, the fire was growing fast.

Somewhere behind them, an engine growled, the noise getting closer with each second. The engine was large—eight cylinder, probably. Not a sports car or anything small. Van. Truck. Not maneuverable in cramped quarters. Kindra needed to find some cramped quarters. It wouldn't necessarily mean safety, but the chances of outrunning anything on wheels were . . . not good.

Kindra had memorized pieces of the area map, but it was incomplete at best and she couldn't be sure where she and Daelan were. She'd lost all directionality in the frantic flight from the warehouse. The warehouse that had become Ryce's pyre.

At least I get to attend his funeral this time.

Pain clogged her throat. Her eyes burned in a way she couldn't blame on the smoke.

"There!" Daelan's scream yanked Kindra back.

Kindra followed him toward a narrower alley, not wasting breath responding. Hopefully it would lead them away from the disastrous, landmine-riddled chessboard their decisions had landed them on.

The engine drew closer. A bullet flew over Kindra's shoulder, cracking into the wall. More followed, each one getting closer to its target. To Kindra. To Daelan.

They reached the alley.

Two more bullets struck the wall. Both were far too close to Daelan's head.

Kindra grabbed the back of his shirt, pulling him toward a dumpster they could use for cover. Daelan jerked and overcompensated. Bullets barely missed her shoulder. His foot slid on a piece of cardboard. Losing balance, he fell, his head striking the dumpster with a solid *thunk*. He crumpled, collapsing on his side on the grimy concrete, eyes open but unfocused.

Kindra needed to run *now* if she had any hope of escape, but leaving him alone in this condition was a death sentence. Staying might condemn them both.

In the few seconds she dithered, a car door opened at the mouth of the alley. A fresh magazine was pushed into a gun. There wasn't enough time for Kindra to turn around and shoot with anything close to accuracy.

"Don't move, Kindra."

Slowly, so slowly she almost wasn't moving, Kindra closed her eyes. She didn't need to look to know how the scene she'd found herself in would be laid out. Her father would be standing half-hidden behind the dumpster or the door of his vehicle, turned to the side to offer a smaller target and give himself the ability to keep an eye on his six. His rifle—or his Remington 1911 if he planned on moving for the up-close kill—would be ready.

"Hands away from your sides. Turn around. Slowly."

Why hadn't he shot her yet? Sure, he didn't have his old accuracy, but at this range he should've been able to hit *something* vital. Amett's victims rarely knew he was there. One thing he was good at was invisibility, ending lives before the victim even knew they were in danger. Talking to them wasn't usually part of his plan. Ordering them to physically face him *never* was.

But, then again, killing his own children probably hadn't been part of his plan before this week either.

Kindra had to force her eyes open as she followed Amett's instructions.

About fifteen feet away, her father stood almost exactly as she had imagined him, his Remington aimed straight at her head.

"Was that really him?"

The question threw Kindra. "Who?"

"Ryce."

"You should know. Weren't you the one who called the shot?"

Amett closed his eyes, his expression collapsing. His hand shook but stayed level. "No. I didn't."

Did she believe him? It didn't matter. If he hadn't seen it happen, Kindra would make sure he had to live with the memory anyway, that it was embedded so deep in his mind, he'd never be able to dig it out and throw it away.

"He was gut shot with a fucking sniper round and bled out, smelling like death." Kindra shoved each word across the distance that separated them and hoped they lodged in Amett's chest like individual darts tipped with a time-release poison. She hoped they killed him in bits and pieces like he was probably about to kill her.

Eyes open now, Amett stared at Kindra, the lines and micro expressions on his face hinting that whatever was happening inside his mind was enough to cause physical pain. The signs were subtle, enough that Kindra was sure there weren't many others who would be able to read them, but to Kindra—whose life had depended on her ability to read Amett's and Odira's moods—the agony was written clearly in his unfocused eyes, the tightness of his mouth, the deepening of the lines between his eyes . . . the way the tremor in his hand worsened.

Kindra expected that pain to transform to anger. Outrage. She expected him to pull the trigger and kill her with the same painful efficiency someone had used on Ryce.

Amett's face went blank. His gun didn't drop, but no bullets flew from it either. Words were what he flung across the distance at Kindra.

"Lillian French is the one who ordered the hit on Hadley. She called it in as soon as you grabbed him."

"The military liaison?" She had barely come up on the Calvers' radar. There'd been nothing about her in the thousands of files Isaac had sent them.

Amett nodded, but otherwise continued as though Kindra hadn't spoken. "She's heading out of the country. I don't know where. She'd never trust us enough to tell us that much. There's almost nothing tying her to anything you have on Hadley, because what he had her working on was separate. Something with weapons."

But what was she doing? Selling military secrets? Shipping weapons meant for the United States to foreign militias?

"She'll be prepared to help the company and the Feds lay the blame for everything at Hadley's feet within the next three hours, if she hasn't started already." Amett sucked in a breath. Frowning, eyes turned down, forehead creased, Amett looked on the verge of tears. "Going after her won't do you any good. You have to look into Jenna Tanvers. You have to follow the money and the people who disappeared. It goes back years. More than a decade."

It had to be a lie. A setup. It'd be a good plan, to feed her false intel and send her back to the enemy camp like an . . . information grenade or something. That *had* to be what was happening. It was exactly Odira's kind of twisted.

And yet . . . and yet Kindra had never seen as much devastation on her father's face as when she'd told him how Ryce had died. Not even when Ryce died the first time.

"Why are you telling me this?"

"Because she won't stop until all of you are ash, and I need you to know what you're up against. Because Odira convinced Javier, John, and Nuura to join us, and they won't make it easy for you to hide. And . . . and because I'm sorry." His dark eyes, almost exactly like her own, had never looked so old. "I'm sorry for shoving you into this life, and I'm sorry we never gave you a choice. I'm giving you this one chance to run and disappear, because Odira will kill you if she sees you again, and she won't think twice about it."

"What about Sera?"

"I'll try if there's a chance to get her out, but . . ." Amett shook his head. "She's always been her mother's daughter."

Daelan groaned near her feet. In the distance, fire roared and gunshots echoed off the buildings. Reminders of the world outside the alley, and hope that she and Daelan weren't the only ones left alive.

"You should be able to find a car if you head west a block. Parking garage. Get him out of here," Amett ordered, nodding toward Daelan. "And, if he's still alive, tell Hugo I should've listened to him in Sarajevo."

Would Amett run? Turn his back on Kindra, get in the van, and drive away?

He didn't. Keeping his gun trained on Kindra, Amett stepped away from the cover of the van's door, both shoulders squarely facing Kindra and his jaw clenched. "Shoot me."

"What?"

"Shoot me, or she'll know. She'll know this conversation happened."

She brought her gun up quickly and leveled it at his head. "I could kill you." *I should kill you.*

"You could." Amett didn't move. Didn't argue or barter or hide or attack. He stabilized his footing, rolled his shoulders, and waited, never looking away from Kindra's eyes. He put his life in Kindra's hands and waited for his daughter to decide what it was worth.

Shit. Kindra knew as soon as she pulled the trigger that she would probably regret her decision.

The bullet thumped into Amett's left arm. He grunted, hissed in a pained breath, his gun clattering to the ground as his grip weakened, and he curled over himself, turning to protect his injured arm.

Without letting herself think about the choice she'd made, Kindra turned to Daelan. He was sitting up on his own, one hand braced against the side of the dumpster as he tried to push himself to his feet.

"Was that Amett?" Only the slightest hint of daze lingered in his eyes.

Kindra ignored the question. "We need to move."

Pulling him to his feet and keeping a tight grip to make sure he stayed balanced, Kindra strode out of the alley as quickly as she could pull Daelan along. She followed Amett's directions despite a whisper of doubt in the back of her mind, a warning and a reminder that he was the enemy now. That this could all be some elaborate trap.

Didn't matter. She had no time to come up with a plan B. Smoke from the warehouse was getting thicker. The gunshots in the distance had died off—meaning everyone had bled out or moved on. Sirens approached, a ways off still but getting closer every second.

Kindra and Daelan needed to be gone. Now.

Daelan regained most of his equilibrium by the time they reached the road, so he pulled away. Not completely—his hand gripped Kindra's elbow hard enough that she knew he wasn't out of trouble yet, but the added space between them made it easier to pick up the pace.

They ran.

Turning west brought them into a slightly more populated area. Low rent, which was good. Low rent usually meant old cars, and old cars were blessedly easy to steal.

Kindra spotted the garage Amett had mentioned and nudged Daelan toward it. They approached from the rear, and she peered over a low wall, scanning for cameras. She spotted two on the ground floor. Two quick shots destroyed the one with a view of the north end of the garage. Daelan pointed at a dingy silver Accord, heading in that direction.

Kindra slammed the butt of her gun against the glass, shattering the rear passenger window so she could reach in to unlock the doors. Daelan dropped into the passenger seat while Kindra jogged to the other side. By the time she was sitting in the driver's seat, he'd popped open the cover of the steering column and yanked down the necessary wires. Buckling herself in, she was ready to shove the car into reverse as soon as he kick-started the engine.

They rolled the windows down to make the missing one less conspicuous. Kindra forced Daelan into a baseball cap they found in the backseat and ordered him to hide his face and pretend to sleep.

"What about you? You'll get spotted by traffic cameras," he argued despite his compliance.

"I'm driving, moron. Can't exactly pretend to be sleeping, can I?" But he was right and the exposure made her nervous.

The hat landed on Kindra's head. When Kindra looked at Daelan to argue, he was curled up with his backpack as a pillow and his arm flung over his face like he was trying to block out the sunlight.

"Shut up and get us there fast," he muttered before Kindra could say a word.

Relaxing just a touch, Kindra pulled the cap into the right position on her head and did as she was told.

She didn't think about how shot to shit their excellently executed plan had become. She didn't think about Garret's half-missing head. She didn't think about watching her brother's life slip between her desperate fingers. She didn't think about Amett's warning, or how soon she'd sincerely regret not placing that bullet straight between his eyes.

No.

Kindra thought about Aaron. Cassidy. Hugo. *Dru.* She thought about arriving at the rendezvous point and finding it empty. She thought about what the fuck she would do if she and Daelan were the only ones left alive.

Her next breath shook in her lungs. Her eyes burned.

Using a lifetime of practice, Kindra gripped her spiraling emotions and shoved them deep into the darkest recesses of her mind.

She thought about absolutely nothing for the rest of the twenty-minute drive. Until she could see for herself just how badly her life was fucked.

Chapter Twenty-Seven

1057 : TUESDAY, MARCH 1

K indra and Daelan abandoned the car on a stretch of highway between cameras, a spot that gave them easy access to a residential street through some trees and a chain-link fence that probably hadn't been fixed or thought about in a decade. It took another twenty minutes of walking through side yards and backstreets before they found the not-quite-complete apartment building.

Construction had stopped six months ago when the company funding it went bankrupt, and its future was still in the hands of banks and attorneys. It had never been properly lived in, but right now it *looked* abandoned, and the sight caught Kindra by the throat, weakening the walls she'd built to keep her fear at bay.

It was code-named Quebec because this had been plan Q, the one they'd hoped they wouldn't need. The place to go when everything went to Tartarus in a tutu.

Would they be the first ones here? Were she and Daelan the only ones to make it away from Odira and Martinez alive?

Beside her, Daelan adjusted the strap of his backpack and squared his shoulders. "C'mon. The longer we wait, the worse the suspense is going to get."

They'd been somewhat hidden in a line of trees, but to reach the rear stairwell, they had to sprint across open ground. With no electricity running through the building and no legal owner to care about security or vandalism, Kindra wasn't worried about cameras, only eyes from the street. Neighbors noticing something off. Avoiding easy lines of sight as much as possible, Kindra led Daelan across a yard littered with leftover supplies and broken construction equipment. When they reached the metal door, she scanned it carefully, looking for any sign it had been opened recently. Something like . . .

There. A smudge of dried blood just below shoulder level, as though someone's hand had slid while pulling the handleless door open.

Someone had been here, and that person was bleeding.

Shit.

Kindra used the small dent in the metal frame of the door to wedge her fingers in and pull it open. Holding it wide enough for Daelan to pass through, she wiped away the signs of blood and whatever clues she'd left herself. There wasn't much she could do about the footprints in the yard, but storm clouds were rolling in. Hopefully rain and wind would wash the rest of their presence away.

Closing the door quietly, Kindra turned toward the stairs. And stopped when she saw Daelan leaning against the wall, skin gleaming with sweat and eyes closed as he breathed deep. Too deep. On the verge of hyperventilation.

"What's wrong?" Maybe he'd been hurt worse than she thought. How had he hidden it this long? Kindra hadn't seen—*didn't* see—any blood, but not every death blow bled. "Daelan, what—"

"Fine." He flapped his hand at her, but the way he sucked in air like the oxygen wasn't settling in his blood definitely wasn't fine. "Dizzy. Nauseous. Just need to . . ." He gasped again and gently straightened, tilting his head back to rest against the wall. "Need to catch my breath now . . . now that no one's shooting . . . at us."

Kindra looked up the stairs, quickly spotting three more smudges of blood—two on the railing and one on the gray wall. There was no body in sight. Whoever left those marks had made it at least to the second floor. Hopefully they'd made it all the way to the corner apartment on the third.

"Go." Daelan nudged Kindra's shoulder, gently but firmly pushing her toward the stairs. "Tell them I'm on my way up."

"Fuck you. Cassidy would pull a gun on me if I left you here alone." At least, she might if she was in the room at all. That blood wasn't a good sign.

Daelan seemed to smile a little at that. Or maybe that was an attempt to stave off his nausea. He needed water and lots of rest if a concussion was the worst of his injuries, but first he had to get up these stairs, and to do *that*, he needed a minute.

Clenching her teeth against a sigh, Kindra moved to the middle of the first flight of stairs, standing with her back against the wall and her gun held lightly in her hand. Her line of sight from this position was about as good as it could get inside a stairwell, giving her the option to shoot anyone who tried to sneak down the stairs or through the ground-floor door.

She couldn't keep her eyes off the bloodstains. Couldn't stop picturing the trajectory a human body would have to follow and the injuries it might've sustained in order to leave those exact stains in those exact places. Worse, there was no effing way for her to figure out whose blood it was. Not until she climbed to the third floor and saw for herself.

Daelan's breathing changed, shifting from shorter, forcibly steady breaths to one longer pull. When Kindra looked down, he heaved himself slowly off the wall.

"You sure?" Atropos knew she didn't have the strength to carry him two flights.

Rolling his eyes—but keeping his hand braced heavily against the wall—Daelan trudged up the first few steps and poked Kindra in the side. "Move."

She turned without further argument, climbing the stairs slowly to keep pace with Daelan. Eyes alert, she scanned the floors above, watching and listening for any more signs of the people who'd passed through here recently. She saw two more bloodstains and a black streak that might have been grease. The door on the third-floor landing had been left a tiny bit ajar, like whoever had come through last had been too intent on the destination to secure their rear.

Kindra tried *very* hard not to think of reasons why that might've been the case. Or why there was a much larger bloodstain on this door.

Ignoring Daelan's muttered curse, Kindra cautiously opened the door and cleared the hallway before letting him follow. She led the way to the apartment in the northwest corner of the building. To the left of the door, a smear of blood. More on the handle. Kindra's heart pounded. Gun at the ready, she knocked out the Morse code for *S-K-D-Q*. Safe. Kindra. Daelan. Quebec.

The signal would either keep whichever Calver was alive inside from shooting them or alert whatever enemy was lying in wait to their presence.

The door swung open. Cassidy grabbed Kindra's shoulder, tears in her eyes, and hauled her into a hug. A breath later, Daelan slumped against Kindra's back when Cassidy pulled him in too.

"Are you two all right?" Her voice was thick with tears and worry. "Where have you been? Are you all right?"

"I think he has a concussion," Kindra said before Daelan had a chance to downplay his injuries. "He needs water and rest and probably painkillers."

Cassidy's hand pressed against the back of Kindra's head, and she pulled Kindra down to kiss her forehead. Releasing her grip, Cassidy turned to her son. "Sit down before you fall over. You look sick."

She led Daelan to a thin, cushioned sleeping mat along the left wall of a room that must've been intended as a living room. She forced him to sit and drink something while she checked his head for bumps and monitored his pupillary response. Kindra watched them as she closed the front door behind herself and locked it. Only then did she take a breath and let herself—force herself—to look at the other occupants of the room. The huge blood smear by the apartment door hadn't come from Cassidy—her injuries were too minor—but it *had* come from someone.

Aaron leaned against the far wall, his head tilted toward the window. He had a bandage on his neck, another wrapped around his left forearm, and blood on his jeans. Hugo sat on the floor next to him, shirtless, with several bandages and wraps—some of them already bloody—covering his torso. A laptop sat open across his knees, and his fingers rested on the keyboard, but his eyes were closed, his face several shades too pale to be healthy, and his head tipped back.

That only left . . .

Opposite from Aaron and Hugo, Dru had been laid out on one of the thin sleeping mats. Bloody gauze and several empty water bottles surrounded her. Bandages covered her right biceps, and her beige bra was bloodstained, which Kindra could see because her shirt had been cut off, obviously to make room for the bandage covering half of her stomach. The left leg of her black pants had been cut off to dress and tightly wrap a wound just above her knee. Watching from the doorway, the one thing Kindra couldn't spot was movement.

No twitches of pain or agitation, no resettling on the uncomfortable mat. No *breathing*.

"We had to sedate her, Kindra."

Kindra sucked in a sharp breath, barely stuffing down the reflex to strike out.

Cassidy didn't flinch. "Dru is alive, and we think she'll be fine, but she was in a lot of pain, so we sedated her."

Sedation. Sedation, not *death.*

Now that she knew what to look for, Kindra could see the incredibly slow breaths Dru was taking. The relief made her dizzy.

"I saw Amett." Kindra tore her eyes away from Dru when Cassidy gripped her shoulder.

"What happened?" Hugo gingerly got to his feet to stand next to them. Aaron looked in their direction but didn't move.

Haltingly at first, Kindra poured out the whole scene. She started with running from the sound of the van and didn't let herself stop until she reached the last message he'd passed to her before she shot him.

Looking at Hugo, she said, "He told me to tell you that he should have listened in Sarajevo."

Hugo laughed. The laughter was sharp and frantic, each burst so loud it sounded pained. It didn't seem like he could stop, either. One hand rose to cover his eyes, and the other landed against the wall to offer balance.

"Now?" he gasped after several helpless seconds. "The fucker decides to listen to me *now*?"

He kept laughing, and Kindra began to doubt he'd come out of it on his own, so she asked the question that had been itching to escape. "What did you tell him in Sarajevo?"

Hugo wiped his eyes and then dropped his hand. "It was about six months after we split. Cass and I were trying to keep their target from dying, and I managed to get Amett alone for five minutes without either of us bleeding for it. I told him . . ." He looked up at the ceiling. "I told him to take his kids and get the hell away from Odira before she destroyed everything he loved."

Cassidy made a noise like a dying mouse, simultaneously reaching out to comfort Kindra and Hugo. Kindra let herself get pulled into the hug, unused to this much physical comfort but finding herself relishing it. Maybe needing it. Everything about the last two hours was beginning to crack through the mental defenses she'd constructed. Losing their hostage, watching Ryce die, Amett's possibly truthful confession—Kindra couldn't handle it all at once like this.

Then her eyes found Dru's eerily still form again. The urge to curl up next to her and fall into the same oblivious state was . . . almost overwhelmingly strong. It wouldn't fix anything, but it might delay the pain long enough for her to cope. Without meaning to, without consciously deciding to, Kindra turned to Cassidy with a naked plea in her eyes.

Help me. Make this stop hurting. Just for a while. Please.

Cassidy seemed to understand. Leaning closer, she kissed Kindra's temple and then gently guided her toward Dru.

It only took a couple of minutes to unroll a second mat next to Dru, fold up a jacket to use as a pillow, and swallow the pills Aaron pulled out of their med kit. Kindra knew she had scrapes and bruises and burns, but the physical damage was minor. It could wait.

"Rest now." Cassidy smoothed Kindra's hair back from her face. "We'll wake you when we have our next move."

Kindra nodded and curled up on her side, back to the room and face toward Dru. The position should've left her feeling vulnerable. It didn't. Maybe because the sedatives were starting to kick in and she couldn't dredge up the energy to care. Or maybe because she was beginning to trust the Calvers and Aaron Tanvers to watch her back.

Probably a little of both, she admitted to herself while she clung to the edges of unconsciousness.

There would be a lot of secrets to hunt and uncover, a lot of decisions to make, a lot of grieving Kindra knew she couldn't run from this time. She pushed all that away and let herself sink into the soothing grip of sleep, let herself reach out and place a hand just under the center of Dru's ribs so that she could feel the warmth radiating off her skin and the rise and fall of each breath, let herself be grateful that at least *this* hadn't been lost today. At least she wasn't alone.

International Airspace over the Pacific Ocean

"**I**t's done, ma'am." Charles Upton looked up from the report he'd just received to meet the obsidian eyes of the woman sitting across from him, comfortably ensconced in the plush luxury of the private jet's seats.

"Specifics, Charles. And 'ma'am' makes me feel like a grandmother. Lillian." She tilted her head, seeming to consider what she'd said for a moment, then shrugged. "Ms. French if you're really that uncomfortable with the idea."

"Sorry. Lillian." Charles cleared his throat and sat straighter in his seat. "Mr. Hadley is dead. Apparently from gunshot wounds and then fire, so it appears as though Odira isn't taking any chances anymore."

"Hmm." She sipped the mimosa in her hand. "I should hope so."

"Additionally, Matthew has been found. Initial reports are ruling it a heart attack. Special Agent in Charge Altair Ameen Zaman has opened an investigation into Isaac Marks's death, but we don't expect that to get far." He checked a file open on his laptop. "The only remaining issues are the continued absence of Sergeant Aaron Tanvers—his sister, Jenna, worked at Genesis—and Marks's missing kid, Blake."

"Kid?" She raised one eyebrow. "I thought he had a teenage son, not a little one."

"Umm, well, not little. Blake is . . ." Charles checked his screen again. "Sixteen. And listed as 'intersex' on medical records."

"Interesting. But not excessively worrying, either of those," she said, waving it off. "I would like to have Garret's little disaster of a side project wrapped up before we activate phase three." She took another sip of her drink and then smiled. "You'll take care of that, won't you?"

"Of course." Charles nodded and looked down, reopening his encrypted email program. He seemed to be pretending not to notice the way his fingers trembled on the keyboard.

"Susan," Lillian called.

"Yes, Lil?" Susan Phan poked her head out of the galley kitchen at the back of the plane.

"Any word from the lab yet?"

Susan shook her head. "Middle of the night there. I'll try again if I don't hear from them in a couple hours."

"As soon as possible, Susan. Odira may have handled Garret without a hitch, but this whole fiasco just proves that it's been too long since I sent her a reminder." Her frown might have seemed sad if not for the glimmer of sadistic satisfaction shining in her eyes. "It's almost as though she's forgotten why it's so important that she performs well."

Charles's eyes remained on the screen of his laptop, hints of confusion in the faint lines that appeared between his eyebrows.

Susan smiled, the expression more predatory than joyful. "I think I have something in mind that can fix that."

"Wonderful." Lillian practically purred the word. "I knew I could count on you."

Relaxing back in her seat, Lillian took another small sip of her drink and turned toward the window.

Chapter Twenty-Eight

"**H**ow is she?" Cassidy kept her voice low when she entered the room. It was probably unfair of Kindra to commandeer one of only two available bedrooms, but she couldn't bring herself to feel bad about it. Dru needed the space and the quiet.

"The fever's pretty much gone." It had broken a day ago and was disappearing in immeasurably small increments. "The soup I got her to eat last night helped, I think."

"That's good." Cassidy sat on the other side of the bed, picked up a washcloth from the nightstand, and gently wiped the sweat off her daughter's face. "She'll be fine. She's a strong girl, and you're taking good care of her."

Kindra desperately hoped she was right.

For the first two days after they'd "jacked up Jacksonville," as Daelan told the story, injury and exhaustion and really good painkillers kept Dru asleep. Better that than suffering through the worst of the burns on her abdomen, the gunshot wound in her leg, and the shrapnel hole in her arm. Kindra had become Dru's personal nurse, which, though usually a tedious job, she was grateful for. It meant Dru was alive and recovering, and it gave Kindra a chance to grieve Ryce in relative solitude.

After those first two days, the Calvers had headed north, leaving the whole mosquito-infested state of Florida in their blood-spattered wake. Four days after Jacksonville, they settled into a safe house hidden in the mountains of West Virginia, and an infection took hold of Dru. Her fever spiked. Kindra had pushed aside her guilt and focused on forcing broth and medicine down Dru's throat. When Dru threw it up, Kindra had expertly shoved an IV drip into her arm.

For a week—two days on the road and five days in this tiny two-bedroom cabin—Dru had been Kindra's sole focus. She hadn't listened to the murmured conversations happening in the living room turned control center. She hadn't offered opinions on their next move or their next target. They hadn't asked.

"She'll probably be awake soon, and it'll be impossible to keep her in bed. Let her take a shower, and then come out to the living room." Cassidy stroked the sweat-slick strands of Dru's dark hair out of her face. "We want to see what you think about some information we picked up recently."

Kindra nodded slowly, but her eyes stayed on Dru, who was shifting restlessly. "We'll be out as soon as she's ready."

Cassidy smiled, leaning over Dru's body to kiss Kindra's cheek. "Thank you," she said before she left the room.

Spending most of a week with only an unconscious Dru for company hadn't offered Kindra much in the way of conversation, but it had given her a lot of space to think.

She thought about growing up under Odira's and Amett's watchful but rarely kind eyes, and how different life must have been with Cassidy, whose first question when Kindra walked through a door wasn't "Did you get what we need?" but "Are you all right?" She thought about Ryce being forced to seduce people he had absolutely no desire for, and how badly he must have hated his life—hated them all—to disappear like he had. She thought about the promise he'd tried to extract from her as he bled to death.

Don't disappear. You need them. Stay . . . Promise, Kinny. Stay.

There hadn't been time for her to promise anything. She thought about it now, about what it might mean, realistically and logistically, to stay. The Calvers had lost Ryce too, and she knew that she'd be able to help fill in the hole he'd left in their team. They seemed to trust her—mostly—and even like her. A little bit.

If she stayed, she'd get to experience what Ryce had so admired—loved?—about Cassidy and Hugo. Daelan would tease everyone, spit out trivia, and occasionally blow something up. Aaron would stay too, at least for a while, his surprisingly steady calm balancing everyone else's insanity. Hugo and Cassidy would plot, looking at what they'd learned about Garret and finding ways to use it against Lillian.

And Dru? Dru would be *here*, with them.

If Kindra stayed like Ryce wanted her to—like *she* wanted to—then she'd be near this girl who knew Kindra was a bogeyman and still looked at her like she was worth something. Like she was special. A normal kind of special. The kind of special that people who worked nine-to-fives and hung out at coffee shops or bars or bookstores seemed to spend their lives searching for. The kind of special Kindra hadn't known she wanted to find.

Dru shifted again and moaned. Kindra looked down just as Dru opened her eyes.

"You're still here." Dru smiled, and Kindra couldn't help smiling back. The girl was in major pain and smiled just because Kindra was there? It had to be the cutest, sweetest, most ridiculous thing she'd ever seen.

So Kindra confirmed the obvious and slipped her hand into Dru's. "I'm still here."

"Tha's good. Mmm, c'mere." Dru's grip was weak, but she tugged Kindra down to lie next to her on the double bed. "I don' wanchu go."

Kindra sighed and settled, sharing the pillow and resting her palm over Dru's diaphragm. "I'm not going anywhere."

"Said you were gonna leave," Dru mumbled, snuggling closer. "Don' wanchu go."

Now was so not the time for this conversation—Dru might not even *remember* it—but . . . for Dru? If Kindra was being honest with herself, she was willing to do a hell of a lot for Dru.

"Hey, look at me." She brushed her nose against Dru's cheek and hummed happily when Dru turned quickly enough to catch Kindra's lips with her own—and she was happy *despite* the chapped lips and pretty hideous breath Dru was sporting. "I know what I said before, but that's not true now, okay? I'm not going anywhere."

"'Cause you got nowhere else to go?" It came out as half question, half accusation.

"No." Kindra sighed, but she couldn't exactly blame Dru for doubting her. "You really think I couldn't survive on my own if I wanted to?"

"I guess." Dru looked hopefully, adorably confused, but still sounded so skeptical.

There had to be something Kindra could do to make her believe it, if only for now.

Something she could give *her* . . .

As soon as the idea hit, Kindra tried to roll off the bed.

"Said you weren't leaving," Dru complained, gripping her shirt.

"I'm not *leaving*." Kindra carefully extracted herself from Dru's weak hold. "I'm just getting something."

Dru groaned and grumbled, but didn't fight it as Kindra slid out of the bed. The bag Kindra had taken out of the town house in Manhattan almost a month ago was sitting in a corner of the room. It didn't take long to find what she was looking for.

Kindra opened the two velvet jewelry boxes as she returned to the bed.

"Here. I thought you might like this." She picked the cuff up from its cushion and gently fit it on Dru's left wrist. She saw the moment recognition hit. Dru's lips parted, surprise widening them more when Kindra clasped the matching necklace around her own throat.

The jewelry was nothing but silver with a design stamped in. It wouldn't bind Kindra to the Calvers any more than blood had bound her to Odira and Amett, but it was a symbol of a choice. Kindra was making this choice, and she intended to stick to it.

"You're really staying? Why?" Hope and relief bloomed on Dru's tired face.

"Because I'd rather stay here." Kindra cuddled close, stroking Dru's skin above the cuff. "Because I want to be around the people Ryce loved so much, the same people who have risked their lives to save mine." She leaned in and brushed their lips together again. The warm touch gave her enough strength to finish what she wanted to say. "And because this is where you are."

Wonder lit up Dru's captivating moss-green eyes. "Oh."

Kindra smiled. "Yeah, oh. Now will you trust me not to vanish while you go take a shower? You really, *really* need one, Bomb Squad."

"Don't be mean to me, baby. I'm sick." She coughed twice, the fakest, most pathetic coughs Kindra had ever heard.

"Nope. Not going to work this time." Kindra rolled off the bed and then, much more gently, hauled Dru to her feet. "You've been slacking off for a week. We have to catch up."

Afraid to leave her alone in a slippery tub, Kindra stayed in the bathroom while Dru showered, washing her own face and pretending she could wash the stress of the past week off as easily. Once Dru was clean and dry and dressed in clothes Kindra had to carefully help her into, Kindra supported her out to the living room, where everyone else was waiting for them.

She scanned the faces, looking for—

Oh.

Looking for Ryce. But he wasn't there. Wouldn't ever be there again. His absence hit her like a bullet—the shock of *something is so very wrong* lingering before the agonizing pain of the wound set in.

This time, she didn't brutally beat it into submission and shove it to the back of her mind. She acknowledged the wound that she guessed would never completely heal, let the agony of it wash over her for a second, held a little tighter to Dru's arm, and forced herself to move through it.

"It's good to see you up." Hugo ran his hand over his daughter's wet hair, kissing her forehead.

"It's also good not to *smell* you coming." Daelan's quip was offset by the obvious relief in his smile.

"Like you haven't smelled worse?" Dru asked as she shuffled toward the couch.

Daelan smirked. "Yeah, after I ran through a sewer, maybe."

"I miss the quiet already," Cassidy said with a sigh.

"I know what you mean." Hugo flicked Daelan's shoulder before moving to the desk where the computers had been set up. "Remind me why children don't come with mute buttons?"

Dru winced when Kindra helped lower her to the couch. Only after she was safely seated did Kindra take the open space next to her.

Daelan was perched on the small dining room table just off the living area to their right, his legs swinging free. To Kindra's left, Aaron sat on the back of the couch, his feet planted on the old, musty cushions and his elbows on his knees. Nodding hello, Aaron scooted over a bit, then turned his attention to the leaders of their little enclave.

"Some of this everyone knows, and some will be new," Hugo said without preamble. "Don't ask stupid questions until we get all the way through."

"Aye, aye, sir." Daelan mock saluted and then mimed locking his mouth shut.

Hugo muttered, "Oh, I'll believe *that* when I see it."

"With Garret 'missing,' the FBI has officially announced their investigation into Garret Hadley and Redwell," Cassidy said. "The executives and the board seem pretty desperate to shovel the shit onto Garret, so we think the investigation will go as smoothly and quickly as government-run investigations can."

"It helps that we basically handed them everything they needed on a silver flash drive," Daelan griped.

"Yes." Cassidy's completely serious agreement made Daelan roll his eyes. "That's the only reason they're moving publicly at all."

"It won't be long before they begin to work with Echemorro to return the land bought by the company and redistribute money stolen from public works projects." Hugo rubbed his jaw. "The problem is Lillian French. There is absolutely nothing implicating her. Nothing."

"Her name so rarely came up over the years we've been watching them that we missed it." Cassidy looked frustrated. "We didn't see the connection, so there's nothing we can add to point the Feds in her direction."

"Where is she now?" Kindra asked.

"The flight plan she registered with the FAA had her heading to China." Hugo pulled up the records. "The plane arrived on time, but there's no sign of her after that. She might still be in China, but she may have decided a nonextradition country was a better bet and hopped over to Mali or Indonesia."

"If she has any survival instincts, she won't be back until she knows where the fallout will land," Kindra said.

Cassidy hummed in agreement. "The woman was on a plane before anyone but her little cabal knew Garret was missing." She looked up from the computer. "Charles Upton and Susan Phan went with her, in case I haven't mentioned that yet."

"And we don't know what she's involved in?" Dru tried to sit up but hissed in pain. She didn't resist at all when Kindra guided her back again.

"Considering her background and her military ties, it's likely weapons or information—something in that arena." Hugo sounded less than confident. "We're looking deeper, and we have several contacts doing the same."

"Great," Kindra said. "What do we do in the meantime?"

"While the alphabet agencies are trying to hobble the giant, we look into what happened to Jenna, as Amett suggested." Cassidy turned back to the computer screens, flicking through open feeds and files. "Some of Daelan's spyware was missed when Redwell scoured their servers, so we still have a few fingers and eyes inside the network."

Daelan snorted. "That sounds so horrifically disgusting, I don't know where to start."

Aaron laughed. Cassidy ignored them. "From HR's records at different subsidiaries, we've found six other deaths spread out over the last four years. Four apparent suicides and two slightly suspicious accidents. There may be more, especially if we go back to the deaths that *we* were involved in more than a decade ago, but . . ."

Hugo put a hand over her shoulder, squeezed, and picked up her train of thought. "But in order to find them, we're going to have to look into every single person who's died while working for a Redwell-owned company."

"Shit. That'll take . . ." Dru shook her head. "Years. And we might not even find anything useful."

"Precisely." It was obvious that this thought had not just occurred to Cassidy. "So we'll drop a hint to Isaac's buddy, Special Agent in Charge Altair Ameen Zaman, to take a look. We can make him think the message is coming from Bernard, that he found new information, and hope Altair bites."

Kindra saw where they were going with this and smiled. "And if we have a line to him, we'll have an eye on the investigation."

"Exactly," Hugo said, looking pleased.

Dru grunted, but didn't try to move this time. "How do we know that this investigation won't lead us back to everything the Feebs are already shutting down?"

"Because none of the companies that these people were working for had anything to do with agricultural import/export." Cassidy ran a hand through the strands of her ponytail, still favoring her left arm. "There's no guarantee that some of the deaths we find won't fall on

Garret instead of Lillian, but the whole thing is a little too . . . subtle for Garret."

"He's the guy who ordered a sniper assassination in the middle of Manhattan," Hugo said. "The same mind isn't then going to fake a suicide—with a note in the victim's handwriting."

Kindra had to admit that they had a point. It was like comparing the work of a quarry miner to the precision of a master sculptor.

"So that's what we're going to do. See if we can spot a pattern and then make that pattern work for us." Cassidy smiled ruefully at her audience. "I really believed we'd be done when Garret was gone. I thought we'd be able to walk away and let the suits take care of the cleanup." She glanced at Hugo. "I guess there's one more job to do first."

"If anyone wants out, now is the time to jump ship." Hugo's eyes scanned the group.

"Fuck that." The sudden noise from her left startled Kindra; it was the first thing Aaron had said since the discussion started. "I went AWOL to figure out what happened to Jenna, and I'm not leaving until I do that. Actually, if we . . ." He cast a quick look at Kindra. "Uh, if we need an extra gun we can trust, I've got someone we can bring in."

"The boyfriend?" Kindra asked, purposely ignoring the oblique reference to the hole in their team.

Aaron nodded. "I checked in with him again a couple days ago, and he— Well, I'm pretty sure Geo is about to do something monumentally stupid to find me if I don't find him first. You'd be doing me a favor letting him in, honestly."

"We'll probably need to take you up on that," Hugo said. Then he and Cassidy looked at Daelan.

Their son laughed and asked, "Really?"

"Give me a few weeks to grow some new scars and I'm in," Dru murmured before her parents asked.

Everyone looked at Kindra.

How could she possibly explain how badly she wanted to be here when two weeks ago she was trying to get away? The Calvers were a piece of the childhood she barely remembered. They could easily become the core of a new life if she let them.

Ryce had begged her to stay. Dru had practically seduced her into staying. Even her father had seemed relieved that she'd been adopted into their clan.

But how could she say any of that aloud?

In the end, she kept it simple. "I'm in, if you'll have me."

Dru pressed a clumsy kiss to her cheek and relaxed against Kindra's side. Daelan, Hugo, and Cassidy smiled. Aaron didn't go quite as far as smiling, but he didn't look surprised by her answer, either.

"Well, then," Cassidy said, her grin growing wider and turning more than a little vindictive. "Everyone sit down and strap in. We've got a lot of work ahead."

Miami, Florida

O dira flicked through the pictures she'd downloaded from her email, lips pressed tight. This was the fourth time she'd cycled through the images, and they hadn't changed. That didn't seem to matter. When she hit the end of the gallery, she went right back to the beginning and started again.

This time when she reached the last picture, she stopped and stared at the face filling the screen. If not for the easy smile and the friendly light in the woman's eyes, she would have looked almost identical to Odira.

The bedroom door opened, and Amett walked in. "I'm waiting on word from one more person, but so far none of our contacts or Javier's have any lead on where Hugo and Cassidy are." He rubbed one large hand over his face and then sat gingerly on the mattress. There were deep circles under his eyes, and he held his left arm carefully. The response he seemed to expect never came. She was sitting on the armchair in the corner of the room, her fingers tracing the not-quite-invisible scar behind her right ear.

"Odira?"

Her eyes flicked up to meet his for a moment, and then she handed him the laptop.

Amett blinked. "Adila?" His finger hovered over the icon that would minimize the photo. Haltingly, he asked, "Is—is she all right?"

Odira nodded once, the motion sharp. "For now. Read."

Exhaling slowly, Amett switched windows, pulling up the email the pictures had been downloaded from.

I'll be in touch as soon as I have a way for you to make up for the absolute mess you've been making of our jobs.

Your next chance is her last one, Odira.

Make it count.

"I'm going to kill her. Slowly. As painfully as possible." Odira took the laptop back, closed the email, and shut her eyes tight. "I swear to Atropos, Amett, if Lillian even gives my sister a *haircut* she doesn't want, I will end her in the worst possible way I can think of."

Amett's right hand traveled to his left shoulder, but he didn't say anything. He didn't look at his wife at all.

There was resignation and regret on his face when he nodded and said, "I know."

Don't miss book two of Erica Cameron's
Assassins series, Nemesis.

Dear Reader,

Thank you for reading Erica Cameron's *Assassins: Discord*!

We know your time is precious and you have many, many entertainment options, so it means a lot that you've chosen to spend your time reading. We really hope you enjoyed it.

We'd be honored if you'd consider posting a review—good or bad—on sites like **Amazon, Barnes & Noble, Kobo, Goodreads, Twitter, Facebook**, **Tumblr,** and your blog or website. We'd also be honored if you told your friends and family about this book. Word of mouth is a book's lifeblood!

For more information on upcoming releases, author interviews, blog tours, contests, giveaways, and more, please sign up for our weekly, spam-free newsletter and visit us around the web:

> **Newsletter:** tritonya.com/newsletter.php
> **Twitter:** twitter.com/TritonBooks
> **Tumblr:** tritonbooks.tumblr.com

Thank you so much for Reading the Rainbow!

Tritonya.com

TRITON
BOOKS

AN IMPRINT OF RIPTIDE PUBLISHING.

Acknowledgments

This book quite literally wouldn't exist without a nudge from Michael Stearns and Danielle Chiotti. You guys offered me a beginning and let me run with it. Somehow it turned into this. Thank you for all your support and guidance along the way.

Many super-duper-special thanks to Ricky for his *invaluable* help on all things guns, explosives, knives, fighting, and Marines. I don't even want to think about how many hours of research I saved by being able to message you random questions. Thank you so much.

Lori gave me the right advice at the right time to get the first draft of this book done. I still think the way we met and became friends is a little surreal, but I don't know what I'd do without you now. At the very least, I wouldn't have a phone that tries to autofill "LORI" after both "OMG WTF" and "HAAAAATE YOU," and that would be sad.

I don't know where I would be without my beta-readers/friends/ cheerleaders: Haley, Lani, Katrina, Tristina, Marni, Cait, Ann, Kara, Lindsay, and Melody. Your enthusiasm, support, and emails/texts/ reader comments—the critical ones, the threatening ones, and the squeal-y ones—helped me drag this book to the finish line. I adore you all immensely.

My work-family at Inspirations was so understanding every time I came in looking zombified because I'd stayed up too late writing or editing. Gratitude isn't enough for supporting me through the insanity that has been my deadline schedule for the last year. I probably owe you guys all dinner or something.

To everyone at Riptide who made me feel like part of the clan even before my books were contracted, but *especially* Sarah Lyons, Caz Galloway, and Kate De Groot, who patiently helped me turn this from an incomplete mess of a first draft into something streamlined and sharp-edged. You are all brilliant and irreplaceable.

And as always, of course, to my wonderful family. You guys are so patient with me, even when I spend days talking about people who only exist inside my head. I love you!

ALSO BY
Erica Cameron

Assassins
Nemesis (coming soon)

The Dream War Saga
Sing Sweet Nightingale
Deadly Sweet Lies

Laguna Tides, with Lani Woodland
Taken by Chance
Loyalty and Lies
Dealing with Devalo (coming 2016)

ABOUT
the Author

Erica is many things but most notably the following: writer, reader, editor, dance fan, choreographer, singer, lover of musical theater, movie obsessed, sucker for romance, Florida resident, and quasi-recluse. She loves the beach but hates the heat, has equal passion for the art of Salvador Dalí and Venetian Carnival masks, has a penchant for unique jewelry and sun/moon décor pieces, and a desire to travel the entire world on a cruise ship. Or a private yacht. You know, whatever works.

In addition to the Assassins series, she is also the author of The Dream War Saga and coauthor of the Laguna Tides novels. You can learn more about her books at ByEricaCameron.com

Website: byericacameron.com
Twitter: twitter.com/byericacameron
Tumblr: byericacameron.tumblr.com
Facebook: facebook.com/byericacameron
Instagram: instagram.com/byericacameron
Goodreads: goodreads.com/ericacameron